"Tom Wolfe rewrites American Gigolo." — *Kirkus Reviews*

"Boys In Babeland. No scruples or psychological doses of saltpeter daunts the narrator of Coerte V.W. Felske's *The Shallow Man*. This novel's hero, Nick Laws, is a club-hopping hedonist who exclusively targets models as bedmates and makes no apologies. Rather than waste time with names, he refers to each of his model-dates as Thing. After greasily chomping on nubiles and discarding them like spareribs, the narrator flirts with the prospect of maturing and settling down, a momentary lurch which takes the form of an affair with a non-model. The frustrating interlude leads him to decide, The hell with it—real women are nothing but hard work. The novel is crass, entertaining, slangy, egotistical, and reeking of sun bronze and the fresh turnover of fleshy delights makes the narrator's decision to become an aging roué instead of a responsible adult seem like an honest, if not admirable, choice. He's willing to go with the flow even if it leaves him stranded. Where *Zoe* belongs to the sadder-but-wiser category, *The Shallow Man* ends up neither sad nor wise, which seems right. Felske writes like a gigolo and treats seduction as a dirty sport."

— James Wolcott, *Vanity Fair*

"Model Citizen: the story of a man who never met a stunningly beautiful woman he didn't like. Love, H.L. Mencken said, is the delusion that one woman differs from another. Nick Laws, a marginally more enlightened fellow, claims that one in every 50,000 is quite different from the other 49,999: she's drop-dead gorgeous, and he's determined to sleep with her. Nick, who narrates Coerte V.W. Felske's amusing first novel, "The Shallow Man" is 30 years old, lives in Soho and works by day as a hand model, by night as a party promoter for clubs with names like Café D&A. He knows how to ask "Would you like to take a bubble bath with me?" in 10 languages, and he has committed to memory the Victoria's Secret 24-hour toll-free number. With the exception of his Harley, all he cares about is what he calls collectively, "Thing": "Fashion models, beautiful women and general hotness." He happily acknowledges his obsession right from the start. When Nick contemplates "the sweetest joining of limbs known to man," his company is agreeable. But during the couple of week she tangles with his brother, his confidante, and of course, models' boyfriends, all of whom demand he re-evaluate his life. By his own account, he is neither very bright nor very witty, and a dullard's earnest ruminations can only be dull—or, as Nick would put it, as exciting as York Avenue. Before long, though, he is back to his old, unreflective self, proving that the unexamined life is well worth living. To Nick, everything resembles conjugating the verb, and if your mind works in similar fashion, you'll probably understand his ruling passion. One feminist writer has used the term "penised humans" to refer to men. Mentally, at least, Nick Laws is as penised as a human can get. When he awards Audrey Hepburn the crown for "pinnacle hotness," it is only because Mr. Felske has nodded. Nick detests the beach but this novel is perfect for it. "The Shallow Man" is also perfect for shallow men. On the other hand, women may think the title is redundant."

— David Kelley, *The New York Times Book Review*

"Coerte V.W. Felske's novel *The Shallow Man* turned the fashion world on its head—and introduced the term "modelizer" into the collective consciousness. One of Nick Laws's dictums is "don't judge a book by its contents" ostensibly delivered in support of his "beauty = truth" theorem. The novel is presented as a comment on our society's obsession with models, and therefore its cultural relevance outweighs any criticism of its craftsmanship.

It's a notion that had its day during the genre of the hip urban novel of the 80's, a genre characterized by its most prominent literary agent Amanda Urban as, *"and then they fucked."* *The Shallow Man* fits in perfectly with this body of work. It's an entertaining book, a pleasant diversion. Like its protagonist, *The Shallow Man* doesn't take itself too seriously, and it urges you to do the same. It's a fantasy, a lark, a good time. The Shallow Man has his moments of doubt and pain, wherein he questions the basis of his existence, but they are brief, and far from mending his ways he vows to indulge in as many in as many places for as long as he can, in retaliation for all the "politically correct bullshit" he's been assaulted with. And, in a way, after several years of that "politically correct bullshit" *The Shallow Man* is refreshingly moral-free."   — *Detour*

"In his first novel, *The Shallow Man*, Coerte V.W. Felske spins a clever tale of the narcissistic world of fashion modeling. In this comic send-up, Nick Laws is the shallow man whose every thought and word reflect his sole interest in life: boffing models. From the late-night clubs of Manhattan to the art deco bars of Miami, Nick searches for beautiful women to take to bed. That's all he does. He's so perfect, he's hilarious. Is there a man with a soul so noble that he has not entertained this fantasy? In real life, no one could stand around all day in his motorcycle jacket and sunglasses, purring platitudes to curvaceous dimwits. But Nick's relentless, self-conscious pursuit is very funny. Nick reminds us, "Never judge a book by its contents." Certainly not this book. *The Shallow Man* is fun, flash, and filigree–a sexy, witty spoof of the Nineties."

— Digby Diehl, *Playboy*

"Shallow waters run deep. This stunning but unreflective man knows a lot more than you think. Behind those big blank eyes and that deep tan is…well, something that women find hopelessly tempting: a healthy disdain for thinking too much. Since he can't be bothered connecting the dots, he maps out the politics of the jejune and Gitanes with an easy straight line. Reading the quick-witted prose, one begins to think less about things and more about Thing, the Shallow Man's tag for the women he dates: gorgeous, seemingly unattainable models. Nick Laws is like Hamlet without the mental baggage, tumbling Ophelia by ActII. So what if behind all that cigarette smoke and charm lies a lean mentality. Felske's *The Shallow Man* makes a case for the unexamined life."

— *Esquire*

"I may not have been the king of Generation Face," proclaims hipster Nick Laws, invoking his superficial peers in screenwriter Felske's first novel, "but I was definitely one of its princes." Nick can't get enough of "Thing" his catchphrase for models and other impossibly stunning women; his every waking moment is devoted to bedding them and their friends—as long as they're not Civilians (regular-looking women). It would be easy, but inaccurate, to dismiss Nick as a misogynist. For one thing, his acidic classification system extends to men too. "Guys can be Dialtones," he concedes. Spiked with original Nickspeak and hilarious dialogue, Felske's depiction of the physically elite is so clever in its anthropological detail that we can forgive his protagonist for just about anything. Besides, *The Shallow Man* harbors a few glimmers of Nick's humanity. You just have to dig to find them."   — *People*

"Deep thoughts from a hand model, *The Shallow Man,* by Coerte V.W. Felske, humorously portrays Nick Laws, a model and club promoter who's happy to let "Thing" (the allure of beautiful women) dictate the conversation if not his life—to the point where he's mastered how to say "Would you join me for a bubble bath?" in every language spoken by supermodels. Aware that his lifestyle annoys "dromes" (average-looking people who resent the beautiful), Nick argues that it's not his fault that "4-B girls" (beauty, breeding, brains, and bank account) were created, or that men are compelled to pursue them. He frequently hauls out his tattered copy of Van Gogh's letters to prove that history's purest artist was also a model muncher. Set up by a "catsuit feminist" (one with beauty and brains), wary of "donuts" (male models who are stuck on themselves), a too-frequent partaker "the Dracula nap" (sleep all day, come out at night), Nick is a lot of laughs even as his promiscuity takes on the aspect of an addiction passed from father to son. Fans of Jay McInerney and P.J. O'Rourke should be amused." — *Glamour*

"Cruising Manhattan's young and beautiful scene on a Harley Davidson, Nick Laws is on a desperate search for supermodels or, as he puts it, "Thing." Whether throwing parties for that one in 50,000 who is "hot, Thing hot," fending off "Civilians," (everyday girls with everyday looks) or convincing Thing to dump "Guy" (everyday boy, everyday looks), Nick is driven by Thing—how to get it and how to enjoy it. Though the world Felske paints is self-consciously hipper-than-thou, he holds his portrait of it in check with a ribald sense of humor and an understanding of the limitations of Nick's ways. Tight prose and smooth dialogue impel the story along, while the names of so many trendy New York night spots dot the text that hipster wannabes can use it as a guidebook. This first novel captures the gloss of its characters with a smart shine of its own."
— *Publisher's Weekly*

"Make no mistake, Coerte V.W. Felske's literary Lothario Nick Laws, the Shallow Man, is no ordinary ladies' man. He is an uberstud for the '90s, otherwise known as a model hound, modelizer, beauty junkie, or, as fashion insiders prefer, model fucker. Is this an accurate depiction of modelettes and the men who pursue them? While the book may be fictional, the modelizer phenomenon most definitely is not."
— *Details*

"The *Bright Lights, Big City* of the 90's." — *Buzz*

"A Model Wordsmith. " — *New York Magazine*

"PLAYBOY CENTERFOLD DATA SHEET, "Favorite Book: "The Shallow Man" by Coerte V.W. Felske. It's about a very shallow man and his involvements with models."
— Priscilla Lee Taylor, Miss March, 1996, *Playboy*

"'People Are Talking About: Books,' Favorite Novel: *The Shallow Man* by Coerte Felske (Crown Publishers) which begins with the line 'I never met a model I didn't like.'"

— Candace Bushnell, *Vogue*

Chandler for the 90s:**** There are two reasons to write a Hollywood novel, and they're both the same: everyone will shell out for a peek backstage. Some Hollywood novels—Jackie Collins's oeuvre, for example—exist to perpetrate the fiction that stars' lives are as glamourous off-screen as on. Others are written, with equal commercial savvy, to expose the shocking vice and greed of the industry. Ultra-glam or ultra-scum; we love to read about either, and the very best back lot potboilers dish out both at once. Coerte Felske is and ex-screenwriter and he seems to have dug enough dirt during his time in the industry to fill several bookshelves. His hero in *Word* is Heyward Hoon, who must surely be an exaggerated portrait of Felske: a failed screenwriter whose hobby is Hollywood anthropology, observing the local Wannabeasts, 8x10s, Noguls, Starmen, and Muffin Heads, and so on. Girls, though, are Hoon's real area of expertise—all 2,000 of them that he happens to know. When lonely studio magnate Sidney Swinburn sees him stagger out of a bathroom with four lovely Bullets on his arms, Hoon sees the perfect opportunity to sell his years of research for a slice of success. It's an old story, and in a way this is an old book. The flicks and chicks may represent 90s excess but the style of *Word* is pure 40s cool, all choppy sentences and dry wit. It's a pastiche but no more than anything else these days; people are getting used to judging authors on what they borrow rather than what they create. And if you like the original—in this case, the work of Raymond Chandler—the throwback can be terrific fun to read. Felske knows this and has gotten his chosen style down perfectly. Whole paragraphs swing with voiceover rhythms that put Harrison Ford's famous Blade Runner monologues to shame. 'He told me work was totally uncommercial. Sure, I'd heard it before… But I was damn good at producing work that didn't sell. So why ruin a good thing? He told me I should look for new representation. I told him he should look at my tallest finger.' It's all good, punchy stuff and Felske never falters. Beautiful babes, New York wasps and sleazy zillionaires all flit through *Word*, larger than life and twice as interesting. The only bit of Chandler that Felske has chosen not to pilfer is the labyrinthine plot, which is a pity in a way: a long, zippy book like this could use a few more twists and turns. In the end, though, *Word* is lovable for the addictive dry wit of Felske/Hoon: 'As I massaged number 4 into her back, my mind drifted from its search of all that is original, and plopped splat on the cliché.' Can you blame him?"

— Carrie O'Grady, *The Guardian (England)*

"Magnificent Obsessions: *Word* is the book Bret Easton Ellis didn't write. It's a satire of Star Camp, USA, Felske's term for the movie colony. His narrator, Heyward Hoon, is a winning and wicked Ivy League prepster trying to conquer Hollywood. He's a screenwriter, and things are going miserably except for his not-so-little black book of gorgeous LA women. Felske does a great job with female characters, and his playful language introduces Strugs (struggling actors), WAMs (waitress-actress-models), and Noguls (wannabe movie moguls). Felske also has one eye on the screen, still, sometimes a book is meant to be just a good read, and we're grateful for it.

— Christopher Napolitano, *Playboy*

"His first novel turned the fashion world on its head—and introduced the term 'modelizer' into the collective conscious. Now, with his tough-talking *Word*, Coerte V.W. Felske is back, red-eyeing it over Tinseltown's turf, but navigating much of the same Faustian topography. Catch a ride on this tale of a street-savvy screenwriter who sells his soul—but meets a lot of 'Wams,' 'Fundies,' and 'Mom-I-Got-the-Part girls'—on his trek toward the fabled Hollywood sign." — *Detour*

"*Word: The Talk of L.A.*: By page 3 of this sharply funny send-up of all things Hollywood, you will agree that author Coerte V.W. Felske shares his lead character's talent for language. While threading his way through the Tinseltown jungle, Felske's wannabe screenwriter Heyward Hoon desperately tries to maintain his sanity. You will be patting yourself on the back for having discovered Hoon's story before *Variety* announces its inevitable arrival at a theater near you." — *Marie Claire*

"If We Gave Out Book Awards: Great Read Gift Guide; Edgiest Girl, *Bridget Jones's Diary*, Edgiest Boy, *Word* by Coerte V.W. Felske. Felske's hero, an out-of-work screenwriter who calls himself a 'Blip' on movieland's radar, hilariously manages to find some beating hearts inside the hippest Hollywood hyphenates."

— *Glamour*

"For all his mastery of the L.A. scene, we are taken by surprise to discover, fifty pages into the novel, that Heyward's primary income comes from his day job as a temporary filing clerk. Both his fortunes change when Sydney Swinburn, head of Novastar Studios, takes him under his wing. Swinburn is impressed by Heyward's social ease with beautiful women, and he makes a pact with him. In exchange for lessons on how to successfully score with women, he will let Heyward stay in a bungalow on his estate and encourage him as a screenwriter. The only rule: He must keep his hands off Teal, the beautiful woman who also lives on his estate and who, of course, is the only woman Heyward really wants. Like Peter Farrelly's *The Comedy Writer*, Michael Tolkin's *The Player*, and Peter Lefcourt's *The Deal*, *Word* is a worthy new member of the growing genre of Hollywood novels in which idealistic would-be screenwriters and filmmakers experience disillusionment as they come up against the madly illogical Hollywood system, in which liars, con artists, and charlatans occupy almost all of the positions of power."

— *USA Today*

"Language is what this novel downloads—a torrent of L.A. buzzwords and insider cynicism unmatched since Odets and Lehman's 'Sweet Smell of Success' took on Manhattan's nightlife. As with Tony Curtis's Sidney Falco, Felske pumps Heyward Hoon with so much film babble he's ready to burst. Insecure but WASPish Heyward, who's written scripts on spec, with not one green-lighted, tars everyone around him; leading men dismissed as 'Starmen,' struggling actors as 'Strugs,' and pretty faces with few goals, '8x10s.' When Heyward, accompanied by his beautiful but alcoholic arm piece, Baby Garbo, meets mega-mogul Sydney Swinburn, he sees a way of perhaps getting his masterpiece, the script of his 'Age of Astonishment,' sold at last. A wonderfully literate script, Sydney says, but, sadly, uncommercial, and he is in the business to make money. Still, he sees in Heyward a bookish ladies' man who can bring into this boorish super-producer's life just what he needs to fill a void: intimacy with the type of woman he has always challenged himself to attain. They strike a Faustian bargain to help each other as Sydney attends Heyward's charm school. Heyward, however, must not pursue Sydney's sought-after and mysterious Teal. When Heyward and Teal find each other irresistible, Sydney, the fearsome dark lord, assures Heyward's destruction in Hollywood. Cynics may snap their fangs at that big-bucks ending, but for film lovers the Hell-A hypechat will flick all of your fuses."

— *Kirkus Reviews*

"Heyward Hoon is yet another brilliant but uncommercial and unproduced screenwriter careening around L.A. looking for a life amidst the clichés. His tale? Hollywood newcomer strikes a Faustian bargain in exchange for entrée into inner circle. It's winningly told, with often ferocious humor, including a fresh, funny argot (e.g., 'Wams' are waitress-actress-models). Recommended for fiction collections."

— *Library Journal*

"People Are Talking About: Books; Novelist-cum-boulevardier Coerte V.W. Felske explains how to marry a billionaire…The outtakes from the life of Coerte V.W. Felske teem with glamour: The portrait of the novelist as a young man by good friend Peter Beard; a snapshot with model Frederique Van der Wal; another with his book party hosts director Peter Berg and Janice Dickinson. To Felske, whose previous book launches were held at Joe's Pub and Lot 61, the velvet rope simply does not exist. For tonight's out-on-the-town interview, Felske suggests we start with drinks uptown at Fifty Seven Fifty Seven ($110). From there, perhaps we'll move on to dinner at Harry Cipriani ($500) before finishing up with nightcaps at Au Bar ($175). An evening with Felske is enough to make a girl's Prada habit seem positively economical. By 7:30 P.M., Felske is stretched out at a table in the cavernous bar, ready to talk about his new novel and what inspired it. He runs a hand through his shaggy Caesar cut, cocks his head forward, and tries desperately to be heard above the din. 'It's a good night, Wednesdays,' he says, surveying a room of Armani-clad tycoons, endless martini glasses, and the high-pitched laughter of well-dressed women. 'The men have finished their business day; maybe there's a meeting tomorrow, but now they have a night or two before they have to go home to their wives. And you get everyone here—Europeans, South Americans, everyone. It's prime Digger territory.' A 'Digger,' mind you, is Felske's term for a woman who targets wealthy men like a heat-seeking missile. And Diggers are at the center of *The Millennium Girl* (St. Martin's Press), Felske's much-buzzed-about new novel, a fictionalized account of his gimlet-eyed social observations. *The Millennium Girl* takes the reader through the marriage market of the nineties. His heroine, Bodicea, is determined to land herself not just a husband but a husband who meets a strict set of financial and social criteria. According to Felske, it's women's lib for the nineties: Bodicea's point of view takes a quick tussle with the fifties (for that perennially chic retro feel), spins through the eighties (for a dose of glamour), and lands firmly in the next century—the goal is still the same (landing the guy), but the white picket fence has morphed into a classic six, several vacation homes, and a Gulfstream V for the commute. The difference is that these women, like Bodicea, approach finding a husband with the steely-eyed acumen of a CEO: Wine and dine at Le Cirque 2000, shop at Gucci and Manolo, summer in the Hamptons, and winter in Aspen. Beyond having the money that allows them to traffic in global finery, these women are looking for men who can spend it with style. But *The Millennium Girl* is not just another collection of insider's jargon and 'Page Six' gossip. Felske is the real thing: He knows his territory, and he writes about it with wit and style. *Girl* may have taken him only a few weeks to write, but he's been steeped in its culture since childhood. He grew up in New York City and on the Eastern Shore of Long Island, navigated his way around Manhattan from a very early age, spent his undergraduate years at Dartmouth, and then did graduate work at Columbia University's film school—after which he co-wrote *Homeboy* for actor Mickey Rourke. Then came two novels that, like *Girl*, glitter with a diamond-sharp deconstruction of modern life in the fast lane. Both got solid reviews, including *The New York Times's*: both are being produced for the big screen by New Line Cinema. 'It's all about the voice,' Felske says, describing what makes his novels different. 'I believe the book is honest. It's not an indictment, rather, it's in praise of women, in a reverse angle way, who are trying to better themselves, empower themselves, any way they can. To not be dependents, but independents. Occasionally, you write a certain piece of music and people respond to it, and I think TMG strikes those universal chords.'"   — Dana Wagner, *Vogue*

"How to Catch a Man at the Century's End. This happens to be written by a man, the novelist-journalist-screenwriter Coerte V.W. Felske. It's a face-to-face encounter with 'diggers,' women who troll resort towns in search of the perfect millionaire. *The Millennium Girl* is based upon Felske's own research. We all know women like this exist, but until now we didn't have all the gory details. Our heroine is a nubile 28-year-old named Bodicea, who dies her hair incessantly and has a wicked habit of giving her fellow diggers nicknames like 'Operation: I Do,' and 'Ellen B. Generous.' We go on tour with the charming Bo as she uses men and vice versa, and along the way she dispenses various nuggets of self-analysis like 'if women weren't so jealous of one-another, we'd be the rulers of the planet.' The book is hilarious and sympathetic and even stops to examine a gay man's search for the perfect mate in the midst of all its heterosexual sex scenes. Bo gains her humanity and has a real soul which is perhaps the surest indicator that this is fiction."
     — Melanie Rehak, *The New York Times Book Review*

"His debut novel, *The Shallow Man*, introduced us to Manhattan 'Modelizers.' His second novel, *Word*, brought us Tinseltown's 'Blips,' 'Bullets,' and 'Strugs.' Now, in *The Millennium Girl*, pulse-of-the-Zeitgeist author Coerte V.W. Felske sets his sights on 'Diggers,' a.k.a. the globe-trotting hotties on the hunt for 'Walletmen,' the ultra-rich men of their dreams."
     — *Detour*

"Let's Hear It for the Girls: They're baaaack, and in the latest reads, they rule the world. So much for that un-p.c. term 'girl' becoming as obsolete as 8-track tapes. It's back with a passion. Who are these lit It Girls? 1. The Millennium Girl, by Coerte V.W. Felske... 'I'm not a hooker...but I do live off men,' says the title character. 'Why shouldn't I take what I can while I can?' Bodicea is a 28-year-old knockout with lips she's tattooed an even deeper red. Her work alias is 'Digger'—she globe-hops in search of filthy-rich 'Walletmen,' some to be kept by in high style, and one to marry before she turns 30. I wanted to hate her, but I couldn't: She was too shameless and too hilariously over-the-top."
     —*Mademoiselle*

"Another from the resourceful and amusing Felske, whose satire of the fashion industry, *The Shallow Man,* and knifing of Los Angeles, *Word,* are both in the pipeline at New Line Cinema. His latest topic is international gold diggers, the sweet lovelies more shark-like than Anita Loos's or Truman Capote's who speak of Walletmen (fat cats of Fortune 500 and Forbes 400 fame), of Chanel, Bulgari, and Armani, and of the seasons of Gstaad, Cannes, Nice, and Ibiza. Felske's narrator, Bo (Bodicea), has jade-green eyes, has had her lips tattooed deep red for a strong lip line, changes hair color every six weeks, and has just gone off-Tour and arrived in Manhattan to see an English sugar daddy whom a fellow Digger (Travels With Men) has asked her to entertain. Bo, part Native American Zuni, builds the ego of her Walletmen with wise words lifted from astrology columns, and, since seeing *Dances With Wolves,* she nicks all her fellow Diggers with names like Earns Every Penny and Every Little Bit Helps. She has a Ten Year Window, from 20 to 30, to hit the Mother Lode, a Walletman she can mine for lasting, lifetime security. For the time being, she lives in a cute two-bedroom on the 34th floor of Trump Tower (rent: $4,800 a month) that she shares with her best friend, the snowman (that is, gay) budding psychologist Napoleon Dieudonne, to whom, as his only patient, tells her steamy life story: her pursuit of the Rich Rebel, Bradley Lorne-August; her tie with late sister Vicky's daughter, Maximilia; and her own rise to true self-empowerment. Felske laces every page with a masterful cynicism that Bo sees as her own Millennial Smarts while still charming all. A novel with legs.

— *Kirkus Reviews*

"Meet Bodicea Lashley, 'the millennium girl,' living by her wits, and various other attributes, as a 'digger'—a species of jet-set hooker who gets paid for her tricks in clothes and rent instead of cash. She travels an annual circuit from Gstaad to Ibiza and points in between, following the money in hopes of catching some crumbs from some generous older gentleman. Bo fills us in on the tricks of the trade as she relates the story of her twenty-eighth year. The digger jargon is kicky, as is the devise of giving fellow diggers pseudo-Native American monikers a la 'Dances With Wolves': Travels With Men, Earning Every Penny, Smiles to Your Face, *The Millennium Girl* is based on a magazine article Felske wrote in 1997 about young women hustling in Aspen. As a novel, it is snappy fun, a box of candy wrapped up with a black latex bow.

— *Booklist*

"Bodicea Lashley has definite goals. She is a 'Digger,' a woman who makes her living sponging off of supremely wealthy 'Walletmen' and an active participant on the 'Digger Tour.' The tour takes her all over the world, from Gstaad to St. Tropez, Palm Beach, and Aspen, to trade her feminine wiles for wearables from Prada and Gucci and for cold, hard cash. The goal of the Digger Tourists? To marry a Walletman, and Bo is trying her hardest to land the big one. A likeable character despite her excesses, Bo speaks in catchy phrases and, for her compatriots on the Digger Tour, finds hilarious nicknames like the Three Minute Princess and At These Prices. This is a strong follow-up to Felske's previous novel, Word, which delved hilariously into the Hollywood screenwriting scene. Here he uses his trademark insight and detail to peer into the lives of sassy but sad women. Learning how Bo got started in her line of work and observing encounters with the richest of the rich is a complete hoot. Sexy, hard to put down, and 100 percent fun, this is recommended for all fiction collections.

— *Library Journal*

"That classic opening line from *The Shallow Man*, "I never met a model I didn't like," defined an era. Coerte V.W. Felske has given us a run of texts which skillfully chronicle the skin-deep and shameless age with laser-like precision. There are pretenders to the throne of this genre but this resourceful and amusing novelist has it down. Like the late Stanley Elkin, Felske masters the pedantry of various trades and milieus, then creates a joyous poetry of jargon to float his novels on, setting sail on an ocean of buzzwords which continue to creep steadily into the daily vernacular. At the same time, he's not merely an inventor of neologisms, rather, a sorcerer of language and the written word, lacing each page with a masterful cynicism. I suspect we'll be talking about this author as the one who captured certainly the Nineties best. He one-upped fashionista literature with *The Shallow Man*, bested Nathaniel West with *Word*, and took Capote a step beyond with *The Millennium Girl*." — *The Guardian (England)*

Scandalocity

Also by Coerte V. W. Felske for The Dolce Vita Press

The Shallow Man
Word
The Millennium Girl

Completed future works

Chemical / Animal
The Ivory Stretch
A Touch of Noir

The Dolce Vita Press editions of Coerte V.W. Felske titles
available at the author's Web site,
www.coertefelske.com,
www.thedolcevitapress.com,
as well as Amazon.com

Scandalocity

Coerte V.W. Felske

The Dolce Vita Press, Inc.
New York

This book is a work of fiction. Names, characters, places and incidents are
either the product of the author's imagination or are used fictitiously
and any resemblance to actual persons, living or dead,
events, or locales is entirely coincidental.

Cover art and photography by Peter Beard
On front and back cover: Irina Shaykhlisamova photographed by Peter Beard on Giant Polaroids,
March 2009
Interior design by Jackie Merri Meyer / www.MeyerNewYork.com
Cover design by Chris Toms / Christoms@live.ca

THE DOLCE VITA PRESS is a trademark of The Dolce Vita Press, Inc.

Manufactured in the United States of America
Library of Congress Cataloging-in-Publication Data
Felske, Coerte V. W.
Scandalocity / by Coerte V. W. Felske—lst ed.

1. Title.
PS3556.E47259S53 1995
813'.54—dc20 94-47947
ISBN 978-0-9840786-1-5

10 9 8 7 6 5 4 3 2 1
First Edition

For Bodicea

Acknowledgments

I would like to thank the following individuals for their inspiration, help, and guidance, now and through the years.

Alex and Jacob Agam, Peter Allen, Alessandra Ambrósio, Ana Beatriz Barros, Peter Beard, Peter Berg, Christian Berman, Frank Berman, Bono, Chris Clausen, Chris Cooney, John Cooney, Bruce Cox, Doug Cummins, Stefan de Kwiatkowski, Jennifer Eatz, Cary Elwes, Norman Felske, Milos Forman, Yann Gamblin, Kevin Gannon, Douglas Greeff, Grace Hattersley, Jeffrey Jah, Diane and Jeff Jennings, Richard Johnson, Brad Kaplan, Robby Kravis, LuAnn de Lesseps, Connie Cromien-McAdam, Roger Moley, Kenneth Nichols, Theodore Owen, Chuck Pfeifer, John Rassias, Brett Ratner, Liz Rees, Tom Rees, Chris Ridenhour, Patricia and Peter Riordan, Amy Sacco, Neil Saltzman, Kim Sozzi, Irina Shaykhlisamova, Yulia Sukhanova, Nancye Simpson, Chris Toms, Anneke Van Wagoner-Felske, Ellen von Unwerth, Keith White, David and Stefanie Wilson, Charles Winslow, and Brad Zions.

Once again, I give special thanks to Peter Beard for his uncommon eye and creative magic, Chris Toms for his high-tech wizardry, and Jackie Meyer for her tasteful touch.

To friends and fallen soldiers, great souls and spirits taken too soon, you will always be remembered and I'm honored for the time we shared: Alan Beeber, Noel Behn, Joe Cole, Frank Daniel, Robert Hattersley, John Kennedy, and Billy Way.

I dedicate this book as I do all my work to my one and only treasure, Bodicea.

Though I have said that I envy the normal man to the point of the bitterest gall, yet, under the conditions in which I see him, I do not want to be one. And so, hurrah for the underground!

—*Fyodor Dostoevsky*
Notes From Underground
1864

There're a lot of sleepy people out there.

—*Jimi Hendrix*
The Dick Cavett Show
1969

Take the Paris Hilton phenomenon. I think a novelist could have thought up the story of a beautiful heiress who gets involved with a pornographic videotape. A novelist could have conceived of a beautiful heiress who has no particular talent getting a ten-million-dollar television contract. But I defy you to locate the novelist who could have conceived the actual plot of Paris Hilton's life, which is that she got the ten million dollar contract because she was on the pornographic videotape.

—*Tom Wolfe*
The American Spectator
January 10, 2K5

Dedication

To the ugly duckling darlings of yesteryear, all summarily afflicted, considered too lazy, underachieving, and uncontrollable in days past, the sensitive ones, the high-velocity ones, the ones brimming with a unique, rare, and glorious form of sensitized life, and now the envied ones, as the world huffs and puffs trying to catch up. And by all means, dearest diamonds, let the world stay winded; it's our time...

This one is for us. Behold ADD Nation.

Scandalocity

Prologue:

Notes from Scandoland

I must confess I spent most of my days convincing others I was better than they were. That's the gruesome truth. It wasn't that I sported finer clothes or a swankier address or had a faster car or even more influential friends. I possessed something far more significant in our dubious day and age: better name recognition. Indeed, enhanced NR was proof of one's significance, proof of the superior life. All that the watchful media types had to do was to crack open the morning paper or snap on a laptop and I was in their face reminding them they'd been socially and professionally outmaneuvered, outmatched, outwitted, and outgunned.

But I wasn't alone.

I belonged to a generation within a generation particularly talented for, savvy about, and consumed with this hollow pursuit. At the time it didn't seem so frivolous. On top of that I was a New Yorker, which made regrettable drives and preoccupations that much more anabolic, sinewy, strident, and fierce. In the process, I earned my share of enemies indirectly promoting the devastating reverse angle that coupled this questionable sport—causing others to feel less important, lacking, unaccomplished, perhaps inadequate. Because make no mistake, in this town it wasn't how affluent or elitist or café society or recessionary-proof or Broadway hip or downtown cool or even famous you once were. It was: are they still writing about you in flattering, glowing, even antiheroic, scandalous, or unflattering ways? And do your media feeds and boldface mentions still inspire envy, even spitball hatred? If the answer was "yes," you were likely still a fabulicious force, shooting down the cannonball tracks in a plush first-class car of the Love/ Hate Express, whooshing along on the crest of a spoiled, narcissistic,

Do-You-Know-Who-I-Am? Generation in a post-millennium, post-9/11 blaze and haze, followed, even adored by, those who never had a chance and hated by those who thought they did.

Many certainly found a lot in me to dislike from this standpoint. As absurd as it sounds, for those keeping score, people in print mattered more and bettering one's boldface was a full-time job.

At the same time, everyone, fan and foe, the admiring and jealous alike, waited with bated breath for the most succulent, ripe, and inevitable part of the boldfacer's story: their demise. It was the mandatory profile chapter linked to our life and times. Society required it, media barons provided it; a social Newtonian "what goes up, must come down" tale depicting that tragic ending, that proverbial crash and burn, a falling back to earth in a fiery fuselage from a rocket ship whose launch garnered so much attention only weeks, months, years before, with flames fanned at the crash site, rising higher and higher on a toxic, incendiary mix of lethal gases given off by residual traces of hubris, self-obsession, self-absorption, self-aggrandizement, and ego. Never a pretty sight. It was the type of devastation nearly impossible to recover from unless one possessed that special swirl of DNA alchemy which produced a thickness of skin to rival that of a rhinoceros, the ability to wear psychological horse blinders, as well as an uncommon capacity to blot out embarrassment and shake off layers of shame; at the same time, have the will and wherewithal to dust oneself off and rise again. But rarely is such a societal Iron Man ever seen.

All I can say is welcome to Scandoland, in the waning years of The Fabulous Age, for better or worse.

It was glam age, a fab age, with the members of its generation collectively screaming, crying out for their fifteen minutes, packs of press-desperate, big-fanged glory hounds all looking out for themselves, the world their mirror, true Legends of Shallow Hollow, all afflicted with the same virulent illness, the disease of me. It was a group no longer attempting to keep up with the Joneses. Rather, they hoped to stomp the Joneses right out of media contention and into extinction with a social climbing work boot with Vibram waffle tread to the neck; all searching for "lines," the head-type, the by-type, the tabloid type, and, as often is the case in the big city whether one succeeded or not, the nasal type. They were stardust seekers young and old trying to chin themselves up the notoriety bar to stave off any life sentence in anonymity, the modern equivalent of mediocrity, of failure, the only reward left for no-namehood, nobodyhood, namelessness and facelessness; a fate resulting in tortured corpses left to rot to the ribcage in the dank, dark, and desolate Dungeons of the Unknown. For many of this era, it was a fate worse than death. The Tomb of the Unknown Soldier was not an honor, it was a curse, and indeed, to some the uncelebrated, unrecognized, unrenowned, and undistinguished life, may well have been not worth living.

The speed and ease with which fresh media heroes were born, blasted into living rooms, downloaded to computer screens, and uploaded to handheld techie toys, made NR seem understandable, accessible, and more importantly, *possible*, like anyone could get in on it. Overnight sensations no longer required the overnight, nor did they need to demonstrate any sort of admirable quality, talent, or virtue. Instantaneous "stars," fab folk, as well as infamous, scandalocity antiheroes appeared on new and old media landscapes faster than the time it took to light up, or add water to their dust or powder, even less: more like the interval required for Facebookies and Twitter-twits to finger-dance an IM. A by-product of the Information Age, instantaneous NR was a cultural and societal phenomenon unknown to previous generations. With these new technologies at our fat little fingertips, we've been our own guinea pigs and I'll admit—we've behaved piggishly.

Yet these tech-driven, self-obsessed, "but-back-to-me" times have yielded more than questionable drives to be famous. Fame had its name recognition muscle and potency and may have worked wonders for appropriately contaminated souls, enabling them to successfully separate themselves from the pack; but to be "fab" was something extra. It was fame with a boost, fame with a carnation, fame with a maraschino cherry. It was sultrier, sexier, it was so of-the-now it oozed, it blazed, it scorched, it popped, because it had that extra spark, thrill, and zing, like the exhilarating dazzle of a shooting star. The boldfaced and fabulous were shooting stars. And I was one of them. Tangentially, anyway.

Where I differed from the vulpine pack was, it had never been a personal goal to possess any form of notoriety, much less to demonstrate it, prove it, show it, and throw it in everyone's face on a daily basis. Unlike most fellow I-Agers living in Manhattan at this time I wasn't consciously trying to socially outgun anyone. My DNA was messy, too flawed for its maestro to entertain, much less sustain modern Machiavellian drives. I was too busy trying to survive, plain and simple. It just so happened a name and reputation came with the territory and my chosen profession. And granted, as an online scando scribe with a daily media feed I wasn't on the All-Fab, All-Glam first team. I worked the sidelines, albeit a ubiquitous and significant fixture on the scene, a necessary cog in The Machine, perhaps even, its most useful, powerful, and feared type of member, a cyber J.J. Hunsecker in the flesh. You don't now know of what I speak, but you will. Then you can judge for yourself whether my tale of "success" had any sweet smell to it.

What I mean to say is that landing in New York and becoming a known and celebrated commodity happened by accident, tragic accident, an event I'll share right up front. For it was this event that shaped me, that led me to that high profile in those intervening years, and what also brought me to my knees, yes, to the juiciest part of my life story; oh yes, my crash, my burn. And, thereby, this calamity made me what I am today. A survivor.

This is my account, a snapshot of a generation, if you will, a misguided generation, a new "lost" generation, not lost to any other cause, continent, or field of battle but lost here at home. It's one man's story and even I can hear the hissing and spitting right now of a fuse that's burning, burning, burning on its way to the powder keg.

Do you know who I am?

You don't right now, but you may soon. And if you do find out, by all means, *Ssshhh!* Keep it to yourself. Don't text, write, or speak favorably or ill of me. I hate it when people do that.

Unless of course, they don't.

1

The Name's Harry, Dammit!

Lockhart, Massachusetts
February 10, 1984

"Harvey! Wait up!"

I hear Caitlin. I want her to come. She's so slow, though. I don't want to hurt her feelings. But it's the first day of ice at the Creek. Burt what's-his-name says it's ready. If the police say it's ready, it's ready. And I'm gonna be first!

My hockey skates keep smacking me in the back as I run. Youch!!! But I don't care. I'm too darned excited.

"Harvey!"

Caitlin is way behind. She always wants to come. I don't know why. She's too slow. I want to go fast. She knows it. If there's anyone I would wait for, it would be her. Caitlin makes me feel good. She doesn't call me names. Not "Crazy Harvey." Never. I hate that name. And "Lazy Boy." That one makes me wild. But what can I do? If I sock 'em, then I look crazy. If I don't do anything, I look lazy. Then it's true! So what can I do? But get madder. Sometimes I get so mad I want to scream. But screaming is no good, Doc Swenson says.

Caitlin looks out for me too. Always. She's an angel, I swear. If she gets a haircut and they give her a lollipop, she always brings back one for me. She always asks for the "one for my brother," no matter what. Even the cherry one if I want. If she got a Corgi car from Mom and Dad, she'd ask, "Can I have one for Harvey?" On her birthday, she makes sure they get me something. And she picks it out! Usually a crazy bright shirt. She says it's *so she can spot me easy. I don't mind. I love her though I never told her. It would sound queer. I used to say that stuff when I was little. Babies do. Then they get older and they don't say it anymore. They say it in the movies. My parents don't say it. The people who say it in the movies are really old, so... and they're the movies...*

But I can't wait now. Not for anyone. I want to get there fast. Going fast makes me feel it. Free. No "dammit Harvey!"s. Nuh-uh. Just me alone. The only time I ever feel it. Just free. I'm sprinting! From our house to the Creek. The last time it took five minutes. Ten minutes tops. Can't wait! I'll be there in a jiff!

I can see it now! Whoa!!! It looks like a sheet of glass. And there's no one there! It's all bare trees reflecting on the ice. It's like the whole world shining on it. Like a mirror! I want to make the first marks! No one's here. No one from school. Not Ridge Billings either. He's the best darn athlete. But he's not here. I'm the only one. I wish Cindy was here. To see me skate. If she saw me skate, she'd have to think about me. Not Ridge Billings. But he's a damn senior and he scores touchdowns. Coach Twilly's favorite. She has to think about all that crap. But if she could think the way she wants to think, then I bet she'd think of me. 'Cause I want to know what she's thinking.

I hope I don't get sent away. Not now. Caitlin is here. And Mom and Dad too. I like Doc Swenson. He's like my friend. He always has an answer. Not a crappy answer. I'd miss the kids in school too. Even though they tease me a lot. And I like the Creek. And Miss Barnes. She told Mom I was smart. Mom likes it when I do good things. But Mom is strict. She's tougher than Dad. She has that killer look. The one that places it all right. The blame. And you know where. That killer look gets me punished. Dad doesn't talk much. He stays out of things. But Mom scares me.

Like the time they didn't know I was home and they were talking about me. More like yelling. Mom said I was "tearing the family apart." With all the stuff I was doing. It's good Mom went away. She was getting real nervous before she left. She had a swell time in Florida. She came back all pretty and tan. She's been okay since she came back. No killer looks. Not even one. And no "we're sending you away"s. It's just the best when she's nice. The day after she heard I was smart, she let me have a study break and let me come out of my room and join everyone when we had the Lincolns over. I was having such a darn good time. 'Til I broke the lamp. Grammy's lamp. I never should have been swinging it. I was just so excited. I pretended it was a sword. And I yelled, "On guard!" like a Musketeer and swung it around. Caitlin thought it was funny. Shoot! Why did the darn thing have to break? Caitlin always laughs at what I do. She thinks I'm funny. That's what she tells me. Caitlin is just about the nicest girl there is. She always sticks up for me. With her friends and all. She's an angel, I swear.

I'll put on my skates by the big pine. I'm doing a crummy job but I want to get started! I'm too excited. And in such a hurry! That cool air going in my lungs. It's like eating mint candy. Here goes, stepping on the ice... Man! It's so smooth. And slippery. Like glass. And I'm the first one! Boss! But my legs feel weird. Off balance. I'll do some figure eights to warm up. Caitlin's coming through the clearing. She's real slow and it's making me nervous. I have to be patient. Like Doc Swenson says. 'Cause I'm eleven.

"Harry! Why didn't you wait up?"

"Oh."

"Can you help me with my skates?"

"Uh, yeah. I guess."

She's got brand new figure skates with purple laces. Purple is her favorite color. Actually, light purple is. There's a name for light purple but I forget. She has light purple dresses and socks. Mom got her dark purple laces only because there weren't any light purple ones. She's using 'em for the first time. She's only eight. She'll be nine in two days. So she opened her birthday present already. That's why she wanted to come so bad. Them new skates. Heck, I'd be excited too...

I tighten hers tighter than mine. So her ankles don't cave in. She needs tight skates to keep her ankles staying in place and up straight.

"That better?"

"Why didn't you wait up, Harry?"

"Stop calling me that. My name's Harvey."

"I like Harry better."

"Well, it's not my name."

"Oh, all right."

I don't like that. Her teasing me. She's an angel but she can still get my goat. She doesn't mean it. I mean she means it but in a good way. Not like kids in class.

"That's tight enough," she says.

I watch her step to the edge. As she steps on the ice she lets out a big old *shriek!*

"*Careful—*" *I tell her.*

"*Why?*"

"*They're brand new. And real sharp.*"

"*So what?*"

"*You can trip easy.*"

Then she slips and goes down. As soon as I warned her. She's laughing. She can be real silly sometimes.

"*Harry!*" *There she goes again.* "*Help me up!*"

I do. But I want to take off. "*I'm going to go fast.*"

"*Harry, wait!*"

"*Practice here first!*"

"*I can go with you—*"

"*Get used to your skates!*"

"*I am!*"

I dig in and push off. Pumping my legs. I can see all the way to the other side of the Creek. That's where I'm going.

Caitlin is coming. I hear her yelling. But there's no time to listen. I'm really ripping.

"*Wait up, Harvey!*"

Now she's using my real name. To be nice. But I'm not stopping. Not for anything. I'm a machine. Feeling free. Feeling big and free!!!

I stand straight and coast to take a breath. My breath shoots out all thick and white like smoke. I'm halfway across. Caitlin's moving slowly, her knees knocking together, her ankles caving in.

"*Harvey!*"

She knows I want to go fast. To go fast, I have to go to the other end of the Creek. Or I can't go fast enough. I've explained it to her a hundred times. Darn! But, well, I don't want to hurt her feelings. I look back and see her trying hard. I'll turn back. She's having a hard time. She's really huffing and puffing. Like H.R. Pufnstuff. I hate that show. Boy, are her ankles caved in.

"*Take my hand, Harvey.*"

"*Okay.*"

Her hand is so small in mine. And soft. I'll hold it tight. I start pumping when I get the good grip.

"*Faster!*" *She's now commanding me.*

I don't want to go that fast. Not with her. "This is fast enough," *I say. I've got to be careful. Mom wouldn't like to see this already. And I'm not even going fast!*

"Is not! Faster, Harvey! You can go faster. I know you can. Come on!"

Jeez, that Caitlin is something else; she really wants it. I'll hold her hand tighter and pick up the pace. I love going fast. So does Caitlin, but she can't do it. Not by herself.

"Come on, Harvey. Faster!" *she keeps saying.* "I'll call you Harry if you don't go faster!"

We're cruising now! Like the wind! Feeling free! Wow! I see her smiling. And laughing. We're almost at the end. I'm getting bushed. But it's great! Whew! I'll coast. Just coasting. But fast coasting. She pulls free. So she can glide all by herself. As she veers way off, she yells, "Thanks, Harry!" *To tease me. She coasts slower then real slow. She smiles at me as she stops. She's looks so happy. I see the ice where she is, it looks pretty darn dark. Like real dark. And puddly. I hope it's not thin. And she's too heavy. I'm getting a bad feeling. It's such a quick bad feeling. I don't want anything bad to happen. It can't. It just can't!*

"Caitlin, get back over here—"

Did I hear a crackity-crack sound? No! Did I?

Then she yells, "Harv'—!!!" *And there's all these lines shooting out from under her skates! Cracks explode everywhere like on an Etch A Sketch board! Then, NO!! The ice breaks!! Crash!!! SHE FALLS THROUGH!!! She's IN THE FREEZING WATER!!! SCREAMING!!!*

I sprint over like a maniac! Her head is barely above water!!!

"Harvey!!! Help!!!"

"Coming!"

"I'm sinking!!"

As I approach the hole, the ice breaks beneath me! I plunge on down too! All the way under. We're in a big darn icy hole!!

"Caitlin!"

I look around. WHERE IS SHE?? I DON'T SEE HER!!!

This is really bad! Worst ever! I dive under, open my eyes, and look and it's so darn black! And so cold!!! Like a thousand Doc Swenson needles jabbing me all at once!!! Everywhere!!! My leg bumps against something. I reach way down and find it. I grab her hand and yank her hard and swim her up. She lets out a huge gasp.

"Harvey!"

Thank God she's okay! I'm trying not to panic. How could it happen? I tried to avoid it! But no one'll know that! I'm in for it! Double in for it!!!

Enough of that! I got to get her out!

I see that the thin ice at the edge won't hold her. I smash the crusty stuff. And keep smashing. Until it gets thick. I try to hoist her. Have nothing to hold me. It's so darn hard to swim with skates on. And heavy clothes weighing me down. I'm sinking. Can't lift her. I paddle to stay up, to tread water, and she slips from my hand. I grab, but miss, and darnitall she SLIPS UNDER AGAIN!!! I wrap arms around her and pull her back up.

"Harv'!!!" She's shouting and stuttering she's so cold. "I'm sinking!!!"

"Stick with me, Caitlin! It's gonna be okay!"

I scoop her under and pump my legs to stay up and hoist her with all my might. She weighs a lot. I get her onto hard ice. Seems thick enough. And it holds, thank God! I say a quick prayer. God please make it hold!!!

"Get away from the hole!"

"How?"

"Crawl. To the bank. Slowly. So I can get out too."

But she doesn't move. She's sitting there. Like in a trance.

"Caitlin! Go to the bank. Get on land! Quick!" I yell.

She's so cold and scared. So I holler really loud. "CAITLIN!!!" It snaps her out of it. She gets up and wobbles away. She makes it! That is a darn relief!

I shimmy onto the ice in the same spot I lifted her. My legs don't move well. Have to crawl. Ice cracks beneath. I make it off, barely!

We're so darn cold. It's not needles now, it's knives! Knives in the ribs, it's so cold!!! And she's just sitting there.

"Are you all right?" She doesn't nod or shake. Her face is white, her lips blue. Her teeth are chattering.

"What are we going to do, Harvey?"

"I don't—"

My head is bursting with so many thoughts. I can't make any sense. Find a nearby house! Go to the hospital! Get a car! Gotta make this right!!! Bus! Taxi! Look at her not complaining! And she's freezing!!! Call the police! Call home! Nothing seems right. They all spell the same thing.

TROUBLE!!! They'll lock me in my room. This time for a month! Or send me away! They were going to before. But now they really will! I can see the killer look! "What were you doing at the other end of the Creek with your sister? You know you're not supposed to go to the other end!! Harvey! Harvey! Harvey! That's it!!! We're sending you away for good!!!"

"Harvey? Don't worry. I'm okay…"

I look at her again. She's not even crying. She's no sissy, that Caitlin. And she's my sister. Seeing her strong makes me feel a little better.

"We'll walk back to the other side. Okay? Caitlin?" I rip through her laces and pull off her skates. Then mine.

We walk along the bank in our wet socks back to the big pine. I see the Thermos. "You brought the Thermos!"

"Uh-huh."

"Thatta girl! That was so smart!"

I was so happy she thought ahead that I coulda kissed her right there! I quickly open it and hand it to her. She's so smart, Caitlin is. But then, she drops the whole thing! All the hot cocoa spills out. Her little hands were so cold that she couldn't hold it. It was my fault. Should have thought ahead myself. "Darn!" Why didn't I hold it? Or give her just the cup? Idiot! Why can't I do things right? Tears start in my eyes. But I can't cry. She'll get more scared. Even though I'm scared as hell. More scared than I've ever been! Ever!!!

"It's okay, Harvey…"

We walk a lot. And walk more. Until Caitlin can't walk any more. Her legs just won't go. She says they won't go.

"What do you mean they won't?"

"They won't go. My hands won't, either."

Her feet and legs and hands are so frozen that she can't move. Caitlin's lips are purple. She looks like a ghost. What the heck are we going to do??

I crouch down and grab her legs and give her a piggyback. I leave my skates. But I take Caitlin's. Hers are new. Can hear my mother's voice now. "How could you have left her new skates? You think money grows on trees???"

Holding her on my back, I kneel and grab both blades. The edges stick against my palm, but I don't care…

I start walking. The blades hurt against my hand. They're sharp. Digging into my palm. And she's heavy with sopping clothes. She's gotten bigger too.

*It aches to carry her. But I'm gonna make this right. Make them proud. My
hand hurts, but I can't stop…*

*After a long while, maybe after a mile, I see the pay phone on Lily Pond
Lane. I think I have change in my pocket. I can't call my parents, though.
They'll kill me!*

"Caitlin?"

"Yeah?"

"How are you?"

"I can't feel my legs or hands. But I'm okay…"

"I'm gonna call Mom and Dad."

"No, Harvey."

"I have to."

"No! I'll be okay!"

"What?"

"We can make it!"

"But you're numb already. That's no good."

"I'm all right. What are you doing?"

"Checking my pockets."

"Just put me down."

"No! I'm not letting you go!"

"Harvey—"

"No!"

*I drop the skates. Crouch down. My hand hurts. It's bleeding. The edges
cut me. I'm not letting go of her. I dig my hand in my pocket. There's that
gum wrapper. But no money. I check my left pocket. Nothing…*

"Caitlin?"

I can hardly hear her. "What?"

"Do you have any money?"

"No."

"Are you sure?"

"Yes. I'm sure."

"Darn!" *But wait. I can call the police for free.*

"What are you doing Harvey?" *She asks in that weak voice.*

"You sit here while I call…"

"Call who?"

"The police."

"No, Harvey! Don't call the police!"

"Why not?"

She starts to cry now, not bawling,, but sobbing. "Because!"

"Because what?"

"Because—they'll send you away!"

It makes my heart sink. That she says it. "Who will?"

"Mom and Dad. Don't call them! Don't call the police! I don't want them to send you away. Not ever!"

I don't care about myself. Don't want her hurt. But she must know she's okay. Enough to make me not call. "But—"

"No! Tell me you won't. Promise me, Harvey. Promise me!"

Water starts to fill my eyes. A tear streams down. I love my sister so much. I've never told her. I will. Today, I will. She's my favorite person in the whole wide world. She's an angel. My sister Caitlin is an angel.

"We can do this together," she says. Then she bursts out coughing. "And no one will know. Ever…" And the word barely makes it out of her mouth. "Promise?"

I don't say anything. I'm too mixed up and confused…

"Take me to Dr. Swenson's. He's not far…"

She's right. Old Doc Swenson'll know what to do. He always has an answer. Not a bullcrap answer. And he doesn't tell Mom and Dad everything. He's like a friend.

"I won't call you Harry anymore if you—" I don't hear the end because she has another big coughing attack.

My foot steps forward. Then the other. We are moving on. Advancing slowly. She is heavy to me now. The going is slower as I get weaker. My shoulders ache. My hand hurts.

Another half mile down the road, I'm telling myself, "we're almost there."

"Cait? We're almost there."

She's not responding. I tell her again. Nothing comes back. She's saving her energy. By not talking anymore. Takes too much energy to talk. She's smart that way. Saving energy. Doesn't want me to have to work harder. Kind of sister she is. The best, I'm tellin' ya.

"That's right, save your energy, Cait!"

Ready to quit. But can't. "Fourth quarter." Coach Twilly said it. Give it all you got. In the fourth. Where you win or lose. Old Coach said it. Heard 'im tell Ridge Billings. And the rest. When I spied practice. Fourth *quarter. One to go…*

Going slowly now. So slowly. Don't know what's happening. I'm hurting. Seeing funny. Been thinking. 'Bout everything. Crazy flashes. 'Bout Mom, Dad, Cait, me. Teachers. Classmates. Seniors. Teasers. "Harvey you moron!" Harvey Dumbo. Crazy Harvey. Lazy Harvey. "Dammit, Harvey!" Been a pain. Don't know why. Try to do right. Doesn't work out. Works out for Ridge Billings. Not for me…

Legs don't move like I want. Do what I say. So cold. Tired. Hungry. She's so heavy. See the clearing ahead, the driveway to Doc Swenson's. I forget everything I was thinking.

"Caitlin! We're here!"

She's quiet. She's saving energy. For later.

Turn down the driveway, gasp out loud. Don't see a car. Maybe it's at the mechanic's. And he's inside. Cooking. Some hot and steamy oatmeal. Doc's going to invite us in. And feed us some damn hot, steamy oatmeal…

Reach the porch. Lay her on the ground. The weight off makes me light. Dizzy. Her eyes are closed. She's out. Getting rest. Can you blame her? I need it too. She's bushed.

I'm real dizzy. No balance. I wobble. Knees go. I float down, see the wide yellow hole. Can't stop. Fall right down. Damn deer peed a hole in the snow. I lay there. Dumb. Moron. Lazy. Can't stand. It's red all around. Blood. Damn dead animal. See my hand. Sliced. Across the palm. My damn blood. Hurts like hell. I'm cursin'. Can't help it. Not supposed to. Mom'll kill me. Click! Click! Can't help it. Heck is hell. Can't help it. Darn is damn. Damn it all!!!

Crawl to the front door. Aches to get up. Sore all over. Look through the window. Don't see Doc. Where are you, Doc? He's not cooking no damn steamy oatmeal. Shoot! I knock. With my left. Right hand's a mess. Bleeding. Don't want to get blood all over.

"Doc!" Yell again. "Hey Doc!"

Check the doorknob. Door locked. Gotta punch it. I'm no lefty. But got to. With my left. Yowww! Missed. Hit the damn wood. I'm no lefty. When the hell is it going to get better?? Do it again. Hard. Straight. Cry out. Yikes! But got it. Hand goes through! Reach, unlatch the lock. Pull out hand, blood everywhere. Knuckles. Gashes across the knuckles. Shoot! Two bloody hands…

Turn the doorknob. Swings open.

"Cait, got it! Damn door!"

I go back, pick her up. "You hear me? Going inside now…"

She's still resting. Speak some more but she doesn't respond. Carry her in. Man everything aches. Fourth quarter. Almost over. Bring her to the couch, by the fire, warm coals. She loves the crackles. And pops. Nice and toasty. Crackles and pops.

"Nice 'n' toasty, Cait."

Old Coach was right. Work hard. Then it's over. In the fourth quarter. We made it. Cait and me. We'll tell Doc the truth. He won't squeal. He's my friend. But we need to say it right. To go over the story. Me and Caitlin. Don't want to wake her. She looks like an angel there. But we gotta talk. She better wake up. Wake up now.

"Caitlin? Wake up." I nudge her. "Cait?"

She's resting. Doesn't want to talk. Yet. But maybe she's not sleeping. Maybe passed out. Can be trouble. Call it a coma. Like that movie. Damn!

I look for the phone. Search. In the kitchen. There! I dial. What's our damn number? Is it 8668 or 6886? Get it mixed up… Always trouble with numbers. It's ringing… Answer, please answer! No one answers. Not even Mom… Let it ring… Twenty times… I'll get the police. "Operator? Get me the police!" Hope Cait won't be mad. For contacting 'em. She won't know. Won't tell her. They'll send me away. Don't care now. Care about her. Time to get help. I saw first aid once. But we need help. Ringing, ringing… Damn! Come on police!

"Sheriff's office…"

Thank you, God!!!

"My sister is passed out! We fell through the ice… Wha??… At the Creek… No, Burt! What's his name? Turner! He said it was ready. But wait!… We're here now! She's out!… By the fire… At Doc Swenson's!… That's right! White Birch Road… Please, get here! Quick!!!"

I rush back. Gotta shake her again. Wake her. Coins roll out. Of her pockets. She had money! The whole damn time!!! To give to me. To call the police. But she wouldn't. Told me she didn't have any! To save me. From getting sent away. That's my sister. She's a damn angel. She said go to Doc's. Her plan. To save me. The water is flooding my eyes so much I can't see. I wipe my eyes. When I can see again I check her hands. They're still cold. I look for her beats. Don't know where they are. Must be here. Can't find 'em. *Saw it happen once to a kid at a baseball game. They worked his hands and wrists. But don't know where. Come on beats, come on pulse. Where are you? Can't find 'em. I'm trying not to panic. But can't help it! My eyes flooding up again. Can't see. Sweating. Panicking. Where's the damn pulse? Damn it all! I can't find it! Please God, help me!!! Where are the beats???*

I put my ear to her lips. To feel her breath. Or something! Can't hear it. Can't feel it. Come on. Air, come on. Grab her head, open her mouth. Blood smears on her face. From my hand. Tears fall. On her angel face! I can't help it! I blow in, keep doing it, to fill her lungs. Blood's getting on her neck. I clutch her head hard. I want a life-saver maneuver. Like the doctors. Got to be a strong life-saver maneuver. Please God! Fourth quarter, time running out. Trying so hard now. But she won't open her eyes. Her body is flopping, I'm trying so hard.

"Caitlin! Wake up!!! Please!!!"

Car pulls up. Thank God! I yell at the top of my lungs. "WE'RE HERE! WE'RE HERE! WE'RE HERE!" *I hear big footsteps outside!*

"Harvey!"

It's Doc Swenson, thank the Lord! He knows what to do! He has an answer! "Help her, Doc!"

"What's happened?"

"I don't think she's breathing!"

"She's all wet—"

"We-we-we fell through the ice!"

Then he gave it to me. That look! That killer look! Mom's killer look! The one that places blame. He's never done that before. And it really scares me. Really scares me now...

"She's gonna be okay, right?"

He doesn't talk. Doc always has an answer for me. But not now. Not this time. Where's the damn answer? More water streams down my face.

God, please make her all right! Please make her wake up!!!

Doc Swenson is working so hard. So damn hard! He's sweating. Make that strong life-saver maneuver! He knows. I know he knows!!!
"It's the fourth quarter, Doc!"

His look scares me. Each time he tries a life-saver maneuver. His face doesn't ease up. Not one damn bit! It stays worried. Sweating. Just let go of it. The bad face. Give me the good face. Let me know everything is going to be okay! 'Cause things have never been okay. Been locked in my room a thousand times. Click! Click! Click! Those damn locks. I see that damn killer look. For something I did. But nothing as bad as this! But I don't give a damn! I just want her to be all right. Give me the good face, Cait! Give me the good face, Doc!

God, please help us! I'll never do anything bad again. Just this one time! Make her okay!

Make up my mind. It's not going to happen. Caitlin is going to breathe. Right now. She's going to wake up, dammit. Doc Swenson's face is going to change. Right now, I say! And get nice. And easy. Now! I want it to happen right now! Smooth out your face, Doc!

"Right now!" I yell. "Just this one time!"

"Take it easy, Harvey!"

"Change! Just change your damn face, Doc!"

"Harvey! Sit down over there!"

I sit on the couch. I watch his nervous, wrinkly face. Damn, it's wrinkling everywhere. With worry. Change! Change now, face! But the face isn't changing. Not one damn wrinkle…

I see all the coins on the floor and I look at her beautiful face, her angel face, my sister Caitlin who I've never told I love her, and she loves me so much she won't let me call the police and there she is as white as a ghost with purple lips and she's not breathing or moving or saying anything, not even enough to call me Harry. Oh, God, please let her call me Harry. Please!!!

"I love you, Caitlin."

And the face of Doc Swenson never eases and the good face never comes, but the police cars do, a whole lot of them. And the ambulance too. And my parents come. And my mother, with her tan cheeks cries hysterically. And my father cries too. And they can't find me anywhere 'cause I watch everything from a deep hole in the woods. And they don't find me for six hours. When Burt Turner the policeman who said the Creek is ready sees me on the side of the road in a ditch in the middle of my plan. I am doing my best try, my best damn try to freeze myself up. Just like Caitlin. 'Cause I think it's the only way to find her, to stop breathing and go like she went, to die, so I can go to where she went and find her and protect her because she didn't know where she was going when she passed out and died and I want to find her before she gets lost and hold her hand and tell her it's okay that we're together and I went the same way she did and we're going to have the same funeral together and we'll be buried in the same place next to each other and I'll hold her little soft hand forever. And that I'll never let it go. Ever. And we'll be together. Forever! That's my plan.

So my legs get totally numb and then my hands and that's good 'cause I'm on my way and I'm coming Caitlin! and I'm trying not to breathe too, but every time I hold my breath it comes back after a minute or so, but I can feel it getting easier because I pass out and everything is real numb and I can't hear anything and I can't see anything and it's all getting real quiet and "Yippee!" I know I'm on my way to Caitlin to find her and hold her hand, I can feel it, together forever, together forever, and real, real quiet... and then... I hear sounds again... dammit! damn, damn, damn it all!! nothing ever works right! That damn Burt Turner with his damn flashlight is talking to me and wakes me up, just as I'm almost there, almost right there with my sister the angel who I love so much and I miss her so much already! And he pulls me out of that ditch and he makes me be breathe and be alive, thinking about her all lost and far away, not knowing what to do or where to go and she's yelling to me to wait up!!!

"No, leave me alone!!!" I scream. "I gotta find her!!! Let me go!!!"

The next worst part is I have to stay alive a lot and forever and I'm under kill-myself watch and the hospital does it with all-night nurses and they look at me like I should be glad for what they've done, that they saved me, and I hate them, I hate them all, every damn one of them!!! And I have frostbite and they cut off half of my fourth toe on my right foot and those goddam nurses, they talk to me like, "Harvey this, Harvey that," and say I'm still "in shock" and have some "cute memory loss" stuff going on and every time I yell back at them: "Harry! My name is Harry! How many times have I got to tell ya? I'm Harry dammit-all!"

"Harry!!! Harry!!! Harry!!!"

Harry Starslinger
November, 2K8

As you see, I recently chronicled, signed, and dated this personally handwritten account of what happened that tragic day in 1984. But my story really begins months prior to putting the unfortunate reminiscence to paper, in August, 2K8.

And the story, well, it's about a woman—isn't it always?

But this was murder...

2

Friday with Dr. Van den Heugel
at the Height of the Age of the Asterisk (*)

August, 2K8

"Why do you say 'please leave a New York no-fat message' on your answering machine?" The Ice Princess with PhD opened with. We were having our weekly twosome, going through the compulsory hollow warm-ups.

"I like it lean."

"As in?"

"Fewest words possible. You can cut verbs entirely."

"Why the verbs?"

"Verbs are fat."

"What is fat?"

"Fat is time. They're a waste of time."

"Is that what you're in fear of? Wasting time?"

"Always."

"Are you constantly in need of more time?"

"Unquestionably, Doctor."

"What do you accomplish with these small bits of time you accumulate by cutting everything short?"

"Not much."

"You don't do anything with this added time?"

"Nothing at all." Confirmed, I was having a bit of a low and my initial venti 'Bucks bold tallboy hadn't assaulted my senses yet.

"Why do you need it then?"

"It's the nothingness, the flat void increments I'm seeking out. Mental holidays. Did I tell you about the ADD BBQ I had last spring?"

"Uh, no. What does BBQ stand for?"

"That would be 'barbeque.' I was stressed and depressed because of you-know-what and they were calling in at a speed you couldn't clock, clogging my e-mail, texting me, faxing me with doodles and blank sheets, and taking up extraordinary amounts of my time."

"Who are 'they'?"

"The Militia."

"What Militia?"

"The ADD Militia. All the disorder-addled types I know. Locally."

"So what did you do?"

"I invited the Militia over. For some spring lamb and turkey burgers. I billed it as a 'Foot and Mouth Meat Festival.' It was a teaser. ADDers love teasers. Drives them wild. If you tell them you're having a theme party, they get very excited. And if you won't show them the guest list they go nuts. They just have to show."

"So what happened at this barbeque?"

Though she was an impenetrable toughie with icy Poland Spring running through her veins, the Princess was never terrific toil on the iris. She had long, dark chestnut hair, milk-white skin, and a forties movie star face barely held in check by rimless, retro-feminist Dior specs. The glasses were a pricey but pastel attempt to downplay her gifts. Her only vulnerable spot was a soft spreading mouth and I worshipped the curve of its grin. I could cuddle up cozily there and doze off. The gal was exceptionally stylish and office appointments served as her own catwalk march where she'd debut the latest Marchesa, Escada, Oscar, and Chanel collections. That day she wore a clingy lemon and tangerine skirt with a vibrant silk Pucci blouse which hung low, letting loose the double hints. We'd endured a long winter, and covered-up period and I wasn't immune to the elegant décolletage of those smoldering guns unleashed and pouring forth once more, with a biological accuracy and fluidity of movement as scandelectable proof of authenticity, respectfully so. Her feet were spiked from beneath by Dolce slingback pumps and day-old Tom Ford shades dazzled up the desk. "Could you repeat the question?"

"The barbeque?"

In fact I was thrilled the summer season was back. It offered so many diversionary distractions for the devastated life, a full metropolis's worth. And when you're feeling vexed, victimized, and vanquished, distractions are pretty much the cotton candy of your days.

"Most ADDers. The truly dysfunctional ones. The ones who harangue and harass me on a daily basis—"

"Wait. Why are you the object of any daily focus they may have?"

"Because I have a job."

"Is that all?"

"No. Because I'm one of them. ADDers generally like each other. Rather, need each other. Or despise each other."

"In what way?"

"Normies are lo-stim. We need hi-stim. We need action. Normies can't provide it. Or sustain it. ADDers can. You know that."

"Do members of this Militia group work?"

"Some do, but most don't."

"Why not?"

"They can't get it together long enough."

"How do they live? Are they all independently wealthy?"

"Some are. Others slough around and live off advantaged types or are on the dole. Some are temps or work part-time. They're largely hand-to-mouthers. But most can't concentrate on anything long enough, certainly not what a real job would require. The only thing they respond to are offers for food and drink."

"Why is that?"

"Because they have to eat. And medicate."

"So you had this party—"

"I went to Balduccis and bought the meat, then picked up a high-powered grill at K-Mart, and tiki torches. The problem was the grill required three hours to assemble, the propane tank came empty and needed to be filled, and the tiki torches had no kerosene. It was already eight o'clock and our only hopes for specialized equipment were the delis. It was all my fault. A drat and double drat affair."

"So what happened?"

"Dr. Van den Heugel, even I know this is a detour."

"Let me be the judge."

"We got lighter fluid, which miraculously worked in the torches, but we couldn't eat. Which I guess is what an ADD barbeque is all about. Everyone comes and nobody eats."

"What about the kitchen?"

"No one cooks."

"So what did everyone do?"

"They drank. It was a beautiful night. The downtown skyline was hovering over us with a sweep of starry lights. It would have been a real symphony, but as I said, no one knew how to prepare dinner."

"So it was a total flop—"

"Negs. A total success. So they say."

"You mean you weren't there?"

"No."

"What did you do?"

"I went to Subway."

"What for?"

"The Seven-Layer Monster. My favorite hoagie."

"Wait a second, Harry. You invited everyone over just so you could leave and eat somewhere else?"

"Precisely."

"Why?"

"Like I said, I was feeling harassed and the only way I could get some well-deserved downtime was to assemble all the attention vampires in one setting and let them all hassle and bother each other."

"Did it work?"

"I had a wonderful sixty-five minutes…"

"Before?"

"Before they realized I was missing. Then they phoned and flurried me with texts like a finger-pecking squadron of crazy Mozarts."

"So you came home?"

"I had to; I had to lock up. You don't leave your loft, even a loft as childproof as the Skybox, with people like that."

"Why don't you turn your phone off if you need peace and quiet?"

"I could never do that."

"Why not?"

"I need to know what's going on."

"For your job?"

"In general. It's the paradox of being turbo-ADD. You hate to be bothered, but you need to know what's happening. It's a killer. It's the pits. And best of all, it's a life sentence."

Dr. Van den Heugel was a gifted psychoanalyst with a def beauty boost. After all, I'd known my share of psych pros and semi-pros; the list was lengthy, and I'd laid rubber on a few. Sure, she nipped at my heels, but none of her proddings stung. The reality is, an appointment with her was not work. It was more like going out, meeting someone chic and honey-comely, and tipping cans back. More like play. Good ambience, fine coffee, delightful detours in conversation on a subject I didn't mind discussing—*moi*—and above everything else, real easy on the eyes.

And we had considerable history.

"Okay," she sighed, no doubt realizing she should have redirected our deviation minutes ago, though she rarely admitted to error. The good doctor was razor and intellectually competitive too. "Let's get down to business."

"'Let's get after it' sounds better." I was mauvely competitive, too. "But I'm just dandy with more 'me.'"

Only then did I understand her subtle technique. She'd embraced the pointless detour and let it run its course in an attempt to relax me. I hadn't been forthcoming and open in recent sessions.

"Why do you do what you do?"

"With respect to what?"

"The sex and the serial nature of—"

Her delicate probe didn't survive through the punctuation. If the Ice Princess cared to talk sex with me, I was resigned to it at last. It could warm the cold stove up too, meaning her, I thought. "It medicates me."

"Does it make you feel better?"

"For a while."

"And then?"

"Then I go to work."

"How are you feeling now?"

"Scanderrific." She didn't believe me, but she was accustomed to my snarky banter. I had an interior vision of her then and felt dismayed. I hadn't heard anything about boyfriends in a while and I wondered if she was feeling lonely, detached, or alienated. After sounding out everyone else's problems and hang-ups all day, when she went home and listened to the silence of her heart, what did she really feel? The stoic beauty never let her vulnerability roam free and I tried to expose it, but it wasn't her job to let down her guard. I knew one thing: she couldn't be as detached as me. Good old Harry Disconnect, an appliance plug of a man hopelessly searching for a wall socket.

"Are you still taking the psychostimulants?"

"Only when I must."

"When is that?

"When I want hyperfocus. Otherwise I leave them alone."

"Why?"

"I don't want to miss out on the good stuff."

"What do you mean by that?"

I opted for the medium-wind version. I hadn't had that second 'Bucks bold brew, the 54-cent refill, and was still car bumper dulled and groggy.

"If you think of the mind as an orchestra, the Adderall acts as a conductor who coordinates the music. Directing the players, keeping the whole symphony together. But I enjoy hearing the individual instruments, the independent thoughts. I'm capable of some pretty nifty ones. I'd say it's pretty much the fun of being me."

"Did you take any Adderall today?"

"Uh-uh." I observed the squiggles of her clinny shorthand and found them cute, the kind which likely boasted hearts and sunflowers to top the "i"s only years before, dashed off in tiny love Post-Its to former crushes *du jour*. It may have been projection on my part. Women I found simpatico I always envisioned in youth as "flower power" hippie girls with daisies in their hair and bellbottoms, full of fuchsia optimism, baby blue courage, bright yellow enthusiasm, and orange promise. Then, for the ones with cash reserves to burn, all that verve and idealism ends up in the chosen seasonal color palette of a Gucci skirt, like the one wrapping the doctor's enviable tush.

"And the Zoloft? Has it helped?"

"Fractionally."

"How are your moods?"

"Swingy. And constant."

"Any more headaches?"

"Not recently."

"Blackouts?"

"My unforced errors? None that I can remember."

She broke charitably to it. "And the job? How is it going?"

"How do you think?"

"It's not important what I think. What do you think?"

"I'm a poor self-observer. I think it's why I hired you."

"Harry…" She droned.

3

Infamy is the New PR

I sighed with impetus and loaded up. Machine-gun chatter channeled through me and out my flaps and releasing it was about as difficult as breathing.

"Party girl wakes up, ogles the pressed-tin ceiling, can't find her iPhone, doesn't have a morning-after GPS, can't access a landline, her La Perla strings are missing and her moneymaker pretty much aches. And I'm required to write about this scando-random behavior with cheeky enthusiasm."

"Has it become boring for you?"

"You think? The same rise and demise dance? Desperate people in need of Face, others desperately not needing it but getting it for pseudo-heroic deeds they may not be proud of. And I'm the lone chimp Slinging it in the middle. It's trashtastic; in a little town called Scandoland."

"You the online gossip blogger?"

I couldn't hold it in any longer, so I indulged fully with no mental edits, overrides, or checks for *politesse*. It poured from my sternum like barely digested post-clubbing pizza.

"But let's face it. It's deep 2K8 and infamy is the new PR for boosted NR and the hero is the antihero. Scandochamps Paris, Lindsay, Britney, Kate, Naomi, the Vintage Three M's: Martha, Monica, and scandogranny Madonna. And scandosampler Combs and scandobammer Tyson. A murdering mobster's scandofam gets their own show, a scandopopper gets hers, and Paris becomes an author. Behold the times, the Age of the Asterisk (*)—*ding!!!*—everything getting more artificial, plasticized, metastasized, and distanced from nature; resources are dwindling, overcrowding rules, and with that comes Desperation Nation, the rats-in-a-cage scenario, people on the fringe, modern antiheroes being pushed to perform Darwinian deeds they wouldn't ordinarily perform in order to be heard, get noticed, which includes sporadic and spastic Machiavellian maneuvers and pushing and mashing the envelope on integrity. Sure, this conflicted character interests me and I try to write with full-throttle zest, but it doesn't always work out. Meanwhile every Bloid, Blog, celeb-worship, and irritainment reality show rams and reinforces the Next Big Thing, the Next Big Dancer, the Next Big Nobody down our throats. Why don't today's stars resemble Cary Grant, Gary Cooper, or Ingrid Bergman? How about they didn't have chopperazzi and scandocams aimed at them 24/7/365? Just one shot in black tie and evening gown sent worldwide would preserve the elegance, but today's Machine doesn't allow it, and look what it breeds, *Whatever makes you famous,* the thinking goes; for this fresh snot-nosed generation, fame and notoriety gives them some hope, an instantaneous shot of self-esteem, and here I am to assist them in ways they may not have dreamed. It's beyond hot in here…"

"Harry—" she poked in to derail me, but I wasn't done.

"It's what the kiddies want who've been weaned on quick hits and now it's their protein, MTV, *ET*, IMs, iPods, Xboxes, MP3s, YouTube, 'I know what I want and I wanted it yesterday,' when all we had was AM and FM; it's Generation I-Age creating a disposability rage, in faiths, families, friendships, and relationships, and make no mistake, the notoriety need is superficiality super-sized, but behold the repercussions; kids are evolving faster than the human psyche can withstand without having experienced life's lessons in a natural progression; nine-year-old girls swallowing *Sex and The City* and by eleven, they're joining the Rainbow Club. It's happening too fast for adults to cope, let alone for tiny, forming minds to absorb all that head pollution: look at the surge of prescripto drugs and the re-intro of recreationals, coke is back phat and fifty percent cheaper, if ever there was a primal scream for help, it's a disenfranchised and disillusioned group; to hell with Gen Y, it's Generation 9/11, a group of twentysomethings trying to find meaning in life at the twist of the century with planes hitting their towers, the planet melting, the bees and bears dying, and they can't process it, who can? It's happening too fast, at exponential rates, it's instant grato, it's 'Next!,' it's ADD Nation creating a *dolce vita* desperation, a techno-driven I-Age designed to connect and include but really distances, isolates, and alienates, sending confused kiddies-turned-mouse-potatoes on a terrifying hunt for lifelines in the cyberspace woods, gossip bites, and headline grabs; while vid-games are a safe house, fame is a life raft, and beautiful girls are anesthesia. They're blocking out, fending off, and fleeing to dire places, their PlayStation, SNSs, MySpace, Facebook, Twitter, the scando sheets, the Victoria's Secret mailbox weekly; lest we forget, the nightclub bathroom stall bondathons with nostril intake. Or just being baby podfathers Podding off into oblivion…"

"Detour, Harry," she determined, my scandorant temporarily stunted. "My word…"

"You asked me about work."

"I let it go because there may be something useful in it."

"Nifty, no?"

"But if you unleash spontaneous outpourings at work, it can't be helpful for colleagues or bosses to witness. Don't you see the need for the medication?"

"By the way Doctor, you can call me Slinger." Like most I-Agers, I was a natural deflector and I often blocked less pleasant queries with swift but delicate verbal forearm shivers to the chin.

"I've known that."

"Most of my friends do."

"I'm not a friend. I'm your analyst."

I found some temp mind candy in a study of her perfect nose. The chassis was vintage Turlington circa 1996. Though all indications were Christy's was her own I wondered if Dr. Van den Heugel's had been spliced up in homage to it. "I've always appreciated the form."

She eyed me cautiously, but as a woman, she had to ask. "Of?"

"Your sniffer." I really did. The gal had the cutest button nose.

Ignoring my tosses of sandbox sand, she moved on. "So you're not enjoying the job. Have you considered another field or line of work?"

"No," I said, suspiciously hollow. "Only millions of times."

"Those are two different answers."

I let it go and watched the jackals fight for the scraps.

"How do you really feel, Harry?" She asked with a genuine note of concern. It was so lovely I could have reached for Kleenex.

"I'd paint it for you, but there's no color match."

"You're wasting time. Yours and mine."

The Doctor was right. I was retreating into sarcasm and obnoxiousness, another leave-me-be defense mechanism. I then decided to take a pause so I pulled out m Crackberry to send a sextext teaser to Exhibit A*.

"Oooooooooooooooooooooooooooo… and those aren't 'o's, they're suds bubbles from my bathtub… care 2 get clean with me?…"

 I redirected to my awaiting Doc.

"I will say this: cheerfulness used to come to me naturally and I still try to mine my reserves but something different always ends up stuck to the pick-axe."

"What?"

"Reality."

My problem is a serious one and part of a series. I've been diagnosed with ADHD, the turbo version of ADD, and they claim I'm a classic case. For those who have been chained to a cellar floor for two decades waiting for their daily bowls of unsalted gruel, ADD is a neurological condition called Attention Deficit Disorder and ADHD adds hyperactivity to the package.

It all means I have trouble staying focused. The meds help, but *non mucho*. My thoughts fly; I'm an action-oriented, high-energy guy and I thrive on high-velocity stim. I prefer elaborate vids, van Dyk trance music, Digweed electronica, or "Fuck Me I'm Famous" house, and I relish iPod-enhanced rollerblading safaris against traffic. Oncoming Manhattan traffic, perhaps the most perilous in the world. I cover ground fast and by all means, don't start looping things I've already heard. Be bright, be brief, and be gone. As long as you come back around to compete again.

Oddly, the need for firing-squad stim is terrif for my job. The items I author are bite-sized and have an abrupt finish line. I can do them one at a time and not get distracted or bored because they're over so quickly. Three lines or less, then, *Next!*

My best defense is to leave my mind alone, but it's hard: more like impossible. It's great for scandorants and free-association sing-a-longs, my specialty. But if I want to concentrate at length, forget it. That's where the meds come in. In fact, if my tale gets disjointed or excruciatingly obsessive, let it be noted I gave fair warning. It meanders, it cross-cuts, it spins and comes back, then it lime-twists, doubly so—like my mind and a manifestation, perhaps projection, of it. But I'll connect narrative dots now: it's a love story between two fractured but hopeful people whose time together was cut way too short.

When I was growing up in the eighties, disorders of the Harry sort had not been discovered, much less diagnosed. I was merely seen as "lazy," "underachieving," "unreachable," and "uncontrollable." So I was sent to a special school. Not good. A child with a misdiagnosed disorder spends years being treated incorrectly. A better description for it is abuse.

I did survive the misdiagnoses, and for this reason, Dr. Van den Heugel was instructed by me not to discuss those difficult formative years. The problems were traced to a lack of proper medication. Once treated, I was a different person, so I demanded we delve into my psych life as an adult and the good doctor complied. And took off from the foul line to baby cradle-dunk my checks.

Still, addled with a disorder that featured distractibility and impulsivity as its main tenets while harboring an abusive past, I often referred to myself as a 'human ambulatory explosive with a time-clock feature.' A ticking time bomb. Sure, methods were devised to wear down the pressure and reduce the combustibles in my casing, but I was never totally contained. I had to watch myself and I had to be watched. That's where the good doctor came in. I did my best with her. At times, I even volunteered things though they were often diversionary, questionably anecdotal, or thoroughly self-absorbed. "I have a Dutch roommate."

"Yes, I know."

"He wants to meet you. He's taken though, in a European way. Very frugal too. He'll take you out but make you pay. Half."

The doctor didn't care for my side-tracking indulgences,

especially when I got personal with her. My overtures constituted nothing more than Arctic seal barks to the iceberg. Naturally, her imperviousness was attractive to me, robustly so.

"Did you go to Scores last night?"

Scores is a legendary scandodancer joint on the Upper East Side. The Fonz and I called it the "*Oficina,*" or, *office* in Spanish, and yes, I certainly had gone there the previous night.

"Did you enjoy yourself?"

"Exotica? What's not to like when you're flying solo on Desperation Airways?"

She wanted more and I only had forehead wrinkles across.

"Harry, help me help you—"

If not presented with something compelling to sick fangs into, my mind retracts, recoils, and climbs back into its own entertainment cube and caters to those independent thoughts.

Her first name was Greer. It didn't claim word toy status but I did consider it wordolicious. Greer. Decidedly Greenwich-high-hedger-attends-Yale-displaying-essential-hollow-WASPy-rebellions-while-still-inheriting-Connecticut-weekend-perks-only-to-move-back-to-Greenwich-ten-years-later-to-reclaim-parents-former—life, address, club memberships, Range Rovers, beach chairs, and SPF 45—and-take-advantage-of-said-perks. It's all I knew about her really. It was all she let me know. "How are you getting along, Doc?"

"Fine," she tossed right back without the bat of a lash.

"Can I hold your hand?" It wasn't a pervy pass or even a romantic Hail Mary, but she didn't or wouldn't acknowledge it anyway.

The fact is, Sunday Fairchild had been a patient of Dr. Van den Heugel's too, through me, and the three of us often engaged socially. But after my gal's untimely death, "Greer" would only communicate with me on a professional basis. That's when she became the Ice Princess. I thought it strange. I'd have understood if she didn't want to see me any longer as her patient and would have been happy to remain friends. But she gave me no choice and I didn't want to lose her entirely. Anyone who'd known Sunday I felt a special something with, and in the doctor's case, a special bond, even a cherished one. Perhaps that was why Greer wanted to see me too, if only on a professional basis. Perhaps we both needed to have each other around in proximity, to bathe together in the suds of a silent, unspoken mourning. I didn't know what she wanted. The gal was an enigma to me, another reason I couldn't let go of the sessions.

"I'm concerned about you."

She angled up sharply. "Don't be," she said, bluntly dismissive.

"Okay, Doc," I winded, dejected and disappointed once again.

Then the Princess hurled an ice ball, one she'd never flung before, a filthy slider, and I wasn't ready for it. The bottom dropped out of it and bounced right off my jaw. "Have you been thinking about her?"

I skipped a tick and had to pause. "Only when I do."

"You want to talk about it?"

Don't think about it, Harry. You don't have to. You're not ready…

"No," I produced in a fragile way with a tumbling chin while a melancholy wave passed through me. See, it didn't take much to pierce the boy's exoskeleton. I wondered if she'd done it to penalize me for getting quasi-personal as a form of punishment. There was no way I was going to think about it. In spite of her… *But you can't help it…*

Flash! That still figure clumped on the bed. Lifeless. Shards of yellow-amber light slashing across her body from streetlamps passing through the Venetians. Dried tear paths on her cheeks, salty residue glinting at the eye corners like stardust glitter. Blonde tresses pouring over the pillow. Perfectly greased lips. Jungle red. Pink frosted fingernails. Still beautiful. Even in death. Not even cold yet. And those locusts devouring her—coroners taking endless snaps. Flash!! That front-page coverage; the cycle lasting weeks. It doesn't end. It never ends. Closure? A myth for the luckies who never faced tragedy 'cause there's no such thing. Flash!!! Why so many goddamn angles? Probably assassinazzi in their spare time…

And why did I have to find her? Just when things were going great between us. Who could have done it? And why keep questioning me? Haven't I told them enough already? Why me???

"But the police do."

Weak, Harry. You're too damn weak. She got it out of you…

"Again? Why?"

"I've told them everything. But they keep asking me to come

in."

"Maybe they think you might come up with something new. You've had difficulty remembering."

"Did you tell them that?"

"Of course not," she said. "But you were her closest personal relationship in New York."

"Except for you."

She looked at me squarely and hesitated. "My relationship was professional, not personal. They never mention any leads?"

"No," I said. "I get the feeling they think I might have had something to do with it."

"You're being paranoid."

"She was confiding in you too. Maybe more than me at the end. Don't they ever ask you to come in?"

"Not in a while," she said. "But I thought you didn't want to talk about it."

"I don't."

She tossed a few more questions and I gave a few half-present answers. My head swiveled away and twin tears tickled my cheeks on the ride down as my chest bucked. She deserved better this doctor. Everyone did. I wanted to do better and I felt a jolt to the system, a toxic mix of guilt, dread, and shame. Where did that crack-wise mouth and noirish disposition come from? Perhaps my twistarama life for starters, stashed away in a kit of self-preservation tools.

It was time to go: I couldn't give her any more. There was a sweet boy inside there somewhere, but I was losing him. A nice, feminine embrace would have worked wonders but it wasn't coming anytime soon, not before a California redwood grew tall or the next asteroid strike. Another venti 'Bucks bold sounded good at the 54-cent rate. And she deserved better.

"I'm going away for the weekend," she tossed out parsimoniously, a no less surprising contribution to the silent void. "How about you?"

I expanded up fully to 42 regular, wiped my eyes, and cleared my throat. "You know me, Dr. Van den Heugel, I stay in town on summer weekends. New York in August on a Saturday is just about my favorite time."

"What are you doing tonight?"

I drew a piece of contraband to spark up; another of my favored defensive and diversionary techniques.

"No smoking in the office, Harry."

I nodded dutifully, having secured my out. I extended a hand to shake hers and she clasped it. That press was what I'd been after and suspicions were confirmed. I faded back to the door but felt compelled to spin back. "I'd prefer to call you Coach Vince—"

She squiggled off a Charlie Brown mouth, the worm on the run one, appropriately so, a show of "good grief" puzzlement. "Why?"

"It's just I don't care to think of us as doctor and patient. I'd rather consider you a coach. My coach. And Vince Lombardi was a Hall of Famer."

She half-smiled that curve I'd envisioned seeking refuge in, but my mind was on winning, instead. ADD Militiamen, even the most depressed of the lot, live for games, debates, and contests, the win-lose stakes keeping stim quotients blissfully high.

"If it makes you feel better."

"You're beyond merciful." Unimpeded, I stole a last glisten of her lips and extended my apologies but couldn't ignore the fluid free-rangers still rolling forth. I wasn't a pig, but I was a man.

"The doctors at Columbia Presbyterian are still interested. My assistant said you agreed to the tests. The brain-imaging scan?"

"Why not?" I sniffled, trying to regain my composure. "Let my mind strike a pose, a centerfold cerebellum pinup. Much more revealing than nudity. Don't forget the wind machines, I want action hair. I'm a—"

"'Cerebral diva,' I know Harry, you've made it clear many times."

"Just goofin', Doc. I'd like to take you out for a drink."

"You ask me each week and each week I give you the same answer. You know I can't."

"You can. But you won't."

My words dangled like chimes in the wind and she eyed her notations all too quickly. "Last question. Why are you wearing yellow?"

64   Coerte V. W. Felske

It's always that overly diligent "last question" bunk. She was, of course, speaking of my high-decibel polo shirt. "Colors again…"

"Yellow is happy and upbeat."

"Isn't it obvious? Think fruit."

"Is that how you feel?"

"Natch. Happy as a lemon."

"But you do wear the brightest colors. Your shirts, your ties. And you give me the same sarcastic, unreliable responses."

"That I'm tacky and have no fashion sense, that's the *vérité*."

"I know you better than that." Airball. "One of these days you'll tell me."

"One of these days you'll havumm cocktail withum Sitting Bull."

"I'm afraid not, Harry."

"Why not? We used to do it."

She hesitated a second, almost as if knocked off stride temporarily, a touch thrilling to witness. "In mixed company."

I soured and sighed again this time more forcefully. "As for my shirts, some secrets are for me. And me alone."

We parted on vague grins, our usual way, as in both of us not entirely satisfied, me personally, her professionally, but me more than her, I was fairly certain.

As I left the office, I repeated "Coach Vince" a dozen times while attempting a semi-gleamer. I hoped a macho coach moniker could help my outlook on the therapy, to make me feel like I was part of a team and we were marching down the field toward the red zone, close to scoring; and less like I had loose beams in my psychological infrastructure.

For four years, Dr. Van den Heugel had been instrumental in helping me manage my attention disorder, to her credit. She gave me plans to structure my life and together we came up with systems of organization and routines. This included my morning wake-up alarms set to delicately melodic and docile Shins, Keane, and Coldplay ballads; my 7 A.M. "New York 1" weather temperature check to allow proper wardrobe management, three mealtime Blackberry world phone alarms with randomly shuffled alt-rock ring tones, and two 'Bucks' break alarms set to high-velocity scandoanthems like Guns's "Welcome to the Jungle," Pearl Jam's "Once," and Led Zep's "Achilles Last Stand," my inbox and outbox at "*Slingshot,*" a town car commute to and from work, an HGH-free body defender who doubled as driver, my phone programmed with daily check-off and reminder lists, personal IM laws (e-mails and IMs must be returned within ten minutes), recreational Dell laptop big-wave surfing for 'Bucks breaks, all gaming included (except MMORPGs), and twenty minutes of Twitter-twitting, Skype-typing, or Facebook frolic and friend poaching, beginning at ten of six, as well as the meds. The agreed-upon rules and regulations served to keep me focused and organized, they were the adhesives which kept a fractured and fragile life system together.

Being my ADD coach was a sizable job. I was a complicated case with a curly. Especially when it came to my personal life. I told her certain things about my intimate business, but not everything. Like what I was doing that night, hence the feigned ciggy sabbatical. I sensed she would not have approved for obvious reasons. Our history made it too uncomfortable for me to gush wide and dot the "i"s between crossed "t"s.

As I rode down the elevator, my concern for the Princess didn't abate. I hoped she'd be okay. I had smelled alcohol on her breath during one of our sessions, though it may have been my own. But I couldn't blame her. The gal needed some form of release. Or relaxing of the pressure. She seemed so wrapped up, tight, smothered even, and frozen into that skin, like a Winter Carnival ice sculpture stuck sadly on the campus green. Though slender and elegant, her hand had the warmth of a parking meter in February. Would the gal ever thaw out? I truly wondered. And worried. In the days between appointments I even missed her, as soon as I left the office really. That wasn't a surprise. The fact is, I missed everyone.

4

Downtown Roommate Story

I was slapped by a hot gust as I hit the street. It's true about August weekends in New York: the city is not the city. It may be Vegas or Paris, but it's not Manhattan. It's a Disney World for adults and anybody who's anybody has left town. City blocks are left quiet and stripped but equally hot and unforgiving. It swelters, it cooks and anything can happen because no one's around to stop you. The little urges simmering get acted upon with no chaperones. It's swim-at-your-own-risk time; anything goes. My kind of time in my kind of town, I suppose, for lack of anything better to do. Sex really is the city in August.

The Fonz was waiting for me up the street. The Fonz was my body defender. Alphonso Martinez was from Bogota and he didn't speak much English, just a few words. I spoke a few words of Spanish like "*café.*" And "*oficina.*" Yet the Fonz knew me well: he could feel me. He intuited when I was low or depressed, and his energy was always positive and upbeat. Fonz lived in Astoria and had a son Gonzalo, whom I adored and took on adventure outings or to Met games on occasion. I gave the Fonz salary and paid his health. Though we didn't converse extensively the Fonz was my friend, my best friend, and he didn't even know it. Sometimes you're better off without words. It can really preserve a friendship.

The Fonz was not a bruiser. Vertically-challenged, he was only 5'4" and fit "S"-sized items at Old Navy without making stress wrinkles. Combined with the language barrier, if confronted with a security issue, we may well be in trouble. But the Fonz was hired less to protect me and more to keep me on track and thwart my impulses. He drove my "go green" hybrid town car and got me places punctually. With his mellowed equatorial disposition and cool demeanor he served as a human Valium, a calming force and I needed anthropomorphic valiums in my friend base. As Coach Vince was my psychological coach, the Fonz took care of my physical well-being.

"*Casa*," I supplied for him and he knew the drill.

Just then, Exhibit A* texted me back. "*Rub-a-dub-dub is right up my alley… see you around eight?*"

Such a sport she was. I confirmed. Game was on.

The Fonz dropped me off at the Skybox. There'd be no Cuban diner dinner for us that night and I let him go for the evening. When I entered the loft, all the screaming silence indicated the Dutchies were out: my Dutch roommates Kees and Miep. I'd auditioned them for the part with an ad on Craigslist. When the couple showed up for their interview, our conversation went like this:

"*How are you?*"

"*Fine, ya, ya.*"

"*Do you like New York?*"

"*Hey, ya, these are really big buildings.*"

"*Ya, ya,*" Miep confirmed.

"*How do you pronounce your name?*"

"*Kees is like 'Case.'*"

"*And you Miep?*"

"*Ya, ya.*"

"*I've never heard of your names before.*"

"*Kees is an old Dutch name. Very old. Ya. And you know it is where the New York Yankees come from.*"

"*Say what?*"

"*Ya, ya,*" Miep concurred.

"*How so?*"

"*You know when the Dutch immigrants sailed over to settle here and founded this city it is a fact that the names of most of the men were Jan and Kees. In Dutch the 'J' in Jan is pronounced like a 'Y.' And people used to say 'Those Dutch people are all 'Yanns and 'Keess.' So it spread. Eventually, to describe the people who lived in the Dutch settlements called Manhattan and what is now New Jersey, they were called 'a bunch of Yan-Kees.' Which later became 'Yankees.'*"

I looked squarely at Kees, then at Miep. *"You're in,"* I said. Anybody who could teach me the etymology of something as brazenly New York as the Yankee moniker set themselves apart from the homeless-in-search-of-housing pack.

What was unknown at the time was how miserly Kees was. No sooner had he moved in than he established a reputation as one of SoHo's great cheapies in the great Dutch tradition. There's an old Dutch saying, *A Dutchman expects a front-row seat and wants to pay a nickel for it.* Delis disliked him because he compared notes on their prices. With receipts. I found his cheapness endearing. If he bought a kitchen sponge he ambushed me upon entry for the seventy-five cents. Cute.

Professionally, Kees had ghostwritten the autobiography of a Dutch soccer star and was seeking literary work. I gave him occasional item copy which sounded funny linguistically from that elliptical Dutch angle translated into English. Miep scouted flea markets, grinded the merchants to 25 cents below the last dollar, and pretty much hung out.

You might wonder why I had roommates if I could afford a loft in Manhattan, car, and security man. Simply: I hated living alone. As much as the company, I enjoyed the stim of cohabitation revelry, confessions of the daily Gotham struggle, inconsistent personality offerings, shared beers with demi-naughty chuckles, occasional turd-burgling humor, America is better than Holland, the sometimes turbulent, burning of the nerves' stimuli, the annual "I need my own space!" freak-out and couch summit, regrettable latrine knowledge, life-enhancing nudity peeks, bathroom rights negotiations, and of course, intimate sound effects. Being with Dutch roommates wasn't high-stim, but it was better than no stim at all. And being alone. I even let them skip rent some months. And that's the downtown roommate story.

5

Cosmetized and Blondified
in the SoHo Skybox

The SoHo Skybox was my three-thousand-square-foot loft on
Broome Street; bedrooms stacked me over them. My room had
sliding Japanese Yamamoto screens that, if drawn back, looked down
on the living room flat-screen HDTV, hence the name Skybox. On
rare nights when Kees splurged on himself and took Miep out, the
place was all mine. It was spacious enough to Rollerblade through,
which he did on occasion. A big ice skater in the Old World, he'd
figure-eight around, whistling like he was on a morning glide
through the frozen canals of Amsterdam. The space was big enough
to smoke a cloud's worth in, my preferred intramural sport.

Back to my August weekend.

Exhibit A* came over to the Skybox at eight having gotten
me a Happy Meal at a Hoboken drive-thru, bless her mall-savvy
heart. She wasn't hungry so she watched and after the delightful
meal we got after it. Exhibit A* was a passionista in all significant
ways, boasting a full repertoire. We met originally at Marquee just
off West 27th Street's Club Row and her first words to me were,
"You're not a Harry, you're a Jack." Just like that, she renamed me
and I was decidedly okay with it. And I renamed her too. I'd run into
her recently at Bungalow 8 and had sensed another scandalacious
encounter in the offing.

Exhibit A* was a Jersey girl with an accent that wasn't overtly
offensive. I think she did some low-level high-step stuff out in
Camden so she could afford New York and roam through Manhattan
social circles beneath the judgmental radar. She wasn't with me for
Face and wanted no part of The Machine and I didn't appreciate

her more for it. My behavior was excessively biological in those days, meaning I was performing enough self-abusing with quasi-humiliating sexcapades which did not involve background checks or a prescreening process for discerning an individual's true aims in sharing themselves with me. I didn't care if women wanted to hook up because they truly liked me or if they were looking for some scandoglam time in the morning media feed. I wasn't looking to be loved, necessarily, just relieved. So I stayed away from the warm and fuzzy, lovey-dovey types, the 5G Girls in particular, the ones who couldn't handle my fractured state and methods. I didn't want to hurt anybody, certainly not women: I loved and respected the gender too much.

And now I'll confess the most personally crucial thing I could say about myself:

I knew an angel once. She was a little girl. She's my ideal and she looks out over me still.

For this reason, I only got involved with women who were emotionally unavailable, who weren't starved for romance, who could share a good time and not be offended by any objectionable behavior on my part or me, theirs. As a result, there wasn't a queue of young ladies out there calling me a cad or rake or an insensitive Lothario. Just the opposite: I was so attuned to and respectful of a woman's potential for disappointment, defeat, and suffering that I had to avoid those I truly liked, the ones who could provide real romance or soul nourishment. In this way I was regulated and not free. Trapped? Only the kind of device that could snare a black bear. But I didn't trust my emotions and when a male is unsure of his emotional grid, it's toxic to any union, an instant recipe for disaster. I wouldn't put anyone through that.

I relied strictly on the *dolce vita* girls, downtown vets, the brides of the wild side, scandovamps and baggers, the ones a tad club-callused and shopworn who indulged their own dysfunction and no one else's and were responsible for themselves. Like me, like Exhibit A*.

I hadn't always been so emotionally detached, blunt, restricted, even formulaic when it came to women, but the death of Sunday had taken its toll. Coach Vince couldn't help, the therapy Band-

Aided my brittle psyche and helped me get through the day, but it was a bust for this type of pain. Remember, this wasn't romantic heartbreak or even the death of a loved one by natural causes: this was murder. Who's prepared for that? What got me through were my sad attempts at humor with a disorder-fueled, crack-wise persona and those barely comforting and fleeting erotic moments with emotionally void passionistas in the Skybox.

I kissed Exhibit A* punishingly and I could taste she'd gone chemical. Scandocandy was an occasional hobby of hers, thankfully; the makeup smears, the face caves in, they get soiled and crazy and before you know it you've got a *Tales From the Crypt* casket pop-up before you. Not sexy.

Somewhat jittery, my friend grabbed at the twist of necklaces dangling from my neck. Among the multiple silver chains and pendants were a cross, a Buddha, and a turquoise-inlaid Power Bear.

"Love the bear, Sugar Bear. That new?"

I told her it was. "A symbol belonging to the faith of the Native American Great Spirit."

"Hmmm. Didn't know you were so spiritual."

I let it go. It wasn't the proper time and setting for that sort of discussion. "Did you bring the bag?"

"Of course, Jack. Silly boy."

Soon, the leather ties were taut and Exhibit A* was sculpture in motion and lotion. She was cosmetized and blondified, all right, her worked-on bod awarding her the asterisk as noted. The breast-erfeiter had an amazing figure, clean, trim, and scandotanned, and the rack was nearly hers anyway as in negligible 'plants. Gal had believables or FBL's: fake breasts lite.

As for the bag, I'm not a bagger by nature, but if someone brings out the chromy stuff I'll lend a hand. Exhibit A* wouldn't leave home without it.

"Sing to me Jack," she urged. So I did.

"Singing" consisted of letting my mind throw out free-association riffs, some rhyming, some not, until I slowed at a cul de sac or shouldered over. I call it scandoranting, arguably my greatest talent, and I do it often and even better when I haven't taken meds.

For me it was like showing a little leg.

We went toe-to-toe and toe-to-heel and fluids flew. In fact, while enjoying her convergence, a warm stream shot into my face and the ejaculate flowed for many seconds. I wondered, was it pleasure or was it pee? The results of a Google check later were inconclusive.

6

Spidermen:
Beware or Be in the Lair

More importantly, later on Exhibit A* revealed to me point-blank: "I think I'm pregnant." At the alarming sound my heart leaped a foot, uncharacteristically so. A curious mist even began to glaze my eyes, but the gal remained curiously nonchalant. "Don't worry, it's not yours."

I cleared my throat. "How do you know?"

"I always use protection with you."

I was stymied by the remark, though I understood. She'd been dating a Spiderman nightclub owner with an extensive clubography who'd been stringing her along, the poor donkey chasing the "future" carrot. Imagine that. In essence, he was a man in charge of too many champagne baskets and Ketel One buckets in too many locales, with too many impressionable ladies looking for a social life, extending hopeful, empty flutes at his spider web table; effectively rendering them vulnerable Bucket Girls and Exhibit A* just another Alice in Clubland. Or so it seemed. Perhaps a potential pregnancy had been A*'s only panacea, her last line of defense, or, just as likely, her revenge.

It made me ponder all those Bucket Girls, dressed in their finest, designer nothingness, sausage skin dresses, and F-me heels, magnetized to that "power"—power-to-to-do-what?— table, fully apprised of a Spiderman or Club Louse's sketchy behavior (or that of Club "Lice" in the plural). Club Lice were the Spidermen's henchmen; carefully selected pimps, procurers, feeders, sycophants, ego-strokers and cheerleaders, all working in collusion to keep Spidermen neck-deep in femininity while taking favors and skimming off their own scraps of female flesh. Too often, the shallowcentric gals would put on blinders to that spidermaniacal setup and would reach for yet another fistful of ice from that bucket. How about, unlimited free drinks and low-level booth recognition doesn't hurt?; and assorted other denial psychologies? The problem was, open bar baskets and buckets were seductive, addictive, and dangerous, like drugs, because the price was right and the alcohol flow was endless and thereby the partypology often wouldn't cease there—the Lice would make sure of it—the catechism being, just a cube and a dream. The dream, of course, was finding that missing variable in one's existence—a new man, a new direction in life or temporary escape from the present one, or just an exercise in self-medication to quiet mood swings, depression, or more severe personal demons; or perhaps the dream was "just to have fun," Manhattan party life's sharpest, double-edged sword rationale.

Spidermen were the most dastardly of playboy species as they had the homes, cars, boats, toys, perks, and the money to "fun"-fund it all, while possessing little or no conscience and even less interest in getting married. Spidermen spanned the globe, of course, but in America the most notorious of the lot did their night-crawling in Las Vegas, Los Angeles, Miami, and New York. The silken threads, however, were spun and spread to all points of the seasonal hot spot circuitry—St. Tropez, Sardinia, Ibiza, St. Barts, Punte del Este, Monaco, St. Moritz, and Courchevel to name a few, and all high-fashion and cosmopolitan cities in Europe and South America—creating a vast, world wide web of nests and breeding grounds for true professionals in the "art" of aggressive seduction offensives. Spidermen would scatter, scurry, and crawl across those international threads whenever they'd become bored with feasting locally on present prey, or when holiday time hit so they could divide and conquer with their own deviant kind.

The Sling on Exhibit A*'s Spiderman indicated that, though he traveled the Web, he was the garden-variety type and lucky for her. You see, the more sinister Spidermen were nefarious polluters of women and real pariahs of pathological natures capable of latching onto a Bucket Girl and sending her on a life-altering odyssey into drugs, depravity, even dementia, a devastating journey from which she may never recover. And it would all start at that "power" table. Power to do what? Power to ruin someone's life. If this reveal inspires a chill up the spine or a sudden need to take a shower, be my guest.

Make no mistake, tables topped with 100-proof party favors were woven webs with the eight-leggers aligned in attack formation, sharpening their pincers, ready to pounce at a moment's notice on unsuspecting prey. The more inebriated the Bucket Girls got, the stickier the web became. In this way, buckets and baskets were lubricants, the modern social gateways to madness and mayhem. They turned polite after dinner gals into decadent after-party chippies in a matter of minutes, their compromising Saturday night deeds becoming the subjects of Spiderman gloat and gossip for Sunday's testosterone-and-braggadocio-on-the-rocks brunch. The veteran, girls-just-wanna-have-fun troupe and the nightlife semi-pros, of course, with little concern for reputation management fared better as those types could shrug it off like always. But for the less seasoned gals, the unknowing ones or those less reckless in nature, the reward for their wide-eyed, dolce vita enthusiasm was often little more than a nasty hangover, a nose bleed, missing clothing, spider bites, cab fare home, and patches of arm hair standing on end for the next week in remembrance of what they'd done and what had been done to them—and not necessarily in that order.

How did I know all this? A good deal of my gossip Sling came from the Spiderman World Wide Web. In fact, it was my only professional thrill: outing devious arachnids for their dark deeds and treacherous ways. In this way, I saw my daily online offering for women of the world as, *You've been warned*. Beware or be in the lair. For these reasons, I was never a welcomed guest at Spiderman girlmageddon gatherings and social soirees. Spidermen didn't like me. But I didn't give a phlying phuck. It was my less than subtle way of alerting the better gender.

As for the resilient Exhibit A*, a survivor of the post-millennium club wars and an all-around accomplished scenester, it appeared she'd still been clinging on to that dream. Perhaps, she'd already fulfilled it.

"Have you taken a preggers test?"

"Not yet. I'm not finished having fun."

The logic seemed skewed, of course. "Is this a good thing?"

"Maybe, maybe not."

Undeterred, I vaulted downstairs, opened the fridge, and immediately popped a corkie. "This is big news. Let's celebrate!"

Though I held to my strict code of avoiding romantic vulnerables, of course I had to contemplate my own contributions to the cube and a dream lottery. I didn't have buckets but I did have bottles. Admittedly, I was in a bad way. At the same time, if Exhibit A* had prevailed in her years of unabashed bucketism against all odds, she deserved to be congratulated and fêted, if not honored. Because pregnancy indeed could be considered a victory against wealthy, hump 'em and dump 'em Spidermen. I couldn't help but respect Exhibit A* a little more for going on the Spiderman offensive.

"No," echoed down and snapped me out of my reverie. "Gotta go."

Sudden emotional ebbings I wasn't used to crept up my frame all the way to a freshly ruptured and impressionable grill. I hung on her an extended moment. "I have to ask," I said insecurely. "Why do you call me Jack?"

She tossed a look at me, somewhat late-night surprised. "Don't go deep on me."

"Is that deep? Who? Jack Frost? Jack B. Nimble? Why Jack?"

"No silly, you're Jack Skellington the Pumpkin King." Certainly I knew the ref, from Tim Burton's *The Nightmare Before Christmas*.

"And my loft is Halloweentown to you?"

"Not your loft. Your life."

She smiled wide in an all too unsettling way. In recent times, I would have slapped my knee and agreed, acknowledging a backhanded compliment from some jaded after-party jester's crackling sense of humor. But the merriment was lost on me now. I'd been reduced to a Claymation action figure.

"Jack, you're a prince," she attempted benevolently.

"Of what? Of darkness? Tell me—"

"Gotta go, Jack."

I invited Exhibit A* to stay over of course with a promise of a big breakfast, skimmed vanilla chai, marble loaf, caramel praline muffs, rainbow cookies, the star carb works. The problem was, I think, that her hastily parked car out front had been towed. I covered the expense, of course, and implored her not to leave, but the towage scenario ruined any suave, why-don't-you-stay-over? romantic capital accumulated after aggressively bagging it. She scandoscampered along instead. I should have known better; neediness rarely helps. It always turns you into the Kansas scarecrow, stuffed with straw, topped with a bad hat, frightening off all wildlife.

I couldn't help but mull it over. I was the guy to "have fun with," to get your kicks with, the guy to def use protection with. I served the intimate equivalent of sticking your finger in the light socket and fro-ing out the hair. I was the Pumpkin King, a ghoulish antihero, better than a cartoon but only because of high-tech sorcery from Pixar or Industrial Light and Magic, and I lived in a place called Halloweentown and they all came over to get their dose of fright and leave. Sure, it rang the empty bells.

Whether or not you want to procreate, it's moderately disturbing knowing you're the biological reject. You like to think of yourself as the wanted seed, the needed seed, the sought-after seed, the seed they're fighting for, the seed they want to trap and ensnare you with; the seed whose DNA they want to see impressionistically smeared into the little face of the little one they've been dreaming of all their lives, the seed they want to label and put to bank for the future if need be. They weren't fighting for Harry's seed. I wasn't even Harry. And that guy got peed on.

I politely packed the bing cherries with stems whale's tail she'd left on the couch along with a bouquet of twelve pinkies and called FedEx for a morning pick-up. I slipped in a note of apology for the tow and suggested we get together soon, as in, immediately, and reminded her not to turn her phone off, twice, with follow-up IMs and e-mails.

Feeling abundantly hollow, I texted around furiously for the next hour, but the Militia didn't fire back. They rarely did when you needed them. I scanned the pressed-tin ceiling wondering when the Dutchies would return. I didn't like it when they stayed out late, it was very self-consumed of them. A few bar rounds must have been bought for them. A draft swept through the Skybox and tickled my bangs as I watched hopeful golden bubbles rising and fighting for life in the hastily deflowered, cork-less green soldier. I felt a kinship with the trapped one stuck to the bottom. I named him "Bub." The loneliness of the loft became loud, deafeningly so.

I hummed a pitiful riff in homage to Sonny and Cher, *"I've got you, Bub."*

Then I was reminded who to call. My cherished pal, Pablo. Pablo was real, as real as it gets. He was funny and upbeat and always said the right things. When we spoke or hung out there was no pressure on us. Either of us. We e-mailed and texted more often than we spoke and I tried to see him as often as I could. Pablo didn't judge me and I didn't judge him. He was pretty well battle-tested from the school of hard knocks and could figure out solutions to most problems in a second in the simplest of ways. He was always there for me and me for him and he gave me grounding unlike anyone else. Pablo was twelve years old.

Pablo Hernandez was my adopted buddy from the Make-A-Wish Foundation and he lived in a crowded foster home in the Bronx. We hadn't spoken in a while. I'd called several times recently and he hadn't called back. I suspected he had a girlfriend who was taking up his time. I decided to give him a buzz. I hoped it wasn't too late.

"Hello?" she snapped her usual rude and fed-up way.

"It's Slinger. Can I speak with Pablo?"

"Oh hi," she sang, re-tuning her tone to Sweet and Low sweet, just about as artificially hospitable as it gets.

I apologized for the late call.

"No problem, Mister Slinger," she smoothed like the beguiling cartoon serpent. Then, *"Pablo!"* was hollered into the beyond bursting my drums.

Pablo didn't care to spend much time at home, but if he was there he liked to stay up late and watch the mini TV I gifted him and the cable package I provided for his "family." Pablo didn't want days to end. He couldn't stand the darkness of night. From his past, he knew nightfall was when the bad things happened.

Pablo's "mother," Conchita Alvarez, was a foster home mercenary, meaning she had five other kids she'd taken in to house in her two-bedroom home. She was an entitlement professional who provided for her life that way. The government gave her a full yearly stipend for each foster head. And they were heads to her, like heads of livestock. *This* times *that* equals *I don't work* and *neither does my husband*. I could rat them out to the feds, but I didn't want Pablo to be sent packing again. He said they treated him okay, not like the other homes where he'd been severely malnourished and beaten at times, so much so he was a foot shorter than he should have been. I called him my Little Lightbulb and not because of his height but his smart, snappy answers. "He'll be right with you," the wily one said. She was nice to me because I meant one color to her. I upgraded things in their apartment and was a pushover for short-term loans which never seemed to find their way back. And that was okay.

"Yo, dog…" I heard blasted into the earpiece.

"Don't *yo, dog* me—"

"Whassup?"

"You haven't called me back."

"Been slammed. You know, school, girls, chillin'…"

"Terrif—"

"You and them funny words. Listen bro, I gotta bust—"

I hesitated on that. He was getting more suave by the day, probably due to all the second base successes generated during pre-teen womanizing. Maybe third.

"How about the Bronx Zoo this weekend?"

"B-Zoo again? Slinger, get yourself a bowser or somethin'—*for real…*"

Pablo didn't seem so enthusiastic. He must have been really bushed. Or under the weather. Besides, he was probably right about the zoo thing. Maybe we had overdone it. I loved the zoo, not the depressing imprisonment of animals aspects of course, but the relaxing downtime with non-human species, especially the fierce creatures. I probably enjoyed it more than Pablo did at this point. Maybe I always had.

"Where to then? Yankee game?"

I could always depend on Pablo. And he on me. I would have adopted him myself, but I still had enough trouble taking care of one child, let alone two. I loved Pablo Hernandez.

"Yanks are outta town. Listen, Slinger, lemme hit you back—"

"You bet, Pablo," I said but he had already hung up. The kid must have been really fucking exhausted.

It was then that I decided to fight back and make my uneasiness go away. How? Diversion which came in the form of shameless consumerism. eBay can be your best pal when you're feeling underappreciated and batting ninth on the loserazzi squad. It could have the psychological effect of a puppy licking your face. I had a favorite line of products I eagle-eyed: swimwear. *Cavalli* swimwear. Yes, bikinis. For Skybox gifting, of course. I checked my saved searches to see if any NWT strings had come on the market. Sure enough, there was the killer leopard print with aqua trim number available, a style I bought and re-bought frequently. It always came in handy and made for a lovely ritual. Gals loved swinging by for fittings, especially when Roberto was mentioned. I had new swimsuits stashed all over the apartment as well as the glove box of the Town Car. Just in case. In New York, you never knew. Vegas had nothing on the Skybox in its heyday.

Unfortunately, the Skybox had nothing on my failing psyche at present—I soon learned compulsive shopping didn't raise morale one iota.

After outbidding the masses and grossly overpaying for six sets of strings, I returned to the bedroom feeling no less calmed or neutralized and the hands of panic took a hold of my throat once more. I figured I must have been at some sort of life's crossroads because the overflowing river of anxiety crashing through me wouldn't let up or subside. And then I spied over. Bub was gone too, vaporized to the Skybox sky.

Alone again. Naturally.

I found myself digging furiously into the bottom bureau drawer. My hand swam to the deep corner and I fished around and drew them out. The purple laces had browned over time making them a muddy maroon color and they'd begun to unravel in places. Clutching onto them tightly, I collapsed in bed.

Exhibit A* was pregnant and I was singing Jack the rejected pumpkin seed, voted off the DNA sweepstakes once again. And the fellow usually there for me, a twelve-year old, couldn't fit me into his schedule. I tried to convince myself I wasn't the last sardine in the can. Before I lost the argument, sleep mercifully put me out of my misery. Sleep can be a wonderful form of euthanasia. I was still gripping the purple strings when I awoke in the morning, totally bedlagged, forced to participate once again in something rather unpleasant: my life.

To add insult to considerable adversity, the Talking Heads song "Once in a Lifetime" came on my bedside player as I was getting dressed. The lyrics shattered the brittle psychological barriers I had built against self-reflection with the verse: "*You may ask yourself, well, 'How did I get here???'*"

7

Girl from the Redneck Riviera

January, 2K7

It had been seventeen months before, January 20th, a Thursday. I was in the 'Bucks off Broome Street two blocks from the Skybox. I was my usual upbeat smart-aleck self having my usual: two tallboys of the bold blend of the day with a splash of milk, no sugar. I didn't succumb to the crispy marshmallow square. That's when I met her, Sunday Fairchild, the girl of dreams, unisex dreams, dreams that you're proud spinning around on the same axis, on the same globe, at the same moment in history, sharing the same genus of species with her, standing sweetly nearby.

"Is the bold bitter?"

In midtown, I wouldn't have turned around but it was my neighborhood. There was still a decent sense of community in SoHo, though it was barely clinging on.

"Not to me. But I don't take sugar either."

"Smells strong."

"Gives you a morning will to power."

"I take sugar," she breezed and a shimmering smile came with it. She was tanned and sun splashed giving the appearance of winter holiday fresh. She'd either spent time in oceans or had great highlights. Her honey blonde Rapunzel tresses cascaded down but couldn't hide the curvy-perfect moneymaker. The gal was so stunning that I figured she was a glam girl, a fully hooked and loaded performance cog in The Machine. I made it my job to find out.

"Try it. By the end of the day you may have three job offers."

"I don't need the work, thank you."

Now this gal was gorgeous, white flag gorgeous, so much so I wanted to retire and move to St. Bart's with her. Or Staten Island, for that matter, on corner landfill. Or to hand out pamphlets on street corners claiming I'd actually seen "It" and would anyone like to join the movement. But back then I was shier, more spiritually-connected, a romantic, less reckless and self-destructive, and possessed more self-esteem. So I didn't conjure instantaneous strategies to railroad her to the Skybox within the hour to persuade her out of her jeans and teenies. But I did order her one, with sugar, and she took a taste. "Mmmmm," she uttered. Then she ordered the crispy square to get her sugar fix, anyhow. As she was mulling her "*mmmm*," I was fixated on my "*hmmm*," having processed a spontaneous spark of commonality.

More importantly, there was something ethereal and fresh about her the way she glided, spoke, and smiled, but she seemed also deliberate, wise, and street. Those were the words which came to mind that morning, never to be bettered. She was no refugee of hipster science, all fast-flavor clothes and clanging accessories, or a jaded downtown princess hemmed in by a thousand strains of New York neuroses with a preference for Angelika-only movies. She wasn't any scandovamp or glamorazzo in training. She wasn't indie, she wasn't preppy; perhaps a bit hippy, which I loved, but she didn't seem to be owned by any metropolis. She came free of classification, undefinable, and in that way, perhaps otherworldly. Perhaps my wishful imagination. Perhaps she didn't really exist at all.

We stepped out to the street and let the blast of the wintry cool air move our hair around. She even leaned in to me, as if giving me the opportunity to protect her from the icy winds, an attitude which was soon contradicted by what she said.

"Oooh. Love that fancy-fine."

"The cold?"

"No, the wind. Reminds me I'm doing the right thing."

"Which is?"

"Following the winds of my life." The grin spread gorgeously too, to punctuate a response well worth quoting. "But I don't mind the cold either. It's like jumping in the ocean in May. Don't you enjoy that?"

"I don't like cold oceans. I like Caribbean oceans at bath temperatures and visibility of one hundred feet in case any big bite radiuses are loitering nearby. And a tiki bar with high-velocity slush cocktails in proximity. What's your name?"

She claimed her real name was Azalea, though she'd changed it. Sunday had been the day her mother was born.

"You live in the neighborhood?"

"On Thompson, right around the corner. It's a walk-up but it's charming."

"Do you have rodentia?"

"Excuse me?"

"I'm referring to a potential mice and rat infestations in your building. Rodentia. Do you have them?"

"Uh, no, I'm afraid not."

"Oh," I said in an overtly downcast way, as in bad Strasberg 101.

Her mouth moved around, mostly up. "Am I missing out?"

"Perhaps you are." I decided to come clean. "I'm sorry, I just love saying the word 'rodentia.' It's a word toy of mine."

She broke magnificently into another memorable display, her smile a white gleaming comet, the laugh explosive as though poised on a powderkeg. It seemed she'd wanted to break funny for a long time and finally found release. It was clear I'd inched closer, verging in on a full breakthrough but it was no time to rest on one-liner laurels. With a rare beauty like her, hopes could be dashed in milliseconds.

"I'm right down there," I indicated further down Broome Street.

"473?"

I was astonished. "Yes." I thought she was going to tell me how she knew but didn't. She did ask me where I originally came from. I'd been born at Lenox Hill Hospital on the Upper East Side.

"A real-real New Yorker."

"Apologies." I didn't bother telling her my family moved away soon after to Massachusetts. I didn't want to sandbag the moment.

"Don't apologize. What are you, a satirist?"

"A satirist?" I was pleasantly surprised.

"Tell me you are, *please?*"

She couldn't know how forcefully it struck me. "Okay..."

"Are you? *Really-really?*" Her face lit up like a holiday tree. "I've wanted to meet one for so long. A real downtown satirist..."

"*And?*" It was an empty challenge. I do that occasionally just to see what results, part of the incessant need for gaming.

"And? And, well, maybe you're one."

"Why a satirist and why downtown?"

"They're like dodo birds: an endangered species."

"The dodos are already extinct."

"Aren't the satirists?"

"Good question. You know why?"

"Why what?"

"Why the dodos became extinct—"

"Ah-hah," she said. "Don't want to discuss the satirists do you? I wonder why?" she challenged.

I was stupefied. That perceptive, the gal was hitting me where I lived. I'd always wanted to be a fiction writer. I had a wild rocket-propelled imagination but had enough trouble scribbling bite-sized tattletrash. I couldn't get through pages of material, I couldn't even write silly mag-rag journalism. The forces of distractibility were too great. Being a scandal scribe was a perfect solution, if you care to ignore the frustration of a lifetime's aspects.

Sunday giggled through my frozen pose and led me out of the jam.

"I see, you just want to play, so let's play. Tell me about the dodos—"

Sure, I was breaking across, I'd led her right into my wheelhouse. My method was to send out a little current, just a few volts for the tiny jolt. Showing a little skin, as it were, it was my tactful but intense social lawnmower approach, but I was always careful not to buzz-cut the full garden.

"In 1598, Portuguese sailors landed on the island of the Mauritius in the Indian Ocean where they discovered a previously unknown species of bird. They dubbed them dodos because the birds greeted them with such a childlike innocence that their gentle spirit was mistaken for stupidity. Dodo, in Portuguese, means 'simpleton.' The dodos had never had contact with humanity and they'd lived isolated and undisturbed for so long they'd lost their ability to fly, so they had no means of escape. When the Dutch came later they used the island as a penal colony. The dodos were big and meaty, some weighing fifty pounds. And the Dutch sailors, convicts, and transients rounded them up and roasted them on spits and ate them until there wasn't a one left. The dodos went extinct in 1681."

She angled sharply at me. "Terrifically sad story."

"I wanted to open a joint in SoHo, the Dodo Bar, and have dodo memorabilia hanging and Dutch penal colony mug shots. But I couldn't find the financing."

"In mockery?"

"In homage. A shrine to the dodos. And a Dutch roommate's guilt."

Her guarded look lingered upon me until a smile emerged. Vaguely. She'd wagered I wasn't serious, at least. "You are irreverent; perhaps you are a satirist. By nature."

"Perhaps. I have an arsenal of quirky human interest tales I've always found well, stimulating."

"And they remain with you because they're so damned haunting and tragic and painful, don't they? How awful humans can be…"

I couldn't respond immediately. I had to let it go. She was so right on that it was perilous. Either it was a lucky shot or she'd figured me out in a stopwatch interval. That sea of regret, disillusionment, and sadness which ebbed through me at all times, the one that led to Harry's private island, she'd already intuited and identified. That private island was for me and me alone and I could not acknowledge her direct hit. As I remained silent and unyielding, she dropped then an uncertain, even bewildered look. Double-drats. Giving of yourself or choosing not to was always a double-edged sword. I would slog on, even though I was pretty sure I'd offered too much shock and bizarre, and, spontaneous zap. And lost her. Then it came to me. "Wait for it."

The smile climbed around and found its mouth. She warmed to the audacious dangler. It glimmered like a silver lure skimming the water's surface and summoned her back. She was too cool to inquire, "For what?"

"I respect that."

"Don't be fooled. I can be a crack-wiser too."

"I can tell."

"Friends just tell me to shut up."

"I reject that."

Ooh. Respect, reject. The gal was nowhere near bubbles and fluff. Maybe it hadn't been a lucky shot. "I can't give you everything all at once."

"*Fair is foul and foul is fair,*" she played on.

"Goodness, Shakespeare in the morning. What a delightful breakfast. So, you think the satirists—"

Before I could finish she snapped me right off. "...have gone the way of the dodos? With all that's happened? Sure. There's no money in satire." She had that right. "All capable writers are living in the boroughs, writing crummy pieces for magazines."

"Or becoming real-estate agents."

"The yuppies came in and sanitized everything, remodeling all the old wonderful lofts, jacking up the prices. The satirists had to move out, like the poets before. Look around, it's a shopping mall."

"You mean, like Yankee Stadium just let out?"

"*Exacticalifragelousixexpialadocious,*" she sang, an inventor of neologisms, no less. It was damned inspiring.

"And how long have you been here?"

"Long enough. SoHo has lost its soul, don't you think?"

I liked everything about her point of view as much as the view from which it came. Finally, I told her what I did and where.

"Oh," she said indiscernibly, not necessarily disappointed. She remained undecipherable, intriguingly so.

"Why are you interested in satirists?"

"I'd love to be one. Either that, or, sing."

It was a curious response, but I wasn't taken aback. She did not conform to type, which was refreshing. I asked her where she was from.

"The Redneck Riviera," she volleyed back like a song refrain. Her positive energy and vitality was surging. I asked her if she was talent.

"Talent*ed*," was the answer.

"Do you have representation?"

"I have an agency."

"Who is it?"

"Liberty," she said without hesitation. I'd never heard of them but there were new talent houses sprouting up all the time.

Then she gave me a vague gleamer and a set of twos as in "peace," and initiated a scandoswag across the street with no gesture of invitation to join. No doubt I was being played with like a Slinky on stairs. I took the big block-lettered kindergarten cue and posted up. "So, where is the Redneck Riviera?"

She pirouetted gracefully back around. She had the lightest step for a tall girl, which gave the impression she could just float away.

"You're a writer: do a little R&D and figure it some. Then maybe we can discuss over some 'Bucks bold. I buy."

The final curve of teeth killed me. I was powerless to do anything but watch her go. And the gal tick-tocked off and not shyly but in a dolce vita blaze, perhaps part goddess, part Grim Reaper, someone's personal apocalypse somewhere, no doubt, an entire city's. Or state's. And I envied the distressed Diesels snugly hugging the flawless backside.

She was from the Redneck Riviera, lived in SoHo, admired satirists, possessed a laser intuition, was DDG, and she was following the 'winds of her life'—that's all I knew about her. But hell if that wasn't enough. You could serial date for a decade and not find such deep character richness. Or so it seemed. I Googled it immediately then texted a former colleague at "Page Six" from Alabama. I was informed the Redneck Riviera referred to the panhandle region of Florida, the coastal section, Pensacola and east.

As I stepped into my elevator, I couldn't stop thinking about the infectious smile which was breezy, clean, and fresh. I could sense that as talent she had everything it took. I wondered if she'd been boldfaced or scandoscoped. It wouldn't have surprised me, she was a scandy all right, as in a scandalous dandy. The face and body were asterisk-free, too. A veritable walking scandal waiting to happen, all she had to do was put on some flip-flops and lean against a lamp post.

Back at the office, I first checked the search engines. The name did not pop up anywhere on Google or Yahoo! or Ask.com. I made inquiries and no scandohandlers had heard of her. She was 100% Sling and boldface-free, which to me was Brahms and strings. Bold catsuit feminist or CFF, compassionate femme fatale, I didn't know why and maybe it was instinct but I felt this chance meeting with this chance scandoglam girl was going to take my twistatopia life out of chance and maybe, just maybe, change it for a period of time that just might be longer than the kind of short whiles, disappointing short whiles to which I'd become accustomed.

8

A Date Against Type

I didn't know how to find her and five days passed. I spent more and more time in the neighborhood dining locally like never before. I hadn't achieved full stalker status nor was a restraining order tacked to my front door, but I was closing in on some form of misdemeanor. I'd been thinking of that Redneck Riviera gal incessantly.

I was having Saturday brunch with Amy Nightlife at Felix on West Broadway when she passed by on the sidewalk. I shot out of my chair and intercepted her. "Hey there." She looked positively, well, scandillating.

"Oh, hi."

"Remember me?"

"Of course. How are you, Harry?"

As if on show tune cue I sang it. *And I said how are you Sue?/ Over too many miles and too distant smiles/ I still remember you…*

"I know that song, Harry Chapin. Harry sings Harry…" She twisted and swayed where she was standing. The lips were parted, the sweet smile was beaming.

"I tried finding you."

"You did? Heavens."

"But there's no talent agency with the name Liberty."

"*And?*" She chuckled too. She was gaming me, throwing back one of my patented hollow challenges. Worse, I had to answer her like the freely-manipulated dancing bear on hinnies.

"Well, it doesn't exist. Which means you as talent don't exist."

"I work for a travel agency on 23rd Street."

"Liberty Travel," I grumbled. They were all over the city.

"Am I keeping you from something?"

"I'm having lunch with a colleague. Care to join?"

She said she couldn't, she was late for her yoga class on Lafayette. She remarked that I was lousy at research, but she did give me her number and I had "thirty-six hours to call." She added more teeth on a crescent, then grabbed a hold of my jean jacket lapels and thrust me into her. "Harry, I think I like you."

"Which one? There are several…"

"The middle one—the sexy one. For now…" She leaned in until we were sharing air then launched into song, whispering the chorus into my ear of the tune I'd initiated moments before.

You see she was going to be an actress and I was going to learn to fly / She took off to find the footlights, I took off for the sky / I go flying so high when I'm stoned—

There was a bite on my lobe and she shoved me away. Still clocking me with a white dazzler, my little scandolita retreated backwards, fading away before me like a Monet sunset. "Yeah, I like you, Harry…"

I stood there, all dazed up with nothing to grab on to.

I took an accelerated no-pride approach and called her that night. She seemed pleased I'd called and was "looking forward to" the dinner I'd suggested at Cipriani Downtown, but not nearly as much as me.

I decided on formally cool with a black Gaultier suit, turquoise shirt, and pointed spread collar. She arrived wearing tight beige leathers and matching jacket, stunning. We had a few Bellinis before and during dinner. Sunday claimed that of all the arts her true passion was not writing or singing. It was, in fact, acting, and she'd been performing in plays since grade school. She'd worked part-time for a doctor in Florida while attending drama classes at Florida State.

"I can't tell if you just arrived or you've been here a while."

"I moved here two and a half weeks ago," she said and her smile forced one on me. She had that ability to an embarrassingly extensive degree. "But I've been studying up on New York for years. I've wanted to come here all my life."

"How did you find an apartment in the neighborhood so quickly?"

Apparently a doctor friend, Dr. Carson Kilmer, whom she'd known previously in Florida, had taken a position out west and gave her the place. The rest of the conversation was less ho-hum and more memorable.

"Why haven't you signed with a talent agency?"

"I'd rather have a manager."

"The agency can be your manager."

Once on the subject, Sunday became all business, her sugar coating peeled away revealing a hardened, streetwise persona.

"Agency setups are still corrupt. I don't want to sign on to a cattle factory that's a high-class excuse for those kind of client favors, one step away from an escort service. You know, just another blonde sent out spinning her wheels until I oblige the male agency proprietor or lesbian booker. Sometimes blonde works. It can also be a detriment, like racism, in a way."

It was a difficult point to argue. "I'm not hair color judgmental, I don't have any blonde prejudice."

"No? There are a lot of blonde racists out there. And one day I'm going to cut it all off."

"So tell me; what's the issue with blondes?"

"It can be so alienating, don't you think?"

"And inviting. It's mythical, illusory, striking, rare, and has been associated with enhanced femininity and delicateness; and that all translates to boosted sexuality. For these reasons, it has been preferred by males throughout history because of that peacock advantage. Blonde women stood out and men wanted to mate with them following their Darwinian impulses. Reacting to that, the vast brunette conspiracy came into existence and created dumb blonde jokes. Today, women spend billions of dollars all over the world to harness that illusion, to secure that peacock advantage. As often as not, those intellectually challenged blondes are bottle-blonde brunettes. That's how I see it."

"Either way, it's such an immediate statement, potentially misleading statement…"

"Depends on who is being served the statement. It's true you don't want to be just 'another one,' but being one and an interesting one can qualify as professional or celebrity dynamite. Don't forget those who paved the way, Dietrich, Lombard, Harlow, Monroe, Bardot, and Novak. And those who waltzed through the door, Fawcett, Madonna, Anderson, Simpson, Spears, and Hilton. Whether you respect their careers or think they're just scandotramps who overachieved, it's pretty successful company."

She smiled warmly, but there was something sly about it and she made a surprising request. "Tell me more about blondes…"

It was a strange query. She couldn't have known I had a fertile, ADHD-loaded, word-fueled, from the hip, riff-spinning imagination, or could she? The subtlety she possessed in her mind was perhaps staggering. At worst, her unpredictability continued to rage. But I had my own brand and I wondered if I should serve up a dose.

"Sure you want to hear it?"

"I am."

I told her to strap herself in. She said she would.

"There are all types of blondes. There's the tiny blonde with the little blowhole of a mouth and the nasty-ass temper who's a tough female version of her hard-ass Long Island Dad who wears a Mets hat and hates Steinbrenner and Republicans and she looks too much like him and she's overcaked her face to compensate and is not hot enough to be so opinionated as in a Ramada Inn All-Star on her best day and she makes you wait ten days for a payday anyway and you can't blame her because you've taken her to a string of B-restaurants so as to avoid the other more serious crushes you have rolling around town and then when you finally score you're actually elated you stuck with it because she is a furious little scandodeviant animal who snarls nonstop and who'll do anything you want and invents stuff when you're all out of ideas and you keep her on board for nearly the entire fall with some Ramada and Holiday Inn nights to boot until all her bad viewpoints catch up and some nights you have to argue back and the steamy scandosex never arrives and when it does resume you stop going down on her and do quick in and outs until your own fellatio stops and before you know it she's changed her number and has some faux-restraining order on you and she badmouths the hell out of you and you're constantly looking over your shoulder for a brother of hers to show up and send multiple rib shots your way until you stop avoiding all places you could run in to her friends and it just dies until you see her in a cafe somewhere eight months later and she says 'Hey Harry how ya doin'?' with a shaved smile and you fuck heartily once more for old time's sake and the sex is just a little better than okay."

A bemused grin took its place on Sunday's face.

"Then there's the tall wiry spaced-out blonde with the wafer-thin lips and two dots for tits who's always short of cab cash and she's sexy as hell and leans a lot and the more she leans the sexier she gets and she has hair down to the ground and blades for hip bones and she says all sorts of nonsensical cosmic things that you don't know what to do with like 'I feel like I'm floating on infinity' and 'wouldn't it be great to have water hair?' that 'when you flick it, it goes splash!' but she's so off the charts they sound beyond sexy anyway and then she gets drunk one night and fatally kisses you warmly with tongue incentives but that's all which lets you cling to the hope you're not carving out a brother-sister relationship with her after all and soon it will be deliciously carnal and there's more theater and horse riding and serial planetarium visits and some obstacles you begrudgingly endure because the image of you scandostamping her bony carcass into her mattress in her studio apartment the one with panties bras and heels hanging on animal horns beside mirrors hanging everywhere and Crystal Meth playing apocalyptic melodies on stereo still haunts the hell out of you and somehow someway she knows exactly what's going on and that she's driving you absolutely mad and even madder when after three months of this you find out from some barfly nobodyoso with a how didn't you know? scrunched up accordion face that there's some gym-muscled metrosexual pirate with a man-purse good for two thoughts a minute who plays bass for a fledgling "covers-only" band stone-boning your cherished cosmic trooper left right and center and you finally realize you've never gotten some you're never going to get some and the taxi's waiting to take her to Two Thoughts so he can get his and she asks you for another ten bucks to get uptown and you give it to her just the same."

I cleared my gullet and took in oxygen. "You want more?"

"I could listen to this into the new year," she sent right back.

"Then there's the wealthy sweet perfect blonde with the bluest

eyes and straight hair and a perfect figure and shocking scandofanny
who's always dressed uptown conservative chic and you've been
friends with her for five years and in love with her for as many and
she's been in a relationship all that time with two different guys and
was only single that one summer when you went away so she found
this second guy instead and you've been kicking yourself ever since
but now she's 27 and this guy is cheating on her but you're too cool
to rat him out and she did see him lip-lock some scandoskanky
inferiorata one night but he was 'drunk' and she can't understand
why they're not having more sex and you crack a bottle of bub, tell
her not to fret about it play music pet her affectionately then remain
cautious and distant refill her glass once three times she giggles she
grabs you you spin and scandoplant one on her so softly and her
Town and Country lips are way better than you thought and you
both retreat a step and don't know what it means so you change
the CD to your killer crooning Chet Baker and go right back at
her with impunity and kiss her so hard and long while feeling the
round of her entire moon with both palms and under her black
turtleneck cashmere sweater you unhook her bra and lift it only
to feel the delicate size and shape and peel up the sweater and see
them with your own eyes and gently suck on her right Jujube then
bite her left and calmly take her hand and lead her up to the Skybox
and slowly take off this and that and the bra releases and falls and
they both roll forward into your face and you peel up her slacks and
find the origin to her high boots and unzip both and twist them off
and she's settled on the bed and has beaten you to the button on
her pants and you slide them off and expose the gift-wrapped in the
chartreuse V-patch and you pinky hook it down oh so slowly and
you place two shovel palms beneath her scandofanny so smooth and
well-lotioned and spatula her over and you see the tasteful scando-
portrait goose bumps on her globes from the loft's unseen chilly
winds and you stay totally clothed and keep it a man's world and
kiss every niche and cranny until she pops up like a Pop-Tart and
just has to release the thermal railer you're sporting and insert it
in her mouth and you ask her if it's one of her favorite things
to do, lapping and adoring a majestic stick apprised of the answer
already and she nods anyway and thoughtfully counters, 'only if it's

yours' and you realize it's your turn at bat to be just and fair and clitorally correct and you click the remote and change CDs and put on Floyd's *The Wall* side two and proceed to cliff dive below and scandosnack her for the forty-nine minute duration and then you gently make multiple loves to her in and out so slowly watching her eyes roll each time you surge in until a tear blazes its way out of her eye and finally you're so comfortably numb in love and you want her so much to be your girlfriend and move her clothes rack right in and she could salvage your entire tedious nightclub life in your empty scandomaniacal world and she prepares to leave and you can't stop kissing each other and your lips are raw but she has to go he's waiting and you unzip your fly and fully dressed with overcoat she postscript fellates you in the middle of the downstairs parquet floor but won't finish you off because she'll be kissing other lips soon but it still registers she tasted some which is some mild consolation to your chick predic and she dashes off and you call your Queen of Cosmopolitana and for every three calls you call her she calls you back once and, four agonizing days later, she comes over finally in the afternoon and asks you to play *The Wall* again and you do it all over again except this time you spend less time down there on her because you can't wait to get up there face-to-face and you find seven different configurations in an hour and she pushes you off her to take you whole and this time drinks you fully and looks up at you and flashes a beautiful, satiated, mysterious smile that defines what making love is all about, but while dressing she seems removed and detached and she leaves and you can't function anymore the thoughts of her and your love for her are killing you and you can't write you can't eat and you can't play anything but Pink Floyd and it's only been an hour since you last called her and you're spending way too much time on your back reliving events while cracking off and she calls you back that night and tells you she can't see or talk to you again and the thought you've been scandowham-bammed leaves you flatline fucked for the rest of the year and you suffer the severest form of aching heartbreak only to remain in a low-level depression for the next year and a half and if anyone plays any Floyd in your vicinity you threaten to rip their fucking face off. Enough?"

She tossed it through an emerging grin. "I think I know all I need to know about you."

It sounded too sadistic for comfort. My face iced over suspended and not knowing what she'd meant I wondered if I'd IEDed it. I'd had a lot of experience blowing it regally in my formative pre-diagno years. Her vague and tattered smile didn't help.

"It's not a negative," she added charitably, processing my nervous uncertainty. "You should put that in a book."

"I've thought of that."

"Why don't you?"

"Let's just say thinking and executing are two different things." I didn't want to explain further. "Are we done?"

"Nuh-uh."

"Wait a second. Does this zaniness qualify as good courtship?"

"Good? No…" she returned sharply sending my thumper into a scandopanic. "*Excellent* courtship."

Relief. "You sure?"

"One more," she added with a note of challenge to it.

And in that there was only one thing she could have meant.

"Then there's the honey blonde gorgette who spins magically into your life she's scandotanned with perhaps-you-can-Carlyle-me eyes needs no makeup but applies light mascara and she's got the shapeliest scandocan which looks just as scanderrific in jeans as an evening gown she's not afraid to show it or anything else she's got it's your problem if it melts you and you just know for her islands and dunes were made to walk starkie scandodance and fuck on and she's unpredictable she's sharp-tongued she's playful she's a hippy, she's feminine, she's all woman and mysterious, but it's chemical/animal too and she even has cute and adorable phrases indigenous to her region like 'fancy-fine' and with all the above she has the ability to carve you and your life up into shreds."

I paused as she took a final draw from the Bellini flute. "You don't seem so sure about this one…"

I was about to say, "Well, I just met her," but I needed to focus.

"Her family is something she doesn't care to talk about her last boyfriend is alternately sucking on a Glock nine-millimeter handgun and a bottle of Jack wondering where he went wrong and where could she be now and if he ever finds out he's going to find her because even though she claimed it's over he knows it's not just like the other half-dozen previous guys would say if they could ever locate her and she appears at your doorstep and tries out your morning bold brew and tries out your sense of humor, challenges your POV and doesn't tell you where to find her, but indicates you should come look, gives you the feeling she's looking at your buns when you're walking away while she knows the entire block is looking at hers and you ponder whether or not you're going to fall for her too and it's completely her choice as to whether you do or not and this little scandolita is used to having that power and nine times out of ten she restrains herself knowing what tragedy might or could ensue but maybe just maybe she sees something different in this guy that might—"

And she broke into a stream of c-snap all her own, "…want to make the little scandolita take a closer look so she takes another sip of peachy champagne leans in to him parts her lips just slightly as she closes in on his—"

Yes, she was doing it. It was a first kiss on this side of magic and it was enough to propel us over to Thompson Street and her apartment. I twisted away as she undressed, though I unintentionally yet fortuitously found a mirror which gave me an eye on the exposure. She was beautifully nude with full breasts turning skyward from a savagely natural hang; she had a long, rising, and elegant back, sinewy and strident scandogams, and a perfectly pear-shaped rear. She was among the best biology had to offer. Her eye lasered mine in the mirror and she remained there, undaunted in the buff for an extended moment so I could take her all in. She wasn't insecure; why should she be? Her look was a blend of pride and fragile wondering perhaps concerning the degree to which I was enjoying the First Nudity. A weak smile followed and I returned it with more grit. With a Degas dancer's grace, she floated a nightgown over it all and asked me to tuck her in bed. She kissed me again sparely but softly and closed her eyes. The gleamer glistened and spread from ear to ear.

As I was closing the door she said, "Harry?"

"Yes?"

I could see pupils now glinting in the dark. "I'm not the blonde you think I am."

I suspected she may be right.

"Harry?" I spun again. "I had a pretty okay time tonight."

I concurred my evening had been "pretty okay" too.

She was still reflecting, I could tell. "Harry?"

"Yes?"

The words came almost silently. "I want to go to the Skybox." My nod was lost to shadows and dark. "That'd suit me fancy-fine."

There was yet one more pause. "Harry?"

"Yes?"

I saw her roll into her pillow snuffing out a terrific white comet. I left her apartment floating. And I counted the hours until the morning.

9

The Chic Emergency

Those first days with Sunday were intimate ones and we did not discuss her career. It may have been the best week of my life as we alternated between her Thompson Street digs and the Skybox with quick, touchy dinners at Nobu, Indochine, and Tribeca Grill. They were quick because we always had something better to do. It was over some Bond Street panna cotta that I asked about her professional goals. "I want to show the world what I can do," was her best phrase and I offered to help. She thanked me.

I knew what it took to give Sunday a career boost. We needed some strong pictures, including headshots, high-glams, au naturals, demi-nudes, miles of smiles, in essence, full-spectrum body and beauty coverage. She needed a formidable, and I mean kick-ass, portfolio that would make ad campaign people drool. I called in a few favors and arranged several photo shoots. I had her work with D'Orazio for beauty and portrait, Verglas for body and bathing suit, and von Unwerth for the best in feminine eroticism. To get something totally different, I brought her by Peter Beard's home studio. I knew she'd be perfect for his Blood Clots and Savage Beauties retro glam art. Sure enough, he threw a lot of cow blood on her, faux-choked her with a reptile skin, and had her crawl around half-naked, post-car crash-esque, scandological and savage-like, to give her the look of, as he termed it, a "chic emergency."

We bypassed the fashion modeling agencies and went directly to supertalent manager Ruth Gunn-Glaser. She represented young Hollywood starlets as well as famous models who were making the transition to acting. Ruth was a hard-nosed negotiator and her clients often landed big campaigns. She was tight with guys like

Perlman and Hayes and Dorn and their account people as well as the advertising execs at the big agencies. She had the heavyweight contracts for feminine beauty products covered.

Ruth loved Sunday and found her book better than outstanding. Even so, she was determined to bypass the typical fresh hottie debut strategies like sending her on go-sees for magazine covers and having her attend silly modelpalooza events. She didn't want to make her a big-name model. Her formula for a Sunday launch was the fast white-hot track ad campaign then television series or movie. She'd need to take acting classes at Carnegie Hall at night. Ruth knew a hard-ass Marine acting teacher who'd had a lot of success with women who were a lot too beautiful.

Of course I'd Slung a "Who is that white-hot scandoglam beauty all the top photogs are clamoring to shoot??"-blind item on the Web site. I followed up that with a "That's who!" picture two days later from the D'Orazio sessions.

In less than two weeks, The Machine was in gear.

How did Sunday react? Completely in stride and true to her down-to-earth constitution. She charmed everyone and was considered a joy to work with. And sure, everyone wanted a proverbial piece.

Wait a sec, didn't we meet somewhere?, I'll give you my number, take my card, are you on Facebook?, come to Cabo, pardonnez-moi, un momento, por favor, this is my e-mail, come to Punta, do you have my cell? call me, text me, BBM me, MySpace me, FB me, Twitter me, Plaxo me, Skype me, sextext me, come to St. Barts, scandotext me—please!!!

Sunday deflected the barrage well, the gal was juicy-cool.

The best part was we fell deeply for one other. She kept her job, but only did it part-time. At all of twenty-four, she was patient with herself, her career, she was confident, and she was in love. And in our union she found the grounding she needed to handle it all.

10

The Birth of Paris

I rented a house in Bridgehampton that spring. Sunday had never been out to eastern Long Island and we made our initial pilgrimage there the first weekend in May. The Fonz picked us up after work.

"*Casa* Hamptons, Fonz," I directed.

The drive was smooth once we passed the commuter traffic in Queens and we watched the news on the inset backseat television. Then a Woody Machine show anchored by one of the interchangeable Stepford Wife blonde hostesses came on which prompted the following exchange.

"Let me ask you: what do you think powers The Machine?"

"Money."

"That fuels it, but what oils it?"

"Tell me—"

"Sex."

"Are you trying to tell me something?"

"But it's not necessarily obvious or direct sex, it's silent sex. It's the little prickly sexual urges and yearnings pulsating beneath the surface of all these little worker bee drones and their bosses who comprise The Machine."

"You included."

"Check."

"Are you suggesting I find another career? Or another boyfriend?"

"Just watch out. Entering The Machine is like being thrown to the wolves. Some get nicked and run away, others get pawed and mauled, others get violated then eaten alive, and others make it through without a scratch. And others bleed to death drop by drop."

"I'm squeamish. What if I don't want to lose any blood?"

"It has a funny way of keeping you going even if you're bleeding. Some become accustomed to the sight of their own blood. Of course, others are trying to bleed."

"Love the carnage analogy. You make a career in entertainment sound so inviting."

"My pleasure, but, *forewarned is forearmed.*"

"Tell me, how did Paris Hilton get to where she is? She seemed to appear out of thin air, out of nowhere, like she didn't pay any dues at all."

"More than thin and less than air. The fact is, the tabloids were desperately searching for something new to follow. The older generation of celebrities had gotten tired of the media circuses surrounding them and began altering their routines to circumvent them. Don't forget: Lady Di had been killed in a paparazzi crush. There was a huge backlash. Celebrities started lashing out, fighting back, making media types look bad, taking paps and scribes to court. The very ones who'd help boost their NR for years and thereby, their careers. Celebs ramped up on security and attended fewer events. Some were growing up, too: living more conservative lifestyles, and not going out in public. So the hot feeds dried up. And the daily sheets needed to locate and mine new reserves. It was 'Page Six' that really shifted the paradigm and decided to go on the offensive. To target a group and make them famous. And what did they do? They went 'young.' Why? Because young people are just that: they carry on foolishly and make silly mistakes in the public eye. Perfect fodder for a column. So 'Six' found and followed a group of rich teens and twentysomethings running around behaving ridiculously, drinking, dancing on tables, hooking up left and right, like kids do. Easy pickings. One of them was Paris and she seemed like a team leader and focal point with those Rapunzel locks and Americana name already logoed globally on the tops of buildings. What made it more explosive was her group really *wanted* the notoriety. They were craving it. After all, they'd grown up in the era of celebrity and it had been advertised that that was the thing to be and do: to become one. The Whatever Makes You Famous Age. Though they'd never done anything in their lives, they were thrilled to take the instantaneous NR. Don't forget; planes had hit the towers, we were at war, the shadow of AIDS still hovered, and the globe was melting. So, why not? It was pure escapism for Generation 9/11, pure escapism for readers. And with it, the columns hit the jackpot. Inventing and promoting this group was like inventing buried treasure. These media-starved do-nothings who craved all that attention actually fed us—let us know where they were, what they were doing, when, and with whom, stayed late, performed, danced, canoodled, and played it up for the cameras. This way Paris and her minions were a tabloid goldmine."

"And once one column followed her, the rest followed suit."

"End of story. Except for one thing. In the era of scandalocity, by behaving scandalously, homegrown, manufactured boldfacers like Paris without portfolios actually then were awarded what was missing—their portfolios—with contracts for movies, reality shows, book deals, endorsements, and paid-for appearances..."

"All because of the NR given them."

"Lest we forget the homemade sex tape that sent her over the top—"

"And the newfound portfolios only added to their fame."

"And income. Paris marketed herself well, too. But the genesis of all this was that a verbally-hindered Goldilocks was in the right place at the right time with the right look and behavioral patterns to become the target of a desperate media needing to create new darlings to follow—"

"And sell papers and magazines."

"Amen. It was a strange time, a perfect storm of geopolitical, domestic, and sociological forces really, causing a certain chaos and unrest that ushered in a new brand of escapism rooted in superficiality, really; and the populace embraced it and her as Queen and made her an icon, the icon of the celebrity-obsessed era. Imagine that, a wealthy, unaccomplished little girl becoming the poster child for an era. It's Andy Warhol's 'fifteen minutes' run amok. And it's a phenomenon that can't be replicated. Not now, not in that way."

"Excuse me?" Sunday shot back on the defensive. "I don't mind recognition but—for something I've done. I'm not in it for fame. In fact, that part worries me. It always has. That's why I never came to New York before. Even though it was a dream of mine."

I could see her eyes had widened and a nervousness was gripping her, perhaps fear or something else behind it, but it was unsettling to see.

"What's the matter?"

She was locked on to something, seemingly not hearing me, and she remained entranced, before snapping out of it and responding.

"Reminds me of *Breakfast At Tiffany's* when Audrey Hepburn says, 'There are certain shades of limelight that can ruin a girl's complexion.'"

"It can be a mean little Machine. Do you have a little Holly Golightly in you?"

She pondered it a moment then angled my way with a playful grin. "Only if I can have a little Harry Gohardly in me too…"

"Mmmm. Good answer."

We clasped hands and sat in silence a short while.

I thought to switch subjects, but felt my dissertation on fame and celebrity culture would not be complete if I didn't issue the final warning. So I finished off with the oft-repeated axiom that constituted what I considered to be the ultimate "scando no-no" of the media-obsessed times.

"But when you do make it, whatever you do, *don't believe your own press.* That's when the trouble begins."

"You mean the lies and negative things that get reported?"

"No. Lies and distortions you can dismiss easily, because you know the truth. It's the exaggeration, the overly flattering, positive media feeds that deep down you also know aren't true. About yourself. Your own hype can suck you in and you see people treating you differently and before you know it, you've swallowed and embraced your own exaggerated tabloid persona. What results is an inflated sense of self. And then you're contaminated. And your particles are changed within. They buzz with a different energy, resulting in altered behavior. Entitlement behavior. In essence, *you've* changed. Which is the recipe for your demise. Because people will see the change. And they won't like it. And they'll root for your comeuppance, then your crash and burn, and wait hungrily for gossip scribes to break news of it. Because mooks in my field are salivating for it. And so are their bosses. *What goes up must come down* is the tabloid formula because you get fierce newspaper sales on both ends. And that's where this conversation started…"

"The money," Sunday mouthed dreamily as if she was thinking in parallel about something else other than the subject at hand. And she was.

"If it becomes too much, I'll just pack up and go. I'm not some small-town, identity-starved girl with one part passion and nine parts need for ego satisfaction."

"Who are you, then?"

"I'm the small-town girl with ten parts passion," she countered, "who wants to perform a talent uniquely hers. If it doesn't work out, that's okay. Life has so much else to offer. There are hundreds of things I want to experience." She sat up straight to add, "I'll do it. But I'll do it my way. Or no way."

"Are you that tough?"

"Yes," she shot back and her expression was defiant, severe enough to convince me of something. She believed everything she said.

I angled over and noticed her still clocking me. "Being part of this Machine puts you in a pretty powerful position—"

"I suppose."

"Should I fear you?"

"On my good side, you're Catherine Zeta-Jones, Oscar-winning movie star extraordinaire, the queen of the glam-glams, and gorgeous wife of Michael Douglas and mother to his children—"

"And on your bad side?"

"You're the classless, nouveau riche, commercialize-your-nuptials-with-a-faux-royal-Plaza-wedding, pass-the-trust-fund-money-plate, whore-out-your-child-for-photos-mercenary; the true daughter of a milkman in every sense and gold digger extraordinaire who shagged her way to Oscar with the body of a chambermaid, a piggy snout, and stumpy little hands…"

"Ouch."

"I'll add that both versions are, perhaps, true…"

"Depends which side makes it to print…"

"We can do this the easy way or the hard way. Depends how I'm feeling, really…"

"Or how you're treated."

And I hated what I was saying. But it was no less true. It came with the territory. As a gossip scribe, it was what you signed up for.

She seemed to be weighing something. "Think I'd like the brunt of your bad side…"

"Oh?"

"But only if you'd whisper it in my ear while hmm-hmming me."

A scando-cardio response, for sure, but the curve at her mouth was so dazzling that I had to attack it. And I did, momentarily. But something was eating away at me and I withdrew from our embrace.

It was that reverse epiphany hitting me again, that devastating moment of fraud; the one where if you possess any talent for introspection and can take leave of that often impenetrable fortress of denial, it screams out at you that you're not what you're purporting to be, that you're really a con, a fake and that everything you've established for yourself and built up, the persona you've carefully devised, sculpted, resculpted, refined, and projected, has been predicated on some form of lie. Or self-deception. It hits you like a brick to the chops until you find a way to rationalize it all over again and let it fade because you have something more important to preserve. Your survival. Of course, our related discussion had brought that "moment" on. I almost let it go, too; but unlike others who I generally hid from out of self-preservation, this person was someone with whom I wanted to be on the level. I wanted her to know.

"Sunday, I'm not proud of what I do."

"All right. I'll be proud for you," she sent right back benevolently. "Look at what you've accomplished. You've got a plum job in a highly competitive field in the most competitive city in the world. Do you know how many people would love to be in your position?"

She turned into me.

"A kid comes to the big city and makes it. That's a terrific story. New York is not for the faint of heart. You wanted it, you accomplished it. So, sorry, your success is not such a bad thing."

"But at whose expense?"

"Harry," she addressed me intently. "Everyone has to do what they have to do. *Everyone.*"

She kissed me again. It hit me right then how lucky I was to have met her.

As Sunday dozed off, I iPodded mellow to the Shins and the Thievery Corporation and mulled my erratic romantic ledger. I'd tried my best at relationships but they'd never lasted long: six or seven months at most, but the majority lasted approximately two. I sensed something special was brewing. I wanted longer-term, perhaps even full-term, an interval I had never considered possible. I'd never trusted myself enough. But I was fully aware honesty and transparency with a partner was a first step.

It was nightfall when we glided into sleepy Bridgehampton. I could see Bobby Van's still had some action going and there were a few people at the bar at Pierre's. We made the right at the statue off Main Street and turning down Ocean Road, Sunday awoke from her slumber.

"Where are we?"

"Home." We turned in and down the long gravel driveway. When we got out of the car, our ears were filled with ocean sounds, the subdued shore break offering its consistent but intermittent rhythms.

"Hear that?"

"Hear it?" She sent back excitedly. "I hear it, smell it, feel it. Harry, let's go!"

"It's pretty windy."

"*And?*"

And she was off on a full sprint, following the winds of her life as advertised. I unlocked the house and the Fonz brought in our bags. Then I headed out back and ascended the dunes. I located Sunday's silhouette back-lit from silvery moonbeams at the shore's edge. I slowed my pace and stayed back to let her have some time. To herself. When I joined her, I sat beside and basked in the delicious quietude. The silent aspects of togetherness were nice, rather, incredible.

"So peaceful," she whispered softly.

I could see a lone tear had made its way down her cheek, the tear's path reflected in the moonlight scattered on the water. I couldn't tell if the tear was from her seemingly elated state or from the chilly winds. I clasped her hand in mine. Hers was cold and she was shivering.

11

Casa Hamptons

The house was a Cape Cod-styled structure perched on the dune with weathered brown and gray shingles and marine blue shutters. There was a small garage and cottage to the side, a black-bottomed pool, and a fine green lawn which ran to the base of the dunes. The dunes were high enough to protect the grass from the winds and salty air. The house belonged to a real estate mogul and he'd given me a sweet deal on the full season through Labor Day. I wouldn't normally have been able to afford a rental as nice as this.

The next morning Sunday ran into the bedroom wearing my white Chateau Marmont robe, her face ablaze with excitement.

"Harry, they're amazing…"

I was groggy, but I knew what she'd meant. She'd been to the garden.

"—so, so beautiful…"

"I'm glad you like them."

I watched her wipe the water from her eyes. "Harry?"

"Yes?"

"The nicest thing anyone has ever done for me."

Breakfast was awaiting on the patio beside the gardens as Alphonso had cooked up *huevos rancheros*. There had been a lot of rain in April and the gardens looked spectacular, featuring rows of salmon-pink flowers specially planted for the spring arrival of my guest. Not ordinary flowers; they were indigenous to the south, the type aligning the fairways at the Augusta National Golf Club in Georgia, the site of the Masters. Azaleas, Sunday's real name, and favorite flower. It was a risky choice, as azaleas don't survive in windy sites, but the high dunes offered protection and the gardener had devised a great drainage system while adding a special type of peat moss. But even if they only lasted that one weekend, it was worth it. She was worth it.

Sunday was kneeling before the rows, nosing them when I came out. She charged up and sacked me to the lawn like a helpless Sunday QB, giggling all the while. Straddling me, she pulled a lone stem rising from the grass, made a wish, and blew the dandelion fairies all around and over me.

It was a gorgeous afternoon and we stayed on the beach, taking a long, big-sweater walk and playing foot-chicken with the chilled and lapping shore break. It was then she noticed my injury. I'd lost the second toe in after the big toe on my right foot.

"An accident," I offered, and left it at that. There was more to the story, but I knew to leave that for another occasion.

Later, we drove around Watermill eyeing vast tracts of subdivided farmlands from which now sprouted incongruous and ill-conceived Sopranos houses, one ghastly architortural structure piled after another.

"I want to bring up what we touched upon before," Sunday said as we coasted along the lazy residential streets. "In college, I took a sociology course and it focused on human interaction in society. And one thing I'll always remember was how an individual's chosen topic of conversation was often an indicator of his or her intelligence. My professor claimed bright people and intellectuals spoke in ideas and concepts. Mediocre minds discussed current events and trends. Less advantaged types talked constantly about people, they gossiped. You brought it up before, Harry, and I didn't feel I knew you well enough to speak my mind. And I still don't know you well…"

"You know me. Tell me." The fact is that I'd come to value what she had to say in a very short time.

"You said you weren't proud. Of what you did. That bothered me. Because you're lucky in many ways. You have a gift, you're articulate, and the way you speak is the way you write. There's wit, there's humor, you invent words, you're a master of language, truly exceptional at what you do. And you have the following to prove it."

"Quantity is not necessarily you-know-what. Goes for readership too."

"Harry, people are striving for a fraction of what you have. You're stuck on what you don't have, what's missing. Like the rest of us, I suppose. Here's where I'll agree. I'll agree with what I think you were trying to say…"

"Which is?"

"That you're capable of more. Some sort of higher calling. That's really what you were saying wasn't it?"

She couldn't know the extent she was piercing my core. I was stupefied. "The thought has crossed my mind."

"I'm inclined to think that you're not sure if you're up to it. For whatever reason. I need to know more about you to know why that may be. But I'm here to tell you if there's anything in this life I'm sure of it's this. You are capable of more. Much more. And you will show it. One day."

I nodded neutrally.

"So reach further. To the next level. Set a new goal…"

"Which would be?"

"Well, write a book. For starters."

The gloss which had formed over my eyes at *capable of more* had already dried in the enduring silence after she'd finished speaking.

"I've wanted to. All my born days."

"So?"

"The easy answer is, I'm distracted."

"Any other answer?"

"I tried once, actually."

"Fiction?"

"I wasn't that ambitious. A children's book. Silly, I suppose…"

"Not at all, tell me about it." And she was eyeing me expectantly, even excitedly.

"All right," I began, "it's a story about a colorful house with big windows and no doors and a little boy Rufus who lives there. Rufus doesn't ever leave the house but has a wonderful time imagining what's going on outside."

"Why won't he leave?"

"Rufus is happy in the house, he travels freely from room to room and plays with his toys and animal friends. But the outside scares him; he's heard terrible stories about it. More importantly, it was where his mother went. And never came back."

"So what happens?"

"You tell me."

She considered it. "Well, he goes outside and finds it's safe. And he learns about nature, he learns to trust, and to try new things. And he also learns a lesson about his mother dying."

"Thematically correct. For a different story. In my version, Rufus goes outside and finds he was right all along, that he should have stayed inside."

She said it smiling. "Is that the right message to be sending to kids?"

"I didn't say the book got published. But," I quipped, "perhaps I could have a career in indie children's books."

She laughed and redirected her gaze to the passing scenery. We coasted past an enormous house under construction, the bare blond wooden beams exposed, the interior opened wide like a massive rib cage, Port-O-Sans still dotting the property.

"Funny…"

"What is?"

"In recounting the story, you described the house first. Before the boy…"

She was right. In storytelling, one usually begins with character.

"Did you dream about Rufus's house?"

"What are you referring to?"

"A structure with no doors. And rooms always open." I spied over at her. "Or the nightmare versions, you're locked in. Or locked out. Were doors closed on you when you were a kid?"

I was suddenly serious about my driving, eyes locked on the road.

"No doors in the loft. None in the bedrooms here. I saw them stacked in the garage. You removed them didn't you? There aren't any locks or latches. On anything."

I drove silently still, to a conspicuous degree. "You hungry?" I asked even more conspicuously.

She was still fastened on me which resulted in a kiss, her lips noticeably heated, smoldering even. "Turn around," she whispered.

"You mean, now?"

"Right here. Please—"

I made a U-turn and we glided past the same large house under construction again.

"Pull over, Harry."

"It's private property."

"Thematically correct. For this story. We won't be anything *but…*"

Sunday got out and advanced ahead and surveyed the skeletal palace as I waited by the car. She circled the entire place and, upon returning, she squared up before me her nose a ladybug's leap from mine. She clasped my hand and led me away.

The sun was slamming down hard and the cloud count was negligible. The house wouldn't be ready for a few months, maybe September or October if the builders got their act together and worked diligently, to make less money of course. Fat chance.

We stepped in the front doorway and Sunday moved to a corner of the main floor and unzipped her blue jeans and let gravity take them away. With no elastics or undergarments, the baby blue "Pretty Vacant" T-shirt was her last thread of camouflage, aside those flip-flops. The lady of the house now, ever the proper hostess, she beckoned me over.

My beach fatigues were soon undone and she knelt low and took me as I eyed the street, the jittery Puritan. There was no one in sight. After a dreamy while, she stopped suddenly, rose up, and lip-smacked me hard. She tour-guided me onward and up the main staircase. The planks smelled freshly cut. We scaled another flight to the third floor where only half the roof had been added. She left me there with my jean flaps open and catwalked over to a bay window, leaning into the empty frame, her back to me. She was poised gorgeously, waist-down naked and eyeing a softly shimmering ocean, vineyards, potato fields, nearby maples undulating in the wind, the old Colonials, other semi-constructed moderns, and the mossy green Sound at the other end, extending further, to the dreamy wipe of Connecticut coastline. No less picturesque, there was the delicate sway to her carriage and the twin dimples above her Diesel-perfect rounds. Right now, she was more than a hostess, she was the establishment's proprietor, her private invitation being delivered to me to the house warming party, folded open already, its decorative flower on the envelope glistening in the sun.

I RSVPd. I would attend. And show early. I maneuvered behind to peel up her baby blue T, her arms rising and hands bracing the window frame.

"No doors, Harry."

It may as well have been Chinese.

"No locks, no roof. Harry like, no?"

It was Chinese. She didn't need a response.

"Fuck me, Harry. In the *casa* with no doors..."

The wind was blowing her hair back to my face and my chin dug in to her soft, fragrant nape and I dutifully granted her request.

"Harder, Harry."

I had a suspicion that she was reading my mind.

"No rules, no restrictions..."

The notion was not lost on me.

"Everything open. For the taking. So take it, Harry. It's all yours..."

I could only remit primal scando sounds, she could only offer a man's favorite octet in the English language, make that, a woman's too.

"You can do anything you want to me..."

We made love in that window with no glass, a room with no furniture, a floor with no doors, a house with no roof, a man and a woman with no inhibitions, a couple with nothing but time, for a couple hours.

A dog barked intermittently. He was our only witness.

12

It Could Have Been Different

In the evening we had lobster on the deck and the Fonz made a potent pitcher of *capairiñas*, his very own recipe, as in Columbian-style. Wonderfully wasted, we snatched a blanket and charged out to the beach to make clumsy love that verged once more on the exploratory. The exploration party took effort and we were soon a sandy mess.

Though our physical desires had been met, we hadn't lost our senses of humor. Our 80 proof senses of humor, anyway. I started in.

"Want to hear a dirty text someone sent me?"

"Of course."

I told her it was from one of my kooky Militiamen pals, a noted cheapie. "It's pretty off-color. You sure?"

"Poz— "

And I was just drunk enough to oblige her…

"'Sixty-six dollars for a Mexican dinner with tip… Thirty-nine-ninety-nine for the Motel 6… Seven-ninety-nine for the condom… But knowing she bought the burritos, brings a girlfriend, they both swallow, hate condoms, and take it up the road less traveled: priceless… It pays to Discover.'"

… And Sunday was just drunk enough to laugh. I apologized anyway and when I did I saw a smile curving along her face. "But I have one for you…"

"Bring it on."

"'Kay," she started, before pausing to get it right. "'The ride out to the Hamptons, one hundred dollars… The lobster dinner, one hundred–seventy-five dollars… Azaleas imported to the garden, five thousand dollars… the house rented in Bridgehampton, one hundred thousand dollars…'"

"All right, all right,' I said, my morale ebbing in on embarrassment. "This is too close to home…"

"No, no, wait!" she erupted and hesitated, her head bowing. Finally, she turned up into me, eyes flooded with tears, and said, "'But giving someone their life back and a chance to become the person they always could have been, and can still be? *Priceless*…'"

Though I didn't know exactly what she'd meant, it seemed to say everything. And I would never forget it. We hugged until neither one of us had any strength left in our arms.

"I think I love you, Harry…"

"I know I love you."

On Sunday, we found another unfinished structure to our liking in Wainscott. It was more modern and angular than the three-tiered one in Bridge. But the ambience was no less charged. The ritual was repeated and again until it pretty much became a weekend scandomatic. We'd spy out sites with deep estate lawns and partially constructed homes and if the architecture was pleasing enough or the place had the right vibe and aura we'd do it on sight, the style, design, and architectural grace dictating the mood. A dilapidated beach shack converted to a duck blind was a find and things there got pretty nasty. Delicious, self-centered, grudge-like, scandotantric. Stately constructions would make us exhibit more decorum and *politesse*. For a while. We enjoyed the thrillies of disrupting all that elitism too, bringing it down to the savage and classless, unbound by social conventions. Sunday welcomed both ends of the aesthetic spectrum and implied symbologies, and, other spectra as well.

We got to know the area quite well. Sunday learned the offbeat street names, the cul de sacs, the back roads, and shortcuts and where things dead-ended. In an alternative Pavlovian way, I became aroused as soon as I put it down in the driver's seat.

We hit our stride by mid-August, becoming avid Hamptons construction site sex tourists. We pretty much covered the east end from Southampton on, invading Montauk when we tired of Easthampton. There was a lot of building going on there too, we learned.

As far as that first weekend was concerned, however, it was a splendid beginning, a time when we became closer, forged a stronger bond, and our union became more deep-rooted and profound.

I decided I would drive back to New York early Monday morning because I wanted one more night with her away. At long last, I had incentive to put my personal life ahead of business.

We went for a sunset stroll on the beach and warmed our feet in thermal pockets posited in the sand by the day's penetrating rays. We held hands and settled in a wind-protected dune recess and enjoyed the pink and mauve watercolor sky and the season's beachy silence. Eventually, I spoke.

"About me…"

She angled over at me sensing something weighty, as in deeply personal. "You don't have to, Harry."

"No, I don't but—"

"I know enough. Enough to know I want to be with you. We can live in the present." She paused a moment. "Sometimes it's better. Healthier…"

"But you picked up on it. You were right…"

She looked sharply over at me again.

"Doors were closed or locked on me. To keep me in. Or out. Twice a week I was held down by force, by 'teachers' at a 'special school' who were doctors and so called 'psychological experts' all supposedly 'knowledgeable.' And they all took turns misdiagnosing my condition and prescribing the wrong medications and therapies. But they didn't know any better. No one did."

"Why did your family send you there?"

"I was a difficult child. High-energy. Impulsive. Your average wild Indian times ten. My mother claimed she couldn't handle me. So the family left New York City thinking it might be better for us to grow up in a rural setting. Which could have a calming effect. On me, the hyperactive child. So we moved to Massachusetts, where my mother grew up. And things were fine. For a while. I was doing well in school. For the first time. But that winter the accident happened. My sister and I were ice skating at the local creek. She fell through the ice. I hauled her out but she died hours later. From hypothermia."

122 Coerte V. W. Felske

I could see Sunday's eyes beginning to glisten.

"For my mother, that was the last straw. So I was sent away."

"She blamed you?"

"For not taking proper precautions with her, yes …"

"What did your father say?"

"He was passive, as usual. Mom ran the show. So off I went to that school. But Mom didn't get any better. She was never the same after Caitlin died. She never recovered. She suffered from awful depression. Not long after, my parents split up. Then Mom had the heart attack. I think she willed it upon herself. I have this image of her ordering her heart to stop; she was that strong-willed. So in two years I lost the two people—"

I couldn't finish. Sunday had welled eyes and she leaned to embrace me. I wondered if I should have divulged that aspect of my past so soon.

"I didn't mean to upset you."

"You were so young," she said, "to have lost your mother." She clutched my hands tightly.

"You know what really hurts? The fact that she never knew who I was. Like I was just some rotten kid. Causing all this mayhem. She never saw the real me. And I always think that it could have been different. But for her, it was like," I pushed as my voice splintered in pieces, "I was never there at all."

Sunday took her time, perhaps a show of respect for the confessional. When she was ready she turned in to me. "You were there, Harry. And she knows you were there. Thank you…"

"What?"

"For sharing it. Your most precious."

She wrapped me with her arms. We didn't say anything for a long while, until she reached for my twist of necklaces.

"Now I understand…"

"Hmmm?"

"How you became a big success in New York," she said. "You were loaded. And layered. Psychologically. And all that came before has given you something you're taking for granted, Mr. Slinger. You wanted to make your mark. Most people pass through life without ever getting an opportunity to make something of themselves.

Because they don't have it. Or anything to spur them on. Yes, much was taken away from you. Too much. But you were also given things. Like the qualities most essential to becoming a success: talent and drive."

She hesitated a second. "And I want to tell you: Your mother knows what you've become. Do you believe in angels, Harry?"

I remained silent. The question came seemingly out of nowhere, yet it was speaking to my soul, another direct hit.

"Why do you ask?"

She took her time. "What do all these mean?"

She was referring to the jewelry piled at my chest suspended from silver chains and black-waxed twine necklaces, each pendant representing a different religion and culture.

"You could say I'm over-Godded. Make that multi-Godded…"

"Does that mean you're confused?"

"Of course I am. But not about religion."

"So what do you believe in?"

"Everything, Sunday. I believe in everything."

"Tell me why."

"They all communicate the same message to me. I think…"

"And what is that?"

"Love, perhaps. And compassion."

"So, you do believe in angels then…"

I didn't have to think it over. "Yes, I do."

"Why?"

And it rolled off my tongue. "Because I knew one once." It was, perhaps, the most personal thing I'd said in my whole life. To anyone.

"You did?"

"She was of this world, until she took to the bigger sky. And she's still with me. Guiding me. And looking out for me."

"How do you know?"

"I have proof."

"What proof is that?"

"The fact that I'm still here. Alive."

She smiled sweetly and went quiet. "*You're* an angel, Harry."

"What?"

She repeated it, the comment so overwhelming it rendered me speechless. Again. "I don't know what to say."

"Don't say anything."

"I've been called things, but never that."

"Not in the traditional sense. You're *my* angel."

"Am I?"

"Yes, you are. More than you know."

"That sounds—" I was stunned to the point of losing my train and I could feel a certain heaviness in my eyes and water filling them.

"How religious are you really, Harry?"

"I don't go to church every Sunday. It's personal, but no less significant to me."

"Did you ever attend church?"

"Early on, then… I always got sent home, and my parents were too embarrassed to bring me back."

"Why did you get sent home?"

"I couldn't sit still. Because of my condition. I would shake my knee, fidget, play with the hymnals, look around, laugh because I wasn't supposed to, all that pressure, all that sit still and be quiet stuff. I felt like I was trapped. It was too much."

"Harry?"

"What?"

"Even angels say good-bye."

I twisted one over at her but gave it some time. "It's too beautiful to consider."

"Think so?"

"So beautiful that it doesn't sound so good."

"Why not?"

"It scares me. For a lot of reasons. I hope it's not a warning."

"No warning, just a thought. Do you think it's true?"

"Is what true?"

"That angels can say good-bye?"

"Don't know," I quick-winded. "Maybe they can. Let's hope not."

"No. I'm serious."

I could see she was, her eyes moistened and alive with nascent tears. But so was I. "Okay. I believe angels can say good-bye, yes."

"Really?"

"But 'good-bye' to one person might be 'hello' to someone else."

"Or to some place else—"

"Yes, and so on, and so on. And that's how angels get their work done. But, I believe this: a good-bye doesn't have to mean forever."

"No?"

"It can mean good-bye for now."

"That's right, Harry, that's so right. That's how angels can say good-bye."

The wetness in her eyes produced a glossy shimmer though she had the most peaceful and contented expression on her face. It stayed there a while.

I woke up suddenly at about four in the morning and saw Sunday standing in the doorway to the bedroom, her back to me.

"Baby? What's up?"

She spun around to engage but I could sense she needed to pause. "Can I meet him?"

Sunday was so unpredictable in a good way that I thought she was asking to meet my father, so I asked to make sure. "Who?"

"Dr. Van den Heugel." It took me by total surprise. "I saw his name on your prescription bottle."

"It's a her," was my startled response. "She's a psychoanalyst."

She waited in thought. "I've always wanted to talk to someone."

Then she came back to bed and gently pretzeled herself around me.

13

The Two Lips Girls (*)

When we returned that Monday from the Hamptons, Sunday stayed at her apartment and her answering machine boasted some unbelievable news. Ruth, Sunday's manager, informed her she'd landed a three-year, seven-figure contract with Two Lips Cosmetics, an Internet-only lipstick and mascara line advertised in all the major mags, *Vogue* included. She was now their million-dollar girl. Apparently the company had been searching for a new face, a fresh face, and they'd wanted a blonde. It brought to mind our blonde prejudice discussion and the irony of it all. It was timing and luck and, of course, that unique, *je ne sais quoi* X-factor Ruth and I both thought Sunday possessed.

Sunday called me, ecstatic, and I joined her at her place and we had a bottle of champagne and celebrated in every way.

From that moment on, our downtown lives were never the same; the campaign she'd landed was bigger than we'd originally thought. She was billboarded in thirty cities. As you drove into Manhattan on the Expressway, she was there to greet you, when you zoomed down Sunset Boulevard in L.A. she was flashing you that Trident White beamer. She was in all the newspapers, magazines, Web site sidebars, pop-ups, blabbering blogs, on bus stops and bus panels. She was the new "Two Lips Girl."

Rather, she was one of two Two Lips Girls*.

They hadn't used a famous photographer for the shot, but they still adopted a controversial style. It was nouveau Post-Millennium Lesbian Chic at its best, pure von Unwerth-rip-off, and it had a massive scandalocity index. The shot showed Sunday cheek-to-cheek with another brunette, both sets of ruby lips opened wide with slanted verticals, the parted teeth showing dark slits, each holding a tulip. The other model selected was Tanya*, whose body was so cosmetized she deserved the asterisk, but her inclusion in the campaign made it no less va-va-voom. It was advertorial scandocandy, the subliminal element so blatant it wasn't subliminal, so much so that the red state anti-sex police were protesting wildly. Kids were stealing the bus posters around town as fast as they were being pasted up, and Georgia O'Keefe was smiling proudly in some corner of heaven.

As the campaign dropped, Sunday put the "I" in "It-girl" and it was pure chaos. The TV shows, from morning to late-night, requested interviews, as did the dailies; *Vanity Fair, Harper's Bazaar, Allure,* and *Maxim* wanted to arrange shoots, Bounty Bob hounded me for snaps, and my competitors Slung and Faced the hell out of my girl. Movie offers trickled in. Ruth hired Sunday a singing coach and a record producer booked studio time to have her cut two demo tracks. Don't forget: it was the era of horizontal cross-pollination in entertainment. You get one, you may well get them all. And she started to. The Machine was in full swing and Sunday Fairchild was becoming the Next Big Thing.

Sunday happily quit her job at the travel agency and was inspired to attend acting classes, as well as work with her vocal coach, and date me. She was in total control, as she'd claimed she would be, and our relationship became ever stronger.

14

Love Letter to *La Grosse Pomme*

Sunday Fairchild was born in Pensacola, Florida in 1982. She was a July child, a Leo, a little blonde princess and I'd seen the photos to prove it. She got her fine looks and features from her mother, but her slender, knifing figure came from her father. He was tall and lean with an athletic build and possessed a washboard stomach well into his fifties. Her mother died of cancer when she was nine and she was raised in a church shelter. Her father was never around. Sunday didn't speak of him other than to say he was a retired Air Force pilot. "I'm going to introduce you; you make up your mind," she said.

I was actually looking forward to meeting her family, and happier she had invited me to.

One night, I returned from a news correspondents dinner and found a letter on my pillow. Sunday was lying asleep beside it.

June 25, 2007
Dear Harry,
   I know you're coming in late so I'm leaving this note for you…
   I love New York for the following reasons:
   The blast of horns from the yellow cabs, the shop windows on Madison Avenue, the Mad Hatter statue in Central Park, the protesters of the downtrodden horses who circle the Park with tourists, the Sabrett hot-dogs with sauerkraut and mustard, the DJ's at Pink Elephant, the constellations on the ceiling of Grand Central Station, the interior design of Joe's Pub, the privacy of Double Seven, the food at Nobu Next-Door, Sylvie's in Harlem, the black beans and yellow rice at Las Brisas on Broome, Halloween in New York, Harry's funny scando world, his cute scando words, his 'scandospective'

on everything, his sexy scandotext messages which get-me-get-me, making love in the Skybox, the pretend-we're-away hotel safaris at the Gansevoort and the Mercer, the Giants away uniforms, the red La Perla bra and 'teenies' Harry gave me for Valentine's Day, Starbucks bold coffee with sugar and a marshmallow square, my billboard on the Long Island Expressway, Yankee knit ski caps, making love in the Skybox (again!), Old Navy on lower Broadway, Joe's Shanghai in Chinatown, Bungalow 8, the music at Cain, the 'New York Post''s horoscope, 'Slingshot' when Harry writes it, the Public Library, La Guardia airport, Ruth my manager, the putrid air fresheners in yellow cabs, the fact that the theaters are there, the fact that the museums are there, the fact that culture is all around us, the swimming polar bear at the Children's Zoo, watching Harry sleep in the Skybox, the fact that you can call the Big Apple the Grosse Pomme, the see-no-evil drivers of yellow cabs, the great-tasting tap water, the fact I never feel like I'm missing anything anywhere, making love in the Skybox (3x!), and in the Canal Jeans changing room, bathroom at Bond Street, the backseat of cab #3YZ89, my fire escape, the half-built houses in the Hamptons, the parking lot of Montauk State Park (not in the Hamptons but as beautiful), those Brazilian V.S. models, reading off someone else's newspaper in the subway, the baristas at Starbucks on Spring, the firemen at Ladder 42, Yann and Yann's sailboat at Port Liberty Marina, rollerblading in Central Park with Harry, yoga classes at Jivamukti, the angel painting I bought Harry, that Evian billboard on Houston with the cute girl in the bathtub with the long leg sticking out, Kim's Video, the Skybox naked waiting for Harry, my apartment on Thompson, and, most of all, what I love about New York is—the fact that Harry, my angel, lives here!!!

I love you very much,

Your Little Scandolita

P.S. Don't bother asking. Just do it.
[Big red-lips kiss print]

As previously noted, we were very much in love.

15

Wally Foxx, the Jack In The Box

September, 2K8
"Hello?"

"Say, Slinger!" the Militiaman said all revved up and winding like a Suzuki dirt bike. "What's shaking?"

"Uh, my job, Wally. I'm at work."

"My Google entries are up! To five-thousand-ten!"

"Terrif," I said, though I was concerned. "How did you swing that?"

"In Vermont. *Burlington Free Press* ran the story…"

"What story?"

"Well, I got in an argument."

"A fight?"

"I suppose…"

"You call the cops on yourself?"

"*Slings*," he droned downcast, as in busted.

"Not your old trick…"

He paused. "Which one?"

"Pre-emptive Mace maneuvers…"

"No Mace. I swear."

"How did the newspaper find out?"

He hesitated again, hemming and hawing. "Nah, Slings, waved off," he decided at last to avoid a full confessional he'd planted the story. He modified it though with a sigh, a mild attempt at transparency. "People in print matter more. You know that."

"Unflattering press is still unflattering."

"Yeah, well, there's always Google Reputation Management. If things get out of hand."

"Just cautioning, Wally."

"Be happy for me. My NR's getting lift-off. Finally."

"Okay. Congrats," I said.

Wally Fox wrapped his fragile esteem and sense of worth around his NR quotient and I was sensitive to his needs. It resulted in potential notoriety-generating, press-desperate deeds no matter how compromising of his character. It was his only job and one of two passions in life, the other being vid games. He performed Google entry checks throughout the day, monitoring movements, hoping his name recognition had been boosted. But Wally wasn't alone. Many I-Agers watchdogged their Google stats, the era's dubious indicator of achievement and seeming importance.

Abuzz with self-satisfaction once again, Wally launched into a manic, high-energy, and long-winded rant into neurotic nothingness his Jack In The Box persona was known for, at the end of which he posed, "*Wanna play?*"

"Can't right now."

"Come on! One game of *World of Warcraft.*"

"Not on a weekday. You taking your meds?"

"Winner take all!"

"Wally, are you taking your meds?"

"I can spot you, Slings—"

Wally was broke, of course. "Wally, I'm asking you a question—"

The pause endured until his television volume spiked loudly, and, punishingly.

"Can't hear you, Slings!"

"*Wally?*"

"I'm at the Stadium! A-Rod's up. *No can hear!* Text you later!"

I knew already the Yanks were out of town playing a night game.

16

Welcome to The Machine

Scandoblind: What Fortune 500 biggie known for his rodeo roundups of the better gender takes them on his yacht, anchors out at sea, sprinkles the mandatory passion fruit punch with dementia dusts and doesn't return to port until he's had his offshore fill?

In the days before Sunday's murder my personal profile wasn't half bad. I'd attended but never finished a state university you've probably never heard of. After being diagnosed for ADHD at nineteen and treating it properly, things turned around. My father called on an old colleague on the Admissions Board at Harvard University who got me in. The appropriate medications helped me to pull it together to receive a Masters degree in the Fine Arts creative writing program. Politically, I was a Whoever-Can-Deliver-crat and my religious views, well, let's just say I was viewing religion. But enough about me, what did I think of me? Stick around.

Physically, I was handsome enough, I was thirty-five years old, had enough hair to get a good cut and enough fashion sense to dress fashionably, except for the loud shirts. More important, goods and services came easy to me and I had *beaucoup* offers. My profession? I was a glorified gossip columnist in a business which thrived on "scandalocity." **Scandalocity** *is the speed at which scandal, measured in velocity, can turn you into a star.* A former word toy, this nasty formula, perfected in the nineties, paid off big dividends in the post-millennium era peaking in fuchsia neon after The Fall; that is, after the World Trade Center attack threw the Golden Age of Unnecessary News, Hollow Publicity, Dirty Laundry, Smashmouth Sarcasm, and Invigorating Shallow Tidbits (ISTs) into a temporary four-corner stall. With the passing of time however scando came back more robust than ever.

Scandalocity blossomed decades ago with the *Playboy* centerfolds and then the Kennedy scandoclan raised it a notch. It buried Marilyn in her lifetime, but Madonna took up the mantle and made it her art. Following suit were cats like Lewinsky, Rodman, Combs, the J.Lo gangsta boost, Eminem, *PamAndersonium Artificialis**, and, of course, Paris. It saved the Clintons. It got Hillary her seat in the Senate and almost catapulted her back to the White House while it turned Bill into a global star of matinee idol proportions. It gave every O.J. trial player an afterlife, spawning numerous prime-time pundit television shows. Though it backfired on O.J. in the end, the Juice had still been on the loose for years signing scandographs and getting decent tee times at golf clubs while Kato was still weaseling scandoglammy odd jobs somewhere.

Twenty years ago, scandal still ruined you: ask Gary Hart. That all changed. Scandal handled in the right way with the proper accents became profitable. Scando became *scandough* but it also became power, the most potent social phenomenon in the media-saturated, post-millennium era turning yesterday's nobodies into overnight sensations. It translated to millions of dollars in publicity and often big-time contracts unless you were a corporate scandoswindler like Koslowski or scandoskimmer Skilling, or a pervy scandocandidate like Foley. Only then were you disgraced. Or alleged scando-'roiders like Bonds* and Clemens* though the lying, juiced-up jocks still got the coin.

You must be thinking, *tell me something I don't know?*

What you don't know is that I was founder and editor-in-chief of "*Slingshot.nyc*," an online gossip and scandal sheet Web site that provided the commodities most sought-after in America in the fresh new century behind platinum and gold. And corn-pulped ethanol. New York was the world's premier scandotropolis, a veritable scandotopia for the scando scribe. My position offered a prime post in the New York-therefore-America-therefore-the-World star-making machinery, an excitingly dangerous media complex I referred to as "The Machine."

As an officer of The Machine and daily distributor of said

commodities, I was awarded VIP status and extensive Manhattan privilege. Socially, I had carte blanche: access for me was called Anywhere, Anytime and rarely did I have to fork over a nickel. They all wanted what I could give them, Face, as in boldface, slingshot to the masses. Anyone who was no one was looking for Face; anyone who was anyone was looking for more. And that went for people's businesses too. Because with Face came enhanced NR and if enhanced NR was the currency of the times, "There's no such thing as bad press" was its rallying cry. As I held an individual's or corporation's NR in my hands, when all was said and done, I had so many daily perks coming my way I had to wear a hockey goalie's mask and duck.

This is not to say that I didn't have enemies. If you scandoslammed people harder than they expected, then you were in for some pretty serious grudge time. But they'd snap out of it pretty soon. After all, they were only as good as their last blurb which went for "bad" pub too. So the Crushed, Disappointed, Embarrassed, and Disturbed would just as soon bury their hatchets with me and get on to some new, good, bold, electric, and kinetic Face for the future, their future. Good Sling was truly worth its weight in gold and sought after as such.

"*Slingshot*" was funded by *The New York Herald* and our online column appeared in the daily paper, too. We all shared office space on Spring Street near the Hudson. "*Slingshot*" occupied a cozy corner niche of the fifth floor and if you sashayed thirty meters and twenty cubicles of the cube farm into the paper's advertising department, you caught the sweeping view of Lady Liberty, Ellis Island, and Jersey City.

I made it into the office around ten. My grunts 2 Late and Amy Nightlife both dialed in with new dish involving Brangelina. The era's hottest scandobrand, they were the new Liz and Dick of the scandozilla era. Lest we forget scandocandy Jessica. Or scandorandy Paris. Or scandofannied J.Lo. Or scandomammaried Pam. Or scandodandy Elton. Or scandotranny RuPaul. Or scandomammy Britney. And her Baby Wars. Or scandomannequin Naomi. Or scandogranny Madonna. Or scandogramps Trump. Or scandoskeletal Ritchie. Bet your ass I was tired of writing about them. I would have been happy never hearing another thing about their press-desperate and fractionally scandoglam lives but their scandohandlers worked overtime scandocramming them onto the site for their daily blast, and these scandozillas sold papers which is what *Herald* publisher Arthur Lawrence enjoyed most about the paper business.

Let me say this now: scando gave me work and a paycheck, a nice paycheck. Sure, I'd dreamed of being a professional writer, but a gossip scribe? Never. The fact is, it was all I could handle.

"*Slingshot*" had an adequate budget with which to work. 2-Late had a scandoscoop rate of four hundred dollars an item and why did I call Will Braddock "2-Late?" If he got word of something sexy, illegal, or shameful you'd done, it was too late. Shoulda thought about that before you got into the scandojam. Nightlife only received three hunnies, as she'd only been at it a year. She was scandosavvy and a beast when it came to the parties. If the column was boldface light, I could depend on Nightlife to get out there, gnaw at some quasi-reluctant feeders, and deliver some semi-precious gems. She worked the room at events like no one I'd ever seen, the way I used to do it. Now I was lazy and without will, depending on my grunts more as the year had not been excessively kind to me.

I didn't drink every day at work but I did most days, as I squirreled away a Tiffany flask of Mount Gay for the afternoon stretch. It medicated me. If I became manic and had an ADHD flare-up like, taking a phone call on my mobile in the middle of a sit-down meeting with clients, leaving my office to find a wastebasket, draining watercooler water into it, returning to my office, tipping the filled wastebasket over my banana plants and watering them, all the while barking into my phone, and, hand gesticulating to the astounded clients awaiting, colleagues would neck up from their cubes like a colony of meerkats and decide whose turn it was to take me out for coffee.

Who's on 'Bucks duty with Slinger today?

Strong coffees loaded with high-test caffeine served to calm me, in the same manner as the psychostimulants. ADDers need stimulants for focus though it has the opposite effect on normal folk, also known as, 'normies.'

With the flask, my thirsty banana plants, a hunter green Dell, smokes, prepaid 'Bucks cards, some shoddy work habits, and an understanding staff, I was one hell of a captain of industry.

My real name is Harvey Starslinger but I never liked that Harvey handle or the memories associated with it. I'd heard it yelled too often for things I'd done wrong. Back in the day, I signed it plain "H" and, after a while, I changed it to Harry and then in college they called me "Slinger" and that stuck. I like Slinger, actually, and if you're my friend you're welcome to call me that.

Along with the gossip grunts, I had two dependable photographers, Clyde Kinopka and Bounty Bob who, covered most social events. I stayed away from lone wolves who'd hammer you with their pricey one-shot fees, but if you needed a snap and the other assassinazzis hadn't delivered there was nothing else you could do but ante up.

"Hello?"

"Steve? It's Slinger." Steve Cipone was a homicide detective and the point man in my loved one's murder case. Like most dedicated cops, he wanted to get together in meetspace. Phoning or e-mails wouldn't do.

"Say, I have an appointment today I forgot about. How about Elaine's for dinner tomorrow tonight?"

"Rather not, Slinger. Don't want to talk about this stuff publicly. Too many open ears and mouths up there."

I knew Steve was right and told him so. He asked me if I could come down to the precinct the following day at noon.

"Danderoo," said I nonchalantly to filter out any traces of dread in my voice.

17

Meetspace Meeting

Steve Cipone headed the Homicide Division for the Fifth Precinct in SoHo and we'd known each other a while, as he'd been a consultant for me in scandofed matters. He wouldn't give me scandoscoops, but he'd make sure I didn't overindulge or get journalistically irresponsible. I could run things by him which could, in turn, avert me from getting in trouble or being involved in potential lawsuits.

Sunday had been murdered in her one-bedroom on Thompson, a few blocks from my place. She'd been asphyxiated and I remember the night in a horrific sequence. She hadn't made it to a movie audition in Astoria and I left work after lunch and stopped by her place, as I had a set of her keys. She wasn't there, but came back soon after and we spent a beautiful afternoon together. We'd had a lot of them recently: I'd never felt so bonded with another human being.

In the early evening, I went home to write, but not blog-item copy, the guilty pleasure prose novel I'd been putting off for years. I'd been feeling unwaveringly good with Sunday, with everything. I'd stopped drinking and was taking the proper meds in proper quantities. After all the mixed-up years I was finally feeling in control of my life.

That night I experienced a waterfall of ideas, so many that the book began to write itself and I was simply a typist channeling it. The page count was up to twenty in a two-hour burst. I even had a title: *The Dolce Vita Diaries*. When I turned off the computer, I called and texted Sunday but received no reply. I figured she was taking a shower so I scurried over to her place to show her pages. She'd been trying to get me to write for a long time. I sensed she'd be proud of me.

When I arrived at her door, the stereo was playing. I inserted the key, turned the handle, but the interior manual lock was latched. I hollered for her through the gap. There was no answer and no shower crackling which was strange. How could the door be latched if she wasn't there? An iPod bath? I waited a while there, calling into the space repeatedly. Finally, I went outside and scaled the fire escape. Her third floor window was open and I saw her when I peered through. She was lying on the bed, iPodless, her eyes open to the ceiling as if studying it.

"Sunday?"

She didn't stir, so I climbed in and rushed to her. I wasn't a pro but I found no pulse. She wasn't chilled but she wasn't alive-warm, she was tepid. Tragic tepid. Dead tepid.

Give me the good face, Sunday!! I cried repeatedly. **Give me the good face!!!**

I suffered a torrent of emotions, ones I'd felt previously: the pain, the panic from the tragedy I'd experienced many years before. When I regained a semblance of control, I called the law enforcement person I knew best, Steve, and the cops soon arrived, the paramedics wheeling her out, shrouded in white, atop a gurney: the real life evening news method. Then they yellow-banded the apartment.

Sunday Fairchild had spun into my life like magic and just as fast, she was gone, *poofed!* to the larger sky.

The murder gripped the city unlike any I'd ever witnessed; the fact it had happened in Manhattan right under everyone's noses and that she was beautiful of course, and white. The papers front-paged every new development in the case, no matter how small or seemingly inconsequential. Sunday's murder had taken over the town.

I left my office shy of noon as the precinct wasn't far and it was raining. I'd worn my slicker to work but hadn't brought an umbrella. This was okay: I enjoyed the prickling sensation of rain on my grill.

Once I arrived at the police precinct, I took the elevator to Homicide and moved past the cubicles to the back where Cipone had his office. He was a tough Italian with a squat body and no less force than a bleeding bull. He was on the phone so I patiently put it down.

"No, I'm an independent. That means I'm capable of my own thoughts… When was the last time you voted Democrat? … It ain't about ideas… You're a cheerleader. And the GOP is your team… Hey Dad, why don't you try an original thought this year, huh? … I hear Cheney has a new running mate for 2012. Bill Belichick! … I got a meeting. See ya." He hung up. "My old man," Steve proffered afresh. "Election years make him nuts. And he's still going on about it."

"How often do you speak to each other?"

"Every day. He sits out there in Queens swallowing that cable news stuff and tries to get me into a dialogue. All I got to do is say one word—Hillary—and he threatens the will thing. He ain't got much to give. Just the same."

I thought about what it would be like to have a daily dialogue with my paps. We had such different outlooks that there was no point in discussing serious issues with him, politics especially. We were safe with irrefutables like penguins or polar bears. You couldn't argue *Animal Planet* certainties.

"How are you, Slinger?"

"Ticking."

"Alive? Nice. I just want to follow up on our last chat."

It'd been several weeks since our previous one as the case had gone cold.

"First of all, you heard anything on the street, whatever, about this rapper guy?"

"No."

"Did she have a sexual relationship with him?"

"Still don't know for sure. Have you contacted him?"

"Claims nothing happened. And he has an alibi. Pretty tight."

"He has a big career. Even if he knows something, I suspect he wouldn't want to get mixed up in this. The daily sheets will report the linkage and a record company will drop him like hot cakes. Either that or make him a bigger star. But doubtful."

"Doubtful is right. She's white."

"Career risk no one wants to take. With respect to her, she's from down south, as you know. Her father was pretty bigoted. So that could mean either-or."

"Either or what?"

"Could be a deterrent or an incentive."

"To be with a black guy? You mean rebellious urge?"

"And she was rebellious."

Steve looked rather glum all hunched there, jotting away, like a tired old Bassett hound. He'd had his fill of perpy creeps, I was sure. Even upside down, I could glimpse the grade-school handwriting. And spelling.

"What was her relationship like with her father?"

"Strained. They hadn't seen each other much. She only visited him once when he went to prison. But I could tell he had some power over her. Have you spoken to him?"

"Pretty uncooperative. Listens to a few questions, calls us a bunch of fuck-ups, then hangs up."

"Sweet guy."

"He's got another year before they spring him."

"Did he sell the club?"

"No. And local cops there tell me he's going right back into it."

"What about Nina?" Steve angled up sharply. "No luck tracking her?"

"We've searched fifty states and Puerto Rico. The morgues, the shelters. No one's heard anything. She disappeared without a trace."

Watching him take notes, I was reminded of things. Everyone seemed to have pen in hand when it came to me. It had been going on all my life. Must be one hell of an interesting guy, I mused, though I never let it go to my crown. And that attempt at merriment was a diversionary coping mechanism. I hated *tête-à-têtes* with authority figures.

"How about you?" He flung out in a freshly sterile way.

"What are you referring to?"

He cleared his pipes and dug elbows in, his carriage pitched forward like an offensive tackle ready to make a trap block. He didn't resemble any sad sack now and it made me more uneasy. I was a veteran of sit-downs and they generally gave me a bodily stew.

I called them the Terrible Twosomes because it was ingrained in me from way back I might have done something wrong. Even when I knew I hadn't. Just the choreography and placement, me, desk, an interrogator, and the hot lights were enough to make my limbs river. But this setup was more intimidating. This was a homicide cop.

"I mean, your health. Still get those blackouts?"

The question took me by surprise. "Sir?"

"It's in a former G.P.'s file. A Dr. Lewis."

"Oh. They weren't blackouts," I corrected in a jiffy. "Bad hangovers. And you forget stuff. That was a long time ago."

"Four years," he stated neutrally, which wasn't overtly neutral.

I wasn't going to fill him in further on the occasional fits of memory loss, what I called my 'unforced errors.' Sure, I was swaying toward the defensive. He'd done some additional homework on me and I didn't know why. It made me tense and I shifted in my chair. "It doesn't happen anymore; I don't drink as much."

He nodded along for the ride and recoiled back again like it was little to him. Maybe. "Just for the file, Slinger, give me another quick rundown of your resume. You know, how you landed at the *Herald*."

Again I was taken aback by the line as we'd been through it before. In actuality, I'd had four outings at local scando camps.

"I was a production assistant for *Hard Copy*, then I grunted for *The Daily News*'s 'Rush & Malloy.' 'Page Six' hired me then fired me for some protocol bullshit, so I defected to *The Drudge Report* then *Gawker*. Then I founded my own site and called it 'Slingshot.'"

"And the *Herald*?"

Keep cool, Slinger…

"Arthur Lawrence made me an offer I couldn't refuse."

"Which was?"

Surprised again by his need for detail, I answered him just the same. "I wanted *Slingshot* to be an authentic I-Age feed, not beholden to any stodgy gray lady paper. I demanded complete autonomy and he gave it to me along with the proper coin. I still own forty percent."

I noticed he'd been eyeing me cautiously. "Good," was all he said, and he finished off a note. "So tell me more about Alphonso Martinez."

"He's my driver. As you know."

"But he was not with you the night of the murder. Where was he?"

Sit on it, don't get impetuous…

"He had the night off and was home, remember? He lives in Queens. Haven't we gone through this?"

Steve didn't respond to my return queries. "I'm going to ask you a couple of questions, Slinger, and don't take 'em the wrong way. Okay?"

I nodded as he lit one up. He offered me one and before my frame could ball up entirely into a French-cuffer's monkey fist, I took it.

"Now, you loved this girl…"

I bobbed again as my first drag bellowed out.

"So why didn't you stay? I mean, why didn't you feel compelled to stay with the body?"

Don't do it…don't crack…don't push the button…

I held off answering until he came at me again. His eyes were narrowed, taut, and firing. *Beaucoup* banditos had faced the pressuring posture of this law dog. These guys can be all Budweiser pop-top buddies until they flip that burner switch. I remembered it well from long ago.

"You fled the scene. Why on earth did you flee?"

I didn't like the "on earth." It had weight with an implication sidecar.

Control yourself… smooth and cool…

"Like I told you before I had a rush of emotions when I found her. None of them good. I was shocked. Devastated. Upset. And I hadn't taken any medication either that day."

"You said you had—"

"I was taking my medication in those days, yes. But not that night specifically." Sure I had the conscious feeling of being pressed. My palms were running oil and water and I hid them furry knuckles up in my lap.

Easy does it… but… it's not easy… don't… but you need to know…

you have to know!

"Why not?"

"Because I was writing. Not for the site, for myself. Which takes more imagination. I wanted my mind freed up without being controlled and focused. Which is what the medication does."

Don't, Slinger, don't! You may come off sounding guilty… but, but… I have to know!!!

"Steve, am I under suspicion here?"

He looked up from his pad then with eyes sparkling and abuzz. *Shit!*

"Who said anything about that?"

"Well," I said clearing a fragile throat. "We seem to be going over the same stuff every time…"

"Yes," he avowed. "And no. Your memory gets better each time. And I learn new things. Which may be important to the case."

What new things? Things about me?? Important to the case against me?? Damnitall! You blew it!

I sighed. "Okay…"

So unnecessary! Why did you do it??? Why, Harry? Why???

I followed his pen desperately but couldn't make out the newest note.

Moments later, he came back at me again like a veteran pro, as if the regrettable exchange had been forgotten. Though I knew better.

"So, no Ritalin?"

Remember the previous subject… so you don't look flustered… Writing, yes, writing the book—no!!—why I didn't stay with the body!!!

I coughed. "Adderall is what I take, actually. But no, not that night, so I was stripped of anything emotionally stabilizing. I was a raw nerve reacting to horrific stimuli. So I took off. It was panic. Pure panic."

Steve scrawled lines, twice underscoring the last thing I said. It seemed like punctuation indicating our session was ending. The liberating sense of relief passed through me. He angled up, his face no longer pinched. He employed a softer tone, more upbeat too. Thankfully.

"So, how you getting along?"

I released a big wind from my chest and wished I hadn't. "I have my good days."

"The Web site doing well?"

"It goes."

It was exhilarating to see him stand. "Coffee for the road?"

"No, thanks." I rose up, too. And I started to gain composure. "Tell me. Wasn't there anything in the apartment to go on?"

"Bunch of things," he said glancing off, like a pitcher warily eyeballing a runner on first base. "But they haven't turned up much."

"What about that doctor? The one who gave her the apartment—"

You're sounding like the guilty perp trying to deflect the blame! Shut the fuck up, Harry, and get the hell out of there!!!

"Kilmer? He was in L.A. at the time. Hadn't seen her in a while. They lost touch." He scratched his head a tad artificially. "Hey, we're only five months into this. These things can take a long time. Don't worry, we'll get him. We go the distance, Slinger."

I pivoted halfway around and scanned the wide wall behind, focusing on the police scandosketch of an alleged serial killer. I knew of him: his deeds had been pretty much page one. "How's the serial case coming?"

I was on the idiot roll now and nothing could stop me…I was going to ham it up until he locked me up and threw away the key…

"He's quiet for now. Which is the scary thing. Naturally."

I spun to scram, but feeling more emancipated and chipper the session had ended I had a thought and swiveled back around to face him. "Got anything for me?"

"Told you about that Amy Winehouse vid, right?"

I said he had.

"And the Kate Moss-in-the-act pics?" Ditto nods. "Yeah so, not at the moment." We stalemate-glared in a mutual something. "Tell me, Slinger, why do they call the kid a 'waif'?"

"A borrowed coining from the Twiggy years."

"Twiggy was a bag of bones. Kate was Twiggy on her worst day." Everybody had formed opinions on scandoplanet celebrity. Even cops.

"Silly names endure. Especially these days."

"Kid's been around for years. For all that self-abusing she does, she only gets better lookin'. Life ain't fair, really…"

"News just in. But you should know better than me."

He had one more for me, too. "So what's it like hangin' out with all that pretty wool?"

I curved him a disingenuous frat boy one and he thanked me for coming in. I left the cop house and welcomed the cool summer rain on my puss again. My palms had nearly dried but I was pretty certain I'd been grilled up there though I wasn't entirely sure. Either way, he'd flicked on that switch like many had in my life: the doctors, the shrinks, the galloping run of psychological analysts and semi-pros. They had different methods to their interrogation ballets but the facial compulsories were nearly identical—those damned critter eyes, that needling nose, the wrinkles folding in all the skeptical places. Had I been interrogated? Was I a suspect? Again, I wasn't so savvy. He'd done further background on me, though, which was unsettling enough. Damn those accusatory looks. And damn my paranoia.

Who said anything about that? haunted me all the way down block.

To clear my bean of the enduring trepidation buzz, I took a turn down Elizabeth Street and forced thoughts on old Kate. She'd been racking up fresh contracts, including Calvin Klein's new perfume. Calvin was a scansational pioneer, lest we forget a prepubescent Brooke and no one getting in between her and her Calvins. No wonder he re-signed Kate. Sometimes, I found comfort in the laws of scandalocity. Like when they gave people second chances. Now Kate can tell everyone to fuck off.

For that, I envied her all the more.

18

Mr. Confetti Guns

"Don't hang up!"

Of all my Militia friends, Mr. Confetti Guns was the greatest purveyor of the big pop and accompanying fizzle; all talk and no follow-through, just a blast of rainbow confetti shot to the lawn. And, as was often the case, I didn't have the time for the talk. I had a job to hold on to.

"Gotta go, Guns—"

"Let me finish. As I was saying," he blasted theatrically, and knowing him, clearly thespianizing it for his better half's benefit, "when is that agency party, Slings? Because I need a replacement model; Tori's almost hitting thirty, she's knows that's the cut-off, her eyes are bagging, the pumpkin's sagging, she's Rollerblading past her peak, cottage-cheesing on the rear thighs before my very eyes, and the face is not popping the way it used to on her composite card. So where is that IMG model party? Or was it Next?"

"You're horrible, Guns, is all I can say—"

"Good thing she's laughing."

I'm not laughing! I heard Tori bellow from the beyond. *Just spending all my money on this professional D.O.R.!*

"You get a job yet?"

That's drain on resources!

"Big step for me."

The only thing he has to offer is text messages!

"*Pssssst! Slinger...*" Guns brought it down to a whisper. "You know they say overseas, every time a woman pays, her pussy dries up a little more..."

"Charming. What misogynist all-star gifted you that?"

"Don't get technical. Think that's why we're not having much sex?"

"Dunno. But wouldn't rule it out."

I heard wrestling. "One more peep outta you nottie-hottie and I go into full Facebook predator mode!"

That's all you do every day, anyway! Just remember about pussy-puss: I can give away a lot more than you can pay for—

Good line, I thought. Chalk one up for Tori. But still. "Guns, it's too early in the day for this. Night, too."

Then I heard more sounds of a struggle. Guns was preventing her from either hanging up the phone or grabbing it.

"Put her on," I suggested against my better judgment.

He did just that. "Hi, Harry. He's feeling his oats 'cause he thinks Alessandra Ambrósio friended him on Facebook. Little does he know it's not even her. She has fifty entries founded by cyberstalkers. Like *him!* He'll friend anyone! Like 'Kandi Kaktiz.' He says she's Turkish, that I'm an Arab-hater. 'Candy Cock-tease?' *Duh! She's a total whore!…"*

He snatched back the phone. "Yeah-yeah sure, granny model…"

"She sounds bold, Guns. Schedule employment interviews soon, before she dumps you flat."

"Anyhoo, where's the party?" He resumed with the ill-advised tease. "I need more composite cards. Anything Brazilian or Latvian… Come on, hook me up, Slings—"

I could almost taste the heartbreak on his horizon and it's why I tried to intercede. He'd need a big shoulder to cry on, for at least a year. Most likely *mine.* But enough was enough. I needed to jump which would be a bonus for Guns anyway. It would enable him to return to his favorite place. Bed. He'd had enough excitement for the day and I was sure it was time for him to re-rack until the next TCM film noir matinee.

"Gotta move; I'm late for an appointment."

"With who?"

"Coach Vince."

"Still seeing her? Don't you know, Slings? Rehab is for quitters…"

19

The Spontaneous Crazies

I was late for my weekly with Coach. We'd missed a session, so I was to see her on Saturday: bad idea. I'd gone out late, slept late, and had downed no bold, no meds. I had little defense. Coach could pretty much have full violation with me. Again. True to form, the Ice Princess dug right in.

"One time, during your descriptions of sexual relations, you mentioned a bag. Is behavior of the sort prevalent in your circle?"

I'd already decided to let it rip. Granted, I didn't have any caffeine going and counterattacks and psychological Cover 2s were not options, but I didn't see the point in hiding things any longer. I hadn't wanted Coach Vince to know the extent of my biological activity because I felt ashamed. After all the good doctor had known my girl. I didn't care to come off like the incorrigible Lothario, a promiscuous cad and thigh-high hedonist, that I'd spiraled so low. But that morning, I decided to put a halt on the charade. Owning up might be helpful to the therapy, I thought. Of course, I wanted to heal and didn't feel I was making lengthy strides.

"Women have bags. Sometimes. Their friends have them too or so they tell me."

"Do you have a bag?"

"No, but the Love Child left hers, so—"

"Do you enjoy the sexual activity involving the bag?"

"Toys can be, well, entertaining."

"How so?"

"An ordinary physical experience can be enhanced by the theater induced by the bag. It takes you to another place. Some feel it's rather transcendent…"

The good doctor appeared absolutely stunning that afternoon.

Her hair was tacked back and she was wearing a tight gray Chloe cashmere sweater and matching skirt which highlighted her ample chest and terrific sidelines. Her lips were painted with a glossy glaze, her feminine scents and fragrances dancing around me like butterfly breath. I'd been missing all her wonderfully feminine prettypology recently and couldn't help but be aroused.

"I find this strange all these people having bags. Am I missing something?"

The nature of her query escaped me momentarily. Did she mean missing because she didn't understand it? Or because she was missing out? I was punchy enough to proceed with the more personally intimate interpretation.

"Maybe you are. Maybe you spend too much time uptown."

"I didn't mean that—"

"Ask your dates. Can we discuss your dates?"

"No, Harry," she said, though not terribly forcefully.

After all, we weren't just doctor-patient, we'd been friends, as noted. I considered some warm interaction between us healthy and if she didn't feel the need to connect, maybe I did. Selfishly perhaps, I ventured on.

"Can we, someday?"

"If we discontinue the sessions and no longer have a professional relationship, perhaps."

"Okay. You're fired."

She chuckled all too thinly, my attempt at warm and chummy denied once again. Rejection was becoming a daily routine for me.

"So tell me, why do they all have bags?"

"You'll have to ask them. I'm not an expert on bag culture. Just the occasional tourist. Rather, enthusiast. I've always seen it like Felix's magic bag."

"In your opinion—"

I let out a weighty labored exhale and thought about it. "The perception of the American dream has changed."

"How so?"

"I can tell you what it's not. It's not a house, a couple cars, a color TV, a chicken in every pot, and some Brady Bunch pseudo-paradise in which to challenge street curbs with Sting Ray bikes."

"What is it then?"

"It's to have the life of a rock star. Or celebrity. Or notable. And join the dolce vita follies—"

"Why?"

"Because it's the latest cure for the age-old pains of the human condition. Death and the like. People seek out money. Beauty. Fame. Enhanced NR. That might include a magazine wife. An of-the-moment husband with good Sling. A palatial Fifth Avenue apartment. A house in the Hamptons with dune-perch. A Ferrari, the latest Range Rover, all techie toys, you name it. They know the good life is out there. It's advertised, packaged, and rammed down everyone's throats by The Machine, Spinternet included. Everyone wants to join the glamorazzi and The Machine has raised the bar. The problem is competition is increasing, the numbers vying for the New American Dream are increasing, it's overcrowded, and resources are finite. So statistics are not in anyone's favor to be a rock star, or to get a cover girl wife for life; there's too much information, it's running too fast, it's ADD Nation, and everybody is trying, and failing, to keep up. So they take prescripto and non-prescripto drugs and try to party as if they were rock stars and the bags and the kinky sex is part of their feeling that just maybe they're getting a piece, however small, of that New American Dream."

"So it's an illusion?"

"Certainly. And delusionary. That's how The Machine works."

"How does that make you feel?"

"It's perverse. But it's where we've come to in the big city fueled by Generation Green."

"Which generation is that?"

"Mine."

"Does Green mean money? Or the conservation movement?"

"It means green in war. And life-threatening experience. It's the younger generation on the front lines against the terrorists. My generation was skipped over. It's a spoiled generation and we're increasingly coming into positions of power. And we don't know how to handle it. Obviously. The last two presidents never experienced combat. The New American Dream is a spoiled dream.

New gennies' dreams will be healthier. More cautious, careful, connected to and respectful of—nature. Cause they've felt the fear. They took the fall of the Twin Towers on the chin at age ten. And a globe dipped in tar and melting. And they're fave zoo creatures disappearing. It's largely Darwinian. They'll have to correct things, out of the most basic of needs: survival. They'll be the planet's Fixodent for our fuck-ups; or it's game over. And that's as Hallmark card-hopeful as I'll ever get. Because human beings are the big C. The world's big tumor. Pac-Manning their way across the landscape, metastasizing, devouring, destroying. And as much as Generation 9/11 may see the need to fix things, they will also adapt to the new damage humans will surely cause—like humans always have. That's our tragic flaw. And it's Shakespearean in its scope."

Coach was now finger-twirling the coarse undergrowth strands at her nape, lost in thought. Her eyes were glistening and if I didn't know any better, I would have bet she was about to shed a tear. Then she awoke from her trance and broke the lull.

"Do you engage in this unconventional sexual activity because you feel you're getting closer to that spoiled American Dream?"

"I do it to get through the day."

"To forget the past?"

"Also."

"Would you consider yourself a sex addict?"

"Perhaps by clinical definition. But I'm not comfortable with full reduction to the primitive. My drive is not so one dimensional or uni-directional; that it's all about sex. I don't see my serial interactions deriving from some insatiable need to press the flesh. Yes, sexual activity can spell relief for me, but it's the overall connecting that's important—making life-enhancing connections. Probably the best thing this planet has to offer. In a world that's becoming increasingly disconnected and distanced from nature. It's communicating, really. Mentally. Physically. Biologically. Perhaps even spiritually. With another of the same species."

Dr. Van den Heugel eyed me evenly and held it a second. It was a curious look, pained and feeble again, and could actually be mistaken for vulnerable. I couldn't remember having seen anything like it before.

"And by the way, it's not the only thing I appreciate."

"Unconventional 'communication' with pretty women?" She posed rather snidely, and, I might add, surprisingly. The 'pretty' was the give-away.

"You sound skeptical. Either that or jealous," I added for levity's sake.

She didn't answer, not even to tell me to "stop playing games." There was curiously little fight in her.

"So, what else do you like?"

"Brains."

"Why don't you speak of that in our discussions?"

"I don't know. Maybe our discussions have become uni-directional."

It was obviously a mild barb and she did not react to it, much less challenge it. Just then, I realized I was going on the offensive with her, having perceived her weakened state. Shockingly, she was taking it.

"Has intellect become less of a priority with respect to your partners?"

"Not by choice. I've always been inspired by savvy Catsuit Feminists. Like yourself. But you're diamonds in the rough. Not easy to find. And look at us; I have to pay you to be with me…"

Her eyes remained dug into her notepad.

Every instinct told me not to go there, but, I had to. "For instance, would you care to tag along with me tonight?"

She hesitated. "I knew it was coming," she said, though her tone of voice had gone soft, even frail.

"Was that a 'no?'" Again, no response. "See? You're proving my point."

"I'm proving to you…" She attempted and trailed off.

"What?"

"That I'm a professional…" I could now see a heavier gloss to her eyes and I was transfixed, watching her eyelids steadily fill with water.

"We used to do it and it worked out fine."

Her voice cracked in two as she said, "Never one-on-one."

All of a sudden, she couldn't suppress it any longer. She broke.

Her face folded and it was the most harmonious, sad contortion of skin to witness before she hid her face in her hands, shaking her head. I'd never seen her get emotional and there's no other way to describe it: it was beautiful. She wept in an altogether pleasing way. Maybe it was just reassuring to see her fall from her ivory tower. I did feel for her, however, and as a natural reflex, I rose to comfort her and embrace her fully.

"No. Please…" She raised a hand too, which kept me put. "I'm sorry, I haven't been myself." She got up, reached for a tissue and blew her nose then. "I get this way. On my period."

It was the most private comment she'd ever shared with me. But the window had been opened and seeing her slip into the intimate and personal I was encouraged if not emboldened. "So—"

"Harry, things have changed since then. As you know."

"Shouldn't that be my worry?"

"Yes," she sniffled. "And I'm doing the worrying for you."

"Why?"

"Because you're not strong enough, by your own admission. And, it won't help you."

"Want me to be honest with you?"

She wiped her nose and paused before answering. "I told you I did."

"Or else there's no point in any of this, right?"

She settled into her chair again and sat up straight. She seemed to have collected herself. "Go on—"

"Right now I want—" And I slammed on the brakes to reconsider.

"You want what?"

"I can't say it."

"Say it."

I turned it over again. "I can tell you anything, right?"

"Yes."

"You *are* a professional—"

"I am."

"We're engaging in professional business—"

She nodded swiftly.

"No, I can't—"

Her expectant expression died, but in a dissatisfied way and I was pretty good at spotting it. What I wouldn't say was indeed loaded.

"Tell me, Harry. I want to know. " And then I believed she wanted me to, she wanted me to express it, unbelievably so. "You have my permission."

"I'll let you say it—"

She leveled resolute eyes on me. "You want to fuck me."

Hearing the words stunned me. It sounded harsh, so overkill for what I'd been yearning to articulate. It wasn't what I'd wanted. I'd brought her there in an aggressive attempt to get friendly and it would appear I'd oversold it.

"If having sex with you means connecting with you, okay, that too. But hugs work wonders, too. Or so I've heard—"

The sexually-charged detour to our discussion hovered there between us, though she didn't react, really, just nodding to herself while reaching in her purse and flapping open a compact to check for smudged mascara. She would find it. She tapped at the corners of her eyes with tissue.

Of course, part of her assumption was true. I found the doctor extremely sexy; how could you not? But any desire on my part was not raw or animalistic or conquest-oriented, it was something different altogether. It had to do with her, Sunday, someone for whom we'd both cared deeply. And joining ourselves in an embrace, even in a more indulgent way, was perhaps a natural way to handle the pain. I believed that. I naturally felt close to this woman, I wanted to hold her, the Ice Princess, and she'd never let me close. She'd never have any of it.

"But you've proven to us both," she countered finally. "You are weak. Besides, it's not being 'honest,' as you say. It's just fantasy." Her voice was taut, her constitution stoic once again. It would seem she'd pulled herself out of the emotional dip and side-slide.

The good doctor then launched into a spiel, likening her feminine gifts to heroin and I was the junkie who wanted to shoot her into my veins. For a quick fix. I felt misunderstood and rebuffed again and that was that. She took a note and asked me if I had any questions concerning the therapy, the consummate professional once more.

I wasn't nearly that schooled. It took me a while to recover.

"Okay, I have a question. Why do you think I'm a sex addict? Not in heroin-junkie terms, in psychological terms…"

"First of all, I wouldn't say you're an addict."

"Then what am I? A scandosexual?"

"More like, hypersexual."

"I know the term."

"Like most hypersexual individuals, you crave sex, but unusually so. Because of your neurological condition, ADHD, you use sex as a form of intense stimulation to help you focus. Like most adults who are drawn to highly stimulating activities as a way to alleviate boredom and clear the mind of distraction. Sex acts for you become a type of medication. You take pleasure in the orgasm but also the act of seducing which enables you to focus as well. You constantly seek out flirtations and liaisons with women and, from what you've told me, you're incapable of resisting any sort of sexual temptation. The act of seduction is like going to the medicine chest, a way of self-medicating. Unfortunately, your endless need for new seductions, the focus they bring, and the resulting ceaseless infidelities, don't allow you to maintain any long-term romantic relationship—"

"So I derive the structure I'm craving in life in that quest for orgasm?"

"Not only the actual orgasm, but the whole process of seeking it and achieving it. The seduction as well as the conquest. The hunt, as it were. You can wrap yourself around the stimulation these activities provide and feel comforted and structured by their systems. But it's more complex because your issues are more complex. You also do it to forget, to drive away the memory of someone you loved. The satisfaction an orgasm brings helps you forget her. But the relief is only temporary. So you continue to seek out erotic consummations to achieve that sense of relief however fleeting it may be, hence the serial nature of your exploits. It's a difficult and dangerous cycle you're in."

"So, short-term romances help me forget…"

"For a while, maybe twenty-four hours. Then the emptiness sets in. Doesn't it?" I didn't respond and didn't need to. "Again, there's more to it but that's for a future session."

"No, tell me. I need to know…"

She paused. "Well, I'll tell you; in part, it has to do with the types of women you choose. Remember discussing your past relationships? Before Sunday, I mean. The Match.com gals? The 'Slingerettes?' 'The Mascots?'"

"Mascots I don't get involved with—by definition."

"I mean, how a woman didn't turn you on unless she was a little crazy or unpredictable?"

"The 'Spontaneous Crazies'—"

"Or that she was attached. It turned you on if she was married or had a boyfriend, even if you knew the boyfriend."

"But it wasn't to be a prick, to get over on a boyfriend, it was the fact that she was taken. It was the challenge, the game, and I'm a gamer. And I was excessively biological, yes. And don't forget, I was single."

"We are biological beings. But we're thinking beings, too. With you, it was more than biological; it was a powerlessness to your male biological impulses. Knowing it was exceptionally wrong, you still couldn't help yourself in trying to screw-the-girlfriend and you did screw them, didn't you?"

"I poached. My scandosexual days. I was weak, in a bad way, looking for quick fixes. And I have regrets. But New York is a candy store for relationships. It's choice-intensive and the gals like to lollipop-shop too. As much as men or more nowadays. It's always taken two to tango. But ladies are more liberated than ever. Having said that, I don't do online dating anymore. I'm stronger now. I'm better now."

"You go to strip bars now."

"Look but don't touch; Perfect solution in an imperfect world."

"I wouldn't call that healing, but we can leave that for another session, agreed?"

I said I did.

"What I'm saying is that in these whirlwind romances there's an element of danger and you're attracted to the danger, the complicated high-risk situations and predicaments. Attached women naturally become a turn-on, the challenge, the thought of doing something illicit and taboo, someone else's woman. The 'spontaneous crazies' as you call them too, the ones who cause emotional as well as physical pandemonium. Women who can have wild exploratory sex with you one night and then don't return your calls for days because they've gone on vacation, likely having unconventional sex with someone else and you sense it deep down—the fact that they can't be kept, controlled, or held in a relationship, or, can't behave monogamously."

"Genus 'Chemicalis/Animalia.' And I was at my worst. *Lowest.*"

"It's a turn-on; the fact you don't know what they're going to do next is thrilling. All that obsessing is terrifically stimulating though you may not like what's happening. In the same way adrenaline junkies enjoy sky diving and bungee chord jumping, you like danger in romance. Remember your favorite book?"

"*Dangerous Liasons.* The movie too."

"It's more than high-stimulation that you find your axes of comfort, it's high-risk, it's danger."

It was true: I'd relished waking up to Spontaneous Crazies jack-in-the-boxing me from the pillow in the morning. If I was at a table with three women, two of them polite and attractive while the third was a little rude, outlandish, narcissistic, weird, high-energy, a stress puppy or a true duchess of dramalocity, or even complicated in the most pastel of ways, she'd be the one for me; that's when my antennae would go off. I would pick up on the odd abnormal frequency. The signal of the others would not register on my instrument; they'd be dead to me. In essence, I'd step over the "good" girls and go straight for the baddies or those who were less than virtuous or trustworthy.

It made me think of her. When we met, I immediately sensed the unpredictability, the spontaneity; I knew that Sunday had another life rippling beneath her surface. And I wanted to get at it. Now I realized why Coach did not care to delve into the subject. Because of *her.*

"The dangerous conquest for you is the ultimate. Not only does it medicate you, as you're attracted to the acts of seduction and conquest but also it thrills you because there's danger involved, something you can't pass up. It's like a double-barreled shotgun blast of stimulation."

She was looping, but I played along like the patient student.

20

The Biological Yang

Just then, the Doc's secretary buzzed in on the intercom notifying her that her appointment after mine had canceled. When she placed the handset back down, I had one more for her.

"What about you?"

"Excuse me?"

"Do you enjoy our sessions?"

"I will if you get better, I mean, control your condition. As a patient, you are interesting and I must say *educational*..."

I felt something brewing within and it was not necessarily pride. Perhaps Coach Vince had begun to attract me in that "odd, abnormal" way too, but I wasn't sure.

"How did it go with the police?"

The question suddenly spooked me and I gripped up defensively. I responded in an evasive, knee-jerk way. "Fine. Why?"

"You were worried about it."

"Just routine," I feathered back and I didn't know why I was suddenly fibbing. "You were right," I added, perhaps less truthfully. "They wanted to see if I remembered anything else."

My behavior was puzzling, even to me. I guessed my reaction to the doctor's query was protectionary, an exercise in self-preservation. It had always been a natural reflex to deflect blame, the result of years of accusations leveled at me in my youth. At the same time I didn't really know to what extent I had been interrogated by the police. It could have been my paranoia making me think the worst: that I may be a suspect. Perhaps also, I didn't want to invite any unfulfilled prophecies by airing fears that were potentially unwarranted. Beyond that, I wasn't entirely sure why I clammed on the police issue. That was unsettling in itself.

"Anything on for this evening? Any plans?"

Thankfully, she'd switched subjects. I didn't care to be thrown further on edge.

"Yes. I'm meeting someone."

"Who?" I told her.

"Frauka?" She repeated mauling it.

"It's pronounced 'Frow-ka.' She's a German model."

"I thought you didn't like models."

"I said I didn't like the 'Model Trap.'"

For some reason, she sat there eyeballing me though her mush was semi-relaxed. She posed it even more airily. "Which is?"

"Really? You want to hear silly Slingerisms?"

She said she did. It was a welcomed relief we were leaving that police business behind.

"Where do I begin? Well, I can't tell you the number of men I've known or written about who've married Illusion Girls and suffered for it. The women, too."

"How so?" Again her expression was less doctorly and more scando-famished. But who was I to deny her? After all, I could always trash-rant. For me it was like whistling in the wind on roller skates.

"In the late eighties and nineties, you had this collection of world-class beauties advertised by The Machine beyond all limits of the imagination. They were in our magazines, on our televisions, and pasted on billboards, hip-checking the movie stars off the red carpet. Like all good products advertised, people grabbed at them. Shallow men, particularly, who tried to convince themselves there was something deeper in it, or tried to force something deeper out of it. But the dynamics are no diff than for normies not involved in this phenomenon. It's tough enough for a relationship to endure when you're drink-from-the-same-cup soul mates let alone when you're a mismatch. A lot of these unions were mismatches. Gross mismatches. Whether there were class distinctions, educational or intellectual differences, or they were just plain old erotic friendships which went too far or lust unions which seemed to promise more." I paused. "Brakes, Coach. Isn't this a detour?"

"Somewhat, but let me be the judge of whether it's helpful or not." Her mouth curved, too, and her teeth released, but vaguely so.

"Proceed for sport?"

"Please—"

"The problem is, erotica can be lethal, and it often results in absurdist thinking. Beauty is not a life and lifestyle cure-all; it's often a cruel mistress, and many of these guys have made their decisions that way, for the wrong reasons. And months after matrimony even weeks into these unions, they find out the hard way. Some make the mistake of having kids and end up tossing and turning in court. I'm not blaming the women; it takes two. But models and beautiful women have never been treated like normal people, so how can they behave normally? Beauty warps their way of thinking. I call it 'beauty contamination.' Is it their fault a guy marries them for their beauty? Perhaps, perhaps not, but I've seen cases where the high-glam run in the limelight for an Illusion Girl is over and the daily praises and tongue wags stop wagging. So they look for and seek out their lost attention fields. In other places. Outside of the home. And when you look like that there's always a forest full of hairy-assed 'Yes'-Apes lurking around, two hemispheres full, avowing, 'Yes, beautiful, you're terrif, talented, original, gifted, and smart'—to offer the instantaneous self-esteem injection. These women who've become junkies for that type of attention grab at it like a syringe, as you say. It's how the human psyche often responds to all that flash. They're not all illusionists, obviously, and some are as real as Kentucky meadow muffins and I know several couples in this arena who have found their bliss, but—contamination rules the day. They become addicted to their own beauty. Like opium. It's unreal. And unhealthy."

"And the men?"

Strike, I thought, bowling pins down—the men. That's why Coach had been encouraging the rant; to know more about men in general, or one in particular. My brain was being picked, not shrunk, and that was fine. From this angle on this subject it was rather flattering.

"Of course, they're no better. The ones who abuse these women and rope-swing from one mag face to the next in an insatiable appetite for self-esteem jolts. It's a seductive and destructive complex and makes relationships in this milieu nearly impossible. For the long-term."

I took in some wind and cleared my throat. "It's what I've seen. Men bludgeoned by Illusion Girls and the Model Trap. And Illusion Girls blinded by their own uncommon DNA and aesthetic gifts. In essence, each compromised by their own shortsightedness."

"Your conclusion?"

"Having driveled on so, I like communicating with models just fine. A steady number of Exhibits have been models. The agencies are all downtown. And they do walk by. And, you know, the biological ying meets the biological yang…"

"You mean, '*catches* the biological yang—'"

"But anyway, Frauka's just a pal."

"A twentysomething?"

"Something like that."

"Why so young?"

"I follow the cougars' lead on that."

"Clever, Harry," she said in a pleasing way. Pleasing meaning, personal. "Just what men need: encouragement to go young."

"Nice, Coach. Love it when you get sasscastic."

She jotted some more even though her last questions hadn't seemed so cutthroat pro. Though she'd recovered from her emotional display earlier, the good doctor was def off her A-game. Left idle, I scanned the walls for more disposable mind candy. You can only game with letters of med diplomas for so long.

"And you're not going to 'communicate' with Frauka?"

For some reason, I didn't care to divulge now. I was having a correction, feeling uneasy about transparency. Again. "No. Frauka put me in the Friend Box."

The dreaded Friend Box was that excruciating state of being designated a friend and friend only by someone who's not romantically interested in you. If I had a crush on a gal, but the crush was not reciprocated, I did not see any point in sticking around. I found the Box demeaning and torturous. I did not react well to it. Hanging out with someone who unlocked my valves of sensation, but who would only offer me friendship status, I considered a living insult. This is not to say I couldn't be "friends" with women, but only if I wasn't interested in them in that other way and I explained this to Coach.

"So what are you going to do with her?"

I couldn't help but break one. "Play *Panzer General.*"

"Where do you do that?"

"On my Xbox. I take the Americans, she takes the Germans. She's pretty talented, especially during Panzer tank raids in the Black Forest."

"And no sex? Beautiful girl comes over to the Skybox? At night? Knowing your tendencies, I'm finding it difficult to believe—"

"I told you, Coach, she Boxed me. And I'm none too happy about it. By the way, you're sounding less coachly and more like a vicarious thrill-rider."

"It's your honesty I'm questioning. Lying and fibbing qualify as setbacks."

"Even teeny-weenies?"

"You know the drill: lying is only lying to yourself."

"Do you think I'm lying to myself?"

"I think you're capable of both. Lying to me and yourself."

"Ouch. How am I lying to myself?"

"You want an example?"

I should have known better than to ask an open-ended question, the answer to which could possibly result in a response I wouldn't appreciate. Analysts are like lawyers that way. They're always prepared and have the branch-covered earth pit ready for the unsuspecting nature stroller. As feared, the response came back at me severely like a trough of cold well water turned over my head.

"You think your childhood and everything that happened in Massachusetts has no bearing on your current psychological condition."

"Correct," I confirmed testily. "I'm over it. I got over it when I was properly diagnosed and given the meds."

"The fact you think that is at best shortsighted, at worst lying to yourself."

"If we're going to rehash that stuff, I'll seek another analyst. It's negative, it's backward, it's debilitating. It's not a help."

"That's precisely why it has to be dealt with."

"Doctor?"

"Yes?"

"*Detour.*" I said it cmphatically.

"Okay, Harry, but I'm telling you, you have to be truthful with yourself, now more than ever."

Now, more than ever, I was ignoring her. Tick-tock, tick-tock...

"Harry? You're tuning out."

I needed to calm myself, so I asked for a cup of coffee and she offered to get it for me. When she got up, her skirt clung to her backside and I could see both buns separated wholly, fully. She had more flesh in the chest and rear than most WASPy types. I wondered where the alien genes had come from, her mother's or father's side, if some pumpkin-butted paramour had slipped his genetic flavorings into the marital line when no one was looking. She noticed I was grinding eyes on her but didn't protest. She certainly wasn't the unflappable, impenetrable ice siren to whom I'd become reluctantly accustomed.

A whoosh of tights passed my way and a waft of perfume hovered and I found myself getting aroused. Again. Moments later, the whoosh sounded from behind as she returned and I smelled her scent once more. She handed me a mug of fresh brew then settled on the front of the desk which left the Y of her lovely form at retina level. From this tight angle I could see that she was braless, the shape and contour of her full breasts coming through the cashmere weave, the upturned forms perfectly rendered, and where they changed color abruptly from porcelain to deep red, nipple red, close to nudity. I held the beverage away to see if my olfactory senses weren't off. They weren't. I was even wafted a most personal scent, her most personal, that of her womanly essence, her nondiscretionary dew. For that to happen, she must have been aroused herself, more like frothing. I crept my hand down a pant leg to cover and conceal a growing gesture of fan appreciation. She leaned in, not far away if you wanted to wrestle.

"How would you characterize the differences in yourself now

from two years ago?"

I tried to focus and reflect. "I'm more isolated. Incomplete. Biologically satiated, but emotionally undernourished. Which means lonelier. Just another lost I-Ager in search of a connection, what else?"

She tilted back again, scratching away on her pad. "Is that all?"

"I feel like Jack the Pumpkin King. Dissatisfied with present life, hoping for something more than Halloweentown."

"Like?"

"I want Christmastown."

"What is Christmastown to you?"

It was her best question to date, I determined. "I don't know."

"How did Jack survive?"

"He found love, the Follywood ending. And love and me, well, you know the story there." Then I drifted off-line. "By the way, if you want vicarious thrill rides, then be my guest…"

She stayed mum and I eyed my watch and noticed we'd gone over by twenty-five minutes. But it didn't seem so, the air was electric; at the molecular level, particles were flying like charged ions buzzing off a big surf wave enhancing the mood. As we seemed to be floating on some sort of carpet ride, it appeared neither of us wanted our time together to end. We were on standby, for something, and it came in the form of a growing anticipation. I said it suddenly: "I've changed my mind—"

It got her attention and she snapped up as if apprised all along I was headed back there, as if we were headed back there, as if there'd been no substantial break in our loaded, intimate conversation previously. The ghost of the charged repartee had never left the room.

"Sure. You want to fuck me…" She'd said it again aloud, using that provocative word once more, and hadn't needed to. She'd volunteered it. "I'm your favorite *type of* fuck."

"As in?"

"As in, the one you can never have."

What was this woman doing? Taunting me? Tempting me?

I was about to toss a *Never?*, but held off, and since I said nothing she felt the need to press it further. She wouldn't leave it alone.

"The gamer in you, as you say…"

She eyed me fully one last time, perhaps expectantly, then retreated to her notes briefly, only to raise her head back up. She was attempting to get clinical, trying to get back to ice and sleet but it wasn't working; the Princess was nowhere in sight nor was the reluctance.

"Another detour," she tossed tentatively, uncertainly.

It was actually poetry to watch her wax personal and I desired to stand and go huggles with her for an uninterrupted interval. I came off that, too. "Sorry—"

"No, I'm sorry. I don't know what's getting into me."

But now I had to. "She has, Greer. She's gotten into both of us."

She stiffened slightly, a sorry attempt to reclaim a professional posture. "We'll talk about her next week." Her eyes were glimmering, mine were misting. And the heat generated in that office was beginning to steam the lower panes of the windows.

"You're wearing orange…" It was a final, desperate arching pigskin toss into the end zone. On her part.

"Flaming orange," I deflected back. She hovered there, swaying in the stark fluorescence, clinging to the fragile stalemate.

I removed the pile of bunched-up paws from my lap. She peered down and took in the lap enthusiasm, gazing upon it steadily, as in, unafraid.

"I'm flattered, Harry."

"Is that what you want? Flattery?"

I shot up from where I was sitting, shoveling a hand beneath her and under her skirt, and I gripped a globe of her fanny and kneaded it like a loaf of baker's fresh, vaulting her up. She didn't defend an inch. Our mouths met harshly and I tasted the vodka in her saliva and we writhed there lips attached, consuming each other, and I repositioned my hand higher, hiking her skirt, exposing her bare ass, and digging down into her moon-crack, deeply between the globes, my finger grazing first a moist, puckered taboo one, massaging circles into it before going on its way to the sopping beyond, the saturated elastics keeping the hand in place and not allowing it to escape even if it wanted to. It was flattery to me, all right, and the tallest flattered digit sunk softly into an abundant honey mix, and curiously, with no feminine tissue to block it, as falsely advertised, it penetrated deeply into her interior cavity, to the end of the line, smothered by those raw, ripe, and flaming hot cutlets, just millimeters beneath her belly button. Millimeters above, the burning railer seared, knifed, and stabbed her flat tummy and she quickly clasped it fiercely only to slash down its zipper and release it, the object of clearly a burning curiosity; to clutch the private flesh in her palm, to feel the rim, cap, shaft, shape, and contour and the smoldering heat of it, too, and something that complimentary and resourceful she had stronger yearnings for, she felt compelled to go low and meet it. She dropped out of sight and redirected her mouth to it, over it, and she sucked it, and drew from it for many seconds as if to clean it, prepare it, and endorse it for likely insertion. As hands rode along on her bobbing crown, clamping it occasionally, my eyes somersaulted back in their caves. She tried to withdraw three times, her attempts met with absolute resistance as I vised her head in place and she went back at it more enthusiastically each time.

Minutes later, as vocal patterns declined to the prehistoric indicating I was about to erupt and let fly, she suddenly sprung back and up and decidedly away from me. She wiped her lip and hung a haunted, fearful one on me. Then she pulled down, twisted, and rearranged her spiked, freshly finger-fucked skirt and the office breathing was labored from all the doctor-patient violations.

"I'm sorry. I haven't been myself lately." She flashed guilt-ridden eyes at me, ones hinting at a pending confessional. "I had a drink."

I had nothing to add. Suffering from a rush of anxiety, I made myself quickly scarce, letting the door shut behind me as my only proactive and available response. I wasn't opinionated or fortified enough to slam it, so it was left teetering open a crack.

The boy didn't get too far. Emerging from the elevator on a lower floor, I bounced off a neutral wall and fell to my side, crumpling and folding inward like a prawn, defeated and antenna-bent. Only then was I able to let go but not the release I'd been prepared for. The tears flowed for an uninterrupted interval. Once again I'd tried to make contact and connect. And once more I'd found no place to plug in and no receptor willing. And spinning on that axis, in that place in time, I'd grown weary of it all.

21

Dolce Vita Daze (Optional)

If you don't care to experience a pathetic and offensive fall into a chasm of scandophoric sex and substance, then skip forward two chapters.

During the taxi ride home, I contemplated a number of things, including the behavior of my good doctor who hadn't been suffering from her period after all. I'd experienced that first hand. In essence I'd witnessed the real her not crippled by any monthly let down. She'd had that drink of course, one, maybe more, but that didn't explain her actions or disqualify them. Legitimate emotions she'd been running on, but ironically the gal didn't come in any clearer. What were those tears? And what was that sudden show of passion? She seemed fractured, perhaps broken. Something was feasting on her, hence the afternoon booze consumption. Maybe from her childhood, maybe something more recent. Behind that six-figure education and those million-dollar words, was she a Spontaneous Crazy herself? I was more befuddled than before, her behavior absolutely perplexing. The only thing I knew for sure was that she'd been curious again about my dealings with the cops.

As confusing as Dr. Van den Heugel was to me, I sensed I'd let it all hang out up there, nearly the model patient. The session had left me raw, stripped, and emotionally depleted. I'd even cried a small bucket's worth. It was a good thing that I had a guest coming by to divert my attention.

Another of my fave Asterisk Girls, poor Frauka* (nose re-sculpture, cheekbone enhancements), couldn't have known what she was getting into. Nevertheless, we began with the patented ritual of ours. In the same way I urge any Australian national I encounter in meetspace or barspace to parrot the infamous Meryl Streep line from *A Cry In The Dark*, "That dingo's got my baby!" I made Frauka repeat *chimpanzee* in German several times, always a modest mood enhancer.

"*Schimpanse!*"

I didn't giggle like usual, but I did smile. "Again!"

After the requisite preliminaries, Frauka didn't have much of a chance. No doubt I was still riled from my appointment with Coach Vince and our clothes lasted mere seconds upon my guest's entry into the foyer. The only thing she kept was her chewing gum, but even that didn't last.

"Ooh. You have a *gummi*-saver," she avowed.

"A what?" In English, it translated artlessly to a *gum-saver*.

With that she took the wad of Eclipse Polar Ice from her mouth, balled it up, and stuck it in my belly button. Then she faded below and mastered the man zone. The symbiotic nature of our relationship had me reciprocate and I took to my knees, nosing beneath her skirt, then we club-chaired it strictly because of the high back, pillow supports, and pleasant view of the alley we could enjoy while in the chosen position and she was considerate enough to keep her knee-high white patent leathers with industrial heels zipped. There was obviously no Friend Box in sight, nor had there ever been with Frauka. I hadn't been entirely honest with Coach, of course, and that gave me an added mischievous schoolboy charge, like I was getting away with something, on top of everything else. It made for a sufficiently aggressive encounter.

"*Oooh, Harry, ja…*"

After the thrillies and shrillies we settled into a game of *Panzer General*. I opted for PG because of the sound effects. When Nazi soldiers get shot, they scream out in linguistically-accurate High German. *Bin verletzt! Bin verletzt!* (I'm wounded! I'm wounded!) That evening, Frauka showed marginal talent, with her troop deployments sloppy, and her ground war maneuvers sub-par. She was post-coital lazy, glossy-eyed, slow and inept which in some circles translates to sexy. The Skybox flesh-festival effectively ruined her Third Reich resolve and I shredded her Panzer tank divisions in minutes. But before I knew it, I was the only one in the game room.

"Frauka!" I called out anxiously, while still gripping both vid control units. "Where are you going?"

"Meeting friends at Beatrice Inn—"

"Wait! Let's play two out of three!"

"*Nein*... Harry..." was sent back in a fractured, labored voice pattern revealing the struggle of someone getting dressed.

White-eyed, skittish, and unmanned, I ran to the foyer and saw her buttoning her blouse. I eyeballed her desperately which further sabotaged the invitation for an overtime gaming session which really was a transparent plea to have her stay on. To bolster my lack of suave and with nothing else to say, I blurted it, asking her if she'd used "protection."

"*Ja doch, absolutistish!*"

I had an idea where she was coming from, but gave her a dead "what?" anyway.

"That's 'of course, absolutely' in German."

The Teutonic sperm-buster greased her lips effortlessly and mirrorlessly, with apassionata red stick and smacked and puckered them in further mockery of her wham-bam-Sammed host. How could she hit the pavement so sprightly after that mutually beneficial, but punishing twist of meat? I thought to say, *You've already had some, you don't need to look so appealing,* but bit my tongue like a debonair fifth-grader.

I did have one last desperate Hail Mary in me. "I have new Cavalli two-pieces in..."

And that gave her pause.

"Leopard," I boosted.

"You gave me one already. Besides, Cavalli is so two years ago. Now if you have any Hervé Léger, you know how to find me..."

Then she reached forward, lifted my T-shirt, pinched the little wad on reserve in my *gummi-saver,* and popped it in her mouth.

"*Danke,* Harry."

As she chomped away, I watched her disappear as the elevator doors collided in a cartoon-like closeout. "*Danke,*" I had to return, even though she was gone. It was the tightest, most perfect punctuation to SoHo loft humiliation, so much more potently ironic and direct than a long-winded, linguistically cumbersome "Thank you."

I pondered my loneliness momentarily, in addition to my declining fashionista sensibilities and déclassé inventory and then ran to the window. When Frauka appeared on the curb I called for it one more time.

Ever the sport, she yelled back up at me. "*Schimpanse!*" It didn't stave off the emptiness entirely, but it was at least some consolation.

I phoned into the Militia to see if anyone was up for a Cuban feast at Las Brisas even though I wasn't hungry. I figured the atomic ones needed protein replenishment from all the mayhem they'd surely been initiating around town the last few hours. No one texted back in time. In fact, no one texted back at all. They must not have been very hungry.

I gave Pablo a call, but he wasn't in. In contemplating our friendship, I realized he was done with the kid stuff I had to offer like trips to aquariums, zoos, Coney Island, and urban athletic events. Pablo was almost thirteen and into girls now, something I could totally understand. I decided to send him a check so he could maybe take his sweetie out for dinners and movies. I stuck stamp to envelope and placed it in the sidewalk mailbox on Broome.

Returning to the Skybox, I went for the sure thing. I called my best friend and asked him how he was doing. He said, "*Sí.*" I told him I wasn't doing so hot. He said, "*Sí.*" I told him the Mets had fortified their pitching staff. He said, "*Sí.*" I told him Colbert was better than Stewart. He said, "*Sí.*" It was an agreeable chat, another one-sided, hollow run of "*sí*"s. But at least he'd taken my call.

I asked him to pick me up in an hour. He said, "*Sí.*"

Like Coach said, I was expected to forget, I was expected to substitute. I was expected to be in search of dangerous romance that would result in emotional and physical scandemonium. A lot was expected of me, and with little to hang my self-assurance, esteem, and faith in the universe on, I didn't care to disappoint.

I showered, using my last remaining Côte D'Azur hotel shampoo mini to smell Mediterranean fresh. I decided on paint-splattered Abercrombie's below while up top I went fall fab with a band-collared white Nehru jacket and beige silk interior. I was hoping the public wasn't going to be too sensitive tonight because I was going to try to live up to my expectations. There was a scandalacious *coup d'état* underway in a little town called Scandoland.

For trips uptown, we took the FDR Drive, allowing me to view the peaceful sweep of lights and bridges and fade into dreamy thought. Very calming. It was another form of sedative for overworked synapses and the *Oficina* was located smack off the exit. On the journey north, I resumed meditations on Dr. Greer and her interest in bag culture. I had an inkling she might enjoy a night out with Team Dolce Vita. She might even like a place like Scores. With so many short-circuiting brains to drain, shrink, and sift through I suspected a full sexposure bar could offer her a nice reprieve. In actuality I had no idea what turned her on, if anything.

I arrived at Scores around eleven and Rocco, the Big Boy with the cut-rate tuxedo, shook my hand with his vise grip. He had that black tie stretched across his bull neck and if the clip-on popped, the tie would propeller through your face like a submarine rivet at six thousand feet below. It'd be a mess.

"How ya doin', Slinger? We got your table ready."

I entered the main stage area with my *Oficina* swag and a run of chest-erfeited lovelies* pecked me on the way to the table. It was perched on the raised right bank that offered a glorious view of the scandocandy. The great feature of Scores beyond the pussypology was they played essential sporting events: an ingenious way to see a game. Love and marriage may go together like a horse and carriage, but so does football and starkie frolic. I sat down cheerfully and caught the last quarter of Florida-Florida State. Coincidentally, Sunday had spent a year at Florida State, but dropped out and had never clarified as to why. She claimed she wasn't happy with the drama department, but I always considered her explanation hazy.

Minutes beyond, Angelo stopped by to have a drink. Angelo was a "partner" in the club. Everyone seemed to be a partner there. In my line of work, I always got people's accomplishments times five, but he always had refreshments and scandalicious company for me. At the time I was drinking my rum and OJ. He preferred darker waters. He liked everything dark, including his women. There were two Equator Girls* (full plastics) flanking him, which means one was flanking me, already getting to know my right thigh. Out of pure politeness, I didn't budge an inch.

"Lots of new faces, Slinger," Angelo proffered, casting an eye over a flock of dazzling semi-starkies crisscrossing on the neon–lit horizon.

"Check. Don't know any of 'em."

"That one next to you, she's Argentinean. They're just like the Russians. Without the entitlement shit. Now you know them."

Ang' was referring to the gals from economically strained nations flocking overseas to find wealthy American men. These fortune-hunting "Tsarinas," the early Wall hoppers in the eighties from Moscow and other Eastern European locales, were particularly scando-scarred. Communist Russia had crushed them and they'd fled to the West like abused and battered women, no wife-beating husband per se, just a nasty little system devised by Karl Marx. That need for green at present, mixed with a fierce pride in the mother country from centuries past, provided them with that entitlement psychology, even if they were out-and-out Prozzies. These Eastern bloc scandovamps wound up often in *Slingshot* arm wrestling walletmen for diamonds and Dior, or as provided-for mistresses and "the other" women to cheating married male boldfacers, as well as no-one-would-ever-know, off-night, under-the-radar girlfriends to scandoskirt chasing playboys.

Similarly, the South American scandodancers had been fleeing their corrupt and impoverished lands in search of a better life in the States, particularly the Argentineans, Columbians, and Brazilians. Their constitutions were less rigid, less prideful, and less entitlement-oriented than the Eastern Bloc-ers, their dispositions more laid back and equatorial. On the other hand, Equator Girls were scalding passionistas, more hot-blooded, eager to please, and jealous than the cooler, colder Tsarinas where sex was more of an ATM transaction. But make no mistake; gals from the lower hemisphere were often savvy and cunning gold diggers and Prozzies on a scando scale.

Before that waiter was murdered at the club, I'd been sending 2 Late to do my boldface exotic bar spotting, but the place died from the Bad Sling. Yet scandalocity re-filtered the negative pub and spun it into friendly-fire Face. Now it was *La Oficina* and I was a "Very VIP" there at the height of my self-medicating, self-hatred period, with morally objectionable habits running at peak performance levels.

"You okay?" The Argentinean girl* petting my thigh posed.

"Just danderoo."

"I'm Coco."

"I know; Angelo just introduced us. It's really a fuckin' pleasure."

Angelo leaned over to me and the scandoprancers spun away as if on cue. "I got east coast and west coast. The west coast is smoother. Want a bump?"

I could have said no, but I wasn't that mentally tough. And I needed some impassioning. "I've got a left hand and a right one. Sure."

I stashed my paw beneath the table, closed my fist on a nice packet of inspiration, then shuffled to the powder room. Anyone who tells you America is winning the drug war is playing ostrich games. Coke is back phat and the post-eighties negative stigmas are gone, but you don't need to buy it because everyone has it. No wonder the terrorists caught us taking a crapper.

I wasn't a gackasaurus and didn't often do bumps; only when I was out, it was late, and I needed a stimulant as in a cup of bold to wake me up. Otherwise I couldn't stay up which means compete with the rest of the nocturnal lustafarians. If you packed it in, someone else scored the passionistas you'd had your eye on. That was the scandosexual addicts' credo and only Martial Law, a Green Zone, and a curfew could change the system.

Those afflicted with ADHD respond to inspiration the same way they respond to Adderall and Ritalin: they become clearheaded. It temporarily alleviates ADD symptoms. Most feel a rush of unfocused manic energy when they do coke, but the ADDer can lock on and execute.

I did a quick sniff and my head rocketed back. Angelo always had the good stuff, East Coast, West Coast, South American. Quick-toss thoughts launched on the subject of my dearly departed, the coke enabling me to handle it. I'd go through some rationale as to why it had to have ended the way it did. Inspiration was kind that way, rerouting your greatest disappointments in life, convincing you that that was the way it had to be. For twenty minutes anyway.

I returned to the table and my head pinballed around like a prairie dog's, searching for an opening, ready to dig in somewhere with a new dash of hyper-focus.

I saw Coco target-eyeballing me, hungrily so. Before she could offer me her talents in a private setting I got a tap on the shoulder.

"I'm a gift," this platinum Contessa* said.

"And gift*ed*," I cracked, the pitiful frat-boy. "You don't say…"

"From a friend of yours."

I spied a look at Angelo, who sent both wings back and shrugged indicating it wasn't he who'd sent over the thoughtful scandoGram.

"Who?"

"Does it matter?"

She'd made a good point. I wasn't that hard to get, nor did I need a reference. "No," I said. "But you'll have to ask Coco if it's okay."

Coco said it was, though her nut twisted away in disapproval.

"May I call you Ginger-Pineapple?"

"You can call me anything you like. If I can call you *mine*."

"Ginger-P, you were born for me…"

The sequined dress came off and the Bare-chested Contessa* wrapped my neck with it. She was fluffy and Monroe-esque and rather exceptional the ribboning highway south, her breasts carved, but not blimp fiascos as was the case for full scandomamms. I didn't appreciate cartoon starkies who were so enhanced they punished the laws of the universe, possessing no natural, anatomical credibility. It was Andersonheimer's Disease; Harry no-like.

Ginger-Pineapple knew how to move too and then it happened what happens with all fine scandodances. They end. So I gave her the cash boost in her waist floss just as Bounty Bob appeared and plopped down beside me. I thanked him for the scandogram support. A Scores regular, Bob had a wife and kid in Queens, but he'd stop by every night, watch SportsCenter, and belt a few back before crossing over the Bridge.

When Angelo got up, the Equator Girls stayed put. No one called for an usher to check their stubs.

22

Tooting Up, Trumping Down (Optional)

"How's it goin', Slinger?" Bob put to me as the prancers soared high displaying skill sets with perfect pole precision.

"You know…"

"Feeling better?"

"Hour to hour."

"Better than minute to minute."

"Says you."

"Does Angelo really own this club?"

I took a big swig. "See a guy working the floor, nine times out of ten he's the face. Paid to be there every night. Faces try to make you believe they've got a piece. Owners you don't see. The real money guys behind a joint. Unless they're Spidermen in mistress or modelizing mode, manning seduction offensive booths with welcome baskets. So, Angelo? You make the call…"

"Still gets the fierce fuzzy though…"

"They all do."

"But he ain't no Brad Pitt."

"Nor does he have to be."

"What's up with that? Guys running clubs are always short, fat, bald, and gross. With nothing to talk about. Probably never got any in high school…"

"Bravo, Bobbo. So for them, it's the club biz. Or Hollywood. To score the unfair advantage. To shift the paradigm and upset nature's laws. Because nature's laws have been killing them all their lives. But impresarios provide something for ladies others can't…"

"What's that?"

"A *scene*. Gives them personality by default."

Just then, a tight little herd of drunk Entitlements giggling nearby caught my eye. You know, the north of Fifty-Ninth Street Pack, off Park, Mad, and Fifth. The black dress-uniformed me-firsters were making their obnoxious and outlandish requests, of course, spouting off rude, snappy answers to anyone alien to their self-consumed clique; pointing derisively at the hardworking girls; cutting bathroom queues with their golden oldie ruse, covered mouths with panicked eyes as if about to spray vomit; drifting in and out of their looping, "I'm so bored"/"But-back-to-me" self-absorbed constitutions and self-deception comas, while pushing and elbowing wherever possible; in essence, getting their little faux-elitist, do-you-know-who-I-am? jollies in a lovely exotica bar which was far too good for them—inspiring finger down throat technologies to any passer-by. The Entitlement Girls were a spoiled lot, among the best Generation 9/11 had to offer.

"Think those are real?" Bob posed of a brunette polester*, stage right.

"Silly rabbit. Aquatics are way off."

"Buy you one?"

"Natch."

"The usual?"

"If I told you a Gatortini with a splash of the croc, would you believe me?"

"No."

"All right, then. Order up, but it's on me."

I spied one over to the dimly lit corner by the cigarette closet. A guy was puffing a stick and behind the smog I could see he was clocking me, or it seemed so, anyway.

"Hey Bob, who's the suit over yonder?"

He handed me my drink and swiveled around thoughtfully. "Which guy?"

"The one by the cigs, smoking one."

"I don't see nobody, Slinger."

I spun back and the fellow was gone. I left it alone and took a big haul of my refreshment. "Yeah, yeah, yeah." Shadowy guys like him I called Fifty/Fifties meaning there was a fifty percent chance they were real as in, really tagging me. Sure I gave odds to and handicapped my paranoia.

"Say, what do you think of that shakedown scandal at 'Page Six'?"

"Bound to happen, too many perks flying around. There's always a runaway train."

"You get that J.Lo preggers photo?"

"Yeah, but don't do kids. Even before the fact."

"Since when?"

"Since I thought about it more."

He gave me a funny look. As far as I was concerned, it was enough talking shop for the night.

"Well, heard she may have twins. Love to snap those snotnoses. That's shiny coin."

Mum from me.

"Tell ya, Slinger," he said grumpily, "I got no patience for young Hollywood. Ain't like the old days. These kids, they act like they've had brights for fifty years. Do a couple shitty flicks, they think they're Clarke Fuckin' Gable."

"What's the problem?"

"They don't want to do no pictures. We make 'em Slinger and then they don't want to do publicity, say they're 'private' and 'don't shoot me,' and they give us five minutes at some lousy premiere and there's a hundred damned photographers and you can't get a decent shot—"

"You still smoke those Parlies?"

"Bear shit in the woods?"

He handed me a stick and I reversed it filter-up for that ingenious little artesian well Parliament filters are known for. Then I dug it filter-first into my powder packet of West Coast. "Some inspiration, Bobbo?"

"You know I don't do bumps, Slinger."

"Sorry. Just being a gentleman." With that I whiffed one big and nearly snapped my neck off.

"Tell ya something else, I'm finished with Mr. Nice Guy. I'm going backyards. Gonna sit in the goddamn bird baths if I have to."

"You already do, Bobbo."

"Yeah, but now it's personal. Hell with 'em. I'm going to take my payday."

"How are the kids?"

"Exactly, I got a lotta school bills. That's if they go to a low-budge state u–y. Forget private."

"Yeah, but how are they?"

"Great. B.J. hit a home run in Little League."

"What about scandobanned Pete?" Affirmative, I was pinballing.

"Rose? He lied for too long. Fuck him. But next to these 'roiders he don't look so bad. Hall o' Shame for the lot."

Another round came and I was hoping Bob would settle down. He was a little like social Mace and the starkies were getting restless. I asked Coco to flank me on the other side. Bob had parachuted in and rolled between us, not because he wanted Coco; it was just his way. He wasn't a flesh hound which made him a bit dim to Slingerette catch-at-midnight, release-at-dawn seating etiquette.

"You okay, Coco?"

"Just fine."

"See Bobbo, *es problemo*. There's too much demand for scando and too much money at stake."

"They're jacking up fees by making it so fucking hard—"

"Made bounty hunting stalkerazzi out of what used to be mild-mannered paps. Like yourself."

"Damned straight. But can you blame us? What do real-estate honchos do? Buy up waterfront. Lawyers? Rep 'em, guilty or not. Wall Streeters, forget about it. And stars? They'll take their twenty milly for what? Two month's work? So we'll take our piece too—"

"Stalkerazzi went chopperazzi, now assassinazzi. Ask Lady Di—"

"Free enterprise, Slings, and we deserve our slice. I'll give any star a piece of advice; just sit down, shut up, and take your snap. Like Gary Cooper did, like Bogart did, like Garbo and Taylor and Wayne. Real legends. That way fees stay down and no one gets hurt. That new crop is spoiled. They actually think they deserve all that moolah. There's always a price and we're theirs, we've always been theirs. It's give and take, now they're all fuckin' take. Nope, they're makin' the problems, not us. And they're not even makin' good movies! Go figure—"

"All makes for good Sling, Bobbo-cakes."

"Right? Cheers, Slinger." We tapped lowballs.

"You all right, Ginger-P?"

"I'm Coco. Just told you I was all right," she said to the looping fool.

"Great. Everything's okay?"

She nodded onward with a horse-tooth smile. "How are you doing?" She lobbed back.

"Airborne, baby, airborne." I did have a nice one-two going, pixilated from the alcohol and clamping furiously from the tootski. I was damned inspired. "You're rabid, Bobbo."

"Say what?" he shot back at my verbal sucker punch.

"You're a rabid junkyard dog."

"Sure, Slinger, whatever."

"Stay away from stodgy stars, stick to the press-desperates. They're your bank."

"Like who?"

"The Bimbo Summit. P-Diddly Squat. All the Gangsta-Yappers for that matter. And Ego Trumpet."

"Trump," he muttered derisively. "Don't get me started—"

"They're easy, easy money, and easier on the nerves. They'll pay for college—"

"Tell me Trump ain't Paris Hilton in a cheap suit. Only today could he redo himself from the hack builder and huckster he is. In the eighties, he was known for what he was. Crude. Fat. Columns called him something—"

I remembered all too well and debated divulging. "A 'vulgarian.'"

"Bingo, the Ugly Americano. In every way. The scum de la crème of the new-vo rich. Ask any real New Yorker, not from the BBQ boroughs, Manhattan, the place everyone calls the 'city,' the real city, ask'em who Trump is and they'll tell ya, he's the number one embarrassment to 'em. And he's not even from the city. He's from Queens!"

"Aren't you from Queens, Bobbo?"

"Yeah, but I don't forget where I came from. And I know Queens ain't the city. His whole shtick is a sham. Boastin' about being an

Ivy Leaguer but he started at fuckin' Fordham. He was a transfer. A shitty student. And he invented this rep of being a 'true New Yorker' and put his name on everything in big letters that just sticks it to real New Yorkers. He doesn't do it for love, he's got a chip 'cause he ain't one of 'em. I've talked to 'em. Not the ones riding the sewer rocket in their Nikes, the ones with family ties here for gennies. The peeps who actually made New York, gave it the great rep, those chi-chis and high-breeds who've always made it the great place it is. Cultured, educated, international. The peeps, Trump the climber he is, has been jealous of all his Flatbush life. And despises. This outsider from the boroughs is hitching a ride on all that as if he was a part of it. I mean, how could he be a Yankee fan? The Mets were in his back-fuckin'-yard…"

Bobbo was just a little too wound up for my mood. "Hey, it's cocktail hour, a time for Slingtinis and Slingerettes…"

"Just tellin' ya, Harry, real New Yorkers are horrified on a daily basis that he's identified with the city. Puttin' up Erector-Set, pre-fabby, cut-and-paste, Miami Beachy buildings with his license-plate name on top. He don't represent true New York any more than I do. And when it comes to self-promoting and insinuatin' being with, more like sucking up to, beautiful wool, everyone knows he was a fumbling scarecrow to the ladies for decades. Come on, you were there—"

"My suit was…"

"Well I was. He was striking out with them hotties left and right. No supermodel would take a photo with him let alone touch him with a ten-foot pole—ask 'em. Had my own finger on the shutter when they squirmed away and eased themselves out of the snap. Insiders saw it, the real Donald. Only the desperados, the handout gals gave him the time of day, the easy ones to score, where sex is as simple as a handshake, like takin' a pee in the shower, you know? The digger pros. Classy beauties stayed away from him like the plague. For decades…"

"Bobbo, can't I just enjoy my drip?"

"And to counteract the fumblings, strike-outs, and rejections, he goes out and buys a model agency. And two pageants. Only then did hotties start to take snap with him."

He took another haul on his drink, a welcomed relief from the toxic mix of borough envy and halitosis spewing forth.

"Don't forget, these celebrity-worship times make him less unappealing than before. You got a name for it Slings—"

"Scandalocity. Where *all* of us make our money, don't forget."

"True enough."

"Spark up a Parly and calm down."

He did so, surprisingly, but after the second drag he went right back after it.

"And publicity stunts like runnin' for President and savin' Miss USA, all for the muggin'. Like he's some kinna chick magnet and he'll decide on this hottie's future, like he was some frickin' Casanova. Without the stuff or the style or the class. Or the *results!* 'Cause prior to that this guy with the ladies was Kryptonite, a four-corner disaster. Remember Marla?"

No response required; he was on the Queens-bound, vanilla-chip express.

"For twenty years, real New Yorkers have taken this crap on the chin, all the phony press conferences, watching this monster grow before their frickin' eyes, with paid-for puff pieces by pubbies and collies…"

"Easy there, trigger…"

"Puttin' up with this walrus pretendin' to be a face of New York as if, as a total outsider, he had something to do with it. When all along he's been ruinin' its image and fuckin' it up! Addin' insult to injury it gets worse as the Paris Hilton times take over. And this middle-market schlumpf rolls along, like Paris, instead of bangin' boys on video, he gives it to an entire city, saved by reality TV. Ain't nothin' natural 'bout him, hair color, comb-over, cheapy Wal-Mart suits, showin' no sense of style—like the buildings. Self-bought rep as a New Yorker, self-bought rep as an Ivy Leaguer, self-bought rep as a womanizer, claimin' everything he does is the "best"-this, the "greatest"-that when, in fact, we know it ain't great; it's a total embarrassment! Real New Yorkers'll tell ya. Taken two hundred years for Manhattan to get a rep as a cosmo-p city, only damned thing we got in America close to old-world class. So take your Trump signs and warehouse 'em off the Flushing Line where they belong. Let real New Yorkers stick to maintaining the city. Choosin' the great architects and geniuses they always have to make it the unique place it is. Stop dumbing it down, stop Trumping it down!"

"Bobbo, think you need to get a life…"

"And now his daughter's soundin' just like him! Poor thing. No matter how many ugly license-plate buildings he pastes up, no matter how many modeling agencies he buys, or how many architecture classes he ain't had, he'll never make it across the river, he'll never be one of 'em. Be happy with who you are and where you come from. Shame on you, fuckface. Rosie couldn't say it, she was a climbing borough queen too, neither could Cuban or Jolie or the rest he insulted who don't care to stoop. A real Queens boy had to say it. New Yorkers? You're welcome."

"Sure you didn't do any scandocandy, Bobbo?

"I told you, don't get me started…"

"*Danke*, Bob. I did have a preferred buzz and some willing spontaneosas here somewhere. Where art thou lovely twisters?"

"Sorry, bro…"

"Just take the money and run. We all do."

Just then, I experienced a sobering jolt made possible by sudden a dip in euphoria. It had the taste of shame, really. I truly despised what I did. "It's not hygienic."

"What's that?"

"It's garbage. And it leaves the office, sent over the wire, and gets swallowed from London to New Delhi to Auckland, New Zealand in a matter of baby seconds. We're polluters. On a global scale."

"It ain't tossin' milk cartons on the side of the road…"

"But it's trash. Refuse. Deposited into peoples' beans. On a daily basis. And it originates right here. In the good old U.S. of A. That makes me a First Polluter. Because the world feeds off our Machine. We're whores, Bobbo."

"Let you in on a little secret, Slings: everybody is…"

I nodded along and mustered up some wise-ass. "Even you and Trump?"

Bobbo shook his head and drained his glass.

Just as quickly, I had a fresh spike in morale. The triumphant toots had eased me merrily onward. "Use the times to fit your business model. Tuition, those vacays in Pompano…"

"I'll take his picture… but he ain't foolin' me none."

"Now you're talking, speaking of which," I added, having tried to get it in edgewise for hours. "Let me check the archives someday…"

"What archives?"

"Your files, the snaps."

"Oh, yeah, right."

Of course I meant *her* and the stockpile of photos he'd taken of Sunday at all the Manhattan social events she'd attended.

"Let's go."

"Now? Let's do it when you're not all jacked up."

"Good idea." Then I came right back at him. "You know, Bobbo, you're like a firefly at the end of an extension cord."

"Say what?"

"You're plugged in, but you only flash once in a while."

"Whatever you say, Slinger," he said and it was swell of him not to slug me. "What planet you comin' from, anyway?"

"Live from Scandoland. Hey, Ang'!" I bellowed. He was pressing flesh at the bar and heard me and came right over.

"What's up, Slinger?"

"Play it! Play me my song!"

"Told ya before, the girls can't dance to it."

"Can do anything to it!"

"No-sir, no acid rock in here. They want disco, R&B…"

"What's your song?" Coco put to me.

"Eddie Hotshot sings it."

So much more than a song it was my scandoanthem and I was already going off, belting it out.

I admit it, what's to say?/I relive it without pain/I got a bomb in my temple and it's going to explode/I got a sixteen-gauge buried under my clothes/I pray!!

"Eddie who?" She lobbed a second time.

"Eddie Vedder."

"Who's that?"

Waved off. It was uploaded into my bean already.

ONCE upon a time I could control myself!/Once upon a time I could lose myself!!

"Why you like that song so much?"

My head bucking broncoed at her. "It be, what be, inside my head." Which was absolutely true, when I got fuckied up it was all I wanted to hear. It's called "Once" and it's vintage Pearl Jam, circa 1991.

I rubbed Coco's leg harder than was required. "Go to it, Coco Loco. Give me some of that *thang*—"

The gal did just that with twists and turns and pear-halves in my face and gyrations and little teaser maneuvers like postcards from the equator. And when you're boozied up, the scandogam dream dance fades to a surrealistic wipe. But I had more game and follow-up cracks.

"If you have any guts, Coco, you'll come with us."

"Who's us?"

"Me and my fiefdom."

"I'm coming."

"But I'll only warn you once: don't step on my cape."

Before long, the scandodrama raged in the back room as I was doing rails off her breasts and she was doing them off my private parts and we kissed and cajoled and scandohammed it up and I told her not to step on my cape again and we squawked about each others' lives, hers more than mine, because I'd become the late-night talk show host with an endless barrage of unnecessary questions, a jittery-jawed grind off, the answers of which I had no time for because I was already on to the next question. That's how focused I was and I kept admonishing my dolce vita vixen not to step on my cape, I'd become Count Slinger, my midnight alter ego, an erudite, elegantly-dressed, dark, gothic, and ghoulish superhero, sprung freshly from the fourteenth century and I was on my way back to my evil hilltop castle in the Romanian forest and after falsely accusing her of treading on the Count's cape and after repeated warnings, I held up a penalty card and we performed some sort of involved and enduring scandosexual act as punishment but I can't remember what it was. But it was punishment, taken without protest.

"The bold scandacity of you!" I barked at the faux-infraction.

I'm not sure the act brought us closer together, but we did arrive at an understanding. I do remember quoting Jimi to her profusely especially my favorite Hendrix gem, "Hey, there're a lot of sleepy people out there." It seemed to be the end-all philosophy for everything we'd discussed, or it seemed so at the time.

Then a scandocanned colleague* of Coco's walked in, a Brazilian half-beauty with eyes too close together to beguile our rigid sense of awe and aesthetic. The twin 2K8 Rio D lab-issue projectile mamms didn't help, but the DNA-correct bubble-butt did and she was gritty street and favela-honed and thereby politely cool enough to engage in more powder-on-body-parts and with the two of them bookending me, it made for a delightful scandy sammy. The hoopla was interrupted when a nosey *Oficina* neophyte way out of his element barged in on us and gasped at the nipple rails to which I responded flatly, "I'm sorry you had to see that," as my skull tightened, my eyeballing intensified, and my face skipped. I do recall Coco pleading with me not to do any more blast. She even snatched my stash and hid it from me.

Before I protested though I was going to hit her from another angle, to keep her off balance. "You wearing Hervé Léger?"

"Thought he was an actor."

"Didn't he die?"

That's when I knew I had them. They were unsuspecting and ripe. "You're cahooting it!"

"What?" Came from one of two quizzical faces.

"You can't fool me. You're cahooting it!"

"Slinger, we don't know what you're talking about…"

"You're in cahoots with each other!"

"Say what?"

"Coach put you up to it, didn't she? She's just a freeloading sexcapade joy-rider and you're cahooting it with all those saps who don't approve of my behavior. Now where's my gack?"

As I continued to object vociferously, Coco 'fessed up and thoughtfully explained that I wouldn't be able to perform in a torrid two-fer with them if I continued to Hoover it in an industrial way.

"Never fear," I interjected. That's when I extended a handful of tiny blues.

"*O que e' isso?*" That was her Portuguese for "What is this?"

"See the aura? The magical blue light they're giving off?"

"What you got there, Slinger?"

"They're not blue, they're orange," the other one piped.

"Oh, right." I was pretty damned inspired. "It's the Levitra then. Personally, I prefer it to Viagra. It's like Coke or Pepsi, but both cut right through the gack." They both eyeballed me like a circus oddity. "Don't look so worried, Coco. Anything is possible, if you just lower your bar on humiliation."

I was confident I'd comforted her. Strangely the exchange did seem to calm the Slingerettes; either that or, it initiated their sneaky and unjust scandoplans of escape, the Count just couldn't recall. Whichever, I'd definitely left a scandelible impression on them.

23

Bless You, Triple Q

What I do remember is waking up in the Skybox at five the next evening no longer feeling like a midnight gothic superhero. I'd crashed back to Earth and a woman who wasn't Coco Loco or Ginger-P was sleeping next to me. I nudged her and the face which rolled my way I couldn't recall. She wasn't a scandoprancer; she was heavyset but not unattractive. Not the equator type either, she was honky tank white and def unconscious to her curvy mouth which was passing off a grin. I figured with the pressure of me clamping eyes on her she awoke, took me in her sights, and finished off the curve. It was a pleasant, good person's smile, whatever that was. I searched for a knife in my back just in case. There wasn't one.

"Hi, baby," she said lovingly as if it was already midweek of our holiday in St. Kitts.

"*Buenos días*," came forth naturally, albeit curiously.

I wanted to know her name, so I tap-danced in the vicinity by delicately probing for a timeline. "When did we leave Scores?"

She laughed shyly. "I wasn't with you at Scores. We met at Pink Elephant." Oh. "We met on the dance floor."

"Hmmm."

"I was a friend of Pedro's, remember?"

"Oh right." I didn't know who Pedro was.

"Pedro knows Pat."

"Pat?"

"Yeah, your buddy, the locksmith."

The only professional lock and key man I knew was the one who'd gotten Sunday and me out of a handcuff predicament a couple years back.

"He was there?"

"He was here."

"Cripes. Who else was here?"

"Triple-R left early in the morning. She said to say good-bye."

Mystery guest number two. I'd have to tell Dr. Van den Heugel I was committing unforced errors again. The blackouts were back. In a dark and likely ugly way.

"I can tell you don't remember," she allowed thoughtfully.

"Overserved I was."

"You were having a good time."

"I'm so sure. Get to the scary part. What was I saying?"

"Lots, actually," she said with that clean and cute smile. "That you don't like the color gray, that you want to move out of New York. That there's no 'i' in team but there is in Team Dolce Vita. That you needed 'distance' from people who had trouble with doormen and couldn't get into clubs because they were 'radioactive.' That there were some people following you—"

"Me and my hollow charm. I wasn't rude, was I?"

"No. I didn't think so."

"So I was selectively rude. What else did I say?"

"You said you were an inventor too. That you'd invented a *multi-purpose vacation formula for eternal hipsters.*"

"A what?"

"A preventative creme formula, a five-in-one balm, I think you said."

"A preventative? To prevent what?"

She chuckled more. "It had sunblock, skin moisturizer, spermicide, an STD antibiotic, and bug repellant."

"Targeted for who?"

"Eternal hipsters," she repeated. "And if you *phoned in right now* you could receive the *special Ibiza edition,* which added K-Y."

That's where the *buenos días* had come from, I reasoned.

"I'm so sorry."

"You were funny. You introduced me to everyone as your 'mascot.'"

What a trooper this gal was; a def sweetheart. The kind of girl I always had to look past and beyond, or rightfully looked past me. How did I know? From what she'd said. I often referred to gals I knew not to get romantic with as "Mascots." I mean, would you sleep with the Georgia bulldog or the Texas longhorn? You could be friends with them, party with them, and act as each other's mutual after-midnight party toys, but that was it. Why? Because they were types who wouldn't react well to my lifestyle and methods. In essence, they were too emotionally available and looking for love and that archetypical "good guy." They were too good for me and I didn't want to derail them or their lives with my shortcomings. Mascots were placed in the Friend Box under lock and key.

"Did anyone follow us home?"

"Uh, what do you mean?"

"Nothing."

"I must say that I liked hearing your viewpoints."

"Oh?"

"Especially the 'Age of the Asterisk.' Do you remember having the discussion with that guy at Pink Elephant?" I shook, of course. "Well, you didn't want to talk to him. You didn't seem to like what he had to say. So you made him pay to speak to us. You said, 'Jabber on but I'm going to have to charge you.'"

I wasn't shocked. I did things like that. "Did he fork over?"

"Yes. You made me keep time on my watch. He had to pay another dollar every sixty seconds. I think he liked talking to you."

"What did we talk about?"

"He told you how much he loved fake breasts. The bigger, the better. Once you heard that you started charging him. You had a different philosophy. Then you both pointed out all the 'Asterisk Girls' in the room as you called them, the ones who'd had work done."

I'd levied a tax on another club ape. "Goodness, how obnoxious."

"But you missed one girl."

"Who?"

"Me."

Sure my face fell from within. "I'm sorry. So I was totally rude."

"No, you expressed your point of view very well. That society

196 Coerte V. W. Felske

is headed down the wrong path. Becoming increasingly fake. Manufactured. And away from nature. And I agree," she said, pausing. "All I can say is I was born with unattractive breasts. Which made me embarrassed. And nervous. It petrified me, actually. About relationships. I cried a lot about it when I was younger. But the surgery gave them shape and I didn't feel, well, so insecure anymore, you know?"

"I do know and I know you made the right decision. I have no defense for my actions." I gave it thought and she deserved it. "Cosmetic surgery may be anti-natural, yes, but it's not the artificial aspect which concerns me. After all, I use synthetics to stabilize my moods. Meds. It's just there's a group of people I care about. More than the rest combined. More than myself."

"Who is that?"

"The little ones. The little girls."

The mere act of articulating it brought on the eye floods. The sweet one reached over and clasped my hand.

"The ones who get brainwashed early, you know? Made to feel what they have is not enough. That they're inadequate. That they have to change things. Those ones have to be looked after. And told what they have *is* enough. I worry about them. A lot." I was blubbering now. "Who is protecting *them?*"

"Your sensitivity comes through, Slinger. It does."

"And I see those young women walking around with their redone bodies and I envision them as little girls once and it makes me wonder why they did it and was it for the right reasons? For their interiors? Or for their exteriors? Or for men, the worst of all reasons. I feel intensely for those little people. No matter how old they're all little ones to me still. And it haunts me."

"Because of Caitlin, I know. You told me a little."

I wiped my face. "Don't know if I ever allow little girls … to grow up."

If I'd told her about my sister, I'd told her a lot. More than my coach even. I wondered why I'd been so forthcoming, and with a total stranger, no less. Maybe that *was* why. A no-tabs chat. Or perhaps it was a sign I was cracking. Or ready to open up. I sniffled a bit more. "It's my problem."

"It's not a problem. It's beautiful. I wish I'd had a dad like you."

It was perhaps the most beautiful thing I'd ever heard in my adult life. I wrapped her and gave her one with full Harry behind it.

"Oh, I almost forgot," she tendered with an amused grin. "Before we went to bed you had to watch the turtles…"

I collected myself. "Ah, yes," I acknowledged. "So soothing. On DVD or 'Animal Planet?'"

She said we'd watched my *National Geographic* DVD. "The turts are better than Xanax."

"It was the sweetest thing."

When I was jacked up and desperate to come off a mega buzz, I loved watching the sea turtles. They'd float along, so peacefully, running to their own time clock set in another millennium, with no worries, harboring no fears; if they encountered a predator or any form of danger they'd just pull in their big paddles, duck their head away, and float to the bottom, like a giant hockey puck, and wait. And live to be a hundred. *Soothing.* I longed for that hard-back turtle shell myself and the capacity to just draw it all in. Until the danger of life passed me by. But no shell and no such luck on Planet Harry.

"Stay as long as you like, darling, we'll order in."

"I have to be going."

I wanted to say *"Don't!"* but tempered it to, "Are you sure?"

She nodded and I could tell there was no talking her out of it without bleeding all my pride. "I'm going to get you a car—"

"For what?" She claimed it wasn't necessary.

I made a quick call and told her the Fonz would be picking her up out front. I kissed her farewell and the fresh fragrance coming off her lips I did not remember having experienced. But still.

"There's something I have to ask you. But I'm afraid to—"

"You mean, did we have sex?"

My eyes were obviously burning on it.

"No," she volunteered. "You said it wasn't a good idea. Which was a surprise. Most guys, well… You seemed anxious."

"About what?"

"After the turtles, I got my things to leave, but you asked me not to, you said you hated to be alone. I held your head and petted you until you went to sleep."

Another tear fell out of my eye. I was stripped raw.

"Thank you, beautiful."

"It was a pleasure, Slinger. You're a nice man."

I wanted to ask her her name but didn't have the nerve; she was all too wonderful, if you can understand it. And certainly too wonderful to gift her a passé Cavalli swimsuit. I cringed for even having that brand of thought so easily accessible.

"One last question. How much money did we make?"

"Nineteen dollars."

"Probably covered one drink."

"No, you gave it to the waitress." She hesitated a second. "Slinger? Why did you just call me 'beautiful?'"

"Because you are. You're a 5G Girl."

"You mean I'm worth five thousand dollars?"

"Can't put a price on it. You possess goodness, genuineness, grace, grounding, and generosity of spirit. You're the prize of the lot."

"How do you know? You just met me."

"I suspect."

It seemed she wanted to smile. Or cry. "Tell me," she posed finally, "of those qualities, which do you look for in someone most?"

"Recently and for a long time? None."

"What do you mean? You don't need positive influences in your life?"

I couldn't answer her. It would trigger that tsunami of pending sadness.

"Okay," she reloaded. "Of those qualities, which do you respect most?"

"All of them. Equally. What I *need* most is grounding. I'm a regular Major Tom. But I've never shown much talent for taking care of my needs."

"As in, 'Ground Control to Major Tom?'"

I sighed heavily. "Apologies for the morose energy fields. The fact is, I'm damaged goods. 5Gs need a whole person... Everyone does, as a matter of fact."

She nodded and seemed to understand better. "I'm flattered, of course."

"Don't be. You deserve it."

"Deserve what?"

"Everything good that's coming to you. Your spirit invites it. And it will come. Believe it. No. *Count on it.*"

Water quickly coated her eyes. "Thank you," said the stranger.

In addition to the shame, embarrassment, post-party depression, and general sadness I had a monster bangover. I eased myself downstairs and found a remaining Tylenol and downed it then sat myself in the bathtub and let the shower pour onto my throbbing head. I was there an hour.

From the tub, I saw something I hadn't noticed before. On the sink lay a stubby inspiration straw and the half-forgotten memories sent the chills up my spine. Upon closer inspection, I saw it wasn't a straw, it was a rolled-up business card, the kind of calling card they stick in your front door or mailbox or stack in your lobby. I unrolled it and indeed it belonged to Pat the Locksmith. He'd penned in a home number too. Even locksmiths kick it up from time to time, I processed.

I trudged back upstairs and the good trooper was gone. I spotted a sheet of paper on the pillow that hadn't been there minutes before.

Dearest Count, thank you for a wonderful evening. Love, Triple Q.

I'd called her Exhibit Triple Q. And she'd been dancing at Pink Elephant. And she was more secure with herself now and goodness was coming to her. That was all I knew about her. But damn if it wasn't nice, rather life-enhancing, to know she was out there.

I reflected on the year's Skybox activity and how I'd had quite a run on the alphabet. Already I was on Q again. For the third time.

That gave me pause.

Dread crept in soon after.

That big wave of sadness that was on hold then crashed over me. Because at some point that night, the terrific one had changed profiles. From being a Mascot to an Exhibit. Which indicated something likely had happened. Between us. And she'd let me off the hook for not remembering. In essence, she was too spiritually-connected to let me know. It also meant she had not only cared for me, held my hand through the turtles, and caressed me to sleep, she'd let me have her, she'd let me enjoy her, she'd let me visit her most sacred space; entwining herself and her feminology around me, passing on grace and goodness, all the while giving me the gentle assurances only women can give, with soft hands, lips, breasts, and warm intimates, that everything's going to be okay, having offered up generously and soulfully her most precious to do it; to show me the love she thought I'd needed. To take me away from myself and my life, to help me escape, to make me feel better even if only for a short while. Even if I'd never remember. She gave that to me. And not telling me purposely so that I wouldn't feel tristful again or lower about myself. She gave that to me, too.

I was wrong. She was more than a 5G Girl, this stranger with no name. And I would love her forever. Though I would never see her again.

I cursed myself. Good old Harry Disconnect. So close. But so far.

The whitecaps of melancholy didn't abate. In fact, they lapped on steadily. I returned to the bedroom and went for the bureau drawer. The purple laces were losing their dye from my clammy mitts. They were unraveling into strings and I knew the feeling. I rewrapped them the best I could and held onto them as I huddled beneath the duvet.

I bawled violently into the pillow, chest heaves and abdominal bucks were involved and it went on until my ribs grieved. This was not happiness or conquest glee, this was a destroyed man in his self-demolition heyday trying to better the big blow, with better than measured success.

One of the most plugged-in cogs in the city, in the world for that matter, I couldn't have felt more alone and detached.

24

DeadBeauties.org

Scandoblind: What Wall Street hedge-fund honcho with an appetite for runaway bonuses by day, is by night a spidermaniacal lech who hosts skinny-dipping parties at his palatial Fifth Avenue pad's indoor pool for pubescent maidens from the Upper East Side's finest finishing schools and pays them a thousand dollars for their enthusiasm and lack of modesty?

The brass wasn't thrilled with me and the big boss wanted to see me first thing Monday. The door was open and he waved me in and his mouth remained a stuck zipper across. He didn't mess around, telling me *Slingshot* had gotten sloppy, that recent items were "lacking and uninspired," featuring mistakes and requiring several retractions. A lawsuit had been filed over a Lindsay Lohan rehab story we'd been scanboozled into covering. The Sling was without merit; its scandosketchy lead had been falsely scandoplanted by some scandoscamming *Post* or *Daily Snooze* insurgent.

Bad Harry.

At the same time, it wasn't unknown I was having personal problems.

"Anything else?"

Arthur Lawrence sat behind the desk of a plush corner office overlooking the Hudson in his ornately-carved wingback, wearing his standard uniform, the immaculate Brooks Brothers charcoal suit and requisite Hermés tie. He was still bugging at me through tortoiseshell rims that were fab circa 1940, his hands folded tightly in his lap. With creamy white hair pasted across his forehead, he had an imposing carriage, and a voice that could crack a walnut. He liked responses short, just like his questions and he drove in one

202 Coerte V. W. Felske

gear: direct. "Yeah. You've gone soft."

"Me or the column?"

"The column. But you are the column."

I knew what he meant. I asked him anyway.

"You avoided Swayze."

"Don't do cancer."

"You missed J.Lo's pregnancy."

"Don't do kids."

"You don't do Paris."

I was about to say, "I've taken a break from starlets," but held off.

"You do do Britney and Lindsay."

"Spears is making a comeback. Lohan was getting clean—or so we thought. That was a mistake. But it was positive."

"Picky, picky…"

I didn't say much to that. I didn't say anything at all.

"Too many sleazy men. Not sexy. Women sell papers. Women behaving badly. Without them you're fucked. As you know. Where are they?"

I only had silence again.

"*Vanity Fair* just released their 'Young Hollywood' issue. I'd like to see those gals in the copy."

"You want me to target?"

"You have budget. And boots on the ground. What about that little troublemaker, the 'Transformers' girl?"

"Megan Fox."

"She seems right up our alley…"

It wasn't a bad idea if he'd come up with it about a year before. "See what I can do, Arthur."

"It's your column."

"Yes, it is."

"But it's my paper." It was his first pause of the day and a lovely time for it. "Maybe you need some time off…"

I told him I didn't.

"Remind yourself, Harold," he said, citing the name he liked to call me. "You don't get paid for your compassion. You get paid for your edge. Don't lose it."

Then he told me to get my ass in gear and start delivering or he'd have to "make a change."

The first keystroke concept that came to mind was, *FQ, Arthur.* The reality is that I didn't care, not a swell attitude for anyone wanting to hold down a job. But the thought of an ADD Militia employment emancipation party held in my honor for losing it did not provide proper solace.

That afternoon was like any other, long and brutal and the items bordered upon the trite and ridic. Not to passionate global scando junkies, necessarily, but I wasn't passionate. Still, something caught my attention. Sling scout Clyde e-mailed me an unsettling photograph of a beautiful woman without a stitch of clothes. A woman I was still mourning.

The starkie of Sunday had been downloaded from an Internet site called *DeadBeauties.org*, a disturbing little outfit which offered everything grotesque in the way of celebrity death scandophernalia. From long-deceased beauties as well as the recently departed. Personal items up were for auction, like monogrammed notepads and toilet seats. Gorgeous. And more upscale merchandise like shoes, clothing, and jewelry. There was gruesome inventory, too. Morgue shots of Marilyn, post-accident shots of a decapitated Jayne Mansfield, every conceivable angle of Anna Nicole's Florida morgue sabbatical, and even underwater crashsite frames of Carolyn Bessette-Kennedy. The brother site for DeadBeauties was *DeadLegends.org,* which featured similar inventory in the male category.

Along with dead body portraiture, the site sold compromising photos of deceased stars. Starkies. Most female stars, at one point in their careers, have found themselves saying *"oui"* to a scando-stark session. Whether out of career desperation, vanity, or during a low period, emotionally or financially, most have done it once. If they were not contracted or meant for publication, and the photographer had the slightest trace of the sleaze gene, or they got into the wrong hands, the photos would be sold. Especially in the *Era Escandalo.* A photo like that could yield five hundred grand worldwide or more.

The photograph of Sunday was tasteful, even breathtaking, shot in the Herb Ritts retro-styled, grainy black-and-white *Playboy* magazine portrait tradition.

I called this Web site's corporate office which was, naturally, located in Los Angeles. The star morgues were right there locked and loaded for bear. And corrupt coroners. And min-wage toe-taggers. I told them who I was and put the weight of the newspaper behind me. I wanted to know who they'd paid for the snaps of Sunday. If they didn't comply, the family would sue them for not having a signed release. And we'd pressure influential friends to close them down. After a hang-up, I got a call back ten minutes later with a name and address.

After work, I asked my driver to spin me over to an address somewhere in the East Village. We were in the town car stopped at a light when the Fonz said suddenly, "Signor Slinger. *Coche—*"

"What?"

His thumb jabbed to the rear, to right behind us. A brown sedan, very American, a Chrysler, I identified. We were being tailed and not secretly. Yet as we motored on, there was no attempt to pull us over, or, leave us alone. I dared a swivel back to get an angle on the faces but the windshield reflection obscured any possible make.

"*Casa*, Fonz…" I figured we were best off just going home.

As we pulled up in front of my Broome Street loft, the sedan slotted easily behind. I didn't venture out. But they did and sidled up. One head dipped low to hawk within, a familiar face. Detective Cipone's. So I spread the door and stood tall.

"Hello, Steve."

"Slinger—"

"Cheers to the police escort home. What's the occasion?"

"You know Marty, right?" He sent back instead.

I told him I didn't and we shook. But I did recognize him. He was the Fifty/Fifty hotballing me at the Oficina, the one who'd suddenly disappeared. I'd been right on. He had been shadowing me.

"So, anything break?"

"Mind if we talk?" He was big on questions for questions.

"Sure thing. Gourmet Garage okay? They've got tables and chairs now. I could use a cup of coffee."

"This your building?" I confirmed it though it was certain he knew already. "Think it'd be better if we came up."

Clearly he didn't care to speak in public. And I favored a trip to the precinct less. There was no reason we couldn't talk in private at my place. Steve was a friend. Or colleague. On the surface, anyway. It wasn't the time to get ornery or complicated.

I gave Fonz permission to take off, and so did the cops. The three of us went up. I made a bold house brew and we sat in the living room, real comfy and homey-like. If you like police officers in your living space asking questions for a fifth time. And informing you there've been no real developments in the case. And questions put to you are no longer distant and impersonal and ditto the looks.

"I can tell you what I know," was my opener.

"At eight-thirty the time of the murder, you said you were home."

"That's correct. So was my roommate. I was home writing. I got over to Sunday's place around nine." I coughed just then. "She was laying there when I arrived."

"Turns out your roommate told us something different," Steve proclaimed.

"Really? I don't understand."

Steve was flapping over the cover of a tiny spiral, taking notes as Marty tossed the metal-tipped, feathered darts. "Tell us again what happened."

"I was here. He was here. What do you mean?"

"He confirmed he was here."

"He was. I was too."

"Not according to him."

"He didn't tell you I was here?"

"He told us he thought you were here. He didn't actually see you."

"He heard me. I was typing. Did he say anything about that?"

"No, he didn't."

"Did you ask him?"

It went disregarded. "And your driver? Where was he?"

"I gave him the night off, like I told Steve. I wanted to write."

"After you discovered the body and notified us you took off—"

"Right. I was very upset."

Marty rose and paced a circle which became a fade across the parquet to the high windows overlooking Broome. He gazed on down. Steve angled pointedly away as Marty treaded back. "What's your relationship with Dr. Van Heugel?" he posed tripping over her name.

"She's my psychoanalyst. Still."

"Have you discussed the night of Sunday's murder with her?"

"Not really."

"Why not?"

"It's been painful. We'll get to it. Soon enough."

"When is that?"

"When I can handle it."

This came from Steve. "The night of the murder, Harry, had you been drinking?"

"I think so. Probably."

"Were you intoxicated?"

"I don't remember, really."

"When we talked before, you said you hadn't been drinking."

I hesitated. "I'm not positive. Maybe I wasn't. I can't be so sure right now. A lot has happened since."

"The bartenders at V.I.P.'s said you had six Mount Gay and OJ's. They showed us the receipt."

"Yes, I drink. Often enough. So I don't remember what nights, exactly. I'm not sure what I did. Or said. But if they say—"

"You have trouble with your memory, don't you?" Marty threw.

The question froze me momentarily. "No, not really." Steve had asked me this recently. I remembered my response. Fortunately.

"You always had trouble with your memory?"

"No."

"You ever black out?"

"Never. I mean not in the memory sense. Sometimes when I drink I can forget things, you know? Things said…"

"Things said?" He hopped on.

"Yeah. Said, not said. Whatever."

"But that night you were drinking. Isn't it possible you could be forgetting some things?"

"I was not in good shape back then, if you know what I mean."

"No, Harry. Tell us. What do you mean?"

"I was medicating a lot."

"Doing what?"

"Drugs."

"What kind?"

"Stimulants."

"Coke?"

"No. Prescription stuff. The Adderrall."

"To help you focus right?" Steve interjected. "Adderall helps you concentrate, not fog you out. Correct?"

"Well, yes. I was taking Zoloft too. And I was drinking."

"You remember that now?"

"You reminded me with your bar receipt."

"Last time we spoke, you said you hadn't taken medication that night. You didn't want to disturb your imagination. For writing."

I obviously hadn't remembered previous responses well. "I'm not so sure, Steve. I thought I wasn't drinking, either."

"Where were you later that night? After V.I.P.'s?"

"At my computer terminal."

"Let me get this straight, sir," Marty said. "You throw back six cocktails and you say to yourself, 'I'm all jacked up on booze and scrip drugs and I think it's time to go home, let go of my driver, go to my computer and write.' Is that painting the proper picture?"

"I'd say you were painting a proper picture. Of any writer or artist throughout the history of the world."

"You don't say."

"Minus the driver," I added for silly wit's sake.

It backfired. Steve angled a razor one at me, a flame rising in his eye. I'd lit it with that one "driver" remark. It had to do with the case and it had to do with me and his hidden disdain for people like me and where he assumed we came from. Privilege, the clothes, the background, the cushy job, the basketball gym-sized loft, the Ivy League pelt. The way of phrasing a sentence. All the advantages his old man never availed him of and probably the reason for their ongoing war. In a flash, I had an interior vision of him. It wasn't about politics; it was a boy's disappointment in his father. Which I understood. That brought on his socio-economic envy. He hated my guts and the backstory was there in that flaming eyeball. Either it was my paranoia talking, or I was right fucking on. Now that he surmised I may not have been telling the truth, the gloves were off. Here came his true colors. It was my fault. He'd been laying in the reeds waiting for an objectionable maneuver and I gave it to him. Or not. It was a Fifty/Fifty. Or less. It could all be rounded off to: I was in deep shit.

I crept my palms along my pants slowly, so they wouldn't see me wiping up. I clamped elbows in to shut down my pits. I didn't need to share I was sweating up a pungent storm, though I always did. Whenever authority figures gave me the third degree. It was Pavlovian, interrogations and running palms. They were a matching antique set gracing the shelves of my checkered personal history.

"Okay, Slinger," Steve said evenly. "Thanks."

"Sir?"

"For the cup of joe," he qualified.

Relief spread through my frame. Enough to call forth, "Have you seen this?"

It was the one of Sunday. The naked photograph. They both eyed it dully a moment and unfazed, they nodded briefly to my surprise.

"Yeah. What a waste."

"Did you talk to the photographer who took those?"

They both craned looks at each other then at me with the same deadpan. Their faces couldn't have been more dead.

"We talk to everyone," Marty said. "Everyone," he underscored with even more poetic detective menace.

"We'll be in touch, Slinger," Steve assured.

But it didn't calm my nerves. They'd been tailing me, for how long I didn't know. But their investigation had brought them knocking. My once-chummy relationship with Detective Cipone had carved out new terrain. At best I no longer had an ally. This was not Harry paranoia, this was not Fifty/Fifty. These feral cats in Homicide, it would seem, were closing in on the empty spaces.

25

One More Notch

July, 2K7

Sunday met Dr. Van den Heugel at Jezebel, a cozy restaurant on Ninth Avenue that specializes in southern home cooking. It catered to Hollywood's African-American A-list. True to form, Denzel was there with his wife. It was a couple months after the Two Lips campaign had hit.

I arrived late and the two were busy getting to know each other. They were well into a bottle of red when I sat down, discussing the good doctor's childhood growing up in Connecticut.

"And horses?"

"We had a stable, yes."

"I would have loved to have horses growing up."

While I chatted with the doctor, I caught Sunday gazing across the room, peering into some distant void. When she snapped from it she produced a tentative smile for me.

"Greer," she initiated in a leading way. "I'm interested in seeing someone professionally."

"The answer is, yes," Dr. Van den Heugel said as she reached across the table and placed a comforting hand atop Sunday's. "Only if it would not be awkward for you, Harry."

I fumbled through it. "Me? I don't think it should be a problem. As long as there's an open exchange of information between us concerning everything Sunday says to you—"

"About me?" Sunday posed.

"No. About me."

We all did laugh, me less than them.

They asked me what was happening in the 'bloid world. I told them the Strokes and Tom Petty were going to play at Wenner's *Rolling Stone* anniversary party, that Axl Rose had purportedly undergone loads of surgery including dreadlock transplants.

"What about Mickey Rourke?" Sunday followed. "Have you seen him? He looks like a burn victim. He was so handsome."

"And what else?" I played. "Oh yes, the Grammy Awards are returning to Radio City next month. And we'll be there…"

"Really?" Sunday sent back weakly.

"Surprise." I sensed she'd be excited to hear the news.

"I didn't know," she said in a failing tone. "Because someone asked Ruth if I would go with them. She asked me and I said sure."

I was surprised. "Who?"

"Aeneas Nitr8."

There was a beat of silence.

"Who's Aeneas Nitr8?" The doctor asked.

"He's a rapper."

"Actually, he's a record producer of rap and hip-hop," I qualified. "Pretty controversial cat. But he had that hit CD, 'The Aeneid.' He's known for sampling other artists' music."

Sure, I'd written him up. He'd worked with the late 2Pac Shakur and had become one of the more publicized record producers in the business. A model-muncher and womanizer, he'd just bought a place in Quogue, a once-elitist, WASPy haven in the Hamptons. He was allegedly pissing neighbors off with noisy construction and modelmageddon parties in the predominantly white and uptight neighborhood. That was the recent Sling.

"Ruth wants me to get my singing going. She said he could help me. If he was interested."

"Singing and acting? How great," Dr. Van den Heugel added.

In pairing Sunday with a gangsta rap producer, manager Ruth was going for the white multi-talented rebel who appeals, meaning sells to, all groups. Attending the awards show with Nitr8 would be fabulous exposure. Like the Two Lips Lesbian Chic campaign, it had an enormous scando quotient.

"Has he listened to your demo tape?"

"No. He's been in L.A. doing something with Beyoncé. Do you

mind, Harry? I won't go if you don't want me to."

I told her I didn't mind. Even though I did. But I knew how The Machine worked and I was part of it. I could only stay silent and let my thoughts get hypocritical.

I performed a soggy snap analysis of Sunday and the doctor's instantaneous mutual admiration society. Deep down, Dr. Van den Heugel resented all that privilege she'd been raised on and the elitism, social artificiality, and disconnection that came with it. And a woman like Sunday who came from a more diversified background and who possessed a colorful personality would glam-slam the point home with exclamation. But Dr. Van de Heugel was sage and unpretentious enough herself to know it. She'd always felt her DNA was boring and unoriginal.

Dr. Van den Heugel was easy to admire for Sunday. She was urbane, and spoke articulately with laser-guided diction and precision, and had an expansive vocabulary. She'd had a superior education, yet she wasn't a snob. She was grounded and cool, which is what Sunday warmed to. It made her feel at ease in her company.

"What are you thinking, Harry?"

"Grumble, grumble…"

They both broke up. They knew I'd been tipping the bottle. Sunday's floating gaze then fixed on a certain someone entering the restaurant. "Harry, look at her—"

"Now that's a beautiful woman," came from Dr. Van den Heugel.

"Do you know her?"

"Why? Should I?" It prompted me to swivel.

"If you don't you should," Sunday remarked. "Looks like someone you should be writing about." She landed a soft hand on my leg.

"Never seen her before."

She was beautiful on the galactic side. She had shoulder-length silky black hair and a medium-shaded *cafe-au-lait* face. She was kind of a modern version of model Beverly Johnson only with more swollen, hornet-stung lips. The sister qualified as pure brown scandosugar.

"Sure you don't know her, Harry?" Sunday pressed.

"Positive."

"What do you think she's like?"

Through the haze of my stupor I realized what Sunday was suggesting. She wanted some spontaneous word-dancing. I'd been drinking to the point where I had no defense like fear or embarrassment to encourage me to balk at the request. And I hadn't taken any meds, so I had all the instruments to the cerebral orchestra available. In the tradition of inebriated fools, I went off on a dazzling scandorant.

"She's milk chocolate fantasy in a black catsuit, the type a whitey like you has always wanted to plant because she scares the hell out of you and what she's capable of doing and you've seen her on the floor ruining others' dance step esteem with a take-a-number attitude and her blowtorch passion she's pure art and curves and living sculpture in motion and you've always wanted a piece and suddenly you're out running solo and you slam into her at the bar and she's on a disastrous date with a deflated dot-commer has seen through his hollow curriculum vitae knows she was conned into the evening and she's had no dinner, only tequila, dressed in scando-skintight leopard and leather bustier and you know she's ready to dust him to make him pay for his deception with an all-out flesh war with someone somewhere if you could only crack the formula and she grabs your hand and yanks you out the door and you're some form of The Chosen One and she motors you without asking to an East Village funk place and shoves you onto the floor and she's perilous curves and all big business and you start to believe you actually could keep up and you do better than ever before because one-in-fifty-million gals like this have a way of transporting you to a higher place and bringing out your better game and as you do it all feels so natural the way it should have been all along and you watch her wonderfully formed lips and you just want to scandoclamp them with yours; they whisper wild witty shit in your ear and you've done a couple of black chicks, but they're footnotes compared to this; she's the queen of them all and you're slamming TQ head to head round for round and it's her drink, not yours, and you're wildly fucked up and it's all so scandodamned surreal and you don't remember the ride home to her apartment only the no-furniture with a palm tree in the middle with swaying fronds you don't know if she's moving in or leaving town but there's marble and you know she's making jack she's too ovenmitt-hot not to and she puts on Dr. Buzzard's Orchestra and the Savannah Band and asks you if you mind if she takes a bath and rips everything off from point blank range you can't believe this body exists perfect medium-sizers with dark 85% cacao-content nipples and it's tall and lean and so damned scandoglam and her moon is the size of a cocoa bonbon from the holiday sampler and she places candles at all corners of the tub kneels and takes you whole for a moment and hops in never letting go of your leash and she hops out wet and smooth and you towel her off getting your first feels and she leads you by a graceful, deliberate hand onto the beige-sheeted bed and the lights are deliciously low and she starts circling you on hands and knees like a fierce midnight man-eating predator with night vision because the bedroom is her jungle and she has all the advantages and she lunges and takes a panther bite out of your neck and more aggressive fellatio so beautiful it hurts, but you retreat so as not to go off too furiously too fast and you plant your face in her nest and make a tequila-induced mess until you're upside down and dizzy and she directs you up and with a tiny buzzing motor in hand she fades back and she wants you straddling her hands thrusting you forward into her face, nails ripping your ass as you scandoram her bean against the headboard, filling her windpipe while she has the motor running for long moaning minutes and after she's all content and motorized and done with the harsh, she whispers "*merci* for the skullfuck," at which time she guides you down gently and you fall sweetly back into her arms and kiss gently and softly and for all the scandosex that was, now there's the soft and it doesn't stop until those swollen lips melt into yours and you penetrate slowly slowly deeply and the soft new harmony lasts until the wee hours and she's flying somewhere like Madagascar in the morning and finally tells you she does have a boyfriend and she needs to work things out but it's no revelation, not this one; has she ever been single even for a weekend? and you walk home dazzled and elated but sad too 'cause it's the one-nighter of the fucking century never to be repeated, never to be undone and you revisit it every time you're alone and

aroused and it never fails because it has become your prime of all
time memory and you see her from time to time and you both care
for each other but you know it could never be repeated and you
just move on and live with that but since you know there's sugar
like that out there it makes you a scandoslave to the experience and
keeps you in a subconscious but forever state of random alert as the
taste remains in your mouth strong and instantaneously erotic and
you know you want to taste it again somewhere sometime before
your heart stops beating."

Only occasionally is your timing perfect because my spontaneous
scandorant needed to be hushed as someone was gliding past who
didn't need to listen in, her hand caressing my shoulder along the
way.

"Hey, Slinger," she piped without waiting on intros, a what-
is-this-a-deli?-there-are-hot-buns-but-take-a-damned-number
attitude sustained perfectly, along with the signature Patron tequila
breath.

There was a lull and the ladies stayed silent. They didn't ask any
questions and therefore, I didn't have to tell any lies.

The town car ride home was equally noiseless but when asked
she chose without hesitation. "Skybox."

Upon arrival she cracked open a bottle of champagne, pouring
two flutes, and once we were upstairs, her movements continued
deliberately and in a determined way. She seemed to have a
special vision for what remained of the evening. "Where are the
Dutchies?"

I shook my head resolutely, meaning they were not around.

"Do you have any toys?"

"Uh, no. I mean yes."

"Are they your toys?"

"No. Someone left them."

"In the year B.M.?"

She'd called it right, the year "Before Me." I opened the third
bureau drawer and pulled out the black bag. It belonged to the Love
Child and had been there a while. Oddly, she hadn't tried to reclaim
it.

"Okay Slinger, let's turn it up another notch—"

It was the first time she'd ever called me that.

Sunday rifled through the chrome, leather, and studded contents, the bullets, beads, collars, weights, masks, the mini bullwhip, and items which needed current. I told her all metals and alloys had been put through the dishwasher, the leathers had not. She settled on cuffs, rings, and a strap-on and before I knew it I was prisoner in my own Skybox. Suspecting my sweet tale of brown sugar had prodded her imagination, she did everything imaginable to me. Drunk and willing, I took it like a scandochamp.

Lockdown bondage activity always held a controversial place in my heart and my girl sensed that. I'd revealed my lockdown issues from childhood and it's why she chose the chrome: to enhance my experience. It's one thing to have a phobia of being locked up but when a beautiful woman with beautiful interiors, in essence, someone you love, ensnares you and does the rest, it's an indescribable sensation of pleasure and pain. Sunday played me like a fiddle, she knew what to do and its cousin: how to do it.

It hadn't gone unnoticed that Sunday would take my biggest fears and target them aggressively as in, scandosexually: a form of therapy. With half-built houses and bondage-type lockdowns, these were ways to exorcise me; not through memory strain and psych pressure, but during acts of pleasure, making the process painless and enjoyable. She attacked my fears like Dr. Hoskins, the only doctor I ever appreciated growing up, the one who'd advised me all those years before. She was instinctively cognizant, and, talk about a dreamgirl.

A couple hours, surface abrasions, general redness of the skin, and a bottle of fizzies later, she dug in the bag again and searched. I asked her to check the bedside utility drawer then my desk downstairs. I would have assisted but I had no hands.

The conclusion was immediate. The key was gone. "Yikes," was a thought.

It was five in the morning on a Sunday. I had a limited tool stash, nothing in the league of a metal saw. I phoned the Love Child on the other side of the world in Hong Kong. She wasn't in. I texted her in quadruplicate. I started to get nervous so Sunday slipped me some medication to calm myself. I began to sweat.

I late-rang the super who'd been asleep and became irked when I woke him but he claimed there were stacks of menus and advertorial service cards left by local businesses in the building's foyer. Movers, exterminators, dry cleaners, and locksmiths. Sunday went down to check and returned with a locksmith's card boasting the emergency twenty-four hour service. She tried the number and miraculously he offered to come over perhaps because we'd insisted that "money's no object."

It took effort not to lose it as we waited. I'd been scandomanacled unwillingly for more than an hour, two if you count the pleasurable part. I mind-gamed for diversion, had Sunday make some bold, and I downed several cups to stay calm and cool.

He was an Irish guy named Pat who'd motored in from Queens. Sunday was in such a state of panic she was still wearing strings when he came in. Thankfully, she put baggy cargo pants on me, thanks again for the baggy feature. We sprayed the room with excuses but Pat knew what was up. "I don't judge nobody," he said. Then he sent a metal prod inside the keyhole and the lock popped. Knowing what could have transpired if I hadn't been freed, I was all too aware I'd dodged a calibered whizzer.

Pat asked for four hundred, I pushed for three hunnies, and we settled on three-fifty when he reminded me of the "money's no object" clause, adding the Queens transportation costs for overkill.

Once he was gone, she and I went to bed almost immediately.

"Random-alert," she chimed referring to my choice of phrase earlier in the night. "Were you on random-alert when you met me?"

"No, spontaneous word choice of a former word toy—"

"The fact that you have that toy readily available in your vocabulary would pretty much indicate—"

I wasn't hiding diddly, so I cut in. "All right, perhaps I was…"

"Because that is you."

"Wait, darling. May I ask where this is coming from?"

"Isn't it?"

I paused. "It had been me. Romantic life in New York exacerbates it. Ask anyone single in this town if they're on random-alert or not."

"Don't hide behind an entire city, Harry. Makes you pretty easy to spot."

"What do you want me to say? That I've spent all my years scandotramping around?"

Her mouth curved in a sardonic way. I noted she no longer needed to call me Slinger. She'd been released of some angst and, perhaps, sexual tension. She was riding on something else, some unspoken pleasure. Or pain. Or a mixture, with relish winning over, but just barely.

"Harry, Harry. Sweet Harry. Women are like bonbons to you. You pick one, try it, have your taste, and then put it back in the box. Then you sample another…"

"I'm laughing but it sounds pretty objectionable."

It was her tone which was striking, the voice deeper, most of the southern sugar drained from it. I'd never heard her speak this way.

"On the contrary. It's pearls and chilled Cosmos, the smoothest. Your combination of wily sunshine is deadly. Because when you open that box, you inspect the contents carefully and give the impression of sincere interest. Because you are sincere. In your interest. Then you have your taste. If it's pleasing you'll have another bite but you never eat the whole thing. You put it back in the box. Neatly. Carefully. Oh so carefully. In its wrapper. So that it keeps its form, luster, shape, and shine. So it can be finished off by someone else. And that's what drives women wild about you…"

"You don't say."

"You use a napkin, pay the check, and don't leave a messy trail. Bet they all say great things about you, Harry. Why? 'Cause they never feel used."

"Or strung along, perhaps?"

"You understand their predicament. And feel their pain. It's admirable."

"Too primitive any other way. I'll ask again. What's prompting this discussion?"

"Bet you've had scores of other men's wives. Maybe more—"

It seemed she was trying to make me feel perversely proud, so I let her run with it. There was an element of sly play in her demeanor, too, which was coolly mysterious and thereby, alluring.

"Everyone gets married eventually," I half-quipped.

"But you had the ones everyone else wanted for life, only you put them back in the box."

I gamed along. "Town is full of Zirconias, Standby Guys, and Wham-Bam, Thank You, Sams…"

"Zirconias? You mean false diamonds?"

"Precisely. Women with whom you know there's no potential for a future."

"Worthy of a cubic zirconia stone and not the real thing, is that it? Genius boy…"

"While gals coast along with Standby Guys, ones they won't marry, preferring to hang around in Dr. Seuss's 'Waiting Place,' to rebound or regroup, refortify, and reevaluate, waiting to trade up to more suitable marriageable types. And the Thank You, Sams, the bold brashettes, adopting methods previously reserved for men, who take you for a night and all you're good for. And don't text back."

"Women have made a comeback."

"More like a *coup d'état*. In fifty years, maybe less, you're all going to be sperm bankers. Designing your own tots. And men will be plush toys. Fuzzy, cuddly, but totally useless. And disposable. Puffed away in a cloud of our own shortcomings. Getting slave wages at the sperm bank. With no repro plumbing of our own, we're fucked. And fading away by the day. How's that for a future?"

"Careful. I worked in a doctor's clinic, remember. Top sperm goes for twelve hundred dollars. Based upon the DNA strength. Meaning disease-free, drug-free. The perfect sperm with few impurities."

The smile made its way to my face. "Supersperm, you're saying. What would be my rate?"

"One-hundred-fifty, maybe. With all your medications, you're not very desirable, sorry to say. One strand of hair will tell you…"

"So I'm a bargain, then…"

"Perhaps."

"Would you bank me?"

"What's the name of that web site? You never know.com."

"There's a book—*Supersperm Meets the Perfect Egg*."

"But the offspring would probably result in a boring, geeky, do-gooder. Don't think I'd enjoy his company."

"Are you the Perfect Egg?"

"Harry, Harry… *Hardly.*"

I wondered why she was so self-deprecating and absolute.

"Cripes," I said upon reflection. "All you need now is a woman President. And then you'll have nukes. Nukes and repro equipment: a pretty potent combination. You'll have it all. And the world will be yours."

"See, deep down inside you, there is a feminist trying to pop out," she mused.

I tried to kiss her and she pulled away, still grinding away at something.

"But still," she redirected, "you've never wanted any ''Til death do us part.'"

"It was never about conquest. It was never about what partners were lacking. It was about what I didn't have. I was flawed. And couldn't trust myself. So I stopped seeing normal, caring types worthy of long-term unions. Romance for me became less nourishing. Until now…"

"Mmmm, Harry." She almost granted me that kiss, the elusive one I'd been craving for minutes on end. "But you still show up at the Christmas parties and the husbands slap you on the back like an old school chum, all the while she knows you've sampled her, you've had your taste, you've had her out of the wrapper. Sound familiar?"

I'd never witnessed this provocative, performance side of her. It seemed Sunday could do spontaneous verbal outpourings too. She was on a roll and I was fascinated, more like transfixed.

"Vaguely, perhaps. And only if she had her taste too."

"Sure she did. You're good for that. And you all get your little 'scando jollies' as you say. You and the slut-wife. But her more than you. Slut-wives live for that sort of thing. Especially when things start to crumble at home. Makes them ooze doubly they misbehaved. Careful, Harry. Always take a good peek over your shoulder…"

"Sounds like a warning."

"Like 'never believe your own press.' Never underestimate the power of jealousy. And revenge."

"You sound so noir right now. I have to add, deliciously so."

"You make me noir. And alcohol helps."

"Ava Gardner would be proud."

"See? You're pure silk."

"I like it. A lot. Especially the part when you tell me how you really feel about me."

"Don't get me wrong. You're nice to women. In fact, you're a dream. You're one of the few who truly love them. Women, I mean. You treat them well. As a man you think like a woman and as a woman you think like a man. They feel it and it warms them. Fancy-fine…"

"Surprised?"

"With what you've told me of your life growing up? Especially. You're not unfaithful to *love*. Only to your lover. And you have reason to be, it goes way back. But your sensitivity to it wins the day."

She'd found Harry's private island again. This time I concurred with her.

"The compassion shaves away any perceived awful male edge women constantly find themselves fleeing. No, it's not 'dull,' anything but, the four-letter word women hate most. More than 'c-u-n-t' even. They trust you. With their affections, their secrets, and their bodies. And their preferences. After a few hours with you Harry they'll do anything. Isn't that right? They feel safe and they'll get daring. Has a woman ever told you you couldn't do anything you wanted to her?" She did pause. "Thought so. Oh, how you love women…"

"I won't lie to you…"

"It wouldn't pass muster."

"Sometimes turnover can be crucial, for both. But not necessarily for sex. For company. New and improved company."

"Companionship?" She broke up with. "Sure. Don't worry, I like the fact other women want to meet you. I like the fact women want to fuck you. You're worth fucking. But even more impressive, you're worth keeping."

"Thanks, glamorous. But that's the old Harry."

"Would you say I know you well?"

I didn't answer it and didn't have to. "My life is different now."

"It's a good life, Harry. I like it. It warms me too. You're smart. Sexy. Confident. But no matter what you say or think, or how much you feel you deserve all you get, deep down you have to know one thing. You were given a gift. And in the deepest recesses of your mind you have to be asking yourself that one question. Why? Yes, meaning me. Because I am a gift. I know it. And I'm drunk enough to admit it. I can be responsible for thrills men dream their lives away about. And I get to choose, I always choose. And I chose you. But why, Harry? Why you? Haven't you ever asked yourself that question?"

"Yes. I have."

"Let's make it easy. I'll tell you. Because you feel it. You feel the pain. A *woman's pain.* And I feel you feeling it. That's why I chose you, that's why I fuck you. If you care to know, that's why I love you, Harry."

"I do care to know." The kiss was on at last, our lips pressing together passionately, and it endured.

After a delicious while, she broke back in. "So what was her name?"

"Whose?"

"That cafe au lait siren at the restaurant—"

"Jasmine. Jazzy for short."

"You didn't introduce us."

"She didn't hang around."

"So did she or didn't she?"

"What?"

"Choose you. She is the choosing type too, after all."

"No. She didn't."

"You were just teasing me?"

"Okay. It's half true."

"Which half?"

"The good half."

I didn't say anything more.

"Well, if you didn't, you should have."

Sunday never brought up the subject again.

We made hard, competitive love that early morning which gave way to big releases. The loaded conversation had something to do with it. My phone rang too. I heard the message later. It was the Love Child being her cool, take-no-prisoners self. As for the missing key? She said she'd taken it with her. To make sure I'd call like I promised.

26

PTSD *Plus* (French)

Most people did find me confident in the way I spoke and carried myself. I could bust out alpha male with the magnetism of a Silverback and send a room atwitter with the best of them. But there were corrections. Oftentimes, the composure I projected was an act. I'd had a self-esteem problem since childhood. A misdiagnosed ADD kid often takes all those "stupid," "lazy," "unreachable," "hyper," "different," "weird," "out of control," "crazy," and even, "psychotic" labels on the chin. For eighteen years in my case. I'd made tremendous progress since then, but some residual damage was certain to remain. The exoskeleton was hard but thin and crackable. I was damned fragile.

My fear was Sunday seeing me at my worst. Manic, ill-tempered, and in a state of high anxiety, the dark side of my condition. An episode of the sort hadn't happened in a while. Still, the ticking time bomb was always there, tocking off, ready for any spark to set off the clock and ignite it.

I'd been medicated on alcohol and stimulant pills the night we engaged in the scandocuff stuff. The coffee also served to calm me. So the anxiety, scandopanic, and depression brought on by the pressure of being restrained had been quelled.

Weeks later, I had a relapse into self-destructive thinking and the dark side of my persona surfaced. The fears I'd been suppressing were in a flash realized. Oh so regrettably.

It happened in July. The week had been a rough one. I hadn't been productive at the office. Sunday had begun to see Dr. Van den Heugel and she started becoming reticent. And increasingly distant. She was working hard on her singing, which was draining, but she'd developed a psychological inner life to which I was not privy. We'd stopped making love.

One night we attempted to have sex and the passion was not there. She was going through the motions. I didn't question her, I turned over to go to sleep only I couldn't. My mind was racing on devastating thoughts. It was always how it started and then it came. The Big M was on. I hadn't had any migraines recently, but this one was splitting my crown. Bad news for Harry.

I slid open my bedside utility drawer and silently downed a couple from my prescription bottle. I assumed Sunday was asleep.

"Why do you take those pills?" She asked, awake after all.

"They calm me down."

"Are you nervous?"

I could feel my feet sweating beneath the duvet. The toes were ice cold. "No."

She reached over me to dig in the drawer and pulled out a bottle, but not the one I'd taken from. "Zoloft," she read aloud. "What is it for? An STD?"

"I don't have any STDs, or haven't you found out yet?"

"I'm kidding. You okay?" She studied me close. "Why are you crying?"

"Those are bed tears," I claimed. "Because I'm so happy."

What's true is I had been the happiest I'd ever been but I was in the midst of a serious banger. A migraine to the third, a trigraine. I wanted to let the night go, but Sunday pressed on. "Please tell me."

"I've told you." The annoyance in my voice was unmistakable.

"About the Adderall. But not about the Zoloft."

"*Booze and pills and powders / You gotta choose your medicine…*"

"What?"

"I'm quoting. Keith."

"Zoloft is for depression and bipolar people. Is that how you're feeling?"

"If you're an expert on meds, you should know how I'm feeling."

"Touchy, aren't we? I read up on it, Harry. In your library…"

"Hey, what is this? Why are you badgering me?"

"Easy. I'm just asking. I'm concerned."

I could feel myself falling into the abyss. I was trying to lift the weight. To redirect, to get out of that morose dark corner. But it was so easy to snap and let loose. You knew it was going to be ugly, but part of your psyche needed to let the pressure out, to bring your mind back to a peaceful equilibrium. I was in trouble.

"Please," she asked gently. It irked me more to hear her tone of sugar substitute concern. I tried coaching myself.

You can do it, Harry.

"In addition to ADHD, I have a condition. Supposedly," I added. "That's all I want to say."

That's it, Harry. Easy, boy.

"What condition? Post-traumatic stress disorder?"

"Read up on that, too?" She didn't answer and I left it alone. I had to. *Use your sense of humor.* "America has PTSD. After those planes hit the towers? Why do you think the world hates us? We've been lashing out from our PTSD. The country needs scandomeds. America needs Zoloft."

"Seriously, Harry."

I let it loose in a low tone. "I get headaches."

It's okay, you're freeing up and unlocking your senses. The low, even tone and slow delivery is good. Stay with it, Harry.

"What kind?"

"You know the city of a thousand and one syndromes, disorders, phobias, and conditions. Well, my head hit the jackpot."

Good on you, Harry. Keep using your sense of humor. You're coming out of it.

"Which one?" She'd been holding the bottle all this time.

Stay truthful. Let the pessimisties pass. Define its color. Bright red. Define its shape. Round. Like a balloon. A big red balloon filled with helium. And it's going to rise out of your skull and fly. Fly away. Far away. Fly, fly, fly…

"Can you tell me which one?"

Don't give in. Stay the course. It's rising now. The big red balloon is rising up. Sailing away. Let it go. Watch it go…

She said my name again. Then three times. It was so damned disturbing to hear her repeat it as my brain banged and banged.

"Come on, Harry. I'm trying to understand—"

The balloon seems heavy. Why? Dammit, it's going too slow. Now it's dipping. Why isn't the medication working? The balloon is starting to float down. It's bullshit! Trying to deceive yourself into feeling better. Now it's gonna burst. I can't stand this shit medication! I can't take it! POP!

"Harry, talk to me. Please."

There goes my song. "I got a bomb in my temple and it's going to explode/I got a sixteen gauge buried under my clothes/I pray!!"

My throbbing head couldn't take it anymore. It started in my chest, a rumbling tempest in need of release. It was a rant, with accusations, insults, the words tearing through the air like exploded missile shrapnel. I flew, totally scandoschitzo. The scandotantrum was on.

"I'll tell you, it's an anxiety disorder for people exposed to extreme trauma. Like PTSD, only worse. Why? There's pain. A sledgehammer trigraine. Common associated feelings are horror, panic, and general helplessness. And fear, don't forget. Me, personally? I feel fear, often. And since you've been so southern sweet and exhaustively polite and relentless, I'll tell you my traumatic event. Three years after my mother died, I was fifteen and sufficiently hating life in that Reform School for Unreachables and I got this toothache but they wouldn't let me go to the infirmary. So the pain gnawed away at me for days until I had a full blown abscess with no intervals in between the excruciating assaults. I couldn't stand it. I smashed the window to my room, scaled down the fire escape, and broke out. I climbed fences and hitchhiked and bloodied my knees and ran through yards and took a bus, all to reach my father's house in Durham, New Hampshire. And when I arrived the following afternoon, I stormed in and heard voices in the bedroom. That's when I saw good old Dad in bed with another man. Screwing the afternoon away. So what did I do? I knew you were going to ask so I'll tell you…"

I leaned in and yelled it at her stunned face.

"I smoked a damned cigarette! That's what I did! Why?" I asked mimicking her voice. "Because it seemed like the thing to do! And you know what? While we're on the subject I'll tell you I don't believe this extreme traumatic event affects me. My father's fucking gay. So the hell what? I chalk it up to a genetic jumble in his map, even. He and his pal Maurice live up in that sleepy college town.

They've been together all these years and I'm real happy if he's happy, you know what I'm saying? God forbid if Daddy had chosen the wrong guy. I mean, then he would have been on the gay love circuit and have shallow empty experiences in a careless serial way until he found his true love. Just like the rest of us, right?"

Sunday didn't respond. Water was welling in her lids.

"Right??"

She nodded in a silently resigned way.

"BUT, when you factor in all that delicious backstory beauty to the rest of the saga, you get a marvelous tale of family historical greatness and triumph—the fact that my sister drowned in a creek days shy of her ninth birthday, that my mother's heart stopped thumping in addition to the broken heart she'd endured prior concerning the fact that she'd had a goddamn lemon child or functional retard as it were, HOWEVER! you want to call it—ME—in reform school getting locked up and pinned down on the wooden paddle honor system, then, I ask you, Miss Fairchild, to give me and my family the proper respect we deserve as one of the great dysfunctional stories of recent times. PLEASE! A little applause would do."

"Oh sure, you could say I'd had nothing to do with it. That my sister died accidentally and my Mom died of a disease that had taken the lives of many in her family tree. You could say that. You could say my father and mother had split not because of me but due to the fact that he was a closet soft boy and they'd been mismatched and doomed from the start. You could make that case. BUT, you can't deny I didn't start us off on the wrong foot, that I initiated the Big Struggle, that I got the ball rolling in a most divisive and destructive way, that I broke the big unit down. Give me the damned credit, will you??"

"NOW, was it my parents' fault my disorder was misdiagnosed? You could assume it, that they didn't investigate, that they sent me to the wrong school for the wrong treatment. Then those school doctor wizards botched it too with my medications and therapies, from an entire roster of modern medical whizzes, experts, psychiatrists, psychoanalysts, disorder coaches, and support groups. You name it, they've all said it! That it wasn't my fault. And on the positive side it gets better. I'm in excellent company! The company of geniuses!

Albert Einstein, Mozart, Thomas Edison, and Ben Franklin—all fractured-brained, ADHD-heroic, neurological disorder demigods. The doctors have all said it! The Who's Who of great scientific brains have all corroborated it! To make little Slinger feel better about himself. But the truth of that matter is that no one knew about this disorder shit back then; it is blameless, and the only thing that is absolutely true beyond the shadow of a doubt is the fact that I'm a pure, one hundred percent genetic FUCK-UP! and you can't take that away from me. Now, how does that answer your saccharine-sweet southern belle probe, Miss Fairchild?" I dragged it out with my best caustically sarcastic Dixie drawl.

Sunday was still motionless, sobbing.

"And since you're here with me now and so anxious to communicate regarding the issues at hand, let's get back to something we pretend to care about. Us! Now you know you're using me and I know I'm using you—"

"Harry—"

"Why don't we just have a little campfire Boy and Girl Scout-styled, vent-our-feelings chitchat about the fact that you think you can do a lot better than me and I can do better than you and that we are both mutually manipulating each other and ours is nothing more than a relationship pit stop, that we're Waiting Place people, we're both rolling our knuckles on tabletops, jiggling nervous knees, waiting for *The Bachelor* subplots to reveal themselves and who's going to fly overboard on *The Deadliest Catch* and passing the time until we both find something more to our liking in the shape of the Bigger, Better, Heel! And for you, it's some bloated West Coast talent-combined-business manager slash sloppy, sweaty, and piggish lover who you'll have to let roll over onto you in the A.M. because of all the movie roles, day rate hikes, cosmetic campaigns, and contracts galore he's getting you, and for me, it's some faux-brainy supermodel with oodles of trashy backwoods charm who's just gotten the nod from Fox to host the new *Project Runway* show and I dutifully and enthusiastically take her on so that I can press the flesh with; not only her, but all the other semi-brainy pretty types who will fall in after her because they want a piece of the guy who beds their childhood model icon nightly, and it temporarily anesthetizes them, making them all feel better about their grim and desperate low-glam lives that have been filled with hipster parasites, cyber rapists, dubious mashers, *Dateline* peds and pervs, and general nightclub riffraff wreaking havoc on their little bodies since they were thirteen and I'll be all too willing to accommodate them! Does that sound accurate or was I incorrect about time slots or something??"

I clamped her chin for a response.

She uttered forth, barely audible: "Stop it, Harry."

"Now, it must make you feel totally terrif inside to know all four of my bagged cats."

My worst fear had been realized. The emotional acid had risen up, the time-released explosives had gone off. A stream flowed over my face with a will of its own. Sunday bobbed into her hands.

"I'm sorry, Sunday," I whispered finally. Even though I couldn't recall what I'd said. I was in a state of disorientation, also part of the condition. You don't know what the hell you've done. There's too much static and you never remember.

And the questions echo and reverberate in your head. Where the hell am I? What the hell did I do?

I scaled down the stairway and lit up, paws trembling. I moved into the kitchen and made coffee. My bitter disposition ebbed along with the scandomanic panic. After a while, it hit me. The medication I'd been taking, in addition to the reality of what had happened. It was too late to wish I hadn't said anything.

Bad, bad Harry.

The next day, Sunday dropped off the envelope. She couldn't tell me directly. It would have been too emotional. That's what she wrote in the letter. More importantly she claimed she didn't want to see me anymore.

The letter wasn't any literary masterpiece. The gist of it was that it wasn't because of me or my scandotantrum. It was because of her. She needed to be by herself. She'd been mulling this course for a while, probably for as long as she'd been seeing the psychoanalyst. My psychoanalyst. Another Broadway bonus.

27

Road Trip

August, 2K7

Of course I missed her.

No matter how many people were assembled around me at work or in the Hamptons that August, I couldn't shake the loneliness. Something was always missing, rather, someone.

Fortunately, she didn't drop out of my life. We frequently spoke on the phone. She informed me what was happening with work, her castings, jobs, and offers. The appointments with Dr. Van den Heugel yielded personal "breakthroughs." I didn't know what she'd meant by that. I'd never known much about her past, but she seemed content and we were communicating.

The first week in September, I decided not to attend the MTV Movie Awards. Sunday was going with Nitr8. They were to attend the Grammys months before, but the hip-hop mogul had been in Europe; this was the rain check. They brought Dr. Van den Heugel along with them. Nitr8 was still "interested" in doing a record with Sunday, but I didn't know how serious the proposition was.

Sunday got home at six in the morning the night of the show. How did I know? She'd called me and I tried not to think of the implications. I didn't like the sound of six A.M., for selfish, meaning jealous, reasons. Six is a mysterious hour. If it's five, you just think your lady's been out dancing, had a lot of champagne, maybe a can of Red Bull to keep her going, but it's respectable. Seven or beyond, it means all hell had broken loose. Six in the morning is mysterious, it's not five and it's not seven. It's in-between and what the hell happened in that in-between time? I wasn't the boyfriend anymore, though emotions were still firing as if I was.

When I returned home that night, Sunday was at my place having tea with Kees and Miep. Her face looked puffy; she'd been crying. I sensed a release of the sort was bound to happen as so much had happened to her so fast. And she'd had a late night. I spied the packed suitcase beside the couch.

I gave her a hug and water fell out of her eyes. She joined me in the bedroom and I closed the Japanese screens and we sat on the bed in silence. I would let her do any talking.

"I think they want to do the record."

"They liked the new cuts?" Sunday had recorded two new songs for this meeting.

"I thought they were going to laugh me out of the car."

"You played it in his car?"

"They had a limo for us."

"Who else was there?"

"Sophocles. He's works in the studio."

"How did Nitr8 leave it with Ruth?"

"Said he wants to put a million dollars into it. Thinks I'm a white Sade, with 'more soul,' he said."

"When does he want to start?"

"Two weeks."

"Fast track. Sounds good."

"Fast, right? Too fast…"

"Did Greer have a good time?"

"She met a lot of people. Everybody was there. Except you. I was hoping to see you—"

"It was your night." Fresh tears were blazing a muddy mascara path down her cheeks. "Tell me," I prodded gently.

"I don't know… what to say."

She cried as I held her tight and said nothing. I would let her divulge at her own pace, and only if she wanted to.

"I think it's all the stuff with Greer…"

"The memories?"

"Too many. Coming at me all at once."

"Painful, I know."

"Momma getting sick," she stuttered, chin quivering. "Things I swept under the rug. They're alive again and every day new ones pop up. About her, about…" Her voice, broken by a heave, returned deeper as she added, "…Daddy."

She angled up, more water filling the eyes. "I want to…" she stuttered. "Will you take me home, Harry?"

My head swiveled away.

Sunday needed a flat-out break. She was experiencing emotional fallout from the sessions, The Machine, the works.

"You know I will."

I called my travel agent Linda and she got us a morning flight to Pensacola. She scored my required seat, 11-J. It's on an emergency exit aisle and has the most leg room for excitable ADDers. I brought meds too. All shapes, sizes, and colors. I wasn't going to allow for another outburst. Ever.

28

Scandalicious

The morning papers ran the interracial scandoslant. There was the Two Lips Girl-with-rapper romantic linkage all over town and in cyberspace. The new "couple" was on *Entertainment Tonight, Access Hollywood,* and *The Insider.* I scanned Web photos from my laptop. The Machine-induced hype and scandal psychology was simple. Generationally bear-trapped adults would be thinking, "Oh my God! Outrage!," while the I-Agers emblazoned and imbued with hip-hop culture would be thinking "Sunday, you rock!," rebellious dreams and taboo urges fulfilled. The Sling was juicy, it was fresh and provocative. And most eye-poppingly, it was interracial. A scando grand slam.

A master of the fresh worldwide embrace of scandalocity, manager Ruth Gunn-Glaser had employed appropriate strategies. She'd taken the same-sex angle on the ad campaign. Though an advertisement, a scando-intensive image beamed out globally, would no doubt crawl around in the minds of scandofans, teasing them into thinking the subject was someone to watch, look for, and follow. The lesbian angle gave it the scansational pop. Once Ruth sent her Two Lips Girl and Aeneas Nitr8 out on an interracial red carpet "date," all she had to do was sit back, ride the remote, surf the 'Net, order in from Fresh-Direct, and respond to offers on Monday morning. Sunday was perfect copy for this machinery. She was gorgeous, talented, new, and hot. *Scandalicious.*

In the end, Ruth's strategy was spot-on. Her office became further inundated with more requests for talk show appearances, will-you-chair-this events?, movie offers, and endorsements. It was The Machine at its most efficient, effective, and—terrifying.

29

Riviera Dreaming

Sunday slept for most of the flight. I didn't receive any vacation site briefing. I mulled inevitable thoughts of a reconciliation but was content to go with the flow. I was intrigued at the thought of visiting the Redneck Riviera from the name alone. I wanted to pepper Sunday with questions like a schoolboy on a field trip, but she was sensitive to her background and the recent psychotherapy had been challenging for her. It was risky for me to inquire. I figured the less that was dredged up, the better. After all the spirit-draining dialogues it was no surprise she was slumbering peacefully.

I knew enough geography to know we were flying to the Florida panhandle, the place where the state abuts Alabama and Georgia. The Redneck Riviera got its name from vacationers comprised mainly of Deep South out-of-staters, from Louisiana as well, who gathered annually to enjoy the eclectic beachfront lifestyle. For this reason as Sunday noted, the further north you go in Florida the more southern it gets.

We touched down in Pensacola and the sunshine was blazing. We both had carry-on bags and we rolled them to the Hertz counter, where I picked up the keys of a flashy red convertible Ford Mustang, a fast sucker. Sunday didn't speak much, but smiled weakly in her silence. As we left the airport, however, I needed her participation.

"Take Interstate 10 east to Route 85 south. And look for the sign to Niceville."

"Niceville?" I posed back with a smile.

"Nice town, nice people, Niceville," she half-sang in an upbeat jingly sort of way.

Niceville. Though I was far from being on the job, it was the kind of name an item reporter for a gossip blog could dream of.

"It's home of the Boggy Bayou Mullet Festival. And it has just about 343 days of sunshine each year." I heard her southern accent slip in place, which was sweet. She giggled too. "Known for the most beautiful sugar-white beaches in the world."

We pulled over and Sunday went into a convenience store to purchase a cooler. I Blackberried in and logged on. Niceville had a Web site. The town was part of Okaloosa County and the average year-round temperature was 74 degrees. But April's average was in the low 80s. Eglin Air Force base was located nearby.

I got off I-10 at the Niceville exit and took in the scenery. The route cut through the base and the government tract extended for miles. We came upon more convenience stores and bait shops. Niceville itself was on the water, the Choctawatchee Bay. The names of places were dazzling, the word toyz piling.

Sunday showed me downtown which was quaint and the people were smiley. And took their time. You could feel the relaxed pace, a welcomed respite and refrain from the bustle of Manhattan.

We left town and turned down a street called Bluewater, which carved through a thick pine forest. At the end of the road we followed a private dirt drive that meandered beneath tall oaks with hanging Spanish moss. We came upon a boarded-up A-frame perched on the bay. There was a run-down hammock hanging at left with no cars in the driveway. We got out and I followed Sunday toward the house. She seemed to be in a trance, offering a caressing hand to the trunk of an old, twisted myrtle tree as she passed.

We moved to the back of the house to the water. The house had a wide porch that overlooked a calm sleepy bay.

"This is Daddy's house," she said finally. "My house, too."

"Where you grew up?"

"Yes, sir," she said and angled up sharply, as if she'd said something I might pick up on. A vague smile followed.

Sunday hopped on the porch and pulled away a floor panel to extract a key, an A&W key chain attached to it. She maneuvered back around and unlocked the front door.

We stepped inside, and the house's interior was as modest as its exterior. There was a living room with a window looking out on the porch, the dining room almost inseparably beside. There was a small wood-paneled kitchen with Formica countertops. To the left and down the hall was the master bedroom. Two smaller bedrooms were across the hall to the right. The rooms looked untouched and the house had an abandoned smell of damp and decaying pine.

"Place has been empty a while," Sunday said. "Daddy doesn't usually come here until summer. He has an apartment up in Panama City. And a club too. But he's originally from Port St. Joe."

"A nightclub?" She nodded. I debated asking a question, but it seemed a natural follow-up. "Where is your father now?"

"Out of town."

I'd been under the impression we were going to meet him but didn't say anything.

"We'll see Daddy on Tuesday."

Our next move was a trip to town for weekend supplies.

30

Real Nice in Niceville

The place was cozy and the location by the water made it serene and idyllic. "Lazy" also described the setting. We sat out back and drank a few beers. My shirt came off and I sported an unhealthy urban white chest along with sun-seeking black pants, a silly carryover from my urban metro uniform. Sunday put on a bikini, an automatic wardrobe choice when she returned home. She looked all too terrif in the suit, aqua bottoms and a black top. I lasted all of ten minutes before the urge set in to become affectionate once again.

Sunday's only maneuver was to wrap herself in a pink sarong and gaze across the bay. She was winding down. The quiet allowed me to rid my mind of hollow nonsensical Slingers and daily deadlines. Within an hour of our laid-back, do-nothing frenzy I wanted to move to Niceville and have eight kids. Or neighboring "Graceville," which was close by and apparently moved at similar speed-bump speeds.

Sunday sensed my overwhelming approval. "Not so bad, is it?"

"Beats SoHo with a stick."

Sunday's Blackberry toned in and she immediately switched it off. She remained mostly quiet the rest of the afternoon.

That evening we went straight to bed, taking up in one of the smaller bedrooms. In separate beds. Romance was never in the air meaning her mood systems, not even the slightest flirtation offered up. Early the next morning, she did lay in bed next to me. I felt water seep down my neck where her head was poised.

We were more ambitious the following day. We motored down the Old Beach Highway and visited those deserted sugar-white sand beaches I'd been hearing about. I wasn't disappointed; they were truly amazing. We stopped at Shell Beach. There was no one within miles of us. We swam, we sun-baked. Sunday was showing better spirits and color came back to her face. With a burn on her cheeks and her hair sea-salted, blonded, and frizzed, she reclaimed her knockout status. Freshly so, like when we first met. She was topless for the duration too and yes, my thoughts weakened several times a day.

"You love me, don't you?"

I didn't answer her. She knew.

"I want to be together again with you, Harry. How do you feel about that?"

I hesitated at first because my yearning for her had been considerable and I didn't want to appear too anxious. I informed her I felt "just fine" about it.

"Because I love you. But… I'm not ready. Yet. I've made progress."

I told her I was happy for that.

"When you opened up to me about your childhood it was touching to hear. And to see the strength it took. Not only in revealing yourself, but to have had the courage to overcome those difficulties. It inspired me."

"So I went for help. When I witnessed your relapse I couldn't handle that pressure and get better myself. That's why I had to separate, to get better, Harry. So I'd be ready, to love. You. The right way, with total honesty, and feeling good about myself. It's hard. I'm not there yet. But I'm getting there. Okay?"

She didn't say anything more. It was more than enough.

Sunday slept for an hour on the beach. Her sleep hadn't seemed peaceful, she'd awoken suddenly with a gasp. I placed a hand on hers. She rose up and took another dip. When she returned, she stood over me dripping wet, toweling her strident gams.

"The photo in the bedroom. Is that Nina?"

She said it was.

"You don't speak of her much."

Verticals slashed in at her brow. "Please don't, Harry. It's difficult."

"Is she alive? Can you tell me that?"

Sunday reached in the cooler and grabbed a bottle of Dixie and twisted off the cap. She took a quick swig.

"Yes. But she left a long time ago."

"Ran away?"

She nodded then had another sip of beer. "She didn't get along with Daddy."

"Are you in contact?"

"We lost touch. I think she's in California." She smiled curiously perhaps giving in to memories of Nina, seemingly pleasant ones. "She always wanted to be an actress."

Sunday and Nina's mother had been active in the local Fundamentalist Church. The girls attended weekly Bible study classes and church services. After their mother died, however, the nuns at the St. Mary's Shelter For Young Women raised them in nearby Valparaiso until Sunday was twelve and Nina was ten. When asked what had happened to their father during that time she stated, "He took off when we were young. Then came back to reclaim us."

After the short discussion, Sunday finished her beer, laid flat on the towel, and fell silent. It was the curtain falling. She stayed quiet the rest of the day.

When we drove to Niceville, Sunday showed me the church. It was a modern stone structure but most of what Niceville had to offer had the appearance of recent construction or repair from Katrina, Rita, and all their destructive hurricane predecessors.

On the drive home, Sunday's phone rang again and she scanned the number to see who was calling, opting not to pick up again. I checked in with the office to see if all was running smoothly. The junior scribes had *Slingshot* under control and asked if I wanted to be sent the copy, but I wasn't in the mood to peruse scando items.

We had a picnic the following day in back at the edge of the water. I put it to Sunday again. "Is your father coming?"

"We'll see him on Thursday."

"I thought it was Tuesday."

"Well, I meant Thursday," she snapped. A moment later, she followed it up with, "I'm sorry, Harry. It's emotional for me."

"Staying here at the house?"

"Everywhere."

31

Trip to Daddy's House

Sunday tapped me on the shoulder to wake me. It was already noon. She gave me a kiss and handed me a cup of southern bold.

"We're going to meet Daddy today."

I didn't remind her of her Thursday plan. "Is it far away?"

"Oscaloosa Springs? No. But I want to show you something first."

We drove east on the Emerald Coast Highway, a beautiful drive featuring an endless sweep of deserted white sand beaches at right, as seen in *Summer of '42*, and thick pine forests were at left. There were charming little towns, Seascape, Tops'l, and Surfside, boasting beach cottages, more ghostly white dunes, and golden sea oats. We entered a magical storybook town that seemed to belong on Nantucket. It was called Seaside and it had the quaintest streets and houses.

"Now we head North—"

We hit the highway blasting a refreshing dose of southern rock and roll on FM radio including the cut, "In Memory of Elizabeth Reed," from The Allman Brothers Band, one of my favorite songs of all time. Two hours later, we came upon a run of high chain-link fence with razor wire spooling atop. It went on for miles. It seemed we were passing another military base.

"This is where Daddy lives," she said in an even tone.

Before I could ask, I located the sign which read, *State of Florida Correctional Institution, Oscaloosa Springs*.

The revelation was stunning. I immediately had to reclassify previously logged data and could better understand Sunday's moodiness and reluctance to divulge previously.

"How long has he been in?"

"A year." After a pause, she said, "He has two to go."

"You didn't think I would understand?"

She hesitated a short while before responding. "Your father is a professor," she said finally. "Your parents were respectable people. My father is…" She waited on it. "I didn't want to fill your ears with some cliché stereotype. I wanted you to see and judge for yourself."

Sunday's father's real name was Charles Witten Fairchild. But everyone called him "Chucky." Chucky was in the pen for tax evasion.

We identified ourselves at the security gate and they gave us passes to enter. Two gates were raised and we drove through and parked. A van then brought us to the main entrance, where we passed through security. A guard escorted us to the waiting area for visiting guests of the prison.

At the far end of the waiting area, a door swung open and the guard waved us forward and we stepped into the visitor's room. The man was already sitting there behind the glass and he rose up as soon as we entered. He was a big guy with a fierce mug, sandy gray stubble, and dark penetrating eyes. Glaring seemed to be their natural state. There was an unmistakable power to this guy. He matted a hand against the glass and Sunday matted hers to it. I could see her eyes were misted. Then the well broke and tears trailed down her cheeks. She said it faintly on a sparely breaking curve. "Hey there, Daddy-Mister."

"Hi, Sugar."

I noted the unconventional greeting.

"Daddy, this is Harry. Who I told you about."

"Chuck Fairchild. Pals call me 'Chucky.'"

"Hello, sir."

We all sat down.

"How ya doin', Daddy?"

"Not half bad. Food ain't so hot. But I been workin' out."

"Did you read that book I gave you?"

"Not yet. But I'll get to it."

Then she said to me, "I gave him *The Ivory Stretch*—"

"Road book. Excellent read."

He looked squarely at me then at her. "You stop by the Shack?"

"No. Not yet," Sunday said.

Chucky's face angled toward me again. He gave me another taste of his high velocity eyes, an aggressive and dark beam. And the glare kept coming, enough to force me to look away. I remembered my Discovery Channel warnings to never look into the eyes of a wild cat. Chucky had carnivorous eyes.

"Named the place after her. Sugar Shack. She's pure sugar," he added strangely. The fierce eyeballing didn't abate nor did the tension.

"Seen her dance?"

"Daddy…" She sounded coy now, almost like a little girl.

"Uh, yes…"

"Great dancer, Sugar is. Don't ya think?"

"Yes. I do."

"Havin' fun out at the house?" He posed and I got the impression that he was no longer toying with me. He was full-on fucking with me.

"Yes, Daddy. We did."

"But not too much fun," he said and cracked a laugh at something that was funny only to him. With that he slid away in his chair, sat back, reached in his shirt pocket, pulled out a cigarette, and lit up. He even crossed his legs, a movement which seemed too feminine for the likes of him. Chucky eyed me roughly as twin paths of white smoke steamed out his flared nostrils.

"Hear you're a paper boy. Undie-sniffer—"

"*Daddy*," she protested.

He was a real beaut. I'd never heard the term before.

"How ya doin', Sugar?" He redirected, which stymied her.

"Uh, all right…"

"Been seein' you in them magazines."

"Didn't think you got that stuff," she feathered back timidly.

"We get 'em all. In the library. For inmates. Fellows think you're smokin'."

"Daddy…"

I couldn't help but note Chucky's crude and bizarre way of speaking, especially to Sunday. He'd referred to her as "Sugar," he was praising her dancing, and his fellow inmates'"smoking" appraisal of her. It was pretty chauvinistic, if not borderline pervy.

"You like libraries, Gossip Harry?"

"Uh, I don't get the time. I used to."

"Bet you did. When you were in college?" he asked with more of that gonna-dick-with-you constitution.

"And after, too."

"You looked good," he sang, switching on Sunday, his southern twang extending it out somewhat lecherously. "Lookin' real pretty."

"It's a lot of makeup," she downplayed.

"Not that much!" He blasted with mocking laughter. "Not much of anything." This trailed off, tonally judgmental.

The man was no longer having fun, his anger and upset betrayed by the derision in his voice. Jibing at the exhibitionist nature of her work, the emotional ebbings were obvious. The tenor of the conversation had totally changed. This guy was completely unpredictable and my palms were steaming.

"I'm making money."

He nodded too, but peacefully so. "You get her into this?"

"Harry has nothing to do with my career."

I didn't care to lie to him. "I introduced her to some people…"

"People," he deadpanned. "*You* people…"

"I gave her a push."

"A push? A push in a grocery cart?"

"I escorted her to meet people who could help her. I put her in my online column. That qualifies as a push, yes."

"How about a push off a cliff?"

"Daddy…"

"No, sir. A push up the mountain, to help her make some bread. Are you against that?"

"I'm not against makin' good jack or even a beer or two to celebrate on the weekend. I am against the ways and means."

"He's done right by me, Daddy."

"Step back, Tessy," he commanded. "Get over there. I want to talk to Shakespeare."

"Mr. Fairchild—"

"Don't insult me with that mister bullshit."

"What?"

"Don't talk down to me, fuckface!"

"I'm—"

"Got my gal kissin' butch cunts 'n goin' out with niggers and dogs!"

"I-I—"

"Think I don't know what you're up to? Got her on some PR highway to hell! Tell me, Gossip Harry, what's your cut?"

"Look, Chuck: sorry if you don't approve—"

"Listen to me, city freak, I want her outta that goddam hellhole 'n' back on my front lawn in a week or you'll be one sorry motherfucker, you hear me?"

"Sunday is doing what she wants to do, she's making her own money, and she's doing a lot better than fine..."

"Fuck you!"

"And I don't care what you have to say to me or what you think. I do know, she's better off up there than hearing your ass-backwards shit biweekly through glass down here!"

On cue the man grinned one wide, sickly so. As if he enjoyed the exchange and seeing my display of emotion. His tone became softer, the concepts less so. "You gettin' some, Shakespeare?"

"Guard??" Sunday called out. "I want to go!"

"Must be. You *are* fucking her." And he flared the most ferocious one I'd ever seen over at Sunday.

"*This?* You give it up to *this??*"

"Stop!" She hollered.

"Now I am certain to make it my personal destiny to kick your motherfuckin' ass!" He fired.

We just glared and gritted at each other as I retreated back.

"I'm comin' gossip boy. I'm-a-comin'!"

I craned back to Sunday. She was bracing the wall, her face turned away, sobbing.

"Have a beautiful life, Chucky."

I took Sunday by the arm. The guard opened the door and we stepped back through it and out. I could still hear Chucky cursing as we left. He didn't leave out any member of my family nor any part of the waist-high anatomy, front or rear. Pleasant.

Our drive back to Niceville involved little discussion. Sunday appeared totally drained, but I did apologize for my behavior.

"He's impossible."

"So you expected that kind of reaction?"

"I should have gone alone. But I wanted you," and she held off on finishing her comment. "I had to see him."

"Why?"

"He r-r-raised us," she said, bucking suddenly. "It's his right."

"It's not his right to abuse you."

The flow continued down her face. "He's just looking out for me. In his crazy way. He doesn't understand that world."

I wondered whether it was the time to discuss some things. "I've never heard a father speak to his daughter the way he speaks to you."

She paused. "He didn't do well in school."

His ability to articulate wasn't what I'd been referring to, it was the attitude behind it, but I let it go.

"Who is Tessy?"

It appeared to be the most troubling question I could ask and I regretted it. Sunday bowed her head and, after a moment, she silently broke down.

"That's what he called Nina," she said finally. "It's short for Treasure. We were 'Sugar' and 'Tessy,'" she said between sobs. "He just mixed it up."

"Sorry for bringing it up."

After calming somewhat, she added, "I didn't want to say anything because I didn't feel right about it. But I wanted you to know. About me. Where I come from. I know I haven't been open. I thought the best way was to drive you right up to that place and let you see for yourself. I was trying to show strength, Harry."

I angled over at her still weeping there. "It was more than that. It was courageous."

"Well," she sniffled, "that's it. My family. Just Nina, Sunday, and

Daddy." She wiped her nose with a tissue. "Fernanda was with us a while but she left."

They'd had a full-time nanny, a Mexican woman named Fernanda Malía. She cooked and cleaned and occasionally stayed overnight and prepared lunch boxes for them. Chuck was at the Air Base for long hours and often didn't come home until late. Fernanda ran the household.

"What happened to her?"

"Went back to Mexico. Wonderful, caring woman."

Quiet moments later, Sunday burst out laughing suddenly through the tears. "Now do you want to run for the hills?"

A new plateau had been reached between us interpersonally, a place of mutual understanding. As we drove down the highway, she placed a hand on my thigh to whisper, "I love you, Harry," with her voice cracking. She was still overcome emotionally. "I don't want to lose you."

I pulled over on a desolate seaside road and stopped the car. I got out and opened the passenger door. She rose and I gave her a squeeze deep to the ribs and she groaned with release.

"Never. You're never going to lose me."

We stood holding each other as the occasional car passed. One's horn even honked and collegiate boys on their eighth month of Spring Break yelled raunchy witticisms. It didn't matter; it was our moment when time stood still. It was the most charged and profound sense of love I'd ever experienced.

When we broke from our embrace, I pivoted back to get behind the wheel, but Sunday tugged on my finger. The tug turned into holding my hand and pulling me off the road. I followed her over towering white forty-foot sand dunes and we ascended to the top and leaped down the other side. We came upon a little sun bowl made of white sand walls hidden from view. Sunday kissed me, then released me and took me right there. I thought to engage in the full act but she would not let me go. She was curled in a tight spiral and her eyes were closed. It was the girl I loved and me and a beautiful intimacy we were sharing on a white sand beach of this Redneck Riviera, a place I was beginning to appreciate.

32

Just Kidding

When we arrived at the house several hours later, there was a pickup truck in the driveway. The light was on in the kitchen and I twisted over to Sunday. She didn't appear overly concerned.

"Recognize the truck?"

"No."

"Who could it be?"

"Floyd, maybe. Friend of Daddy's."

As we got out of the car, I moved ahead of Sunday, advancing on the house. I ascended the stoop and a shaded figure of a man in a curved cowboy hat with a Confederate flag embossing it appeared, framing himself in the doorway.

"Left the door open," the man said in a reproachful way.

"Guess we did," I countered with the same stern tone. "Guess it got tested too." Perhaps it was not my place to speak, but the situation was immediately off-putting and I felt it to the core. Besides, if this cat was a friend of Chuck Fairchild's, I was encouraged to be wary of him.

"How ya doin', Floyd?" Sunday asked amiably, a greeting that all but melted the frost of mine. She passed in front of me. I trailed her inside and Sunday introduced me to this guy, Floyd Fanntaski. He worked for Chuck at his nightclub in Panama City Beach.

"Came by to check on things," he volunteered. "Chucky told me to make sure everything was working fine for ya."

"Thanks. Care for a beer?"

"No," I responded as if I was the guest, to fend off any stray notions this Floyd might have been offered an invitation to hang around. Floyd and I stood our ground, grinding eyes at each other. From his pinched look I was now sure Chucky had spoken of me to him.

"I'm asking Floyd," Sunday qualified.

"No thanks, got to get back to the club. Ladies Night tonight. You comin' down?"

"Don't think so, Floyd. We've been out to see Daddy and I'm kind of tired."

"Okey-dokey." He tipped his curved lid and stepped past us. "Be good now," he said with a peculiar smirk.

Sunday smiled that vague one and she could tell I was unsettled by the intrusion. "Daddy's best friend. He does things like that."

"I understand. But when you're here?"

She didn't elaborate.

"What's the story with this club?"

"He's had it a while."

"Who goes there?"

"It's a big Spring Break place."

"College kids?"

She didn't say anything more and she spun around and faded to the bedroom to lay down.

Having met Chucky and now Floyd, who seemed to share the same shady disposition, it made me curious as to what this nightclub setup was. It seemed to cater to twentysomethings. Given the crude, even misogynistic way Chucky spoke, I wondered was he Florida's version of a Spiderman with a spider web establishment?

I sauntered to the back porch. The silences combined with the stunted discussions were disconcerting. I was never one for incomplete knowledge, perhaps an occupational hazard. I thought it time to declare my uneasiness while being precise. Vagueness or too much consideration of her responses would only void the intensity of my proclamations. I'd thought my questions through, but without editing in lieu of anticipated reactions. I knew all too well that needs bite the dust by not asking for enough. When she emerged from her nap, I ventured forth at my own risk, of course.

"How are the sessions going with Dr. Van den Heugel?"

"How do you mean?"

I wasn't going to mince. "What do you talk about?"

Without responding, she moved to the fridge and uncorked a bottle of white wine. She poured each of us a glass while the question hung there like a tacky brass lamp.

"We discuss a lot of things," she said finally. "Everything."

"Specifically."

"Specifically, well, I can't say."

"You can't, or, you won't?"

"Both, Harry. Both."

And she reached over and grazed my glass with hers. "Cheers," she said. "What's troubling you?"

"We're remaining foreign to each other."

She floated eyes over at me and didn't say anything. I wasn't in the frame of mind to be respecting silences.

"I know today was difficult for you; you shared something very personal. But I feel we're hitting a ceiling…"

"I suppose," she said offhandedly. "Time, Harry. These things take time. And that's what we're doing, taking time. Besides, maybe it's better this way."

"Maybe. But maybe it's not allowing us to move forward."

"Forward can be backward, Harry. I don't think people should know every last detail necessarily, about one another."

"The mystery is gone?"

"Not so much. Too much importance is given to things that aren't really important. Like peoples' pasts. It's not right. Or fair."

"I'm trying to understand. You only care to delve into the present and the present only?"

"I'm a fan of it all as long as it doesn't become an issue. Right now it's an issue. Or it's becoming one."

"And I'm making it one."

"I'm still getting through things. I can speak of the past, but for now only with a professional."

"Greer," I said bluntly. *My* professional, I silently chided myself.

Sunday sighed and angled away. "I understand you're a reporter, and it's in your nature, but time my analyst and I spend together does not have to be fact-checked. This is not a news story. And I don't want it treated that way."

"Doesn't avoidance make similar issue of it? Silence can be loud when explanations seem necessary."

"Explanations aren't necessary, Harry."

"Why not?"

She leveled hardened blue eyes on me and spooled it off easily: "'Cause that's how people get hurt." There was a drastic tone to her voice, an otherworldly grittiness that was startling, even frightening. Like she'd been through hell. I'd witnessed it once before, the night I told her she sounded *noir*-ish. Now it didn't sound so cinematically glamorous, because it was all too real.

"And trust?"

"I trust you, Harry. Implicitly."

"Why?"

"Because I have no other choice. And neither do you." Both responses came easy for her and hinted at an understanding of certain aspects of life which were unfamiliar to me. "Besides, we're just getting used to each other again."

The trailing comment was troubling as it underscored our time apart. That during the passage of time, new things had perhaps happened in our lives.

"You slept with him, didn't you?"

"I *what?* Who?"

"You know who. The guy who calls and texts here every twenty minutes."

Sunday took her time with it and never offered up anything in the end. Always a let down in that kind of repartee concerning this type of subject matter. It does nothing to silence the gonging of the rib cage. Or the dreaded mental wanderings or devastating fantasies.

"He wanted to, didn't he?"

"Harry," she droned at the seeming boring nature of my query. "Who doesn't?"

"Did he try?"

If I'd been confused by her behavior previously, what she did next took it to new heights. She came up from behind and gently wrapped her arms around me and whispered in my ear, a sultry whisper, poetic even. Live from the finest the Redneck Riviera had to offer. I was the fool who could do nothing, absolutely nothing, but offer the ear.

Sunday slipped her hand inside my jeans and sent it over and back on me. Sure I was feeling it, all the way. She followed with kissing my ear and sucking on the lobe.

And she continued to whisper, now about what happened. In that limo. The night of the MTV Awards.

Two cooled hands stroked me and the incendiary tale kept on flourishing. Had I not been aroused and played with, I might not have received it so cheerfully.

Enough was enough, I could hear no more. I took her hand and led her into the bedroom, ripped up her tube top, and tore down drawstrings. I didn't take time to rip off her panties and certainly hadn't taken time to shed my pants. Just a thin protective strip pulled to the side.

Our reunion had been a long time coming.

I spun her around too and did it all over again from behind. Then with her atop me. She didn't talk any more, she tried but I covered her mouth.

Eventually she got a message through to me, in my ear, of course.

"Just kidding," she said and tossed a short, churlish laugh. Her story disclaimer tickled her.

The bold nature of her tease made me shove her on her back again and pick up the pace.

While I was on top of her, she clasped both my hands and brought them to her neck, placing them flat on her throat, and her glossy, half-closed eyes widened to take me in. It was a look which required a response. "Pressure," she whispered, nodding slightly to confirm.

So I put some on it.

"More."

I complied even though it felt strange. I had erotically charged sensations rippling through my body and she wanted me to choke her, contradictory measures as it were. There was not a pleasure quotient in it. Only for her, or so I guessed.

"Harder," she urged.

I gave her as much pressure as I could while still able to keep up the forceful penetration. It began to require resolve to stay firm.

It went on for minutes. Her face flushed, she was writhing in ecstasy, in a dream state nearly with eyes closed and a softly spreading smile. Then her whole body shuddered as she came, as she released. She wailed like a banshee and I could hear and feel a rigidness, a distinct tension sailing out of her body. As the cries and shrills got shorter, she curled up, jamming her thumb in her mouth and sucking it like a toddler, as if reversing back in time before my eyes. I still had a hold on her throat as the little girl sucked her digit aggressively, emitting the short, high-pitched sounds. I ceased with the pressure and she unwound in a final series of tiny jerks and whimpers. Then, stillness. She lay there a while, her eyes remaining shut, still doing her thumb business. When the digit slid from her mouth, she was out.

I lay totally awake. Sunday's tale of a midnight romp in the limo intermittently flashed through my mind. It'd made for potent scandosexual theater. She was well-apprised of the dark erotic buttons. I was certain the episode wasn't true or she wouldn't have told me. I was certain he'd wanted her. *Who wouldn't?* Everyone who came in contact with her did, and, maybe of course, she had wanted him. Part of him. In the form of a contract. Or perhaps more than that. The male imagination under siege by potential indiscretions runs more than laps, it runs marathons.

But *she wouldn't have told me*, I reasoned again.

I lit up and sat outside and watched the moonlight smatter over the surface of the water, breaking up in little ripples sent unceremoniously everywhere. Though there'd been discord our reunion had been sweetened. We'd shown our love for each other. Again.

The next day, we stayed local and spent the day on the beach. We picked up where we'd left off right there in the white sand. An elderly couple walking the shore was nice enough not to watch; Niceville, as it were.

"Remember what I told you on our first date?"

"That I liked to fuck in the dunes," she sent right back. "Pretty spot-on, Harry," she added, freshly impressed.

Two days of memorable intimacy later, we flew back to New York. Our vacation in the Redneck Riviera had come to a close.

33

Mad Ted

October, 2K8

"You haven't been returning my texts…"

"Have so," I countered with a heavy dose of grog and hoarseness, wondering still why I'd picked up the phone.

"Have not."

"It's there waiting for you rotting away in cyberworld, in your BBM trash receptacle… "

"Did you have your male enhancement consultation yet?" He waited on a response—and didn't get one. "I had mine and it didn't take long—not a lot of work to be done. You know if your MEC runs the full hour, well, you're pretty much in trouble… *Harry?* Not in the mood for penis jokes?"

"No."

"Okay, okay. Did you hear? Guns broke up with Tori."

"Heavens… Tori tell you that?"

"No, Guns did. But he seems pretty bummed."

"Would check the facts on that one…"

But the Mad One was already on to the next item of niggling news. "Matthias doesn't like you," he said.

"It's late, Ted…"

"Why doesn't he like you?"

"I choose for him not to like me. He's pestological."

"We're all pests, aren't we?"

"To varying degrees. I can handle a lot. But he's too conniving. As well as afflicted. Makes him dangerous. Don't need dangerous people around."

"Okay, well, listen. This is what I wrote—"

"It's three o'clock in the morning—"

"I know—Conan sucked. Are you listening, Harry?"

I had been dead asleep when Mad Ted rang and I wished I hadn't engaged.

"'*Dear Ebert: it's come to my attention you haven't written. And frankly, I'm flummoxed as to why. Perhaps you're still sad. We all are. I miss faxing him. By the way, Roeper can't hold Siskel's jock. Such the cinema critic tourist. His comments are about as deep as a dime in asphalt. He's a lummox and when he puts on those oversized 3-D glasses and calls male romantic leads "studs?" Come on, Rogero. We've got to give him the heave-ho!*'"

"Ted—"

"'*But let's get to the meat of my season. I'll repeat from my fax yesterday. How could you give* Zerophilia *such a deplorable review? There you go again. Let's begin. Perhaps you didn't see the symbiotic relationship developing between the two young men. I mean, that was classic parasitic, character feasting. Rogero, you can't just toss this off as "self-indulgent, sophomoric trash." Holy harshness, Batman! It's symbolic of everything we're seeing at the base level. Men becoming women as the vast lesbian conspiracy froths and foams at the mouth. Get out your Nikes, Rog', men are on the run! Let's discuss the whole kit and caboodle soon. Your e-mail address seems to have changed, so drop me a line. I'm in mostly all day. But night is good, too. You can e-mail, text, and I still have my beeper, so—*'"

"I could read you more, but, guess what, Harry? *Harry?*"

"Yeah…"

"Ebert put a restraining order on me. For that fax no less…"

"Didn't I tell you?"

"A blatant betrayal of our trust."

"What trust? What did I tell you?"

"You said to stop contacting him. That something like this might happen. But he actually did it."

"Ted, you've written the guy two hundred e-mails, texts, letters, and faxes…"

"I'm a movie fan. A *concerned* movie fan."

"You did the same thing to that G.P., arguing and badgering him with your WebMD theories—"

"He needed to be challenged!"

"—calling all the Time Warner, Sprint, and Con Ed switchboard grunts to get into billing and user plan dustups with them—"

"They need to be exposed. For what they are."

"Ebert has never once written you back. Doesn't that say something to you? Don't you see it comes off as—"

"As what, Harry?"

"As somewhat pathological?"

Before I could charge him with being a full-fledged phone-stalker, the aggravazzo hung up on me which was okay. His neurological needs for disputatious dramalocity in the form of senseless confrontational dialogues with professionals, corporate servants, and their supervisors was too much. Besides, it was the only way I was going to get some shuteye.

34

Of Moss and Men

There hadn't been any communication since our last meeting, the memorable twosome that had featured those puzzling professional-patient violations. When I arrived for my weekly, there weren't even inquiring, much less lingering looks on her face. Though she was no longer the Ice Princess, having thawed considerably, the good doctor was all big business once again and on a familiar detour.

"How do you know these people, the 'Militia,' as you call them?"

"Some are fellow patients, some we attended special schools together, others we shared doctors. But mostly you just meet them."

"How?"

"They're buzzing around everywhere, interrupting, gesticulating, making noise, singing show tunes, texting invite-yourself-O-Grams, s'punking girls, creating general dramarama and chaos, and your ADD antennae go off. We're on that same abnormal frequency. It's not hard when you're charged so at the molecular level and humming and firing with sensitized life."

"*Spunking?*"

"Making outlandish pervy passes and creepy come-ons to the better gender. Just to get a reaction—'*s'punk'd.*'"

"Are they still bothering you?"

"I was woken up by one, but mostly no. They're kind of quiet now."

"Why are they quiet?"

"They're all worried about what they want to be."

"When they grow up?"

"No. For Halloween."

She just shook her head. "Why do you call America an ADD Nation?"

"It's not just the Militia. The I-Age causes attention deficits in the population. Techie tool processors have disrupted the human internal time clock. People are trying to run at Pentium 4 speed. The overtaxed brain tries to keep up, but can't. Hence the distractibility aspects. There's no time to focus properly, as in biologically. It's pandemic, and, universal. Of course, mercury in the water doesn't help. That's ADD Nation."

She cleared her throat. "You're wearing fuchsia today."

I let it hang like a seedless bird feeder from a withered elm.

"Beautiful color. Care to comment?"

I didn't.

"I see," she said. "One final thing; in picking up from our last discussion, there's something I'm still curious about—your choices…"

"Yikes… *Of?*"

"Women. The ones you choose to date."

"You know all this."

"We've discussed who you choose, but not how or why."

I took my time, wondering how best to phrase it. "It's a very narrow character trait list and candidate skill set I seek out. Very restricted."

"You make it restricted."

"I have to."

"Why?"

"Most can't handle a guy like me. Nor would they want to try. As you know."

"But you meet all your dates in clubs, bars, and strip bars—"

"That's what's left for me."

"Come on. Don't you ever go to cocktail or dinner parties? Or meet people in more natural settings?"

"What cocktail party do you have in mind?"

"Harry—"

"Or dinner party? How about Greenwich? Then we can have a

big polo shirt sleepover, no bottomsies."

"Stop."

"You know I had to try."

"I know."

All better, I thought. We were done with my usual pick-up compulsories with the good Doc. Then I wondered why I'd even attempted it. In viewing our last meeting, we were way past that. It was as if I was bringing us back to ground zero. As if nothing had ever happened. Like it mattered little to me, which was not the case. To neutralize her, perhaps. But why? Then I knew. I feared this session. The sensitive subject matter to be discussed scared the hell out of me. I was trivializing our recent carnal indiscretion to weaken her. To make her feel vulnerable. Insecure. Used, even. Enough to take her off her game. And thereby take it easy on me.

Of course, I was wary of it all backfiring—and making her a lean, mean interrogating machine.

"Doc, are you trying to reform me?"

"Always. That's the point of all this."

"Or *con*form me?"

"Whatever helps …"

"But these questions about choices and cocktail parties are questions a friend might ask." She didn't respond. "Are you my friend?"

"You know what I am." She wasn't done, surprisingly. "But yes, Harry. I am your friend."

It was so nice to hear it finally. But I still hadn't cracked her. She remained poised and undaunted. I needed to do more.

"Actually, I need big, open, and free venues with massive interaction so I can comb my way through. Thereby, my selections are natural—to me and my code. By the way, I don't find dinner parties natural; they're too contained. Contrived. And confined. Ever taken the Hampton Jitney? Forced to plop next to someone with whom you really don't care to share the same zip code? Besides, I have a low approval rating at dinner parties."

"Why?"

"You know me, Doc. My controversial charisma."

"When was the last time you attended a dinner party?"

I didn't have to think about it; it was already uploaded to my brain. "About five years ago. Real mossy affair…"

"What do you mean by 'mossy'?"

"Do we have time for this?" I added for effect.

"Yes."

"Well, as I recall, it was a sit-down for about twelve with an equal ratio of men and women, and I was asked where I wanted to sit… Mind you, I was a little cocktailed and not medicated, so I outlandishly cited my fave Publilius Syrus phrase and said, 'Since we all know *A rolling stone gathers no moss*, I'd like to perform a moss check. Any objections?' No one protested nor did they know what I was talking about, so I went down the table from one gal to the next sizing up her moss index or potential for plushy green growth. The first was married, not sexy, and had the no fun vibe, so I sniffed her nape and said simply, 'moss.' The next one was single but preppy-uptight, lockjawed, and frowning at me, so I gave her a '*heavy* moss." The third was from Great Neck and 'Daddy'this–'Daddy'that, and she had an absolutely horrified look on her face and charged off when I tried to nose her out. '*Deep* moss,' I determined. And that elicited a high-pitched laugh nearby. The next gal was in an 'it's complicated' union and posed, 'By moss, what do you mean? That's she's clingy or wants romantic commitment?'… 'Not necessarily,' I said, 'but there may be a stagnation quotient involved.' She giggled freely as I nosed her and reported her as 'mildly open-minded with *patches* of green.' The next gal had a jovial grin and I identified the laugh, so I took a big whiff and said, '*Mmmm*, likely a unisex rogue enthusiast, relatively moss-free.' Then the last gal—I kid you not—got up from her chair and spiked her napkin down and said, 'I'm not going to be subjected to this!'—even before I could say "*choke* moss." Instead, I spread my wallet and extended a bill to her and said, 'Here, have a dollar'—for the inconvenience, of course. Her face got beet red and smoke was coming out of her ears, as I suspect she felt doubly compromised, that I could offer to buy her off for her pride…"

"Harry…" the doctor intoned judgmentally before making an unwelcomed comeback. "So is 'choke moss' the worst kind?"

After all that, I lamented silently, she'd adopted my crass terminology—unflinchingly, no less. Drats.

"I'm glad you asked. No, in fact; it's not. '*Gangrene* moss' is the worst. Those types will sap you of all your nutrients, siphon out your originality, extinguish your spirit and spark, take you for all your worth, and watch your life force ripple with the winds, leaving you a ribcage mannequin exhibit for Bio class. Not recommended. But they're a rarity, anyway. And difficult to spot."

"How so?"

"They're transformers. Once they've gotten what they've wanted, they can appear to be the most soulful people you've ever met."

"You're sounding bitter."

"Oh? Well you know me."

"So—where did you seat yourself finally at this dinner party?"

"I plunked down next to the gal with the good attitude."

"Did you sleep with her?"

"Fractionally; but months later I did have multiple choice sex with one of them…"

"'Patchy moss'—?"

"No, 'choke moss.' I had her all wrong. I thought she was a classic free-spirit buster. Funny world. Needless to say, I was not invited back to the apartment. Doc, I'm just not appropriate mixed company fare…"

The good doctor chuckled, too, to my dismay. I thought she'd be turned off by my mildly objectionable if not incendiary tale of Moss Girls juxtaposed to our recent indulgence. She didn't even ask for a personal moss count appraisal. I sighed weightily. She'd let me spew and had allowed the detour to run its course in an attempt to relax me—so I could best handle the disturbing topic we'd been avoiding. Funny; her strategy to confront the pending issues was to calm me. My strategy was to disarm her. But she wasn't fazed. And I was still terrified. She won.

"Okay," she allowed, returning a huff herself, likely unsure whether the perfunctory openers had had any diversionary effect on me—for good reason. Can you really feel at peace before a root canal with no Novocain?

"Let's go through it now…"

I was in the chair with a chest napkin and the dentist's drill began to buzz.

"What happened when you came back from Florida?"

I'd ruminated about it so many times that it was easy to remember.

"At first, everything was great. We were happy. Loving. I'd stopped drinking, I was taking my meds. I was focused, on everything. Work. The relationship. Sexually, we were very intimate. Passionate. Then she suddenly frosted on that."

"Why?"

"I don't know. She became distant and we went through a period of having little sex. Yet those few times we did engage, she seemed to enjoy it very much. Almost too much."

"Was it like the sex you had that night in her father's house?"

I'd told Dr. Greer about the unconventional methods we employed, of course, but always left out the asphyxiation stuff which I considered to be our own private matter.

"It was just hard. And more impersonal. Anonymous. Like we were serially one-nighting each other. Or she, me."

"What do you mean by impersonal?"

"The choreography."

"How so?"

"You want to know positions?" She stayed silent. "Frombe. A lot."

"Frumby?"

"That's from behind. From wide angles with mirrors. In strange places. Sometimes she'd have her laptop glowing behind me tuned into porn on Redtube."

It gave the doctor pause. "Porn? What kind of porn?"

"Lesbian porn, actually. Which was a surprise."

The doctor nodded neutrally and didn't inquire further, which was also curious. "What do you think brought on her distancing herself?"

"I could only think, that she felt I knew too much about her. About her past. And background. And about her father. Perhaps she was regretting she'd told me. Oddly, I didn't think I knew much about her. At all. She was largely a mystery to me still."

"Why would she regret what she'd told you?"

"It might have made her feel vulnerable. Too vulnerable. And I suspect she began resenting me for it. I could feel it. We couldn't agree on the simplest things. I was unnerving her constantly. For no apparent reason. There was something else, too…"

"What?"

"There was some sort of gap, or hole, a wound, maybe. Something seemed to be hurting her deep down. Maybe dark, maybe not, but something. And she knew I felt that way."

"What did you think it was?"

"The logical answer was her sister. Nina. I mean she hadn't seen her in so long. I thought that was what was missing in Sunday's life. The hole that kept it out of balance. Or kept her from being happy. I sensed she needed that connection. She needed her. And it would help if I could find Nina."

"What did you do?"

"I searched for her using all my contacts."

"What happened?"

"My associate located a 'Nina Fairchild' working as a waitress in Los Angeles, where Sunday said she'd gone. So I went out there. I told Sunday I was attending a press dinner with West Coast colleagues. When I went to the restaurant she was Nina and a Fairchild all right, but a different one. When I came back, I told Sunday where I'd been and what I'd been doing. Instead of perceiving it as a compassionate gesture, she got upset. As in, how could I be so insensitive to meddle into her private life? And that I was 'obsessing' about her. I'd already gotten her professional help, I turned her on to you. I'd been forthright with respect to my past, my disorders, family history and such. She'd asked me about it all. So…"

"Did she think you weren't in it for the same reasons?"

"Perhaps, but I don't see how. I was trying to help her. I still don't understand. Did she speak to you about that?"

The doctor took a sip of tea. "We'll get to that. What happened next?"

"She wanted to take a break. So we separated again. For a month. We had lunch a few times, we slept together. Twice. Or three times."

"When?"

"One time she came over. After she'd seen a movie. With you I think. She texted me during it and said it was too depressing."

"Which movie?"

"*City of God*. You remember?"

"I do," she said and paused. "And the sex. Was it passionate that night?"

"Better, anyway…"

"But aggressive, still? Impersonal?"

"Uh, yes. But not so impersonal."

"Was she doing the thumb-sucking?"

I nodded. "And she was becoming increasingly fond of alternative forms."

"Alternative forms of what?"

"Penetration."

"Anal penetration?" Again, I nodded. "Did she discuss why?"

"Only that she liked it."

"Did you like it?"

I was surprised Dr. Greer was asking so many raw specifics.

"Well, I wondered why she needed it so harshly. It was animalistic, less intimate. I was in love with her and I wanted her to get better. But I saw our downtown fairy-tale getting corrupted. Cheapened. It was crumbling apart. Again. So I started drinking, taking other things. Anything to medicate me."

"Then what?"

"All of a sudden, everything was okay again. Something had calmed in her. She became loving, caring. Concerned about me. The way she used to be. We'd rediscovered that closeness. It was beautiful, as blissful a time as I'd ever experienced. It seemed that everything had come together. Finally. It lasted a month. Then she was killed."

Dr. Greer fell silent taking a run of copious notes. "Tell me about that night. The night she was murdered…"

I sat back in my chair. I took several swigs from the cup of second-rate deli-bought bold. It was exhausting to conjure.

"We were at her place in the afternoon. Together. We made love. Then I went home to write. I completed twenty pages of the novel. I was so proud I wanted her to share my excitement. So I printed out what I'd written and went back to her place. I found her laying there…"

"Did you tell this to the police?"

I hesitated. "Well, not exactly."

"What did you tell them?"

"This is between us, right?"

"Of course. You're my patient."

I paused again. "I said I'd been there only once. Later. When I discovered the body. I never mentioned I'd been there earlier. My roommate who thought I'd been home all night corroborated my story."

"Why didn't you say you were there earlier?"

"I didn't want them to get suspicious."

"Why? What were you worried about?"

"Complications."

"Which were?"

"Taken a read of the dailies recently? I didn't want any attention. I'm in a high-profile position. Why complicate life unnecessarily? I loved her so much."

Dr. Greer eyed me penetratingly. Then she angled away.

"I was paranoid, really. I get that way. As you know."

I watched the good doctor jot a final notation and close the notebook. A lightness swept through my frame.

"Wasn't so bad, Dr. Greer. I mean, I feel pretty good." I had the urge to peck her on the cheek, to embrace her, even. She'd done so much for me. I rose up from my chair.

She was fastened on me still, with an uncharacteristically serious regard.

"Harry, listen carefully, I need to discuss something. You know those neurological tests they ran on you at Columbia Presbyterian?"

"The MRIs?"

"No. The CT and brain SPECT imaging scans…"

"My brain pinup? It was full frontal lobe. Did I expose too much?"

"Detour. This is serious. I've conferred with the doctors. They'd like to see you again."

"What for?"

"As you know, you were tested for many things. What they found was an enlarged section in the area of your brain that controls cognition and memory. There's swelling and scarring, which indicates some damage to the neurosensors. You were most likely born with it. They suspect this may be causing the migraine-induced blackouts and fits of anxiety—"

I collapsed into in the chair.

"It's a recently discovered condition. It can occur under intense emotional or physical stress, as in a heated argument, even sexual intercourse. Attacks last up to eight hours with extreme disorientation with the sufferer's perception of activity, time, and place. Even total loss of memory."

I was already gazing off, nearing a borderline catatonic state. She was still talking, lips in motion, jabbering on. I couldn't hear her. I was melting into my seat.

"The blackouts you've told me about? The lapses in memory?"

It nodded. "Yeah," came out of its mouth.

"Harry, isn't this positive news? To get to the bottom of it once and for all? That's why they want you to come in. They think they can help you, which can help others."

It took a while to snap out of it.

"Harry?"

"So," I produced sparely with a sandpaper voice, "what is this terrific condition called? Does it have a name?"

"TGA. Which stands for Transient Global Amnesia."

"Sounds like an airline," I said, hollow and so freshly shattered.

"New word toy for Harry," she tossed back attempting upbeat.

But the water found its way to my eyeballs pretty fast until they were awash and I couldn't make out shapes and figures anymore.

"Are you all right? Why are you getting upset, Harry?"

I didn't make an appointment for further tests. I wasn't playing hard to get with my sexy centerfold mind and I hadn't become a diva or prima donna. I didn't have a problem striking another pose, I just didn't see my schedule freeing up any time soon. I'd been fearing something in that office all right, but what I got was far worse. I was tip-toeing on a burning fault line, dancing between hot, jagged plates of terror and desperation. I felt my neck and whatever was wrapping it tightening.

35

Champagne and Black Air

Thankfully, the unmarked squad vehicle docked around the corner from my loft saved me some bucks, the same car responsible for giving the Fonz consecutive days off. Now I exited through cellars, walked the alleys, scaled fire escapes, and took the sewer rocket express if I needed to travel. That morning I popped out of the station at Astor Place and Lafayette and headed east on St. Mark's Place.

His name was Eddie Morny and he lived on Sixth Street in the East Village. I thought it likely the city had been home to this photographer. For all the glam production work Sunday had done, she'd never made a trip to Los Angeles and at no time during our year-long relationship had she ever scheduled a session for nudes.

Perhaps she hadn't told me or she'd had them shot before we'd met or she'd done them during our break-up. She claimed to be opposed to doing nude photography. She felt being just a woman was compromising enough let alone the exploitable versions. They just set you up for bedroom invitations and little else. Ruth Gunn-Glaser was against them too, though *Playboy* had come in with mid-six-figure offers. So it was one more mysterious event from a series linked to a girl I thought I knew reasonably well.

Unfortunately, I had to know the truth. It was in my nature, a trait Shakespearean in its scope. My scandocentric life ran on an I-must-know basis and that was even true for news which didn't involve me. This was the love of my life. Call it a tragic flaw, call it an obsession. And if that wasn't enough, my need to know took on a special urgency now. I was being implicated in a murder.

It didn't take hours to saunter up to Eddie Morny's walk-up

building. The address was accurate; his name was plated beside the door. I buzzed him and a circumspect male voice responded, asking me to identify myself.

"I'm Harry Starslinger. From *The New York Herald*…"

"Oh… Okay… The paper. No jokes?"

"None."

I wasn't surprised he knew who I was. Machine people know each other. The fact he didn't turn me away was not necessarily a good sign. It meant the police hadn't spoken to him and I wondered why. Perhaps they'd already decided who the murdering perp was. Me. It was a Fifty/Fifty.

"What's it about?"

"Just want to talk to you."

"Yeah-um, okay… Meet me at Aggie's Diner on Avenue B. In ten…"

We did just that, over weak and badly burnt diner coffee.

"What's on your mind?" he posed casually.

He was Bohemian scruffy with long stringy hair, par for the neighborhood. In the East Village, few shower until late afternoon, when they have to emerge from their hovels after a long day of some form of artistic expression that hasn't turned the corner on profitable. For most of them, anyway. Though I was right on the shower part, I wasn't sure Morny had the same routine. After all, he had no-clothesers of Sunday Fairchild and I was certain his bank account had been boosted handsomely, but not enough to warrant a Manhattan apartment change. Morny had also been an assistant for photographer Bruce Weber and he was about five-foot-five.

"I want to talk about Sunday…"

"Sunday Fairchild?"

His eyes went jittery all of a sudden, his hand combing back through oily strands.

"What for? Only met her once."

"Listen. I'm not trying to bust your balls or make problems for you. We had a long relationship."

"You were her boyfriend?"

"Yeah. And I want some information for my own private brain trust. In return, I will take care of you with some solid Face, as in face time in my daily when the time comes, even if the time is now."

"Shoot—"

"The nudes."

"What nudes?"

I immediately realized he wasn't susceptible to the soft approach and a change in strategy was imminent.

"The ones you sold to DeadBeauties for fifty grand."

"Who told you that?"

"They did. And they did because the girl was murdered. And the murder has gone unsolved. And the cops are ripe for any information they can get. You want to be dragged into this?"

That yielded a 'no.'

"Good answer, because you don't. No matter what they say, it's not good Face. Murder linkage hurts future business; it sinks careers. That goes for fashion snappers too, and you certainly don't want to get the ball rolling that way with the scandoscathing Sleazoid Fotog item I could scandoslander you with in tomorrow's edition."

I raised my phone cam and snapped a brilliant Eddie Morny action shot, a medium head shot which, when placed over unflattering item copy, would appear more like a mugshot. His arms were octopussing in protest when I took it. "Hey!" Was his related objection.

When I scandocammed another quickie, I got the angry, I-could-be-a-convict pose which would enhance the Sling's credibility, a lock to be processed by the public as an uncontestable truism.

"Motherfucker!"

"No more than the beauts at DeadBeauties and the scandoscum who sell to them."

He was miffed all right, but he calmed. He knew it was in his best interest to do so. "What do you want from me, Starslinger?"

"I want to know how you got that photo, if you have any more, and anything else you know about her…"

"Like?"

"Did you hear her say anything out of the ordinary?"

"Why don't you let the cops handle this?"

"This is personal. I'm doing it for myself and no one else."

Morny sat back and lit up, hiding the cig beneath the table top.
It seemed to settle his nerves. Then he poked around his genitalia. It
made him increasingly more attractive by the minute.

"Guy calls me up, 305 area code. Says he's a fan of my work…"

"What work?"

"The *Enquirer*. Shots of celebs, the ladies attending premieres
with the hot flash piercing through and showing nipple-tit. Those
were the ones he liked."

It sounded like Chucky, an acknowledged porno-perv. The area
code matched, too.

"He checked photo credits and contacted me through the
paper."

"What did he say?"

"He wanted me to shoot photos for him. Nudes."

"Nudes for him?"

"That's what he said. I said, 'How much?' He said, 'Five grand.'
So I said, 'Who do you want me to shoot?' And he said, 'Sunday
Fairchild.' And I said, 'That's great but I ain't got access to her.' He
says, 'Well I do.' I was shocked, I mean I woulda paid him to shoot
her. I was just the lucky guy, know what I'm sayin'?"

"Then what did he tell you to do?"

"Gave me her number and told me to call her. I said, 'Just like
that? No jokes?' And he hung up on me."

"Just to call her?"

"He said she'd be expecting my call."

"Do you still have the number?"

He did on his iPhone and he showed it to me. It was the digits
for the Thompson Street apartment.

"So you called her—"

"Yeah. And she was real nice, that southern accent, you know?
But she said it was a secret, that I couldn't tell anybody about it. And
I would make more money if I kept my mouth shut."

"Then what?"

"We set a date, and I booked a studio, a real private one in the
Meatpacking District few people use. And we did it. Cripes, that
girl, bless her heart, was something else."

"Was she friendly?"

"The fuckin' best! And I should say, and don't take this the wrong way: open."

"How do you mean?"

"I gave her a glass of champagne and a robe. She took the bubbly, tossed the robe. She had no problem prancing around, and why should she? She was perfection."

Sure, it stung. Not what he'd seen, what I'd seen and had now lost, unable to see her ever again. Discussing her with people who'd had interaction with her was often painful.

"How long was the shoot?"

"Few hours. I mean it coulda been five minutes, she was so great. From any angle. I kept banging off rolls."

"Rolls? You weren't shooting digitally?"

Then he went into his artistic spiel, how he preferred still photography with actual film, the old-fashioned way. The pictures came out grainier and richer.

"I'll be honest with you, Starslinger. When I ran out of film, I made like I had more and shot three rolls of black air."

"What's that?"

"Nothing, no film. Just to keep it going. You don't get opportunities like that. I coulda shot her all year long, no lunch breaks."

"I got it. Champagne and black air…"

"Yeah, well…"

"Did she say what the photos were for?"

"Don't want to twist you up, but her 'boyfriend,' she said. They were going to be a surprise."

"Tell me, Morny, what did you do with the photos?"

"When it was over, she paid me nicely, in cash. Five g's with a thousand-dollar tip, to keep quiet, I guess. Or quieter than I was already supposed to be. She gave me an address to send the photos and the negs."

"Did you?"

"Sure."

"And what about the other set?"

"What other set?"

"The dupes you made."

"Dupes? Who said anything about dupes?"

"I did."

He shot an artificially fierce one at me which soon died because of his Scott Baio acting skills. My eyes didn't budge and guilt was streaking all over his grill. "Yeah, okay, Starslinger, right. How could I not?"

"Where's that set?"

"Kept it."

"Where did you send the paid-for set?"

"Believe it or not, to some guy in prison."

"In Florida?"

"Yeah. Thought it might be the guy who called me up. Florida area code. But I never knew for sure. I was never given a name, only an inmate number. Who is that guy? Another boyfriend?"

The tone came low and the flavoring was disturbed. "No."

"What's the matter? Don't like the guy?"

"'Like' is a funny word."

I asked Morny if I could see the rest of the photos and he was swell enough to bring me to his tiny apartment to scan the series. He had a makeshift photography studio, the space he likely shot most of his photos. And black air.

"Hey, you're not going to get hacked at me are you?"

"What for?"

"I mean, they're pretty risqué. Mostly fried eggs and near 'eagles. You cool with that?"

I just clammed up.

He hadn't left out much, having taken every angle. They weren't porn shots, but the coverage was extensive, which amounts to revealing. And then some.

"They were supposed to be in *Playboy*," he said, defensively.

"You line that up?"

"No, she told me she had. They'd approached her. But when she was killed, well, I never heard back nothing. No jokes."

When I asked him for his negatives, he had a price. I met it. He said he'd have them for me the following day. I said, "no way." He said, "forget it, then," that the photos would be worth twenty times what I was paying five years from now. I told him I'd come by to pick up the negs the following morning. That would give him time to make a third set of prints and negatives. Just another Boy Scout from The Machine also known as, *bastard*.

No jokes.

36

Florida Sisters

I decided to take that week off that Boss Arthur had suggested. The morning flight to Pensacola was booked, so I took a sunriser to Tallahassee, seat 11-J. I was returning to the Redneck Riviera.

I started my investigative odyssey at the Niceville Public Library. An elderly librarian named Mrs. Hutchins assisted me.

"Fairchild? Chuck? It rings a bell, yes. He was in the service, right?"

"Yes."

"I think he was right here at Eglin Air Force Base. We have their newsletters. From way back. Would you like to see them?"

I said I did, as well as back editions of the local newspapers.

It seemed Chuck Fairchild would have been at the Base in the mid-to-late eighties, early nineties. Sure enough, I found records of him as a pilot indicating he'd flown sorties in the first Iraqi conflict in 1990. Then he retired to Niceville in 1994. He'd been with the Air Force for nearly twenty years.

Local newspapers, *The Niceville Press*, and *The Pensacolan*, didn't have much on him. But in the *Panama City Gazette,* I found an article proclaiming he'd bought an old beach cottage and received building permits and a cabaret license to turn it into a dance bar. He'd been met with resistance, however. A group called the Council For A Better PCB tried to block the conversion and his construction proposal. The Town Planning Board, though, in need of tax revenues, approved it as they did with many commercial proposals of the day. It all led to the nightclub boom there which later became the big lure for college student Spring Break vacationers. Chucky and his bar sparked off the explosion in night-life establishments in PCB.

Chucky had paved the way.

Several years later, the *Gazette* ran a feature story on the Spring Break phenomenon in Panama City Beach. The article profiled the popular clubs and the Sugar Shack was singled out as the hot spot for itinerant collegians. There were wet T-shirt contests, even Joe scandoFrancis from the "Girls Gone Wild" scandofranchise had his crews filming there. There were also references to the proprietor's passion for the ladies, *young* ladies, and Chucky was heralded as a local Hugh Hefner. The scandalously flattering puff piece appeared in 2000.

Searching further, I came upon a spicy *Tribune*-esque feature article profiling Chuck Fairchild in the *Gazette*. This piece chronicled his rise and fall two-step. The man who'd pioneered the night-life boom in Panama City and had earned himself the "King of PCB" moniker had also taken a nosedive. First, there'd been word of underage drinking at his club, then reports of drugs being sold out of it, specifically, designer Ecstasy. Chucky was never charged, but the club's reputation suffered. A couple years later, Chucky was arrested for sexually assaulting a fifteen-year-old girl. The charges were dropped for no apparent reason, which was a reason in itself. It was insinuated Chucky had bought her off. The whole enterprise came crashing down when he was nailed for tax evasion. It appeared the Spidermen and women polluters of Manhattan had nothing on this grotesque guy.

Reading between the lines, I assumed Chucky had enjoyed a mutually beneficial arrangement with the local Panama City grease-for-peace police. It was Florida, after all. For this reason his club had been allowed to operate with reckless abandon. But when the feds became involved, most likely tipped off by one of Chucky's growing list of competitors, detractors, and enemies, he could no longer be protected. There was no one else he could scandohand.

Next, I drove my rented Mustang to nearby Valparaiso, where the St. Mary's Shelter For Young Women was located. Yes, I'd opted for the same car in homage to her.

The Shelter had a flower-lined crescent driveway, making for a pleasant impression upon entering. You could leave as freely as you came. I was calling on Sister Sloane Parks. Sister Sloane was the only adult figure Sunday trusted and confided in while growing up. When I arrived, I was met by a Sister Jamison, a warm and pretty elderly woman covered in frock and headdress. She was seated in a chair in the hall performing her pillow needlepoint. When I inquired about Sister Parks, Sister Jamison informed me that she'd died six months previously. It saddened me to hear it. I turned the subject to Sunday and Nina.

Sister Jamison initially couldn't remember any girls named Fairchild. She'd only come to the Shelter in the early nineties. Sunday and Nina had left around that time. "Sunday, did you say?"

"Yes."

"Yes, oh yes, Fairchild," she repeated. "I'm afraid I'm up in years and very bad with names, Mr.—?"

"Starslinger. Harry Starslinger."

"Yes, Mr. Starslinger. Of course, Sunday. The famous one. Awful tragedy. I remember her, surely. Delightful girl and just as pretty as a picture. She had long braids. A bit troubled, but sweet…"

The Sister's cheerful expression seemed to tighten.

"Troubled, you say?"

"Like many chillens without parents, they get down at times. But Sunday, she always bounced back. I think she was Sister Sloane's favorite, though we don't treat the chillens any different. But they used to catch butterflies together in the State Park. Sunday loved taking long walks on the beaches. She loved the sandy beaches here."

"And to swim, I imagine."

"Oh yes, to swim. We all went on a trip together to swim with the dolphins. She had a ball, all the chillens did. But Sunday was happy-spirited, full of life. She told me it was her favorite thing to be in the water. We were so excited when we heard how well she was doing. Such a tragedy. She'd become quite a star, hadn't she?"

"Yes, she had."

A rush of ill-feeling gripped me. Call it guilts. I gave thought to Sunday, The Machine, and my part in it. It had never sat well with me, for obvious reasons.

"They find out anything?"

"No, not yet."

"Just terrible. Like the Jessica Lunsford story. But they did pass Jessica's Law." Then she spoke in whisper. "Secretly, I was thrilled and I'm a nun." I nodded. "Are you with the police?"

"I was a good friend of Sunday's. I write for a newspaper."

"I spoke too soon."

"Secret's safe with me. But I'm going to make sure Sunday's memory does not die and that justice will be served."

"I do hope so."

"Maybe you can help, Sister Jamison."

"Me?"

"Can you tell me anything about her life once she left the Shelter? Did you hear anything? Anything at all?"

The good Sister twitched nervously, caught off guard. "I wouldn't know about that sort of thing."

"She never contacted the Shelter once she left?"

"They were in contact. Sister Sloane and Sunday."

"Did Sister Sloane tell you anything?"

She hesitated again. "You say you're from a paper?"

"*The New York Herald.*" I pulled a business card and handed it to her. She inspected it.

"You writing a story on her?"

"No. I was her boyfriend when she lived in New York. I'm trying to put the pieces together. I don't know if they'll ever find out who did it; it's been almost two years. Her memory is being tarnished. It's not the way it should be and I want to change that. We were very much in love."

"Let me give you some advice, Mr. Starslinger. Remember her in the light, the good times, and let the rest go."

"Please, Sister, I'm all alone in this. My life has been—"

The emotion surged forth. The Sister looked on me kindly and arranged the knitting needles neatly in her lap. "Let's take a walk in the gardens—"

There was a small French brick courtyard in back, and a manicured garden beyond, planted with rows of magnolias and camellias. Two sisters were pruning petals and stems as we passed. Sister Jamison clasped my arm as we strolled along. First, she recounted the story how Sunday came to the Shelter, a conversation I'd never forget.

"You see, Sunday's mother was friendly with Sister Sloane. They were very close because way back, Sunday's grandmother helped pay for this Shelter. She donated a large sum for its construction. Poor thing was so sad when she arrived, her mother dying and all."

"And Nina?"

"What's that? Oh yes, there was a Nina. But I think Nina came to us later."

"They didn't arrive at the same time?"

"How do you mean?"

"I mean, they were sisters and—"

"Oh no, they weren't sisters. But they were best friends."

"Sunday and Nina weren't sisters?"

"Heavens, no. Nina's parents died in that awful plane crash in the Everglades."

"Wait," I said trying to piece things together. "So Sunday's father was not Nina's father too?"

"No sir. We never met Sunday's father."

My breathing pattern shifted. "You never saw Sunday's father?"

"Sunday never saw her father. He left before she was born, never seen or heard from. Sister Sloane had regrets about that too."

"But no, he came back. And got them."

She casted eyes on me sympathetically. "I'm sorry, Mister. Sounds like you've been fed some sort of a line—"

My thumper was slamming the bars of my rib cage.

"Then who took Sunday away from the Shelter when she was twelve?"

"The guardian. That Fairchild man. That's how Sunday got her name. Then he adopted Nina too. Both girls took his name and moved in with him. And," she added in a markedly lower tone, "there were those unfortunate stories."

A hot flash prickled my pores. I couldn't believe what I was hearing. "Stories?"

"Mmm–hmm, yes."

"What kind of stories?"

She sighed the contents of her little lungs, then gave the sign of the cross.

"Well, this man had a fine military record at the local base. War hero, lost his wife to cancer. There've been many deaths locally from it. Some say it's the water, others say it's in the fertilizer. But it got Sunday's mother too, may her soul rest in peace."

"Now this man, Fairchild, Charles I believe, came to the chapel and worshipped and like I said, had impeccable credentials. He was kind, too. Offered to help us when we needed help, a man's help, to move things around and such. Sister Sloane liked him. Each year he rented a bus and took us to Shell Beach."

I remembered the location, that beautiful stretch of surf line off the Old Beach Highway we'd visited once, the place where Sunday remained silent for hours on end.

"And St. Andrew's State Park, and the waterfront area in Pensacola. Of course, the girls took to him when they first met him. He and Sunday became close, in that father-and-daughter sort of way. After a while, he asked us if he could adopt her. It was time for her to start junior high. She wanted to live in a house with her own room. She wanted privacy more than anything, like blossoming young women do. Doesn't happen so often you find a guardian match for orphaned chillens and we thought we owed it to the family, to Sunday's mother and grandmother to try and help best we could. So we interviewed this Fairchild and requested recommendations, from the higher-ups at the Base. I daresay he passed the requirements which deemed him fit. So we held a meeting and decided he had the best intentions. And, he could afford it, so we voted in favor. It's a state issue and it was legalized with adoption papers. Sunday left us this way. Then the man adopted Nina, too."

"What happened?"

"Those stories I mentioned?" She made the sign of the cross again. My heartbeat alternated between hops and leaps.

"It was rumored that this man was taking advantage of the girls. We tried to intervene."

"When you say 'taking advantage,' what do you mean?"

"That he, well, was abusing them."

"Sexually?"

"Having relations with them. Yes."

"Both?"

"Oh yes, Mr. Starslinger. Awful."

"How did you hear this?"

"We have friends in the community. It's a small town. There's chatter. It started with stories of them sunbathing in the nude and skinny dipping. Then, worse. People saw what was going on."

"Saw them having sexual relations?"

"In broad daylight, outside their house, in the backyard, in a hammock. Just terrible."

"What did Sister Sloane do?"

"She tried to talk to Sunday, but she never could break through. Sunday came by one afternoon and cried her eyes out. But she never would speak out."

I flashed through what I knew and gave thought to the nightclub. The Sugar Shack. And how he called Sunday "Sugar." I envisioned all those college girls. On Ecstasy. On Spring Break. How it became a hot spot. And his "Ladies Nights." And that fifteen-year-old in the paper. Charges had been dropped. It was almost too twist to contemplate at once. I wanted to throttle Chuck Fairchild right there.

I snapped out of an horrendous ADHD image stream and saw the water welled in the good Sister's eyes.

"Then he was put in jail for tax dodging. And Sunday just took off. Finally. We were so happy for her. She was free, after all she'd been through. And they got him too! But for the wrong thing!"

The good Sister broke briefly and dipped her head. I stepped in and held her tight. "We loved them so much—"

"I know," I whispered. "Sunday knew too. It's why I'm here."

She hesitated a moment. "I'm sorry I wasn't forthright with you before. Didn't know who you were. We are servants of God, but, well…"

"You don't have to explain."

"We protect the chillens. In life and after."

"I understand."

"May God be with you, sir."

Before I drove off Sister Jamison thanked me for the contribution. I told her it wasn't much though she didn't agree.

"Thousand dollars buys a lot of tickets to the Seaquarium," she proclaimed thoughtfully.

37

Med-Free Harry

I drove without much talent, my circuits flooded and flashers set off. I couldn't think straight. My mitts were clammed and I nearly lost the wheel on a turn. My mind was bombarded with thoughts, most of them dark and vengeful. There were too many directions to take. The safest thing I could do was check into a hotel and try to maintain.

A long shower helped me remain calm. You see, I'd stopped taking the psycho-stimulants, as I feared they were making me a drug-dependent zombie. Sure, they helped me focus, but they numbed me out, too. I determined that I needed those peaks and valleys and didn't want to be dumb-downed and stripped of will and emotional force, for days like this. I needed the force. As for focus, I prayed for it.

Bet your ass my next stop was the correctional facility. I wasn't certain they'd let me see the creep; and if they did, would he agree to see me? He didn't have to. I carried on anyway on the double quick.

The reality is, I was tapped enough to do it. I sensed Chuck "Tomcat" Fairchild was twisted enough to want it too. After all, I'd been bedding his favorite gal, the one who'd given him years of perverted pleasure. He'd received many an afternoon of three-walls-and-a-grill kicks from his jealous meditations on us, I was sure. After brief analysis, it was clear Chucky Fairchild couldn't *not* see me.

I phoned forward to deliver the message and he was waiting for me with a jackhammer knee. He was splayed in that chair, a half-smirk pasted to his mush. It was a goal to keep calm, it had its degree of difficulty. I wanted to murder this guy.

"Shakespeare," he mused. "What gives me the honor?"

"I was in the area."

"Just passin' through?"

"Could say that."

"Y'oughta stop by the Shack. Wall-to-wall twinkies on vacation."

"That a fact," I sent back like deadwood, controlling myself, while my pulse was stammering.

"All stoked finals are over. Don't gotta do much, they're wet-willied 'fore enterin' the door. Just talk to 'em about their major, unless yer lucky and get a freshman. Then you can help 'em decide on one. The best creamy, them high school juniors and seniors, they need to find a college—" He belched out at that. "Goddamn quail shoot."

Chucky had clearly been informed what I'd been up to on my return trip to Niceville and he was trying to get at me for it immediately, with his quick-toss of the young girl thing.

"Guess that leaves you all perved up and nowhere to go—"

"*Shiiiit*," he sang southernly.

His expression went from smug to more so, but I decided to bite my wagger and play along. "Spring Break's been good to you, eh, Chucky?"

"Kiddles love my place. They're the future. Gotta treat'em right. Soon as I get sprung, I'm gonna open up in Tallahassee."

"To tap in to that Florida State young stuff?"

"Sassy Tallahassee. Got your thinkin' cap on today, Slinger. That's what they call you, right? Slinger? Or is it Harvey?"

I didn't take the bait, but registered it had been put out on a line and cast. He'd obviously done some homework too.

"Personally I like 'Slinger.' Anyhoo, FSU? Best jammy in the state. So whatcha up to? Lookin' for Jap flags and skid marks?"

"You know me—"

"What'd you find out? That I'm a war hero?"

"Even war heroes have to pay taxes."

"Don't begrudge Uncle Sam one bitty. Slip o' the pen, won't happen agin," he jingled.

"Found out a few other things—"

"Where you been snoopin', that orphanage?"

"What were the nudes for, Chucky?"

"What nudes, Slinger?"

"The ones of Sunday…"

"Well, yer smart bomb still ain't hittin' no target. From when? When she was twelve? Thirteen? Fifteen? Seventeen?"

He surely was repulsive, but I had to retain my cool. "The ones taken in a New York studio. By a guy named Morny."

"Those? They're for what they're always for. The files."

"Files?"

His demonic little eyes cooked up more sparkle. "Keep photos o' all my girlies."

"You killed her, didn't you?"

I scanned his face for the instantaneous freeze or guilt reflex.

"Which one? Sugar? Tessy? Brenda? Darlene? Gimme a hint, Slinger." He'd blown right through it unfazed.

"Sunday."

He reclined back and added a bigger dose of despicable smirk to the unshaven jaw. His mug looked wholly gruesome to me.

"Now why would I do a thing like that?"

"Because you're a whack bastard."

"Really? Thought you said I was a war hero."

I was boiling beneath my skin. This guy had no remorse for anything he'd done. I realized then it had been a senseless maneuver to come. For me, it was an exercise in humiliation. For him, it was the Super Bowl. He knew how much I cared for her, but he hurt from the fact that she'd loved me, the little girl he'd scandobranded with his hot iron all those years before and considered his property and he was just going to wash my face in shit for four quarters.

"I'm going to get you put away. Forever."

"Are you now?"

"See you in pedophile hell." I twisted up on the pivot to leave.

"Whoa there, Shakespeare. Where you goin'? Where's that Yankee politeness? You may be done with me, but I ain't at all finished with you. We gotta talk—"

"Yeah? What for?"

"We should work together…"

"On what?"

"On finding who killed her. Got me some theories. Should be real interested in my theories..."

"Yeah, right." I'd heard enough and spun and retreated.

"They involve someone real close to you..."

I hesitated. I had to. "Who?"

The man shot up from his chair, screaming and finger-stabbing.

"You, you motherfuckin' gossip faggot! You couldn't handle a thoroughbred like her. She just used your ass to get a little ink so she could take care of things—"

"Take care of what?"

"Us, her family."

"You're not family—"

"You saw it, she was my girl. S'why she did nudies. Letting me know what the body and mind I possessed was lookin' like while I was in the joint. To remember the good times. And I want to thank you our messenger paperboy for helpin' us get the big buckies."

"She didn't give you any money—"

"Check them accounts, Shakespeare."

"You're a liar—"

"While yer at it, check that beachfront property I signed up for off Old Beach. That ain't all Shack money, that's Sugar money. My new beach home when I get out and it don't end there. You know why I called her Sugar, don't you?"

He put two grimers in his mouth as if tasting them.

"She dumped your ass," I threw back. "And came up north to shove it in your face—"

"Come now, Slinger. You'll never make it as a reporter. You can't get the facts straight. Young girl like that, cheerleader legs, ass like a peach and a super sugar-puss? She gotta work out. Bet she gave you them blue pills. Gave 'em to everyone. How 'bout that rapper she was givin' swifties in the studio? and that doctor lady whose steamy she was lickin' down? She was nudin', suckin', fuckin'. Where were you when the good stuff was happenin' behind your back?"

I was stunned by what I was hearing, but took comfort in knowing Chucky was a pathological liar; that this may be his reality distortion field specially laid out to get deeply under my skin all the way to the bone. It was the only way to cope with it.

"Hell, up north she was lickin' ladies, doin' niggers, nudie snap fotogs, even tattle-faggies like you! Whatever it took to get me my thousand acres and a slice of blue—"

"You're full of shit!"

"Why the hell else would she open her slammies to your sorry ass, fool? With yer fruitcake talk, sleazer job, and cockroach life. Prolly think you were somethin' special gettin' a roll with her. Get over it, Harvey! She used you like a grease towel! Gal was workin' the town and I gave her permission to. You guys were the giving tree! E-e-e-asy money!" Sure, he added a triumphant Confederate howl. "Say Harv', if you see that nigger-rapper thank him for that singin' contract, will you?"

"How do you know what she was up to in New York?"

"Got my ways. Harvey boy, you were stockin' stuffin' for her."

The suppressed fury mounted and burned each time I heard the old name, and he knew it.

"Face it: she cooled on you fast, as in overnight. You must not have done enough butt-stuff with her. Sugar loved the butt-stuff. The hearty ramrod? Hell, from behind, Harvey? Cunt was at her best. You done missed out…"

I couldn't handle it. I was shuddering and it spewed forth fast a choppy.

"You raped that fifteen-year-old and paid her off. You sexually abused Sunday for years. Nina too. Who knows how many countless others you raped and abused. Nina ran away. Sunday broke off from you. You had her killed. The whole town knows you're a depraved pedophile. And murderer. They all want you in prison for life. And I'm going to make sure you never get out of your little masturbation chamber!"

"Poor Harvey," he gibed, "gonna put me on Nancy Grace? *The O'Reilly Factor?*"

He sprung up then and pounded the glass.

"Well, bring it on! But Factor this, motherfucker! Who was the jealous one? Who *is* the jealous one? I had her since she was twelve, I had her first time. Right there in that bay water house, under my sheets, drainin' me off daily while I watched Gameday, and breaking it off in her ass at halftime. I had her best days. You came at a time when I couldn't give a good goddamn about her. I was just makin' a payday, but to you, she was the Goddess Supreme. You never thought you'd get something as fine as a flapjacked twenty-four-year-old version o' her. With what I'd done to her, bitch was spent! I had it every night, Slinger. Still get it every night, whenever I step into the Shack. I put it down right upstairs. They know the rules, no flossies. Knows I won't touch 'em if they do. And what do you think they do, drunk little teenies on Spring Break? Run away? Phone home? Text their boyfriend? I get four at a time all season long. If they're feelin' bashful I help 'em along. Tabs o' X, Transformers, Optimus Primes, Rufies, GHB. Until their eyes are swimmin' like goldfish in a bowl. And I'm peelin' them whale's tails down and plantin' my face in the slushie. Then I flip 'em over and raise it up and drill it deep into their tighty until their eyes pop. Nothin' like a teenie queen whose first boyfriend's too shy to fuck her in the ass. That's what Uncle Chucky's here for; I get it fresh and direct."

The bastard then calmly leaned back, lit up a fresh cig, and took a poke off it. To get all contemplative. I wanted to vomit.

"I'll confess, they don't like me much the next morn'. Could call it hatred. 'Cause they feel it. That burnin'. It never leave 'em all day. As they lie in the sun, take a swimmy, wipe on sunny block. But that burnin' never go away. So, neither do I. Sure they tell them sorority sissies 'bout it, it pass around. Details kill 'em, to pieces it kill 'em. 'What a creep!' 'Pedophile!' like you say. I heard it all. And them little piggly wigglies make her feel bad and they'll 'never go back to that place.' Little hypocritters. When all the while it hit'em just as hard, right down there where it flow. And they gone milky thinkin' 'bout it through the day long."

"Yeah, them girlies hate me. As they shower for the night. Wash their little puddies. Twist on that baby jean skirt. Admire their sunnyburn. Put on face paint. And feel that burn. They absolutely hate me. 'Cause deep down they know. They got rocked. Unlike never before. To the core! And they realize somethin', somethin' in life they had no way o' knowin'. They liked it, Slinger. And it grind away on them pure tiny minds the day long. That's why they hate me. And those who didn't get it hate me motherfuckin' double."

He took another haul off the stick and blew through it.

"Then what happen? They suck down rummy punch bowls at din-din. Meet frat-boys. But somehow they find the joint 'boring.' 'N' 'this place sucks.' And boy, do they hate me. That is, until one of 'em mention it. And everyone stay silent. And no one disagree. And they make it seem like a fluke when it ain't no fluke. 'Cause they knew all along they were comin'. Comin' back. To the Sugar Shack." He sang it out, rhyming like the devil's jester.

I was shaking in my heels forced to hide buzzing hands. I'd never heard such a pour of filth. Call it a twist of my own, but I had to know. I had to know just how rabid, how heinous these animals were. The homegrown insurgency, the true domestic terrorists. In essence, what the world was really up against, in addition to the rest of the globe's sworn enemies of civilization.

"And guess what, Slingy? I'm expectin' 'em. Like clockwork, they show. Floyd ring me and let me know. They do a couple laps. Pretendin' not to be aware. O' nothin'. 'Cause they all hate me, 'member? Until one of 'em spy me. 'By chance', o' course. And last night's news hear that and her heart starts a'hammerin'. Until she can't take it no more and she git her nerve and make her way over. For some reason. When she meet my eyes finally, that little hissy fit face melt. And brighten up. She explode from within, in fact. Been talkin' shit about me all day. But deep in her mind I ain't so bad. She know I'm special. 'Cause I know everythin' 'bout her. I seen everything she got. And had it. And she know I know. And she like it. And standin' 'fore me now I know her heart's poundin' and she just as about as wet as wet can be. Hell I know more about her than her damned daddy. Closer to her by definition. Know how she gasp. Cry. Moan when her nipples get sucked. 'N how her wettie taste. 'N' which way her eyes roll when she take a few miles o' redwood inside. Next to that, what Daddy done? Bought her '31 Flavors'? Set up playdates? I been to places Daddy never been. That place deep where she scream out, where 'no' means 'yes!' and 'don't' mean 'don't stop!' I changed the chemicals in her gutty. Just had to be away from that sorority, polite society, hypocritters, judgments, and her old man, to express herself freely. Like the woman she wanna be…"

"You're a real liberator, Chucky."

"Pleased it don't escape you none, Slings. I give 'em somethin' they been yearnin' for all their teeny-tiny lives. Given the choice o' that freedom, in a sunny resort, 'n no watchful eye upon 'em what you think they gonna do? It's what Spring Break is all about." To which the scandoscum nodded proudly at his words.

"You got it right. When I'm done, they got themselves a new one. A new Daddy. I'm their Daddy, Slings. And that's what they call me."

"Daddy-Mister." I had to articulate it though it was an invitation for him to improve upon his despicable, self-satisfied grin.

He accepted. "And so it go…"

"Gorgeous."

"Yah-huh. By the third night o' hollyday week got 'em all up here. Sittin' like duckies in a row. All takin' turns. Bobbin' away on my boy. That's right, Slings. One after the other. Watchin' each other, how they do it. Then I take'em, each one. Privately. In the office. Close the door. And bend 'em over the desk. And choose which way they gonna git it first. Eeny, meeny, miny, mo. And give it to 'em. Them sissies felt no tighter bond than after visiting old Chucky in the Shack, tell you that. See, I provide 'em with somethin' different. Somethin' special. Special is somethin' they can never talk about. To no one. 'Cept themselves. Can never tell their parents, their future hubbies. Why? 'Cause it'll ruin the bastards. But them memories'll be real freaky to 'em. Forever. Best they ever had. They're the ones that'll always do the job. Always make the honey run. Instantly. On demand. As they lay silent and ho'ny in their beddies for the rest o' their lives. They'll always be drawn to them mems of ol' Chucky. And'll call upon 'em. Chucky on demand. In the Shack. When they got rocked. Beyond their wildest imaginations. Oh yes, Slinger, Spring Break bin good to me. And them young slutties."

The creep sucked another one in deep and blew a few smoke rings and waited to watch them disappear until the rings became nothing.

"Course once they broken in gotta kick 'em to the curb. Can't have'em hangin' on, no-sir."

It rolled from my mouth in disgust. "That's how it works…"

"That's the Chucky way. If their parents only knew where their vacation money went, eh, Slings?"

"The Chucky way."

"Damned straight. Then they're beggin' to visit me here in the joint so they can show me their Brazilian bush-waxed twatties. That's how it work—"

"Think I've heard enough…" Really I couldn't take it any longer. Gut fluids were badly brewing, threatening to surge up. Face to face with the sickest breed of Spiderman, the most treacherous and evil of the lot, I could feel my health rapidly deteriorating.

"Nope, them twinkies never forget ol' Uncle Chucky. Shack beats the hell outta them chitty-chat rooms. 'Cause they're already in the damned house! Liquored up. *Shiiit*. If *Dateline* only knew…"

I angled away to pretend I was bored, though I was still trembling from the vile pitch. It prompted him to twist out his stick. His eyes climbed around some and off the wall and he seemed to break from his gloat, only to sit forward again.

"As for you, Slinger boy, you'll never see pretty gash like that agin. Ever. Gash is gone, *POOF!*" He spat and roared with laughter. Composing himself, the demonic one leaned in with burning beams, "'N you shouldn't o' done it, Harvey—"

"Say what?"

"I'm on to you, I know you done it. Yeah, you. For the same reason you think I done it…"

"No—"

"Don't 'member, do you, Harvey? See I heard 'bout you too. Got problems with yer nut, 'memberin' shit. Sugar told me she did. But just think, Harvey, who was crazy in love with her? Me? Or *you?* She wasn't cheatin' on me, she was cheatin' on you, and you couldn't handle it. You cracked! And all your little eggs. You sopped it up, did China whitey. You been cryin' up a storm ever since. Why you here now, Harvey? *Why?* Yer so fucked up you just had to come. You gotta know! You gotta know the real grime and how it all ended. Well I'm here to tell you, you strangled the damned bitch!"

"You're a fuckin' liar!"

He kept right on throwing it.

"You had to know I was first one inside them yammies ten years gone and you had to know how it felt. Felt goooooood. And now I'd like to know how it feel for you to be a killer, a *SECOND TIME!* That's right, Harvey! I know you offed your kid sister! Know all about it. So tell me, how it feel to be a *double murderer?*"

Sounds exploded thrown forth from deep in my gut. I blew.

Reacting to all the shouting, the guards stormed in to haul me out of there. He was still yelling as they gripped my wrists.

"Got a gift for you, Harvey! *They're coming back! Click! Click!* The cuffs are coming! *Click! Click! Clickety-Click!*"

It was too much; I wrestled free of the guards and rocketed toward him head first, pounding the window right where his face was pressed against it. His ghastly features were mashed into the glass in further mocking and taunting me, his barrage unrelenting.

"Official report claimed it was an accident, but I know you killed little Cait! Forget that too? Choked her, too, you did! But that's okay, Harvey. Bitch prolly had it coming, bitch prolly wasn't *FUCKING YOU ENOUGH!*"

He was laughing his damned head off too.

The guards dragged me away kicking and hollering and Chucky just kept it flying.

"They're coming for ya, Harv'! Git ready for lockdown! Cuffs're comin'! *Click! Click! Clickety-Click! You hear me, Harvey?? You hear me???*"

38

Night of No Wonders

I drove to the shore and was only honked at for faulty maneuvers twice. I needed wind, and I needed space. I rammed the Mustang into a roadside ditch then faded over the high dunes and plopped down in that little sun bowl, the one Sunday and I had discovered months before. I let fly a stomach's worth in the dune grass. Cops found me sitting there twenty excruciating minutes later.

"No walking on the dunes," I heard one blurt.

I was in violation and the prowlies gave me a ticket. They gave me a funny look, too, when I asked where'd they been when my friend had been sexually violated by a local perv for years on end in Niceville. And what departmental beauts were on his payroll covering for him. We didn't end mutual supporters or even friends, and I didn't promise anything for their local Police Benevolent coffers. When they saw I was from New York, they tacked on the "insulting an officer" charge with maximum penalty fee counts.

"Nice town, nice people, Niceville," was my final answer. It cost me a buck twenty-five for the significant related jollies.

I drove for a while and slotted the car properly enough. I sauntered down to the beach and studied the surf spray.

It was the beach where Sunday and I had spent an afternoon, not making love. Now I knew why. She'd had that ugly window spiraling in her head to think about, cry over, to ruin another promising day. Having been used by that bastard for all those years. When she was alive I'd obsessed over the growing distance between us and all the whys. Now I understood and I felt like a fool.

No wonder she was concerned for me; no wonder she wanted to see a psychiatrist. No wonder she distanced herself from me as she confronted her past in the those sessions. No wonder she broke with me after the psychotic display, no wonder she stayed in touch. No wonder I was the one she asked to accompany her to Florida to confront her father. No wonder she wouldn't tell me anything, no wonder we reconciled, but had no physical contact. No wonder she was capable of it only after she saw him. No wonder we didn't use the main bedroom, no wonder Nina ran away. It was all piecing itself together, throwing it in my face. Nice town, nice folks, nice boyfriend.

Swapping pasts with Sunday had never been a fair exchange. No matter how much I'd told her about my personal setbacks, they didn't match up. They couldn't. Her abuse went right to the core of her soul. It was pure violation. Mine, a sign of the times and for the most part, accidental. And not sexual.

My stomach churned and twisted, my face didn't have it as cheery. Plopped in the sand there, I cried better than a newborn. Nicely, oh so nicely. In the environs of Niceville.

Could I have done it as Chucky said? No way. As the police implied? Not possible. Could I have? It was too horrific to ponder.

I didn't care to use my hotel room, so I just loitered there late on the beach taking in the nocturnal oceanfront noises. I mulled and rethought everything until I couldn't anymore and passed out.

It was nearly dawn when I heard the pitters. My shoes and pant legs were wet. The fiddler crabs were dancing past anxiously before the receding tide, with no guilts of having helped mess up someone's life, just the simple pleasures. A crustacean's embrace of the new rising day. I was envious.

I collected my bags from the hotel, ignored the pillow chocolates, and flew back to New York. I arrived in the early afternoon floating in shock. I needed the medication more than ever. I'd been experiencing too many full-bore, uncut mood swings. I needed relief.

I'd never been so scared in my entire life.

39

The Gotham Gripster

But the relief I sought didn't come; only disbelief did.

I noticed it first when I touched down at LaGuardia. It was spread across someone's lap in baggage claim. On the drive into town with Alphonso, Radio 1010 WINS confirmed it. I scoped it again in SoHo in the window of my preferred shop of periodicals.

I'd made it all right; to the front page of the *New York Post*. They already had a name for me, too: "The Gotham Gripster." The sultans of scandalocity had scored again. The photo showed my two hands around the throat of Sunday Fairchild effectively, and unquestionably, choking her. Her face was flushed, pressured, and puffy as if she was hysterical and desperately clinging on to life.

"Where to go, Señor Slinger?"

"*Casa*, Fonz. *Casa*."

"*En serio?* You are sure?"

The Fonz maneuvered the town car up to my door on Broome Street. The scandofeds were clustered there awaiting my arrival. Detective Steve led the pack. There were six others, four more in uniform.

"See ya, Fonz."

"*Adios, amigo*," he said with a pitying expression.

I emerged from the vehicle and scandocam flashes slapped away at my face and the scando-video rolled. As I was shoved into the squad car, I could hear the chanting from the sidewalk.

"*Choke!*" "*Choke!*" "*Choke!*" was the repeated message.

It was the scandochant basketball fans all over America employed whenever former New York Knick player Latrell Sprewell came to their arena and made it to the foul line, referring to the incident in which he'd throttled his former coach.

We pulled away with prowler vans in front and behind. I saw long-lensed scandocams zooming in to get an eight-by-ten glossy of the prize: the Gripster's grill.

Outside the Fifth Precinct, the awaiting scandosnappers popped away as news hounds barked: "Why?", "Did you do it yourself or did you have help?", "Is it true Sunday was having a child with Aeneas Nitr8?" And the topper: "Did you strangle your sister, too?"

The worm had turned and it was now me in the scandojam.

Once we were inside the cop house, Steve and his colleagues were actually pretty calm. It was their job to be. They knew me well enough to know that if I had done it, it had likely been a crime of passion. Perhaps. I didn't know what they knew. Or believed.

We sat in a drab, narrow rectangular room that had tape recorders and a flat-screen TV. My seat was plastic and uncomfortable. They offered me a cup of coffee. I asked for three. They offered me a cigarette, I took that too. They were in interrogation formation: a line up of hang-dog faces, the Mount Rushmore of Homicide at the Fifth Precinct positioned in a semi-circle in front of me. Only there were six. Two held spiral notebooks. Steve did most of the talking.

"You have anything to say, Harry?" He'd dusted my more familiar nickname long ago.

"No, not really."

I told them I didn't want to speak without the presence of my attorney. That's when they told me they were going to arrest me for the murder of Sunday Fairchild if I didn't talk.

He started in with the timeline stuff again and my whereabouts the night of the murder.

"Your former roommate is sticking to his story. He didn't see you."

"What do you mean by 'former roommate?'"

"They moved out. Didn't they move out, Turk?"

"Like pack rats."

"I didn't know. I hope he left a check."

"For what?" Marty asked.

"For last month's rent."

"Enough of the bullshit, Harry. Why don't you tell us what happened?"

"I've said it over and over…"

And all the dogs let loose at once.

"We'll go over it a hundred times until we get the straight story!"

"Get your story straight! This is my life, remember?"

"You took someone else's life! Who gives a rat's ass about your life?"

"Okay, okay," Steve said. "The day of the murder. How many times did you visit the victim's apartment?"

I swallowed first, then calmed and smoothed over features so they could not betray me. "I'm not exactly sure."

"More than once?"

My pulse quickened. "Perhaps, yes."

"Dr. Van den-whatever, the shrink, claims you told her you were there twice, with the victim early that night, then later."

My heart sank. Thanks a bunch, Dr. Greer, I thought. Nice doctor-patient secrecy oath.

"I don't remember saying that. I do remember seeing Sunday that afternoon, maybe five o'clock."

"You never told us that—"

"You never said anything about earlier that night."

"Because I wasn't there earlier that night. It was at four or five o'clock."

"So now it's four o'clock?"

"That's what I'm saying, not at night. What do you think four or five o'clock is? Afternoon."

"Want me to read your statement back to you, Harry? It's been years since we fucked up direct quotes."

"Reel-to-reel doesn't fuck up direct quotes."

"So you just forgot a little detail like you'd been with her earlier that night? The night she was killed?"

"I didn't consider four o'clock 'night,' okay?"

"Harry! Night, day, noon, afternoon, it doesn't fucking matter. You didn't tell us you were that at all the first time!"

"I'm not sure what I said…"

The beat down was on. It was rapid-fire, it was high-stim, the kind I didn't find so pleasurable. I was facing a firing squad.

Ready! Aim! Fire!

"Where were you, Harry, at eight o'clock? Where were you at eight-thirty?"

"You haven't been at home writing on your computer at eight-thirty in a hundred frickin' years, Harry!"

"Where were you at nine? Where the hell were you, Harry?"

Steve, all of a sudden, quieted the dogs. "Harry, do you know a Dr. Thomas Skinner?"

"Uh, it sounds vaguely familiar."

"Vaguely? Well he knows you more than vaguely. He's part of a team of physicians at Columbia Presbyterian Hospital. They're doing a study on brain disorders and they've been studying you. Testing you. Ring a bell now?"

"Right, yes—"

"Eureka! He remembers!"

"'Cause that's a problem, isn't it, Harry? Your memory. Sometimes you can't remember so well, when you get stressed or pissed off. You get headaches. Migraines. And the pain is so bad it drives you nuts, isn't that right? And you get all crazy and sometimes violent and when it's all over you can't remember what the fuck happened. Right, Harry? You have a type of amnesia. What's it called, Marty?"

He spat it forth from a spiral. "Transient Global Amnesia."

"Yeah, TGA. Sound familiar?"

"*Vaguely?*"

"It's a theory, Steve."

"It's more than a theory, Harry. Doc Skinner says you got it."

"How could he? I never went back."

"Went back where?"

"For more tests. They wanted me to, but I didn't go back."

"And why not? Why not, Harry? Why didn't you go back?"

The former scandofuzz associate was bearing down on me. They all were. I didn't answer him. It was all big cop macho rot.

"I'll tell you why," he continued. "Two reasons. You didn't want to know. And more importantly, you didn't want anyone else to figure it out—"

"Figure out what?"

"That you killed Sunday Fairchild in a jealous rage!"

"Did not!" I noted I'd answered like a child, no doubt a defensive reflex due to all my frequent "did not" denials as a kid.

"You avoided getting diagnosed! With a condition that proved you got problems with your memory! You knew it made you look bad—"

"That's bullshit, Steve!"

"Then tell me, how do you know? How do you know you didn't kill her? You can't remember shit from that night; we've proven that!"

"'Cause I was drinking! Not choking someone!"

"Who said anything about choking?"

"It's on YouTube!"

"You killed her, Harry!"

"No!!"

"Choked her like a rag doll!"

"Another choke-Romeo!"

"For fuck's sake, Harry, admit it!"

"Confess!"

"We can book you now!"

"On what? What possible evidence could you that I killed her?"

It was a question I knew they'd have an answer to, but I let the whole damned thing play itself out.

"*This*, town car Romeo…"

The videotape was almost professional standard and they proceeded to play it for me in its entirety on the interrogation room flat screen. Sure, I knew when and where and what had happened and how it had gotten to them. It had been shot in that town with all the nice folks a year and a half prior, during our trip to the Redneck Riviera. It was a set-up orchestrated by Mr. Chuck Fairchild, ex-fighter pilot, and known-yet-not-convicted-but-still-practicing pedophile, who had been sleeping with two underage girls he'd legally adopted in their teen years, who was so depraved he had his henchman Floyd come over to his little bayou backwater cottage and hot wire it with scandocams to capture his little birdie in the act, the one who'd flown the nest, to see her naked once more and watch her get it heartily from the New York "undie-sniffer" he hated, to see how they did it and in what positions in order to crack himself off nicely and majestically and to compare notes and size. And that I had just finished accusing him of the murder on my second trip there that very day and this little stunt was his revenge. That was the gift, the forthcoming handcuffs he was yelling about when I left the prison.

I told the cops about this and they informed me I was wrong about the timing. They'd received the scando-video long before that. Hearing this, I figured they'd decided it meant nothing to them, that we enjoyed asphyxiation sex, nothing more, because they couldn't tie me to the actual murder with just that. It was coincidental, too circumstantial. They needed more and that's where Dr. Greer came in. She'd changed their minds. Threefold. She'd divulged what I'd told her in confidence, that I'd been to Sunday's apartment on the night of the murder twice and that I'd been tested for a memory disorder as well as the fact I'd revealed in our sessions every one of my sexual habits and details, but, never a penchant for asphyxiation scandosex with Sunday Fairchild. That gave them the real cause to finger me.

"So why show this to me now?" I posed. They didn't answer. "How did the press get ahold of it? You guys?"

Not quite. A "colleague" of Chucky's had sent it to Barbara Walters of ABC News, then sold it to *Entertainment Tonight*, *Access Hollywood*, *The Insider*, and *Xtra*. It had run all day long, I'd been YouTubed endlessly, and the papers printed photos from the video feeds. Old Floyd had been real busy.

"You're a real media darling now, Harry."

"Look... Fairchild was peeved I'd been asking around about him."

"Peeved? You hear that?"

"He was *peeved!*"

"So he had it sent to the media. He knew you guys obviously hadn't done anything with it, which leads me to ask, why *didn't* you do anything with it?"

"We'll ask the questions here, Harry."

They wondered why I'd gone down to Florida. I told them I'd done it for myself. They already knew about Chucky and his reputation. I'd told them about him a year ago.

"For yourself? For your own peace of mind? Come on, Harry. Get real…"

"We discussed your sex life with your shrink, in detail. Right down to the number of times. We also asked you if Sunday was into kinky sex. You said 'no.'"

"You didn't define 'kinky' to me."

"Listen to this guy. Define 'night,' define 'kinky.' Hey, you ain't Clinton and those kinna answers don't work in here!"

"How about define 'murder?'"

"We want some answers—"

"You know what a jury would do with you?"

"Okay, let him answer," Steve interjected. "You didn't tell your shrink about the choking stuff, either. Why not?"

"It was private. As in nobody's business. I didn't want to betray the woman I cared about."

The home video kept rolling before us for everyone's enjoyment at the Fifth. Floyd was a pro. He'd attached his scandocam high up in the room angled down on the bed. You could see and hear everything.

More! Onscreen, Sunday was urging me to apply additional pressure to her throat.

"So, what was going on here?"

"It is what it is."

"Did you instigate it, or did she?"

"Hear it for yourself."

"We're asking you."

"This was the first time you had strangulation sex?"

"Yes."

"Why did she ask you to do this?"

"She liked it."

"Why didn't you mention it before?"

"Again, guys, it was private. And I didn't think it was relevant to you."

"That she liked to get fucked and choked at the same time

AND she was strangled to death? *Hello?* No relevance?"

"Can you get this sloth to stop referring to her in this way? To hell with you guys!"

"Uh-oh, he's gettin' peeved!"

"And sensitive—"

"Better call Dr. Phil—"

"Look what happened to Hutchence," I said.

"Who?"

"Michael Hutchence. Everyone knows he went down having asphyxiation sex…"

"Didn't he commit suicide?"

"No, but he was alone. They called it autoerotic asphyxiation sex…"

"So the fuck what?"

"What's that got to do with you?"

"The story passed around the world. I should know. And I didn't want that to happen. I didn't want that to be the last word on her. Or us. We had very public careers, a lot was at stake…"

It was swift, caffeine-induced thinking. The reality is I didn't have an answer for them. Surely, her desire for asphyxiation sex was crucial information. Whoever killed her could have done it during the act. Accidentally or not.

"I have a question I want to ask. What happened to your serial killer theory?"

"Let us worry about the theories."

Then Turk, a detective with a slooping brown tie, hacked once loudly, then cleared his throat, and all went quiet. It seemed change was in the air, like the direction of the interrogation. "Let's go back in time, Mr. Starslinger."

"What for? But fine…"

"Let's talk about Lockhart, Massachusetts."

It wasn't the "back in time" I'd imagined. I was thinking two or three years, not twenty to twenty-five. I removed my hands from the table so there wouldn't be any steamy residue. "What about it?"

"The death of your sister."

My ticker raced at the sound of it and what it implied.

"Tell us what you remember of that day," he said with emphasis. And all the rock and rubber faces smirked across in harmony.

"I don't see any connection."

"That's for us to determine."

"Just answer the questions!"

"The police report filed claims you saw her fall through the ice. Is that correct?"

"Yes."

"Then what happened?"

I needed to focus; my neck was on the line. I knew to calm and center myself. To speak slowly. In bite-sized sentences. The longer the responses ran, the more I'd have the opportunity to stumble. And look guilty. The very quality they were scanning my puss for.

Keep it small. Brief. Bite-sized. Like item copy.

"Caitlin followed me to the Creek. I loved to go fast. She tried to keep up. And I let her catch up. And she skated into a part where the ice was thin. And she broke through. She went under the ice. I went in after her. Luckily, she was right there. I pulled her out and took her to shore. She was soaked. Very cold. I put her on my back and carried her to Dr. Swenson's house. He was my doctor. A child psychologist. But he wasn't there. So I broke a door window, stuck my hand through, and unlocked it. I brought her inside to get her warm. But she lost consciousness. I tried mouth-to-mouth on her. I'd seen it done in health class. I didn't know what I was doing. But she never came to. I called my house but no one was there. Then the doctor came home. And—"

"And?"

"Can someone explain what's going on here? I'd like to know."

"You're a murder suspect, asshole."

"Lou!"

"Cripes! Listen to this guy!"

"You'd like to know what?"

"I'd like to know what the relevance is here."

"What is the relevance?" This came from Steve. "I'll tell you what the relevance is, Harry. You put your kid sister on your back and carry her nearly two miles, you pass a pay phone just a half-mile away, you have money to pay for a call if you want to, but you choose not to. You don't call your parents, you don't call an ambulance or the local police. You decide it would be better to carry your sister on your back another mile and a half further to your doctor's house, almost a mile further than the hospital when, during all this time, she's fighting for her life from exposure?? And there are slashing red marks all over her throat and neck when you arrive at the doctor's house. Along with traces of both your and her blood on her. How's that for relevance, Harry??"

My eyes flowed over and the water ran silently down my cheek.

"What do you have to say?"

"Nothing," I said barely audible. "Until my lawyer shows."

Steve let out a big sigh.

"Look. Maybe you killed your sister, maybe you didn't. But more importantly, we don't think you're a serial. We think you killed Sunday Fairchild out of passion. Jealousy. We think you found out about her sexual misadventures. You confronted her, snapped, and you killed her. Strangled her. And maybe you know or maybe you can't remember. Now Harry, we're not going after you for what happened in Lockhart. We're not going to bring all that stuff up; it's painful for everyone. You, your father. We won't bring that up if you confess to a crime of passion with Sunday Fairchild—"

"We can get you a better deal, Harry."

"She was a star, don't forget. They will hang you by your balls!"

"You don't want murder one."

I thought about what I'd been hearing and processed it for a while. I had a question. "When you talk about Sunday's 'misadventures,' what are you referring to?"

"You know what we're referring to."

"Who? What did she confess to? Dr. Van den Heugel?" It was a wild stab, courtesy of Chucky Fairchild.

They all remained silent.

"Did she tell you what happened between Sunday and Nitr8?" Again, not a sound in the room. "Look, I don't know what 'misadventures' you're talking about…"

That got a roar from them. "Bullshit!" was the most common phrase belched.

"I found out about Chuck Fairchild, that's it!"

"You mean to tell us you knew nothing of the relationship your shrink was having with Sunday?"

"Still don't."

"Come on, Harry. You knew they were mixing it up."

"Uh—" I couldn't tell if what they were claiming was true, but it would explain Dr. Greer's icy demeanor since Sunday's death. And alcohol abuse.

"Don't play dumb, Harry. They were getting it on for months and you knew it. And when you found out about it you went in there, flew into a rage, and killed her!"

"That's a lie!"

"You were jealous!"

"Crime of passion!"

"'Fess up, Harry!"

"Just like you offed your sister all those years ago!"

"No! I could never!" I erupted.

"You were jealous of her, too!"

"Your parents testified that you were jealous of her."

I was heaving hard. "You've been talking to that cop Hathaway! He's a nut!"

"Come on, Harry! Make it easy on yourself!"

"Your father thinks you killed her!"

Ready! Aim! Fire!

The scandoclamps were tightening down, the noose knotted and muscling in.

"You get jealous and can't control yourself!"

"Your sister got all the attention! They were threatening to send you away! They didn't give a shit about you, Harry! You were angry! You hated them for that! You hated her for that!"

"No!!"

"And you lost it and killed her and fled the scene just like you killed Sunday and fled the scene!"

"*No! No! No!*" I was sobbing uncontrollably now.

"And you can't fuckin' remember any of it!"

"If I can't remember it, how the hell can I confess to it?" I bawled. "*Huh?* Tell me that!"

40

SoHo Solitary Confinement

November, 2K8

They threw it ugly, they threw it pretty, all to make me crack. In the hopes of getting a confession, to book me once and for all. The interrogation lasted into the night. When it was over, they decided against it, surprisingly. They weren't going to charge me. Yet. I was clearly their prime suspect, however. Eight hours after I'd been collared by that brace of scandofeds, my attorney Jason Schwartz drove me home.

The truth is that I wasn't sure of anything anymore. It was all cloudy. Whether my parents believed I killed my sister, I couldn't say. As for me, if indeed I'd blacked out and had a memory lapse in a frenzied, emotional state and participated in any way in those tragedies, I knew I could never survive it.

I was left to bathe in my own chilly sweats until further notice.

From what I'd learned, one claim consumed me more than the rest. It was the second time I'd heard Sunday romantically linked to another individual, confirmed by the cops in their line of questioning. Sunday and Dr. Greer, it would seem, had been lovers.

A fistful of reporters were camped outside my building. They scandocammed me as I slipped inside. I silently went up the elevator, pretty much shell-shocked. The elevator doors opened and there it was, the Skybox. Quiet, deserted, a peaceful scandovoid, and thankfully so. With a note on the kitchen table.

We thought it was best to leave, Harry. I hope you understand. Good luck. Kees and Miep.

The Dutchies were gone. No more cohabitation frolic. I lay on my bed. I had a swarm of phone calls on the machine. More came in through the night, including one from my father. Upon hearing his voice, I lay there screening the message, listening. He said he was worried about me and thought that I should come up to New England and we should talk.

But the call that really busted me up was from Pablo. He left a message saying he believed me, that he knew I didn't do it. He told me he missed me and asked if I'd take him to the zoo real soon. I cried into my pillow awhile after that.

My life, from then on, was not the one I'd known for thirty-five years. I was now public property. The Gotham Gripster. And assorted other names. Harry The Ripper. The Strangulator. Mr. Death Grip. The SoHo Strangler. The Butcher of Broome Street. And for the real scandalogical sickos who wanted to credit me for my onscreen scandosexual prowess, as opposed to my rep as an over-and-out snuff artist: The Man With the Golden Hands. The cute coinings just scandofanned the scandoflames.

I'd become my own type of sought-after subject matter. I was someone else's item now, and the Face was endless. Every day there was new Sling. I got scandoslammed. Though I hadn't been charged, I was still under severe suspicion. The facts about my past and Caitlin's death came out, and that I may have strangled her too, which made things worse. The ill-repute flourished in the Golden Age of Infamy. Infamy was my new PR which boosted my NR exponentially.

Where I walked, where I ate, what I bought, snippets of overheard dialogue, things I'd said, things I hadn't said, truths, falsehoods, the whole damned scandalocity enterprise. It was all scandofodder for the making and taking, The Machine uncompromising, the Face unrelenting, and the scandophiles ate it up like Gerber's tapioca. It was scandelirium.

The only paper that left me alone was my own.

Arthur Lawrence didn't fire me, but he may as well have. He asked me to take a sabbatical until things blew over. I wasn't so sure if he thought they would. A lot of people believed I'd done it; the video was pretty scandodamning.

Related stories cropped up daily, about Sunday and Dr. Greer and their secret love affair. Photos surfaced showing them necking. There was an item pairing Sunday with Justin Timberlake and John Mayer. Any single celebrity hottie had to go through that type of linkage. It was the era.

The *Enquirer* ran a story about the night of the MTV Video Awards contending Sunday and Dr. Greer had had an orgy in a limo with Nitr8 and Sophocles. It started as girl-girl and turned into simultaneous takedowns and then a scandoswap. It was the way Sunday had whispered it to me the night of our intimate reunion in Niceville. Minus the swap. A veteran of rumor and innuendo, I saw enough scandosmoke in the account to indicate the probability of fire.

The Machine I'd been feeding for years was now chewing me up. The karmic wheel had swung around and run right over me.

Yet of all the debilitating chaos enveloping me, the question most disturbing was, 'Who was this girl I'd been so hopelessly in love with?' Sunday had been living a wildly duplicitous triple life. And it went completely unnoticed by me, the former award-winning gossip blogger, a true pro at getting the story behind the story.

The Machine's barrage didn't surprise me. Once I was involved, I figured it would be open season. No longer did I receive the fellow colleague's protectionary blanket. I was a celebrity murder suspect with a passion for alternative kinky choke scandosex. Delicious. Dangerous. Scandalous. I probably polished my arsenal of M-16s daily with a closet full of homemade bombs and scando-ammo. Now if they could only get a snap of me and O.J. together, the ultimate scando money shot, the thinking went.

My staycation lasted three weeks. My attorney's advice was simple. Don't talk to anyone. If the scandofeds hadn't pressed charges yet, they wouldn't yet. They didn't have enough on me. What was disconcerting was the implication, he was yet another unconvinced of my innocence, my own attorney.

Colleagues from other papers rang in offering their scandolences. Of course, they pined for the "your version" of the story. To "help" me. I heard from Nightlife and Clyde, too, who both wished me luck.

318   Coerte V.W. Felske

But I never lifted a handset.

A rare, uplifting moment occurred when Exhibit A* BBMed me claiming she was four months pregnant. After giving of herself in the most indulgent, pleasure toy ways and getting serially used in the process, it appeared she'd have a life for her and her child paid for. In essence, the gal had triumphed over the Spiders. Good on her. It was mutual manipulation at its best in a town called Scandoland. Chalk one up for this messy swirl of inexplicable chaos we call life, I thought. And her real name was Tammy.

The only calls of a painful nature were from Dr. Van den Heugel. At first, I received one a day. Obviously, I didn't pick up. If I hadn't been shocked enough by Sunday's behavior, Dr. Greer's amoral conduct was an unforeseen bonus. Our doctor-patient relationship had been violated twice, once with Sunday and once with the cops. Lastly, Dr. Greer had been romantic with my girlfriend. Dr. Greer had outright betrayed me three times. Perhaps that was why she had a drinking problem. Perhaps she just liked her spirits in the afternoon. As a coach, the gal wasn't going to be joining Vince and the rest of the Green Bay Packer greats in the Hall of Fame any time soon.

41

Driven to Distraction

"Harry, come on. Pick up. Was it something I said? You can't leave me hanging; I'm beside myself. Okay, here it is. Hair Wars is on. I know you're thinking 'again?' But I found antique products in a drawer. Bleach, I guess. And combed it through. And my hair turned another color. Tangerine. I heard everyone in town was going to that Art Basel weekend in Miami, those hipsters you write about. I don't know them. But I had to fix them good, the ones coming back with tans and big teeth and blond-cocky. I wanted to look like I'd been traveling, too. I was alone. In my apartment. With those chemicals. So tempted. Before I knew it Hair Wars was back. It's worse than the spiky fro-hawk and the putting green slash-cut (with hole on top) combined. I was taking my meds too! Don't know why I can't leave my salad alone. I'm in lockdown until springtime. So please. Come by and walk me. Then we'll have some Spaghettios. And cream soda. I've left sixteen messages. I know you're there. This is seventeen. My heart is on my sleeve. Pick up!"

I did pick up, finally, and it was Marty Collins, also known as "Driven to Distraction," taken from the book title of the same name, the ADDer's Bible. I let Marty know my silence had nothing to do with him, that I'd gotten in trouble recently and now everything was better. Almost. I left out the 'almost' part. Marty was so self-consumed and self-absorbed he hadn't heard of my troubles nor did he bother to ask. I didn't bother to divulge.

Marty had a severe case of AvPD, avoidant personality disorder. AvPDers consider themselves socially inept and personally unappealing and they avoid social interaction for fear of being ridiculed, rejected, or disliked. Whenever Marty felt an urge to go out in public, he attacked his hair to ensure another self-designated apartment lockdown.

I messengered a baseball cap over to his apartment and offered to have lunch with him as soon as my life settled down. I assured him I'd walk him and we'd order in.

As amusing as it was, the image of Wally Fox, the Jack-in-the-Box looking like an orange-blond surfer from the Ukraine didn't provide much solace. I had bigger fish to fear during my very own sojourn into self-imposed exile.

42

A Cube and a Dream

I kept turning it over in my mind, about Sunday and her different lives. I pondered Chuck Fairchild and how he'd contributed to her dysfunction, giving thought to my very own contributions. I'd taken her under my wing, a fragile person with a disastrous past and, though unknowingly, I fed her right into the jaws of the lion, The Machine, in the most scandomaniacal, scandocentric period in history.

I'd supplied her with the cardinal rule: *Don't believe your own press.* She'd obviously swallowed the attention whole, convinced of the veracity of her hype and image, imbibing its spirit; then proceeded to live it, the scando no-no I'd warned her about. Her same-sex sway began with the Two Lips campaign, then a "date" with a hip-hop mogul ending in an alleged limo flesh-fest. Seemingly, she'd gone out with the scando Sling in mind and used it as her script and made it happen as if she needed to believe she was as worth talking about as The Machine was purporting her to be. And more.

It is a mean Machine. It's hard to say how it would have ended with Sunday. We were robbed of finality there. Judging by the direction she was headed, her prospects for a long and prosperous career didn't seem so favorable.

Perhaps the most absurd bottom line to this was, the fact that I still missed her. Terribly.

There was a beer in the fridge left by the Dutchies. I sipped on it and stewed things over. Again. Then I ordered a case of Foster's from the deli on Greene Street. I listened to some coolly smooth Michael Franks jazz and drained a few oil cans. It came to me at once. I was done sequestering myself in my fully disclosed location.

I buttered my nests with Speed Stick and decided to get real scandofab, opting for Far Eastern China-rising. I threw on my black velvet Shanghai Tang top coat with lime green silk interior. On my dogs I sported snip-toed Chippewa boots with the harness rings and topped my bean with a Beijing-starred cap with visor shading my grill for the added please-don't-look-at-me-but-please-do pop. I was going for the Mao Tse-tung revolutionary warrior meets *Kill Bill*. Some irritainment pundit said if you have a problem, hang a lantern on it. Well, I was going to put Yankee Stadium lights on mine. I pocketed the coveted purple laces for good luck.

I wouldn't need the Fonz; I didn't want the complications of being tagged and shadowed. By now, everyone negatively appropriate who could make problems for me knew his face and our car. I took a cabster to the East Side and emerged on the corner of 60th with my scandefarious swag intact.

Rocco the Big Boy didn't drop velvet at first, but when I lifted my Red Army star lid he gave me a black bear embrace, then escorted me inside. Angelo took it from there and greeted me not like a murderer and not like a patron, more like a movie star. He gave me my own naughty boy chamber with the big round table within a cut lime's toss from the booth I usually received at the *Oficina*. Only this one was private, had more room, and seemingly no limitations as to what could be done, hand mammograms and beyond.

In seconds, there was a gaggle of scandocandies* encircling me, Angelo, and another "part-owner," Giuseppe. Each starkie gave me a dance in sequence and the city's latest scandotante didn't complain. One thing was for sure: it wasn't as if nothing had happened. I was clearly being perceived differently. I was no longer a dolce vita scribe, I was no longer Slinger. I was no longer a person at all. I was a star, a scando star, which just happened to be the most sought-after type in the post-millennium era, the class topping everyone's guest wish list and this was my coming-out party, a formal scanduction ceremony. The laws of scandalocity were beaming starlight down upon me. I had arm scandy left, arm scandy right and the scandotante sat there scandohamming it, bathing in his champagne brew of notorious notoriety. And the scandophants continued to swell as the scandophiles rejoiced. Natch. My infamy was peaking in fuchsia neon.

A few high-steppers* asked me for autographs. I respectfully declined. If so inclined, I was sure I could now get decent tee times at most country clubs. Or the choice bowling lanes. Or reservations anywhere worldwide. Access was now anywhere, anytime on any continent where the story had broken. I'd had access when I was a Machine player; a major difference now was that, I didn't have to pay for a damned thing.

Life in that festive chamber was like life in high school when you've returned from summers apart and everyone is ecstatic to be reunited. We went through ten bottles of champagne and an equal number of Grey Goosies. The bucketeers were tanked, booth groupies kept mounting assaults, and so did the arm scandy. The scandotante slipped in and out of moods. They vacillated between the fractional joy derived from the present frolic to more complicated introspection. I received tugs from no fewer than three scandogammers to join in private-private. I was asked repeatedly to play Broadway bumper pool too, but declined. I didn't want any substance-abuser leak mounted atop my chokester rep. I'd pocketed my own sport-meds, Vicodin, though someone tried to slip me a vial of scandocandy. Then I was paid the ultimate scandiment. They played me my song: "Once" by Pearl Jam, a favor never granted to Slinger the online scribe. Angelo had been wrong on this one. The starkies scandodanced up a storm. It was sheer scandemonium.

"ONCE upon a time I could control myself! / Once upon a time I could lose myself! "

At one point, a floss-crotched scandotranny and a floating gay scenester on a Libra Ambition Tour approached me. The tranny posed the question in sassy baritone, "Is choke sex really better?" It was curious how the she-male had made it into the macho club. The surreal fog of scandowar was a good bet.

"I'm a doctor, actually," the she-he followed up with regrettably.

"Of what?"

"Fagulosity."

"Hmmm. I like that."

"I bet you do."

"I like the neologism. Sounds like a word I'd make up. Does it come from fagulous?"

"Of course," came back with a tranny peck to my cheek.

"What's your sign?" the she-male's sidekick lisped my way.

"Taurus, Slinger rising," I said and they squirmed and giggled at the notion.

Then they eagerly recited the Manhattan after-party mantra in unison: "Where are you going next?"

"Don't know. But if there's a sighting of myself, let me know where I am. Or where I've been."

At one-thirty, I was done with the scandohamming. I bade them all farewell, jacked up enough to sign a few scandographs. I even scrawled some 'Nice to meet you's. I was given Angelo's car and his driver named Erez. I just said, "Drive." After twenty minutes of circling midtown, I asked to be let out.

No longer feeling like the scandotante, but still comfortably pixilated, Scandoland's newest superhero, Scando Man, lowered his Chinese star brim and sauntered up Park. Several blocks further up, I came upon a doorman with silvery hair and a dark coat with gold epaulets for trim posed beneath an awning. I inquired about a resident. He inspected me momentarily, then stepped into the lobby. It took a while. He came back out, spread the door wide and uttered, "15-B" for my benefit.

I shuffled down the corridor to the elevators in back. It was an elegant lobby, the marble finishings were uptown-tasteful. I rode up and had a taste of myself in the mirror. Though I was pretty viked up and cocktailed, I didn't look half-bad. Said me.

The door opened and she was waiting for me. She had a silky robe on and her chestnut hair had been freshly brushed. She wasn't wearing any makeup; she didn't need any. She never had needed any. As I stepped out of the elevator, she welcomed me with an enduring hug which was not very professional of her.

"I'm so glad you came."

"I'm glad you're receiving."

"I never do it this late."

"That's a falsehood, Doc."

"You're right. I guess it is."

She stepped back through her door and I followed her. I took in her expansive, expensive apartment. Not only was it big, but it was professionally decorated. It would make a nice layout in *Better Homes and Gardens,* I thought. She even had a small "Jackie O" Warhol. I wasn't surprised; advantage had been her lot in life. She'd come from a few generations of damned good breeding, whatever that means to people to who don't have it. The furs-and-facelifts set. The genetic impurities had been distilled off long ago and taste had been handed down to her, along with the great looks and the sharp figure. And the inheritance-to-be. It was a household that was relatively stress-free.

She asked me if I wanted something to drink.

"Rum and O.J...."

"Sounds like a good idea."

"Go ahead, give me the Ron Rico."

She chuckled at my wisecrack. There were obviously no bottom-shelf bottles in her establishment. Then I spied her. She looked great from behind, those twin moons rendered perfectly by the silken cascade. I watched her pour, too. She had the good stuff, the Havana Club liquid gold. She twisted back at me, giving her once-overs and broke one wide. She seemed happy I was there. I did everything I could not to snort like a razorback.

She returned before me and handed me a squat glass and we settled into a grand living room sofa with pillow high-rises cushioning our backs. We crossed legs and shot it then, afternoon tea-style.

"How's the practice?"

"Not as exciting as it used to be." Sure, she was intimating something.

"Is that a good thing?"

"Not necessarily. I'm so sorry, Harry."

I asked her how she liked my new name, the Gotham Gripster. Acknowledged, I was losing it. Rather, I'd already lost it; the fiberfill was coming out of my corner seams. I pulled out a pack and asked permission and my coach said it was fine. I sparked one and took a big inhale and asked her why she'd gone to the police and told them things about me which were confidential with respect to our attorney-client privileged relationship.

"They threatened me," she said, her pretty bum leaping forward to the edge of the couch. "With jail time. They thought I was involved in the murder somehow."

That seemed ridiculous. I pressed as to how.

She sighed before answering. "They knew I'd been visiting her a lot. They knew I'd seen her the night of the murder."

"You were there?"

"Briefly. I rang the buzzer. She never answered. So I took off."

"How did they know you'd been there?"

"Some tabloid photographer was stationed outside the apartment. He got it all and told them."

I asked her which photographer.

"Someone named Bob."

"Bounty Bob," I repeated to myself, loud enough to be heard.

"I guess. I was later told he'd been hired by your paper."

That was a surprise. *Arthur?* I mulled.

"Apparently, they'd been selling shots to other tabloids since they weren't running any. In deference to you and the relationship."

"Bless them."

"They have everything. Since she became famous, they know just about every move she made. This guy Bob followed her for months."

"Perching in birdbaths, no doubt," I supplied, as promised. I asked her how she'd obtained all that information.

"One of my clients is a policeman's widow. She's still close to an officer with the Fifth Precinct."

I processed that one a moment. "So Greer, it's all true."

She eyed me sharply, registering the fresh name change and then inched closer to talk.

"I called. Many times. I respected your right not to want to speak to me again."

"Swell of you."

"Harry, I'm truly sorry," she sent back. "But, well, here it is.

Sunday came to me for help. She told me about the horrors of her childhood. About this guy Chuck Fairchild and how he took both girls from the shelter into his own home and supported them, then took advantage of them. He made them refer to him as 'Daddy-Mister' and he had sex with both within two weeks of their arrival. He'd be involved with one while the other lay there and he would subject them to psychological torture. He'd play them off against each other, making them competitive for his affections, which weren't even affections. They were submissive acts. He was a scary guy. He threatened them constantly. But they maintained a perverse loving bond. It happens like that. The children can't help but feel close to that domineering figure, no matter how big a monster, seeking approval and love which never comes in the proper form. Only in the form of degrading acts. The more it doesn't come, the more disturbed and unbalanced they become. They'll do anything for it. Effectively, they were slaves, emotional and physical. It was very disturbing to Sunday, who was older. She knew it was wrong, but she couldn't break out of it. She called it an 'invisible prison.'"

"The psychological toll was more damaging to Nina. Sunday was the prettier of the two and Fairchild favored her. When Nina was sixteen, she moved out finally never to be heard from again. You were right when you felt there was a hole in Sunday's life. Nina was the only person she trusted in the whole world, because she knew. Nina was the only person she could talk to. She would never say anything to the nuns. Don't forget; Fairchild had threatened them not to say a word and of course they were ashamed too. Some suspected, but no one found out. You know, one of Chucky's cronies forced himself on Nina."

"Floyd?"

"She hated him, but she wanted to get back at Chuck. So she continued to see him. It's very disturbing. All that had been an overwhelming burden for Sunday. When Fairchild was sent to prison it was the first opportunity for her to break away, so she did. She was scared to death of him. That's why she went to visit him and he demanded you come. She didn't want to bring you; she thought you'd be in danger too, but he threatened her. It's why she hired me and confided in me. She had never been able to tell anyone. It had gone on for ten years. Bastard. He would bring girls back and make Sunday and Nina join in. It's a wonder they didn't kill themselves."

"Couldn't Fairchild have been responsible for Sunday's death?"

"I'm not an expert, but he was in prison, as you know."

"Why not Floyd?"

"Maybe. But from what I learned about Fairchild I don't think he would have let someone else do it. It was too personal. She was his obsession. His sick mind would want her to know it was he—Daddy-Mister—who dealt the fatal blow. To show her one last time who was in control."

Greer got up and fixed us another round. I was sunken into my seat liquored, whacked, with sufficient liftoff. She settled down a half-cushion away. I wasn't craving more space.

"What about you and Sunday?"

She eyed me carefully. Her legs fell open to an uncrossed position, hands dangling below her lap like a benchwarmer waiting to get in the game. She was hunched forward in a masculine sort of way.

"From the moment I met her, I felt a kindred spirit. Maybe the sister I never had. I was devastated and appalled and fascinated and in a state of sheer amazement at her courage. But I confess and it's difficult, but we fell in love. Or I did, anyway."

"And she didn't?"

"I think I fulfilled a role, perhaps the role Nina played in her life. Someone whom she could trust implicitly, with whom she didn't have to worry about judgments or opening up freely without fears."

"She couldn't feel free with me?"

"It wasn't you or your character. Just the gender."

"Same gender as Chucky Fairchild."

"He'd set a horrible precedent, yes. With men, if a woman divulges this sort of darkness it often backfires. Some men can't deal with it and any intolerance will send a fragile victim into an emotional tailspin. She may back away or run. She feared telling you, she feared you'd see her differently. Wouldn't you have?"

I didn't answer. I wanted to hear more of what this woman had to say. She hadn't gotten to the most significant part.

"The whole thing devastated me, Harry. I liked you and you're not even going to believe this, but, I had feelings for you. That's in addition to the anguish I'd experienced for my misconduct. But I did not betray the confidentiality of our sessions to her."

"Perhaps not, but you used what you knew against me."

She angled up sharply and said nothing, understandably so. What she did do though was quickly inhale her drink. The whole thing had been eating her from inside out. I could see it now.

"In effect, you turned her away from me. Because I felt the distance. Our connection chilled. I didn't know what it was. I thought it might have been that awful night we'd had. Or the publicity, The Machine pressure. The truth is, she'd fallen for you."

"Not entirely. I was more taken with her than she was with me. She loved you; she told me she loved you, and she felt very guilty. Even though you'd broken it off. She felt like she was sliding down a chute and couldn't stop. She had deep needs formulated years before from layers of childhood agony. You did nothing wrong."

I finished my glass, took hers and headed to the bar. I scrapped the baby glasses and summoned tall boys from the cabinet. I dumped cubes in each and let the Cuban liquid gold run. I handed hers off and made a trip to the bathroom, where I slapped my face with water.

When I returned, somewhat refreshed, I sat back down and asked her, "When did this all start? The relationship…"

"Does it matter, Harry?"

"Yes."

"Why?"

"Want me to say 'closure?' There's no such thing. Let's go with my sense of understanding, in totality. There's finality to that—"

"Okay." She hesitated, trying to remember. "It started after our fourth or fifth session, a few weeks before the awards show."

That was when I shot up and did a mild pace in front of her. "Tell me about that night—"

"It wasn't a wonderful night, I'll tell you that…"

"Tell me—"

"Harry, you don't want to hear it."

"You bet I do and I deserve it, remember?"

She let out a deep lungful, having settled on a form of resignation.

"It's better if I start from the beginning…"

"Beginnings suit me fine."

"We had an informal meeting at my office to see what she was looking for in therapy. We got to talking, our conversation going in all sorts of directions. It drew me in. We alternated from her personal revelations to mine. About her growing up, about me growing up, about her life in Florida with the nuns. We decided to go to dinner. We had margaritas. During dinner, she leaned over and gently kissed me. We had another round or two. That was when she went in to the dark aspects of her past. I was shocked. She sobbed and I started crying too. Then we came back here and talked until very late. She didn't want to be alone, so she stayed over. We slept in my bed holding each other. You were out of town. We had a couple more formal sessions and then you two broke up a couple weeks later. After that, we had dinner one night and that's when we slept together. Fully. From then on, we were linked. She had a twenty-four hour professional to talk to with me. And she needed it. She needed answers. To questions that had plagued her all her life. And I was there for her. I'd never had a same-sex experience before. In that way, I was filling a different need, one you couldn't. She wasn't at peace in your relationship. It would have been the same with any guy. She had demons. And we, meaning two women, were fighting together to quiet those demons. It was us against the world. Sunday said that and seemed to take comfort in it."

"How did it end?"

"She ended it. We stayed up very late after the awards show. The limo dropped us off and we talked. She said she was still in love with you. But she asked me if I would see her professionally still. I was hurt, but… then she phoned you, right?"

I didn't answer, I was airborne. No one had any pull on me, not even gravity. I was floating high in a relative scandotrance.

"I couldn't desert her, I couldn't not be her analyst anymore. So we moved on as friends and agreed to continue our professional relationship."

I chugged the last of my gold and spoke in a tone uncontrollably low, deep from the diaphragm. "Tell me about the limo—"

"Harry—"

"I want to know!"

She took in another lungful and more came out than went in.

"Mind you, a lot of champagne had been consumed. Sunday and I got affectionate and one thing led to another. We got carried away. It got intense. We were incredibly drunk, but it was really a release, a show of, I don't know any other way to say it, but freedom. Sunday said you'd spoken to her of the danger in believing your own headlines. She felt as though she was trying to act it out, that she was being psychologically drawn to all the scandalous hype her manager had been angling for and was now being written about her. That she'd become seduced by her own hype. One night, she told me about a dream she'd had. She said, 'I went on a date with myself as the Two Lips Girl. And know what I did? I fucked her all night long. With no protection. And it felt great…'"

I reached for her elegant hands, they were slender, white, and bloodless, but they weren't cold. Not now. They were heated and a tad moist and nervous. I raised her from the couch to a full stand. I viewed the points through the silk and took in that belt loosely tied at her waist. How did I know it was "loosely" tied? Robe belts always are. I pulled on the dangler and the lapels silently drifted apart, revealing a tantalizing strip of nudity from head to toe. Both breasts were milky-white, perfectly arranged, fully biodegradable, and nipples partially exposed. I scanned lower, down her porcelain body beneath her ribs to the bikini-perfect concave tummy, and that's when I caught the glint of fire, the diamond-studded navel and the tiny mole beside it and transparent pink-lace panties with a gem-shaped bar beneath. The inner thighs were nicely hollowed and it continued just as harmoniously down shiny lotioned legs, toes painted with a creamy, pearly finish.

"Harry? Are you okay?"

She was a very beautiful woman. And no longer stoic. I stepped in closer until I was up against her. I sent my hands inside the robe and rested them behind her filling my mitts with her moneymaker. Our faces brushed past each other's and settled cheek-to-cheek.

"It's over between us," I announced gently.

"It is?"

"On a professional basis. Dr. Greer, you're fired."

In a sudden rush, I grabbed her by the back of the head and kissed her harshly, as I'd done once before. She was ready and locked on. Our necks spiraled around from the pressure.

Then I undid my pants with my free hand and pressured her shoulders down and she went to her knees. I shoved her head into my waist, making her smother it. "Did you do this?"

Her bean struggled to nod through my grip.

"Did she do it to him?"

The good doctor nodded again.

As I guided her back up the robe fell and I gripped her upright. She was totally naked and eyeing me fearfully.

"Tell me what happened—"

"Harry…" It was the weakest of protests.

I clutched her arm and led her into the bedroom and shoved her down on her back on the bed.

"Tell me!"

As she recounted that evening I listened and held her legs on either side. Without any pause that would exhibit some form of patience, I aimed and smoothed through it. She cried sharply, but then gasped all too excitedly. I charged in and out of her frame as she continued to spin the tale.

"Now tell me about her—"

I withdrew as she resumed, flipping her to her stomach. I vised her beneath her pelvis and raised her backside and she rose to all fours all too willingly and the mammal sounds she made had nothing to do with pain. I leaned forward and clasped hanging fruit which yielded a request, to grip them, harder. I'd arrived at an appropriate gear for her. She enjoyed psychological games, she had a PhD, after all, and she preferred it physical. And exploratory. And new. She was sudsing.

"Then what happened?"

With her arm extended behind me, she dug fine talons into my backside cheek and shoved me forward into her to the rhythm. It was work to hold it, until I couldn't any longer. I had to pause.

Suddenly, her body jerked away from me and she curled and

spun around to sit up and face me. Her eyes were aflame and she said it like a witch, scandosexually possessed and haunted. Which haunted me.

"Then we switched!!"

"*Swi—?*"

"Wild, Harry. The wildest night of our lives!" The witch shrilled excitedly and it had laugh to it. The laugh endured a while.

When she'd exhausted the ecstasy from the charged, taboo reverie, she faded back, eyeing me savagely all the while as she retreated. She lay back on the bed slowly and her head found refuge in the pillow.

She relayed it softly now.

I lowered myself, trying not to think about what she'd said causing myself to lose it. Every emotion imaginable was raging inside me. I was angry, jealous, vengeful, and galactically turned on.

"Come on, Harry, fuck me," she whispered hoarsely. "You've had a night like that. Haven't you? You've had fifty…"

This side of Greer was fresh, a showing I hadn't anticipated. A softer, warmer, and more intimate creature with a sultry pour of whispers, the kind of unique interaction that can make a boyfriend out of you. I felt close to her. She'd done a lot for me, more than any other professional had, and Sunday had brought us even closer especially after her death. But I'd been only looking for the friendly embrace, to share the pain of losing a cherished loved one. Like any male, I'd wondered what it would be like to have her, I'd even considered it, of course. Sure, we'd shared that kiss and quick carcass grope, but this was a surprise. And a reveal. Here she was before me now, naked and open, with sweet, sensual whisperings. It was clear now how and why she'd turned into the Ice Princess. And an alcoholic. But she was ice no more. The wet sheets corroborated it.

"Remember how you spoke of the bags, the breasts in your palms, the panties you coaxed off your Exhibits? Raw female parts drenched with desire? Nights when you had to give in completely, when it should be a 'no,' but it's a 'yes.' It has to be a 'yes,' right? Because you can't say no, you just can't. Fuck me, Harry."

"Ssshhhh," was my response. I still had a fragile hold.

"Okay, I'll shut up. As long as you pin me in place. And fuck me."

We went at it silently in smooth rhythms for another ten minutes. She was chewing on my earlobe, nibbling my neck, enjoying herself, and mouthing gentle words. "Come on, Harry. Do it."

I didn't respond until the command was repeated.

"I am," was returned, labored.

"No, Harry. Do it."

I hesitated. "Do what?"

"You know—"

I told her I didn't know what she was referring to.

"Sure, you do. What you did to her—"

"I don't know what—"

"You just don't remember, don't want to remember. But I understand…"

"Memory is a problem of mine. As you know…"

"Yes, I do. And it happens right now, doesn't it?"

"So they say…"

"While you're fucking. So, do it. Lay down your hands, Harry. Right here. And forget about it all. You know where—"

"No—"

"Please, Harry—"

"I can't—"

"Don't fight it—"

"Stop…"

"I'm here, you're here, it has to be. Give it to me, Harry. Put it to me. The pressure—"

She raised my paw and placed it, then the other. So they both were clutching her neck.

"Know how many times I saw it? I downloaded it, replayed it. Of course I wanted to be there, with you in my mouth while she divided me below? Can you imagine? In the office I wanted to get up from my desk, kneel down in front of you, rip open your pants, let it part my tonsils and suck your cock 'til I choked. And I almost did—"

"Greer—"

"You want to, you know you do. You know what she liked. Now I'll tell you, I like it *fancy-fine* too…"

The words stabbed me like a hunter's serrated knife. "It was you, wasn't it?" I posed. "She didn't do that before. It was you…"

"'Course I taught her. I don't have toys or bags, but I know what I like…"

"I can't believe—"

"Not as uptight Greenwich as you think, am I? Sure, I taught her. Then she brought you on board. Why, Harry? Because you have the force. You have the hands…"

"All along, it was you—"

"Those firm, strong hands, those scando hands…" She was taunting me now. With scandospeak. "Settle down and give me those scando hands…"

"That night—"

"Sssshh. Give it to me, Harry…"

"You were there after me—"

"*Sssshh…*"

"And you did this to her—"

Her eyes were nearly sealed and she widened them to take me in fully, nodding sparely. Then she shook her head even less.

"Couldn't keep our hands off each other. Did it whenever we could."

"You killed her, didn't you?"

She 'eagled her legs, both taking flight apart. "She'd open up this wide…"

"And you told the cops all that stuff—"

"Always the scandal, Harry. *Tsk…*"

"—to frame me—"

"To fuck you? Fuck *me*, Harry," she played, her rendition of scando-semantics.

"You made me tell you in detail, how we fucked, what positions. You were jealous of us, jealous she stopped seeing you. And you killed her…"

There was a pause. "Why, Harry? Does that turn you on?"

The question swirled around and quieted me.

"It turns me on…"

"What does?"

"To know—"

"To know what?"

"You may have done it…"

"Done what?"

"Killed her, Harry."

What poured from her next made me want to tear her apart.

"Look at me, Harry. You've wanted it for so long. To be here. On top of me. Feeling me. Look at my tits, all those times in the office you wanted to jump across the desk, rip off my blouse and suck them. Here they are. Suck them Harry, suck my tits. Take me on the carpet. I knew how you looked at me. And knowing how much you wanted it, my pussy throbbed. I wanted to give it to you. I had to change panties twice on those days together. So, so wet. After our meetings I went right to the bathroom. To finger it. And relieve it. Now everything you wanted, is right in front of you. For the taking. It's all here, Harry, really here. And you are too. Inside it. Take it Harry, take it. And fuck it hard! And while you're fucking it, *give it to me!*" She implored.

She'd gotten me so excited I ratcheted up the pace, sustaining it a while, then slowing. I couldn't let it end. Not this. Not now.

"That's it, Harry," she whispered. "Settle down. And do it. Make me feel it, the force. From those meaty hands. Make me feel it all over my body, the way she used to feel. You know what to do, choke me with those scando hands, Harry. *Choke me fancy-fine!*"

I couldn't deny her. The force was on her. With both. I twisted it's warm, fragile, softness. But she wanted more. She wanted it fierce. And harsh. And brutal. And begged for it. My hands were gripping her throat beneath her jaw, tightening the skin of her entire face. And her face got redder.

"Come on. Like Slinger would. You can do it. *Harder…*"

It felt good fucking her. And wringing her throat. I didn't know where the passion was ending or where my revenge was beginning. They were together. I wrung it hard, then harder, her face cherrying up even more.

Emotions were stacked. The revenge on Sunday for what she'd done, revenge on Dr. Greer for having been with her. The pent-up passion I'd held for the Doctor. How could I not? I was single. And weak. And devastated. Every piece of clothing in her wardrobe I'd seen five times and each time they'd ended up on the floor. But I'd thwarted it, all my impulses and urges, out of respect for my girl. Because I felt ashamed. When all along she'd been doing it with this woman. This woman who had lied to me, deceived me, poached my girl, and ratted me out to the cops. This woman! And now she was here. And I had her. At the other end of my meat hooks, my scandalicious scando hands.

There were whispers and smiles for her too. "Remember what they call me, Doc? How's it feel now?"

I was in charge, glaring into swollen eyes, the red, furnaced face, the saliva bubbles at the corners of her lips, tears streaming from both eyes, while stamping her, scando-manhandling her. She gagged beautifully. She'd been responsible for my misery. And pain. She'd had my woman, shared foursomes, even throated her like I was doing her now. And fucking her. The pleasure, the misery, the pain. She nearly locked me up for life, maybe tried to frame me even, to take my freedom away. Now I was taking the freedom from her, the oxygen that gave her life. I was choking the hell out of her. For the first time, choking felt good. My railer had never been so steeled.

I was worked into a frenzy, a wild state of uncontrollable and melded desires. I'd gone animal and could hear the animal grunting, snorting, howling, hitting vicious notes never uttered before, while the victim let out alarm calls in the brush, high-pitched warnings of a predator nearby, shrieks.

Only the predator was me.

Everything slowed then and sense of place and time was lost. It was as though the whole world had stopped. And the animal and his assault could be seen from afar. From an angle of down and in, as it continued to maul away at its prey. I had nothing to with it. It was between the species. One ingesting, the other getting devoured. Completing the circle of life. And the erotic feeding frenzy was watched until the end.

It soon became a lot of everything, too damned much, and the animal pulsated, shrieked, bucked, and exploded inside the host, blasting the walls of soft and wet interiors, no doubt. The carcass beneath heaved violently along with the animal's, and though it couldn't meet its shrieks, its voicebox throttled, it gagged a ferocious groan and moan while squirming and spiraling beneath, and it half spun over as if trying to get away, as if it was too much. But too much had been its end game. The animal knew that. The prey itself was a master at a frenzy of the sort, with a lesser species; it was its own fault, and was now getting its own taste. From the animal.

I awoke from the surreal encounter what seemed like many minutes later, perhaps a half-hour's worth. My eyes left the ceiling and I looked over to orientate myself, to remind myself, to gauge place and time. But there was only one image available: a beautiful naked body on the bed. Saliva was streaming from the corner of her mouth. She lay there totally still, watered eyes opened a crack, cheeks brightly flushed, her mouth curving up barely, sparely in an impressionistic Monet way.

She seemed satisfied.

She seemed peaceful.

I was hazy on the details other than that it was the last I saw of Dr. Greer.

I stepped sprightly into the elevator, the operator there to greet me. He paced behind me to the vestibule and past the front doorman. Then I went on my way. I felt physically robust. Whatever had happened up there had rebooted me and pulled me out of my stupor. I didn't think another thought about it. I couldn't have even if I'd wanted to.

It was late and only late-night street crawlers were still stuck to the pavement. I had New York to myself. And no scando bounty boys snapping one-shot buyouts for a few hunnies, no one trying to give me Bad Sling, no one shouting "It's the Gripster!" No one making me feel like a scandostar. No scando junkies, nowhere. Just me and all that cosmopolitana for the taking.

I shuffled to Grand Central and moseyed around inside. I hadn't taken an MTA train in years. I saw fractured bag people-types pushing carts. I got a warm roll at Zabar's at the opening. I didn't eat it. I played with it in my cold, clammy hands until they'd robbed it of all its warmth. Then I tossed it for the birds. Or the bums.

After a while, I tired of scandoprancing around and died all at once. I crashed on a park bench my head bent against an iron armrest. That was okay, Scando Man needed rest. As I drifted off, I could swear I heard some rats the size of cats scurrying past. Better them than the scandostarved scandofans. Or maybe it was a dream and it was the early morning scandopervs and scandopeds with out-of-town ankle bracelets having crossed state lines, mapping out the day's crimes, and doing all the scurrying. Giving rats a bad name.

43

Reluctant Star

Kids shrieking nearby woke me. I searched for my Mao star cap, but it was gone. I checked the big rooftop clock on Fifty-Seventh Street. It was already two in the afternoon. I bought another cap, a cheapie Taiwanese knockoff, then flagged a cab home.

There was traffic on Broome, so I decided to hoof it the rest of the way and save a buck. As I approached my block, I saw the reason for the congestion: three squad cars docked in front of my building. My first reaction was to take the scandoclamor head-on, but Lord knows I didn't need another a day of bad Face. Time to scandoscram.

I drew my new lid further down and turned back east on Broome, then up Lafayette. At Union Square, as I was passing Circuit City, I saw a flat-paneled Sony beaming New York One which featured live shots outside a Park Avenue residence. Then a photograph of Dr. Van den Heugel flashed; she was wearing riding gear and a pith and was perched atop a gorgeous horse. It was a tasteful shot, probably taken at her stables in Connecticut, followed by tape of her white-sheeted body carted off on wheels. I read the closed captions.

Dr. Van den Heugel had been murdered, which I considered sad news, but for some reason I couldn't feel the pain. She'd been found in her apartment strangled to death, along with a lost baseball cap. The Chinese kind. A photograph of me was showed, a damned lousy picture. I looked sweaty and unlikeable. No smile, nothing. Sunday's photo appeared then too and the ubiquitous YouTuber of my infamous scandohands and her throat in action in Florida. As far as programming went, it was a scansational extravaganza. I was implicated again for a murder, the second honor bestowed on me in five weeks. The third in a lifetime if you count my sister, Caitlin. You could say I was in another tight scandojam.

My body prickled throughout and I felt that sting on my skin. It wasn't sunburn, it wasn't a flush either. It was the spotlight of the world beaming down on me. I had a rush of uncertain feeling bordering on scandopanic. I wanted to go to my office and check my inbox, but security would squeal on me for certain. I considered returning to the Skybox, turning on my Dell, and checking e-mails, but there'd be too many flatfoots. Maybe the Fonz could pick me up and we could have a chat, I wondered. He was always game for an uninterrupted tête-à-tête, though he wouldn't know what I was saying. Unfortunately, the town car was too identifiable and could get made.

I could use some sedative medication or Mike and Vikes, but they were located in the Skybox medicine chest. And the CVS over-the-counter commandos would not have a med tag on me. Meds were out too.

All systems of focus and structure in times of desperation and menace were unavailable. Bad for Harry.

I pulled my brim lower and stepped into Duane Reade and bought some plastic magnifiers, the kind that resemble prescription horned-rimmeds. With those riding my grill, I crossed over Houston, slipped into Blades West on Broadway, and bought a new pair of Bravoblades. I suped them up with 80-millimeter wheels. Then I picked up a cheapie Discman and a classic Hendrix CD at Tower.

Minutes later, I was on safari. I whished direction uptown listening to *Crosstown Traffic*, dodging and weaving, braking and pumping, coasting past the midday car crawl. It was high-stim at its best satisfying high-action needs. Normally, I would have taken Fifth to go against traffic, a steeper thrill, but I didn't want to be so in your face and noticeable. Still, the action on Third soothed and comforted me which is what I'd been hoping for.

I flowed and coasted back along Forty-Second Street and turned in to a corridor leading into Grand Central. There I bought some slip-on Vans, gave the blades to an unsuspecting commuter, and purchased a rail ticket to Boston. I didn't want any further scandoclamor; I'd gotten too darned popular. Give the Face to someone else was my feeling. I invested in fashionable eyewear to diversify my looks. I hoped to blend in harmoniously with the train hoppers and leave Scandoland with little fanfare.

All aboard, I slept beneath dark frames. It was ten o'clock when I arrived at Boston's Back Bay Station. I took a room at the nearby Sheraton and ordered a pot roast sandwich from room service and turned on cable. I was a real media darling getting scandodamned, -slammed, and -panned in the media. All the usual scando-vigilantes were weighing in. Scarborough was all over me on MSNBC and Nancy Grace and Greta and Olbermann. I closed them all out and settled for a West Coast Kobe Ballhog hoops contest on TNT; it was easier on the brain. I couldn't handle the notorious notoriety.

I was a star of the greatest magnitude now. On the scandolam, my scando index was peaking. My Google entries were in the millions and climbing. It was my time. But Scando Man was reluctant to take the applause; perhaps you understand.

It was nice to be back in Boston; nice folks, nice town, Boston-bound. I hadn't been back since my Harvard fifth ten years before. That gave me a capital idea. I thought I'd go over to the University, poke around, and roam around Cambridge, always amusing. The bookstore could be a real hootenanny. I thought maybe I could stock up on collegiate jocko gear indigenous to the area like crimson shorts. You know, colors that made you blend in. No jokes.

Before dozing, I gave further desensitized thought to Dr. Greer. She was dead now. I realized then I'd never told her my final secret, the one about my loud shirts and ties.

The next morning, I rode the tube and landed at Harvard Square. I walked the Yard a while and eyeballed the facade of B House. Then I passed by the statue of old John, John Harvard that is. I saluted him, but he appeared a touch green. There must recently have been a Dartmouth weekend. Whenever we hosted them in football, those Big Green goths caravanned down from New Hampshire and painted poor John's eternal bronze pose in their school color.

I'd had some of my best years here, I thought. It was the first time I'd been successful as a student and that was no small accomplishment as my ego began to take shape for the better.

Then I was over it. My brief dazzling reunion with my alma

mater was done, the kicks all played out. I took the tube to Back Bay and rode Amtrak's Montrealer further north. Something was driving me, but I did not know exactly what.

44

Silly Silas and Uncle Mo

They hadn't been expecting me and I hadn't known it was where I was going. The train arrived in Durham at six o'clock and I snatched the only waiting cab. My father lived in a cozy white-shingled, black-shuttered New England farmhouse on the outskirts. He'd opted not to live in faculty housing on campus. He wanted more privacy.

I got out of the cab and saw lights on inside. I stepped up and knocked on the door.

The door opened and my father, Silas Starslinger, Professor of English at the University of New Hampshire, was poised there, stalwart, with a snowy white beard. His face sagged a bit, but he'd aged less than I'd anticipated. "My God. Harry."

He remained stiffly, not knowing what to do. After the awkward interval, he reached forward, half embracing me briefly. Then we stepped inside.

"It's Harry!" he called to the bleachers.

"My word," said the voice from the beyond, another man's voice. Soon after, Maurice appeared in a Provençal apron and he finished off my Dad's hug. Maurice was my father's companion, the one I'd found my father in bed with all those years before.

"You know?"

"We know you're in trouble."

"A former colleague from Columbia phoned me, then we saw the television report. How are you, Harry?"

"I said, 'How are you Sue?'" There went those Harry Chapin lyrics again. "Trains are better than planes, I say."

Though I wasn't crying, it flowed freely and evenly down my

cheeks. I didn't feel awful, the damned tears I couldn't control.

"Is it as bad as it's being reported?"

"Is it ever?" I returned. "They're all Scandosaurus Rexes. And they'll get theirs."

The lull dropped into an awkward moment of silence. For them.

"Have you eaten?" My father posed. I mumbled something unintelligible. "Good, Maurice made chili." He then asked if the authorities would be contacting him. "I'll say I haven't seen you."

"Don't be silly, Silas, of course that's what you say," Maurice echoed having shuffled into the kitchen.

"Got a T-shirt for you, Mo," said the good guest. "With 'Naomi Hit Me' on the front and 'And I liked it' on the back. You know, the scandotantrumed scandomannequin... I'll courier it on up."

We ate in the dining room. There were bookshelves on all four walls. My father liked to surround himself with volumes. There were packed shelves in each room. He was a binder-to-binder kind of guy.

The hushed atmosphere was regrettably broken with, "Do you want to talk about it?"

It was Mo's turn. "You're aware you're in trouble, aren't you?"

"Yes, I am. You still have that riding lawnmower?"

Silas attested he did, but with the ball in his hands he dropped the subject. I'll tell you now, it pissed me right off. I hadn't had any meds, not even a squirt of cherry Chloraseptic. So there I was, my mind stripped to the wind, in a sufficiently morose and depressed state, certifiably off the beam.

They wanted to ask me, but they were too timid. My father had always been a coward. He never stood up for me, or himself, for that matter. He wasn't a strong man, he was soft. Maurice was not, he rarely shied from confrontation. He used to shoot pheasant. In their union, Maurice took the masculine role and dear old Dad was his wife. As I watched Silas feeling his way around my predicament, hoping to get some answers but not having the stones to ask, it depressed me more. "How's the chili, Harry?"

"Top-shelf," I said, which was a lie. The chili needed salt, pepper, and something else too. It had no south of the border zing. Maybe

Tabasco. It needed Tabasco.

I took a haul of water. The water reminded me of the rolling rock streams in New England. It was a comforting sort of image. My thoughts were splintering, anxiety mounting, but I could follow a mountain stream and mossy rocks.

"So tell us, Harry," Maurice chimed in. "How much trouble is it?"

I noted that Maurice was the one to direct the difficult part of the discussion. That ticked me too. Though it was the only way it would ever be. Still, my fuse was on a slow burn.

"It's hard to say…"

"Try," my father proffered.

"Try what?"

"You know, to tell us about the trouble."

I was going to make him work for it. "What do you mean, exactly?"

"About the trouble?"

"What trouble?"

"Good God, Harry," Maurice piped, parachuting and rolling in. "What's going on with you?"

"Finding my way in the big city."

"It's a dreadful place, New York."

The comment bulldozed a path. Finally a way in, I thought.

"Yeah, it doesn't have the softness of a place like this."

"Softness?" Maurice challenged.

"Yeah, you know, the cushy pillow existence. Get up in the morning, no job, bills are paid for, just real nice soft living. Worry about what jams to buy, sing-alongs on the campus green, you know the big rural galloping green rot. Nice people, nice town."

"That's no way to speak. Maurice is your supporter you know."

"Well, *danke*, Mo, it's nice to hear. No jokes. And you?"

"This is not about me, it's about you."

"But I want to include you, you're my Dad. Family, see? And I want to share my life stories with you. So come on, bring it on—"

"Harry—"

"Come on, Dad, you can do it. One word at a time."

"I'm not going to listen to this."

"I'll help you. '*Did*—?' Come on, Silas—"

"Is this the boy I raised?"

"No, this boy was raised by serial disciplinary schools. You missed the party. But I hope I've morphed into the boy you wanted to raise. Have I?"

"What does that mean?"

"Nothing, probably. It just sounded appropriate. Come on, '*Did you*—?' You can do it, I swear…"

He was frozen in his chair.

"Ask him, Silas—"

"No help, Uncle Mo—"

"Uncle Mo?"

"Don't be needy, this is Dad's big moment…"

Silas wiped his mouth with his napkin and stuttered through most of it. "Did you kill them?"

"What? I couldn't hear you, all that maple syrup sap drip-drip-dripping outside—"

"Did you kill those women?"

"Very good." I clapped. "Is there any four-berry pie, Maurice?"

Perhaps I was taking all this murder business a little lightly, but as a natural deflector, it was the way my mind in its unpredictable state was handling it.

"I'm afraid not, Harry."

"To answer your question, Dad, 'did I kill those women?,' the answer is that I don't remember. It's more surreal than personal, like a Dali soft watch. I'd been drinking and taking medication and when I do that I have a tendency to forget. One thing I'll never forget is, there may be no 'I' in team, but there is in '*equipe*.' That's French for 'team.' You got to hand it to the French. Can't say they don't know about self-centered, selfish, and self-interest. And make it sound cool."

He eyeballed me sternly, my father did, which made me feel proud. A stern look from him was at least something. It had a point of view. Like maybe he was thinking about you.

"What has gotten into you? This is your life, Harry, are you trying to throw everything away?"

"It's obvious, Silas. He's already done it."

"Double *danke*, Mo. I'm playing the back nine already. In fact I'm probably already at the eighteenth tee."

"What does that mean?"

I rose up; the chili was too bland and it had begun to irk me. I wanted to detach and distance myself from the bowl. We just weren't connected, we had very little in common.

"You're so silly, Silas," I spewed. "There's no 'I' in team, is there? The Militia knows; they've got my back."

"You should be ashamed of yourself."

"Come off it, Uncle Mo. You don't even have the guts to make spicy chili."

"I think it's time for you to go," my father said.

"No, I want to hear it," Maurice shot right back. "What does 'playing the back nine' mean?"

"It means I'm totally baffled as to why I came here. I'm waiting for members of my *equipe* to show and tell me. Anyone seen Team Dolce Vita?"

I rose from my chair, faked a trip to the bathroom, and ducked into the living room. I was searching for something, all right, the photo was standing with the family series on the table. I was surprised to see them out for public display.

"Where are you going, Harry?" One asked nervously.

"What are you looking for?" His wife asked.

I returned to the dining room and they were both standing there, faces etched in worry and maybe even fear when I launched into my spontaneous flight of capital ideas.

"You know, Silly Silas and Uncle Mo, you grow up in a small town as a little prince and not before too long, you find you're pretty distracted frustrated and unreachable and you don't do well in school and you're constantly told you're bad or stupid or lazy, not always by parents, but others and you realize you're not the prince you once thought you were, in fact, just the opposite, but the one person you hold truly near to your heart in this confusing world who loves you to death and who shows you the same kind of love—your angel sister—she goes and dies in your arms and it just may be your fault and you're shipped off to school knowing that and the school doesn't know how to treat you because they've got it all wrong and your real meds haven't been discovered yet, so you do the lockup-lockdown thing for a bunch of years, years that have days which never end with the essential closed rooms padlocked doors and strap-downs to boot and you never seem to be allowed to go home and see your family, but finally you are granted, permission to go and you're so excited you can't stand it and you arrive home only to find out on your one trip you're allowed to go home your mother has died and you are permitted not only to go inside the house, but you're also permitted to go to the funeral too and 'bless everyone's hearts,' you think, 'for being so damned thoughtful and sensitive' to allow you these freedoms especially to attend the funeral which is such a treat...

"So after all that family merriment, you wake up from the haze of adolescence and you're only fifteen years old and you've already lost half of your family and you come home one summer and look at your old 'friends' from school, the ones you had before you were sent away, the ones who called you 'stupid' and 'crazy,' the fat girl and the mischievous boy, the popular guy, the girl you had a crush on, and normal healthy impulses are pulsating in them and you see what all their lives are like from afar and it's pretty cool because all the while, you know there's a guy in your house banging your father or your father's banging him and you're supposed to feel adjusted to that and you want to, but the fact is that you're just a little too young to understand all that live-and-let-live stuff and genetic impurities and crossovers and you learn there's nothing wrong with homosexuals, but you don't know how to process it, even after some good old liberal arts teaching, and you can't reconcile the whole damned thing in your mind and combine it with the rest of the life tragedy series and you have not enjoyed the sturdiest psychological infrastructure from the outset anyway so you move a few states away to live your life and separate yourself from the rest and you're smart and not bad looking and the ladies like you and you find you like them way more than you should and you like doing things with them that most people consider "weird," but you're happy and kicking it and you land one of the plum scandoglam jobs in the biggest and the best and the most dynamic city in the world in the post-millennium era anyway, and you get strong notoriety and unlimited social access to everything worth having access to, and it's all so wonderful and great and you keep avoiding that weakness you have up in New Hampshire and you're way into big therapy to Band-Aid it all and you meet a girl, the greatest girl you've ever been in contact with, and you feel like this is what all the pain and uncertainty was about and how you had to pay your damned dues with all that past crap just to get to this and this gift is beyond your wildest dreams, but then it gets strange for no apparent reason; but there is a reason and that reason, unbeknownst to you, is because of the same damned twisted shit you've been experiencing and that has been a part of your beloved's life all those years and the perps are people who have this what's-your-problem?/is-this-the-type-of-child-I-raised?-attitude and I know and it's clear we should be rising above, but we're only giant water balloons composed of three-quarters water and some boney sticks, ready to pop at any damned time and the circuitry inside us is just too damned fragile to overcome with the mind and mental overrides to our innate homo sapiens fears and what I'm saying is that it's no goddamn wonder I'm wanted by the police and I can't say definitively or not if I am capable of all acts heinous, depraved and gruesome, and so I guess the reason I'm here is to simply ask you bookish little fruit fly impostor father with the unemployed snowball softy sidecar who makes gutless chili tell me if you care to put your mind to it if *I am a murderer???*"

Maurice was watered up and emotional, my father was not. That's when I realized in my fractured way I'd been fooled all along. Maurice was really the catcher, not the pitcher.

"No I don't, Harry," my father said.

I wiped my own face which was awash once more in salty spirits.

"And I think it's such a damned cop-out to play the blame game and call nice men like yourselves fruit flies and soft boys and it's just one big genetic potluck dinner out there that no one's in control of, and he can't help it if he likes men, it's just life and a tiny twist at the biological level; nevertheless, the man still goes out and gives life to me, but then I can't help it if my twistatopia life's interludes and related programming have taken me down the path of unconventional scandosex and scandorandom behavior too, and the girl I'm in love with can't help it if her legal guardian is pervy and creepy and wants sex from her before she's hit thirteen, and then she can't help it if she's attracted to a guy like me who has his own disorders in serial multiples of three along with other hang-ups for frosting and she has to use him as a stepping stone to get to the next platform of personal psychological comfort and security and we both can't help it if the emotional electricity is so big that one of them gets killed and then another perishes in the wake and even if I did kill them am I really held accountable? and when does the cycle end and when does someone become accountable? and should they ever be? because if you look deep down into the hole of all these sordid facts, situations, arrangements and genetic details, no one is wrong for having done anything and everyone is right, according to the limitations of their own DNA, and it's just what they've all had to do to find their way slogging through the quagmire of the human condition with what they're given at the molecular level and how they're genetically configured and in this context they're forced to interact in a world where the odds have been stacked against each and everyone from the start. So tell me who's to blame."

I paused to catch my breath.

"And then he realizes it's just another color-by-numbers, cop-out philosophy and when does the whole goddamned circle end? Huh? Leap forward out of your area of expertise for a second and provide me with the proper analysis. Tell me, Professor Starslinger—"

Neither said a word. I believe their reactions were both in the area of shock, and how could you blame them? I'd been verbally disgorging for minutes on end, a scandofrantic rant, the harshest words and phrases chosen. My only consolation was the truism that if you're going to have a nervous breakdown, it might as well be in front of family, or those who contributed spices and flavorings to the crockery of your unraveling.

But Dad did have a query for me.

"Did you hurt Caitlin, Harry?"

"I don't really know," I gasped through the water dripping off my lips.

45

Ritalin Robby

"Don't worry, Slings. I got your back…But I need to ask: you must be pretty chummy with the coppers now. Next time you're in the precinct, can you get a few of those wanted posters for me? You know, the real Public Enemy Number One stuff? Some sketches, maybe? And anything else cop-like you see lying around. Trinkets and such. It's for my, uh, cousin… I came by the loft and left a note for you on the back of one of those white locksmith cards. To remind you. Anything fuzz-like. Coolio. Off to the dog show…"

46

Checking In

I led myself to the door. I didn't slow my departure in expectation of a last-second invitation to stay for the night, either.

As soon as I hit the foot walk, I found it difficult to form proper sentences. The words wouldn't come. Then too many came. It was a jumble; I'd lost the verbals. I threw out nouns and prepositions and verbs and descriptive words in random order. Conversation was a no-go. I was just left with the sounds.

Ab-bab-bab-bab-ab, dad-dad-da-da-daba-dada! Then it looped.

I ambled forward out of pure instinct and I was lucky I'd had three and a half-decades' practice.

I found myself in the UNH campus's main hotel shuffling through the lobby. I hitched a ride in an elevator on a random floor choice. When the elevator doors spread, I moseyed down the corridor, taking in the New Englandy wall art in the hall: cows and such. I slipped in the first room with the door ajar and lay down on the bed. When the maid returned with her cart, she asked me if I had enough towels. With profuse grammatical imperfections, I requested a robe with pockets and extra shampoo minis and a shower cap, then settled in for a slow doze.

A couple hours later, the maid reappeared with no robe and the concierge. It was he who woke me up.

"Excuse me, sir, this is not your room," the wiry mustached man asserted. "You'll have to leave."

I lifted myself up. I didn't have to find my coat; I was still wearing it. I didn't speak up, either. I must have figured that would only get me into trouble.

Then I did a smart thing. I pulled out my wallet and handed

him the MasterCard.

"Would you like your own room?" He was prompted to ask me.

He led me downstairs and checked me in. In New York, I would have been thrown in jail for the stunt, but in sleepy old Durham, New Hampshire, I was given the considerable benefit of the doubt.

My room was a pleasantly decorated suite with more regional fabrics, furnishings, and moo art. I stayed there and watched cable. I didn't eat at first; I didn't trust myself on the phone. On the second day, my thoughts queued up less randomly. Words came back in their proper order. I ordered Ruebens and club sandwiches and fries with Cherry Cokes and strawberry shakes. And I got my shampoo minis.

Then it hit me all at once: the reason I'd come to my father's house in the first place. No one could help me now and lift me from my throw-away-the-key status. I was either going to extricate myself from these alleged crimes or, implicate myself even further, but at least I would seal my fate once and for all. My exoneration, if I was even worthy of one, rested upon my shoulders.

I latched onto the purple laces. I had a plan.

47

The Creek at Lockhart Hill

The morning I checked out, the concierge smiled, but he wasn't so friendly. He must have heard I'd gone elephant seal on a member of his staff. I signed the bill and he returned my card. He also reserved an international seat for me on the Amtrak train to Montreal.

Striding down my father's street, I turned in at the next-door neighbor's driveway, then snuck into my old Silas's backyard. I slipped in the garage. It was dark; I needed a flashlight. I hoped what I was seeking out hadn't been spring-cleaned away. I found the dusty sleeping bag behind the ski rack and swatted it until I coughed. Atop homemade wine crates, I located what I'd been looking for. It was marked in big black block letters: "*Harry—Save.*" The box was the reason I'd come to Durham.

With the box in my arms, I took back roads to the train station that doubled for a bus depot. I bought my ticket and it had nothing to do with Canada, as I'd told the concierge, in case he'd caught some Dan Abrams or scansational tickertapes advertising the manhunt. I was sending the scandohounds to sniff up a bogus trail.

I had a pair of seats for the trip, which was just as well, though my strategy was to keep to myself. I may have bayed or howled during sleep, but I'm not sure if it was real or part of a dream.

Upon waking, I thought about my father, Silas. Always the academic, I was sure he thought I'd cracked in a Fitzgeraldian *The Crack-Up* sort of way. The thirty-five-year-old cranium split, the severe, life-altering one that hits you with Tyson-to-the-chin clarity as you realize you're not everything you once thought you could have been in life. If he was marinating such thoughts in mind, he'd have been an optimist. It was a full breakdown and there had been seepage. I didn't know if the damage was irreversible or if the breakdown was only in first gear and gaining speed.

The next leg of my New England tour took me to the Cape. On the beach I rehearsed being a real human being again. I tried former systems from which I'd derived pleasure in the past to wing me back to normalcy. I drank a few beers, ate two burgers, and talked back to the roaring November Atlantic seas. It was great to wake in my old sleeping bag walled in by high dunes. Coherent speech was returning and I practiced it in the wind.

I stayed two nights. It was chilly, but the stab at rehab was well worth it.

After the Cape, I came back due west, avoiding Boston. I didn't want a metropolis. I wasn't seeking out urban high-stim activity. Too much chaos, not good for Harry. I was trying to downshift, downsize, and enjoy soft and local village predicaments with few choices and less interference.

Lockhart, Mass. was its usual sleepy self as the bus pulled into the local stop on Main Street. I gathered my box and stepped off and sauntered into the corner country market. Though the ownership had changed hands, the interior hadn't been touched. It had the same unforgettable smells of a thousand jellies and jams and spices and pine and leather work gloves and freshly cut cords of wood. I bought a pen, a pad of paper, a wildflower bunch, and a chartreuse chamois snowmobiler's shirt that glowed in the dark. It was a little nippy.

I spent the first afternoon wandering through the peaceful streets and hiking in the woods. I visited Doc Swenson's house. I was standing in the driveway for ten minutes when the new owner came out. "May I help you?" He asked with an alarmed expression. I was smiling fractionally in a good-natured daze. He informed me that Doc Swenson had died some years back. I turned back to town and stayed the night in the Lockhart Inn under a false name, "Vinnie Vega," the name on loan from Tarantino's *Pulp Fiction*.

I ventured out to Lockhart Hill the following morning. Naturally, I was jittery; I hadn't been back since the accident which clocked in at twenty-three years before. I'd suppressed the very memories which had drawn me back.

I wore my new day-glo shirt.

It was a splendiferous sunny day, though the trees were skeletal, fall's death call and all. The water level of the Creek was the highest I'd ever seen. Of course, scale changes from youth to adulthood. Objects from one's past that seemed so enormous end up shrunken and small. The Creek was different; it had expanded, a result of all the heavy rainfall the northeast had been experiencing.

The big lofty pine had grown further skyward. We used to deposit our personal belongings at its trunk when swimming in the summer or skating in the winter. It wasn't long before I spotted the sign placed beside the tree, courtesy of the Sheriff's Department. It warned, "Minors under the age of twelve must be accompanied by an adult when swimming or skating." Sure, I felt responsible for it.

I stepped lightly down to the near bank and surveyed the water. There was a wooden duck decoy floating peacefully and another mallard coasting circles around it, courting it. He was clearly a romantic hold-out, trying to get a last bit of nookie before the impending journey south, unaware his courtship was doomed to fail. The winter chill would soon be upon us, I thought, and the Creek had a few weeks before it would ice over. The freeze would start at the edges and the ice would close in on the middle until it reached maximum thickness: three to four inches.

I drew out the pad of paper and began to write. I placed it and dated it from memory: February 10, 1984. I tried to record it as best I could, my flight of thoughts.

It took time and forced attacks on memory. But in that setting, that very setting, a purposeful and conscious mind excavation yielded results. I'd always feared this type of recall, avoiding it like the thirteenth-century plague.

I hadn't offered it up, not ever. Not to any shrinks, support groups, psycho semi-pros, or ADD coaches. Not to Dr. Hoskins, not to Dr. Greer, not to Sunday Fairchild. Not to anyone. It had always been too painful.

It came back in intermittent flashes with intervals of nothingness. Then memories returned in another fresh spurt.

The memory banks filled up as I eyed the familiar setting. The more I allowed the gates to stay open, the more memory fluid surged in. It had been so long.

It soon returned with clarity, disturbing clarity, tragic clarity. The fleeting thoughts of the day, long suppressed, surfaced in my brain. It was like reading again a book I'd read many years before. The sights, the smells, the colors, were all coming alive and there I was back in Lockhart, Mass. as though it was yesterday. But for some reason I wasn't scared. I felt empowered and determined. And that tragic day from twenty-four years before, kept unfolding.

It poured out of me, as fast as I could write it down. Faster. My pen could not keep up, the memory flashes hitting me like lightning. I took down what I could. This was no Sling-able item, no short bite of news. This was a spontaneous pour of memory and emotion.

A cold sweat came over me as a stiff autumn wind howled across the Creek and went right through my sweater. Fallen brown maple leaves swirled past and blew over my shoes. My hand slashed across the page with such ferocity it ached. Gripping the pen so tightly, I had to pause to let it rest, only to re-grip it like a vise, lost in reverie.

It was the last day I saw my sister Caitlin.

48

Everyone Calls Me Harry

I signed and dated the last page of the journal, rose to my feet and drifted to the far bank of the Creek. Just opposite the spot where my sister and I had fallen through the ice all those years before.

I peeled away the tape on the box, the adhesives gummed and sticky to my fingers. I spread the flaps and a spunky spider troupe emerged. I clutched the pair in one hand. They had turned a creamy color. Poised there on the bank, holding them tightly, I came up with a better idea.

I drew out the old purple laces I'd saved all these years and had recently pocketed for luck. I threaded them through the eyelets of each skate, then tied the ends in a big knot to keep them together. Holding the knot, I hurled the skates high over the Creek to the spot where Caitlin had gone under. The skates sliced into the water with little splash and floated peacefully a brief instant. Then the weight of the blades took them down and they went under and disappeared.

I remained in place at the muddy bank and wiped my face as the surface of the Creek went glassy once more. I took in a deep one and pivoted around and ascended the bank. I drifted past the body of water, back beneath the towering pine, only to spin around. "She's not playing hard to get!" I hollered at the relentless mallard. "It's a chunk of wood!" But the duck just kept on circling the decoy, hoping for a breakthrough that would never come. I thought, why rain on his parade? As long as he has something to get him up in the morning, something to live for. Many worship what, when brought to their elements, are simple chunks of wood, and that is a good thing. *Go, duck, go!,* was a final thought.

I didn't turn around again. I continued on my way back to town and never returned to the Creek again.

Later that afternoon, I paid a visit to the local cemetery. It was the first time I'd been there since Mom's funeral. I laid the wildflowers between them. The two most important women in my life had been buried side by side and shared the same headstone. I spoke softly and informed them what I'd been up to and what my admittedly sketchy plans for the future were. I mentioned the past as well.

Yes, that awful day at Dr. Swenson's was the last day I saw my sister. But it was also the last day I saw my mother. She was supposed to visit me at my school. I was told it was too painful for her. I believe that.

Standing below her headstone, I spoke to her. "I tried my best, Mom. With what I had."

I contended that she'd never known who I was; she'd never had the chance to know me and I was sorry for that. I thought she might be proud if she'd gotten to know me. She might have even shared some laughs with me as my sense of humor had developed into an admirable trait. But I wasn't sure. I acknowledged our last memories together had been tough to overcome and I understood why she chose not to see me again.

I did not blame my parents for the misguided treatments to which I'd been subjected or for sending me away. I felt that, even with all the locking down I'd endured early, I enjoyed enough freedoms later on. And my mother, who never knew who I was, now I would tell her.

"I'm just a boy who lost his mother."

A spare wind immediately picked up and the nude, leafless branches of a nearby elm, guardian to the headstones, began to sway. The elm seemed to agree with me.

By that, I meant that I was like most others, feeling pain, feeling loss, and moving on, but never forgetting. Like everyone. Like, normal. I felt normal. And she should feel happy about that; little Harvey felt normal at last.

There was no longer a need to worry if she was inclined to. Lastly, I told her I missed her, and that I loved her.

Then I stepped over and took in a deep breath because I was nervous. I laid a carefully selected flower on Caitlin's side of the grave. The color was lavender, also known as light purple.

"I'm sorry I haven't come to see you sooner. I've wanted to, but I was weak. I avoided the memories of that day for many years. A day has not gone by I haven't thought about you before noon. And in my darkest times, when I was at my lowest, it's the thought of you that has kept me going, times like right now. I live my days for you, I have always lived my days for you. I remember your strength and courage and that's how I know you're still with me. Because I could not have endured this life alone. I wear the brightest colors so you can see me whenever, wherever I am. So you can still pick me out of the crowd. And being alive is my proof you do see me."

I let the water seep out of my eyes for a minute.

"I met someone I loved. I was grateful for that. She reminded me of you. She had a similar strength. I think you would have liked her."

A knee buckled. I was pretty watered up.

"I kept the name you gave me. Everyone calls me 'Harry' now. I love you, Caitlin. You're still my angel and I count on you more than you could ever know. And I will forever more."

It was near dark when I left the cemetery. I hoped they'd been listening to what I'd said.

On the walk to town, I spotted critter eyes glowing in the brush. I appreciated those eyes, I liked life a little better than the day before. I liked myself better too, if only wee-bitly. On my way to the hotel, I moved through the darkness with a pale trace of confidence. It wasn't much, but it was something.

49

Oh Yeah, I Almost Forgot

In addition to the photo I'd snared of my mother and me, there was another item I'd sought out at Silas's. Maurice inherited a sizable gun collection from his old man, an absurdly macho Vermonter who bagged a half-dozen yearly deer and mounted most of the heads. Maurice got rid of the rifles but kept the Smith & Wesson .357 Magnum pistol. He'd shown me the piece one day to impress me, I guess, to appear a fuller man than he felt I'd been appraising him for.

I'd glommed the piece when I faked a bathroom run. I picked up a few rounds and a camouflage hat at the sports shop in downtown Durham, an easy purchase. New Hampshire is a hunter's state. You can hoot and holler about gun control and how thin the laws are, but when you're out there doing your damnest to dodge and weave the big heat oppressively coming down upon you, you wholeheartedly welcome the privilege of entering a gun shop and picking up some lead, few questions asked.

I had the resources going for me when I emerged from the southbounder at the 125th Street station in Harlem. I made my move there in case the fuzzies were running around Grand Central looking for missing, wanted, strange, and dangerous MSNBC scandostar folk. Since my mug had hit the airwaves, looking over my shoulder had become pretty much an every-thirty-seconds tick of mine.

As for my mental state and orientation, I kept pushing for focus, fine-line focus. I had my plan, but I needed to execute it with precision. Some meds would have helped, but I remained fearful of introducing myself at a pharmacy.

I avoided the rocket, the badges were roaming through them. The Giuliani years put more cops on the streets and in the subways, and Bloomberg kept them there. I waited for the most foreign-looking hijack cabby I could find instead, someone whose preferred choice of television news would likely be Al Jazeera and not the homegrown propaganda machines of major network or CNN. I had Mustafa drive me over the Triboro Bridge into Queens. His air freshener smelled so putrid I made him deposit me blocks before the Grand Avenue subway stop. I knew my way around from there.

With my back turned away from the sidewalk, I eyed donuts in a shop window and waited for all pedestrians to pass. After a brief, the coast-is-clear-walk, I rapped on the door at 147 Dekalb Street. It was a modest two-story house in a row of forty identicals. They were so close together that you could pass condiments from windows.

I didn't want his wife to answer; I could handle anything but that. But no one responded to my knock. I decided to squat in the shrubs and wait, for nearly three hours, and let my camouflage hunter's hat work its magic.

He eventually came home, alone. He strode up the walk, knee joints knocking and climbed the stoop. I moved in as he inserted the key and pressed the cold barrel against the back of his neck.

"Easy, Bobbo—"

"Christ Almighty, Slinger! You scared the hell outta me!"

"I'm scary right now."

"W-what's up?"

"You were tagging her for months."

"Hey, I'm sorry. Is that what this is about?"

"Let's go inside."

"Please, Slinger. Don't—"

"I want to see them."

"See what?"

"The photos."

"Photos? Of her?"

"All of them."

He nervously led me downstairs into his basement photography lab. His photographic images had been downloaded onto a fancy desktop. He popped on the lights and booted up.

"You got a timetable?" he asked with an artificial calm like he was at ease with his predicament. I knew better; he was shitting in his pants. He'd already pegged me as the murderer like the rest of the world.

"From the beginning."

He played around with his mouse until his database was uploaded. "I wasn't shooting her until she got Two Lips. That's when—"

"Lawrence hired you."

"Yeah, you know that. I'm sorry, Slinger. I never wished you ill, it's just the job. It's gotten more competitive." Now I could see the abject fear in his eyes. "I know you're in trouble, all I say is don't take me out, I got family. They're dependin'—"

"Let's see what you got."

We went through them one by one, all the parties and premieres. Her arriving at the MTV Movie Awards, getting back into the limo after, emerging from it again outside her building her hair a mess. It was Sunday's final months in New York captured in pictures.

Then we came to the night I was interested in.

"Here we go," Bob said. "That afternoon. Here's you walking in. Then leaving. Here's that doctor lady at the front door waiting. Not getting buzzed up. So she takes off."

"Let me see those again—"

"Which ones?"

"With her, the doctor—"

"It's what the cops were looking at."

"And?"

"Think they'd tell me? I didn't see anything in 'em."

"No one else entered the building?"

"Not that I saw."

"Were you there the whole time?"

"Natch."

There was worrisome clamor upstairs. "You hear that?"

"What?"

"When's your wife coming back?"

"In an hour."

I focused on the screen again, watching Dr. Greer as she waited outside Sunday's building. "Did you reload disks at any time?"

"Think so, but I had an eye on it. I always keep one eye on the subject, always."

I went back and forth from one snap to the next. I was dissecting them, searching for something, not knowing what it could be. But I sensed that there was something; there had to be.

"Are these prints perfect?"

"They're digital. Doesn't get any more perfect."

"No hairs or dust marks?"

"There's no film development. Unless it's on the lens and I control that."

"Let's see me leaving that afternoon again." It flashed on the screen and I studied it. "Now, the Doctor pressing the buzzer that night." There was something, I'd seen something. "Look. See that?"

"What?"

"That fleck—"

"Where?"

"That white thing. Can you enlarge it?" He did. "Zoom right in on the door, see that?"

"The light for the door buzzer panel?"

"No, the thing attached, that little white square."

"That tiny thing sticking out?"

"Now look at the photo of her arriving—"

This was the precise moment I heard tires screech outside. "What's up, Bobbo?"

"I dunno—"

I tore up the stairs and peered through a window and spied two squad cars out front. I dashed into the kitchen. Through the window I saw Edith, Bounty Bob's wife, standing outside, her trap agape.

I charged out the back door and hopped a fence into an alleyway, scooted behind an auto mechanic's garage, jumped over dead tires, found another alleyway, climbed over another fence, and ran along that until it ended. I twisted a look back down the street. Two officers were running in pursuit, though they hadn't spotted me.

For lack of any better exit strategy, I scaled stairs to the subway, which ran above the street. I prayed for the Number 7 train, but any would do. I waited one minute, two, then four. It came finally and I sprung aboard and made myself part of the mob. I kept a watchful eye on the platform and didn't see any cops. I stayed real tiny in the corner and pulled my lid even lower.

Three stops later, at the Brooklyn Bridge to be exact, that same pair of cops, an African-American and a ruddy-faced Irish type, advanced on the crowd in the next car. I could see them through the end windows. I reversed myself. When the train stopped, I hopped out and raised the collar of my overcoat and took a minding my own business pace. But sharp voices indicated I'd been spotted, so I dashed down the stairs.

I shot across the street through traffic and charged up the ramp to the Bridge. It was the hundred-yard dash missing from my life all these years that got me to the crest. I didn't have a strategy or plan, just two options. The first was laying back, lighting up, and spewing out low-probability scandorandom theories to the coppers in the face of a mountain of evidence against me. The second involved taking a great leap for and from mankind.

"Starslinger!" One shouted out. "He's gonna jump!"

"There's no point in that!" Yelled the other.

Nor was there any point in chitchatting with these scandoskeptics and nonbelievers. I was badly buzzed and in a state of scandofrantic panic. I had no way of exonerating myself. My last words were whispered to a little face I conjured, that angel face. "I'm coming, Caitlin."

It was a hell of a long way down. Not the seventy-mile-an-hour, four-second interval of a Golden Gate leap, but still.

At two and a half seconds, I topped out at fifty. That last second and a half is the difference between your bony sticks staying in place and the full watermelon splat. But the surge of adrenaline was no less scantastic. After all, I was Scando Man, a modern superhero, taking his artful plunge. At the moment of impact it felt like passing through concrete. It was the last scansation I felt.

50

The Specialist

December, 2K8

The coma broke days later. Though I was laid up with severe injuries, life had a way of continuing without me. No matter how significant you think your impact and contributions to the spinning globe are, people just have to get on with it.

They'd pressed Bob, of course, regarding the brief conference we'd had in his basement. Bob claimed I hadn't been myself, that I'd been speaking in uncontrollable gibberish. That I'd seen "better days" and "damned shame about Slinger."

In the end, the law enforcement dogs were relieved. First, they were happy I hadn't taken out Bob and his rat fink wife. And they'd solved their high-visibility "Two Lips Girl" case, the one that had been embarrassing the hell out of them for the better part of a year. They were thrilled it was all over. The Gripster had been apprehended.

The cops grilled Bob for what I'd communicated exactly, hoping for an explanation of my sick and heinous crimes, but I hadn't been much of a braggart. I'm sure it disappointed them greatly.

The only substantive detail Bounty Bob could recount was I'd been babbling about a "little white square" on his black-and-whites, a fleck appearing in one photograph and absent in another from the same series. That was it.

I don't know what departmental genius came up with the idea because credit went to Steve, but someone suggested the white fleck on the photo was a calling card from a pizza delivery service, a moving van offering, an aggressive Chinese restaurant publicity team, shyster lawyer or locksmith. So they cased the buildings in the area. They found the card's copy in a nearby walk-up, still attached to the mailboxes. That was cross-referenced with the proper ransacking of the Skybox when they found: a bag of sex toys leftover from an Exhibit alphabet sister; toiletries; weapons for mass conception and contraception; little orange and blue pills for those you-know-when nights; and a bedside table full of discarded napkin numbers, business cards, Adderall tabs, and Zoloft push-out mats. And a white 24-hour locksmith card, left over from the time Sunday and I had phoned in for the emergency bondage house call in the hopes of getting late-night scandocuff relief many, many, many months before.

It was a long shot that they'd seen the locksmith's card sifting through my place. It advertised features like high security cylinders, window gates, alarm systems, Medeco and Multi-Locks, and the fact that his service covered all of Manhattan. And it boasted the all-important 24-hour emergency service for the real downtown scandosex addicts, baggers, and general freaks in search of that elusive downtown American Dream. A leave-behind advertorial to a true specialist in every sense of the word.

The lock specialist had turned the card into a receipt. He wrote how much I paid and signed his name, all too legibly for him.

The police went to the locksmith's shop, first at the Manhattan address, but found it closed. Then with the reverse address directory, they found the specialist out in Queens. When Steve and two officers appeared at his shop which doubled for a home and threw a few questions his way, he became cagey. It tipped them off to investigate. It resulted in a take-no-prisoners assault on a garret listed in his mother's name in the projects near Coney Island. His mother had long since died, but the place was thriving. They found a nest of scandophernalia of an accomplished nut.

There were padlocked cabinets filled with more locks, guns, knives and scandoporn. But what interested the prowlies more was the chunk of the L.I.E.'s Two Lips billboard stacked against the wall. The bathroom had wallpaper consisting of the DeadBeauties. org nude photo he'd printed up in bathroom tile-size, pasting up hundreds. A bulletin board showed every print job Sunday Fairchild had done and drawers filled with her personal items: an old Filofax, a photo of her and Nina, a photo of the Azalea garden in the

Hamptons, a pair of pink Nikes, and the red La Perlas I'd given her for Valentine's Day. It was a veritable shrine erected to the Chic Emergency Girl, the one who'd landed the scansational Two Lips contract. More importantly, it was all the chilling evidence of which I'd robbed the police in my seemingly seamless conducting of the murders.

In addition, there was all the essential reportage and news clippings of the three murders, which had occurred locally in Queens, cases Steve had been working on and had been attributed to a serial killer. The very case in which he'd told me the killer had gone dangerously "quiet."

When the self-confessed "I don't make no judgments about nobody" specialist saw the unusual number of two-toned cars flooding his block, he made a dash for it only he was more swift. It took them forty minutes to apprehend him, as opposed to the fifteen it took to ensnare me.

In the Fifth Precinct's interrogation room, the one I'd sweated in, after a few blows to the head by short-tempered, blue-badged muscle boys, Pat the 24-hour locksmith, the one who'd helped us out of a scandojam that morning, cracked, pretty much like a farm egg. The same Pat, the sleepover Exhibit sister claimed I'd invited to one of my after-party benders in the Skybox. In actuality, he'd been stalking me. Pat confessed to the campaign in Queens and also took credit for the murders of Sunday and Dr. Greer in Manhattan. But that run of the mouth wasn't enough for the law boys. What nailed him were the hairs left on the body of Dr. Greer, a DNA match for his own.

The access necessary for the perfect murder was easy for Pat, easier than for a gossip blogger. Lest we forget, he was a specialist. He had real access. He could physically get in anywhere, anytime. I'd always needed a velvet rope dropped. After he'd met us in that compromising predicament with Sunday glowing away in her underwear, he tailed us in our daily lives. He followed her to her appointments. When he knew she was busy working, he'd enter her apartment. Sometimes he would lay in her bed or sit there and smoke a cigarette, watch cable news, eat fruit, rummage around, steal, or play with her computer. Then he would leave. He did it a dozen times and he continued to follow me after her murder.

How did I know? Detective Steve claimed Pat extended a personal thanks to me for turning him on to those two headline-grabbing murders, his greatest triumphs, the one of Sunday in particular. You see his whole serial thing out in Queens had not been yielding him enough far-reaching publicity and, in essence, respect, so he brought the show on the road into Manhattan where he could be assured some more scandalacious Face. He claimed I'd taken him to the "Promised Land," hence the gesture of gratitude. He knew he'd make a terrific splash with Sunday's murder in full embrace and appreciation for the laws of scandalocity in the post-9/11 era.

But what tacked Pat to the wall was that calling card in Sunday's building. The scandoscum would have gotten away with it, had there not been a hack writer brimming with neurological disorders who got involved by chance; a guy who'd endured relentless nightmares of lockups, lockdowns, closed doors, straightjackets, and the general *Click! Click! Click!*s of life; a guy whose familiarity with the world's padlocks at a young age compelled him to write a children's book about it; a guy who possessed a mind so attuned to lock-and-key systems that he was able to identify a tiny fleck out of a grainy snap and make the subliminal association, through some type of holographic mind referral or delivery, to the murderer; or, a guy who left himself open and available to a flock of freaky, afflicted, co-suffering cohorts who hassled and harangued him endlessly and these unemployed, unmotivated, and unaccomplished darlings, his ADD Militia, the ones who covered so much ground with their minds on a daily basis in such chaotic ways that one in particular, Ritalin Robby, left his own wacky personal note on a locksmith's card in Slinger's building, and, having done so, deposited the concept in Slinger's mind, planting the seed in memory as it were, to be called upon in the nick of time; or, more likely, a combination of all of the above. In this way, Slinger was uniquely configured and suited to be the perpetrator's ultimate foil.

Moreover, for all the negative influences The Machine imposed on Sunday Fairchild's life, it was a photograph taken by a bounty-hunting Machine chopperazzo that ultimately nailed her murderer.

The facts were irrefutable, the irony undeniable.

Why had scandoPat left an advert calling card at all? He claimed that when he was leaving Sunday's building a squad car rolled past and he spun around to show busy, only he beat it before he could grab the card back. But Detective Steve didn't buy it, surmising Pat had done it purposefully, that serial killers were narcissistic and enjoyed leaving scandographs, often signatures like this. Old Pat had even left one behind in the form of a scandocandy straw at my Skybox after-party, the scando ego of it all.

Poor old Pat had felt scandobland, despondent over the lack of proper NR for his Queens campaign. He knew he could go out with a bigger bang in Manhattan. He'd made Sunday his mark. But after killing her, he experienced a revived interest with all the exciting scando press and attention. Scando-loco. So he targeted me to help him choose his next victim. Why? I had access to more boldfaced, influential, and media-generating targets. In the end, his murder campaign had been revitalized by The Machine and the sweeping global scandoFace it generated. In that way, too, he was probably good for a few more killings after Dr. Greer, to further boost his Google entries.

But not now. The scando-psycho would be locked up for the rest of his days, scandodamned in hell. That's how I saw it anyway.

51

Fond Farewell

January, 2K9

Unfortunately I missed out on the double-borough fun. I was in the hospital for three weeks, including New Year's Eve. In addition to the mind-numbing restriction of the coma, I had a collapsed lung, seven broken ribs, a broken arm and a shattered leg. With that fateful plunge came the end of the myth. There was no superhero, no Scando Man. I was real flesh and blood and I was still bleeding. But I was alive.

I was shocked that I'd survived the fall, as survival hadn't been an obsession at the time. The only thing that prevented me from exploding my heart was that I'd been in such a bad state from the recent breakdown I basically had no fear. I'd never experienced an event that so thoroughly lived up to my non-medicated and therefore unrepressed high-stim objectives. It was also gratis.

The impact of the solved case was immediate. I beat my Gotham Gripster and SoHo Strangler titles and the shared scando-championship belts they represented. I also changed my line of work. I was going to finish off my guilty pleasure prose number, *The Dolce Vita Diaries,* or maybe some nonfiction. Warner Books offered me a low six-figure deal to write the story of the murders but I declined. I still had two hundred large banked. That could last me a few years in the hills of Vermont. Or a decade in India.

I decided on the latter. Not Goa, but an old farmhouse in Norwich, Vermont located right on the Connecticut River on the New Hampshire border. Dartmouth College was across the river in Hanover. The town offered solitude and tranquility and had excellent library and campus resources to choose from. And no scandal sheets. A lengthy and involved stint with academia would be good for a soul which had been neglected, at best, parched at worst, but thoroughly undernourished no matter how you looked at it.

January 25th was moving day and the city had just had a welcomed light snow. I was overseeing the operation as movers picked up the furniture and boxes of personals at the loft. While cleaning out my mailbox I found a letter inside which raised my spirits.

Sister Jamison, the Florida nun who had helped me with my investigation into Sunday's death, had written me to thank me for my annual contribution. They'd held a memorial service for Sunday on Shell Beach and scattered her ashes on the ocean. They'd invited me to attend, but I was still in the hospital. She also informed me some "exceptional and intelligent young women" had been admitted to the Shelter who were certain to grow up to be "fine strong modern ladies." One reminded her of Sunday because she was slender, blonde, and very pretty. The young lady was interested in becoming a news anchorwoman in New York, not an "entertainment journalist" like me, the Sister noted. All the better, I thought. No scandophiles, no scandophants. Real news, real people.

I kept the letter and quickly hit the road. Word had it the Militia was throwing a going-away fête at my now-empty, unfurnished loft. For me. The party was supposed to be a surprise, but left in their hands, the secret had little chance. I filled the fridge with sandwiches from a catering company and beers and left the doors unlocked and arranged for an industrial team to handle the clean-up. Only later would I learn they actually did show up. They forgot the cake at the bakery, of course, though they did manage to bring a send-off gift. A pogo stick. A random sidewalk choice from a homeless vendor.

But I had to smile. As undependable, self-absorbed, and wacky as they were, Mad Ted, Ritalin Robby, Zeke the Freak, Mr. Confetti Guns, Crazy Jake, Driven To Distraction, Wally Foxx, the Jack-In-The-Box, Adderall Paul and others, all practitioners of the big pop and no follow-through, all lacking the drive, stick-to-it-iveness, and wherewithal to get a job, much less keep it, make their fortune, or some fuck-you money, anyway, sentenced to a life of buzzing around blindly, they were my brothers. In this context I indeed felt fortunate.

Rather than attend the party, I had a final lunch with the Fonz, my friend, a time for us to say a few "*Si*"s and one "*Adios.*"

"*Mi divertidad bastante, Señor Slinger,*" the Fonz confided too.

Lastly, I contacted Pablo to let him know that I was moving and that he could visit anytime, and that I had his back for anything, including college tuition. He apologized for not having been around to see me and told me he loved me. I told him I felt the same way about him.

Hours later, I was on a train heading north, en route to White River Junction, Vermont. I was no longer a player in The Machine, I wouldn't be Slinging it anymore. Scandoland and the petty, insignificant items it generated were now someone else's problem. I didn't turn back once, not even to eye the shrinking skyline. With one final item in mind, I let it disappear all on its own.

Scandoblind: What Manhattan scandoscribe with a regrettable scandospective on life has given up his scandomantle and all the scandobanter that came with it for the quiet hills of New England?

I would see the world in a larger and more compassionate context, not from the angle of a jaded, urban-maniacal, media-intensive, and pop culture-dominated niche. As for the indulgent dolce vita days, they came abruptly to an end.

Thereby, so had my story from New York at the dawn of a fresh century at the height of the scandalocity era.

52

The Visit

February, 2K9

Weeks later, in mid-February, the snow was piled six feet high at Dartmouth College, the campus green's towering Winter Carnival ice sculpture depicting a miner panning for gold. I was returning from a Women's Study seminar at the Hopkins Center. The house was winter dark, as usual, but even darker when I stepped in as it took time for my eyes to adjust from the whiteness of snow outside. The front door had been open, as I always left it. It was Vermont, after all.

He was sitting there in the living room, puffing away on my recliner. His face was half-shadowed by the fading light, but I could still make out the rough features and fierce jaw. I recognized the creases in his forehead. I'd seen what they did when he smiled, I'd seen what they did when he smoked. And I'd seen what they did in my sleep. And Daddy-Mister's accent, of course, was hard to undersell.

"Where is she, Slinger?"

I asked him what the hell he was doing there instead of answering him directly. I was rewarded with a pistol click and a shiny barrel leveled at me.

"One more chance," he said. "That's it."

"I'm sorry, Chucky," I said in a fully resigned way. "You're just going to have to do it."

I thought it was over. I was waiting for a slug to explode in my chest any second, just one big firecracker blast and a red surge and that would be it, so quick there'd be no time to tell my angel I was on my way for real this time. Yet the big noise never came.

"Things haven't been the same since you left."

"Oh?"

"Talent hasn't been so hot out at the Shelter."

"Sweet."

"But it's pickin' up in town since that Alabammy co-ed got snuffed in Aruba. Gal was a spike for business, single-handedly brought Spring Break back to where it should be…"

"America?"

"Florida. Serves 'em right for goin' foreign."

He was a real beaut. "Heard you lost the place—"

"It's the Sunshine State, Slinger. I'm never out, just a couple bank accounts removed. Now where the fuck is she?"

"I only know who you're talking about because it's you. And she is dead, Chucky."

"Dead my ass."

He proceeded to go into a mild tirade about how he'd known Sunday since she was young, that she'd always tried, and failed, to outsmart him. I could smell the aged bourbon across the room. "Bitch is alive," he finished off with.

Then he started to break up, an eerie laugh. Fairchild had a way of packaging everything a mite strangely. A flash drift had me imagining an orphanage down south and little Charles Fairchild, the unwanted child, sitting on the swings with no one to push him. Since no one was there, only someone to lock him up at night, he was going to take it out on someone. As in, the next generation, in a perverse way. I understood his kind of upbringing in an odd way, even to the bad place it brought him. His interior had been twisted and fury had taken up full-time residence, forever. Me? I'd gone inside and beat myself up for twenty years. He did it to other people. I didn't feel sorry for him, even if he had endured an unfortunate childhood. Many start out like he must have, and don't turn into pervs and rabid sexual abusers. He was just too fucking selfish.

"I'm going to tell you something you ought to know."

I was ready for the old misogynist's cheer, the "They're all whores!" speech with a row of legs kicking high, panty peeks, and pom-poms with streamers, but the cheer never came, though something more surprising did. He said it softly, like all good striking freaks do, but I wasn't prepared for the voice choking up.

"Think of the faces, Slinger, them little faces. Remember 'em as tiny tots. Then they grow up and get bigger, with more expressions blazin'. Them little girls 'n' boys," he said, his delivery splintered with emotion. "They lookin' up at you all trustin' to show 'em the way. All fired up 'bout everythin', 'bout you, 'bout their little lives, what gonna happen next. Follow them little faces through time as thing get tough, life tough. And thing start gettin' in their way. Some good, some not so good. Over time, that little puss change. It get disappointed, angry, sad. The little spirit take a hit, git nicked, bumped, 'n' crushed. Was pullin' yer leg what I told you 'bout the Shack and four at a time."

I told him I was aware of it. Perhaps it was only "three."

"Yep. Wanted you to hate me."

I told him he'd accomplished that.

"'Cause I hated you."

I rode along silent again.

"Heard someone once say the greatest damned natural resource we got is the spirit o' them little people. And if that spirit git broken then, well, she git broken. The rest o' her life. I loved that little girl."

He hesitated, I assumed, to collect himself. He then raised the gun barrel and wedged it deep under his chin. A Chuck Fairchild brain salad on the ceiling of my little farmhouse was certainly a death befitting him, but then he pulled the gun away and started up the laugh track until it hit an uproarious pitch.

"Don't worry, Slinger. Not goin' Oprah on you—"

The creep was yukking it up, but I could see the unrest. In his eyes, the ones sunk in the caves of a little boy with sandy blond hair, I saw it register in them: the pain. His little speech had nothing to do with sorrow or guilts for his mistreatment of young women, it had to do with himself. He'd been broken and his precious little spirit long ago. He could hide the damage in the military, but when it was all over he had no more uniforms, no more flying suits, no more shiny boots, helmets, or goggles. He had no more reveilles or pilots' luncheons to attend. He had no more structure. He'd been held in by great traditions with the finest stitching, bandages, and adhesives keeping it all together, but it all fell apart when he got out. The man had cracked. In the way I'd described it to Sunday in my first spontaneous rant to her, the one about ex-lovers sucking on whiskey bottles and Glock pistols and feverishly hunting her down. I'd been partially right about that. Unknowingly so.

In fairness to Fairchild, he was more gifted in the darkest and meanest ways than any creature I'd ever come across. As I sat there, it became my duty to get through the meeting without taking a whizzer. I wasn't looking forward to much of anything, but I still had some pride. Maybe even a foray into the book business awaiting me and one breath let out wrong could end all that.

"When did you get out?"

"Nice o' you to ask. Sure are sensitive. What the fuck do you care?"

"I don't."

"That's right, Slinger. And since you don't care I'll tell ya. Six months ago. And like I promised, I'd be comin' to find you. Now I'm here. See, been watchin' you…"

I regarded him carefully. "Following me?"

"Hell, yes."

Fairchild rose up and took this positioning to interrogate me some more about my movements in the last year. He knew most of them. He was convinced she was still alive. Then he had this.

"Wa'n't so bad as you think, Slinger."

"What's that?"

"Us. My relationships with 'em. Hell, we had good times. Some damned good times. Like family."

I didn't say anything. What do you say to a comment like that from a guy like him? I told myself to stay calm and keep my trap shut. I probably spared my life in the process.

"I loved her—"

Again. Mum from me.

"Say somethin', Slinger."

"Her ashes were scattered on the ocean."

"Which ocean?"

"The Gulf. Sisters held a service for her on the white sands."

"Really…" I even think he flipped my response over in his

mind a moment. "What else you got for me?"

"We're not so different, Chucky."

"Come agin?"

His face seemed to brighten, as if he was pleased to hear that. That, or he'd conjured peculiar expectations of what my offering could be.

"You're bleeding; so am I. Just a matter of time for us both."

He steadied on me a moment almost in a trance. That was the last bit of communication I had with him. I only remember a flash like lightning, an explosion from within really, alighting all I could see.

I woke up hours later in pitch blackness. It was four in the morning. I had to first widen my jaw to release it, as my lower teeth were dug into the floor rug. My eyeballs ached in their sockets, my head throbbed. Fairchild had blackjacked me at the base of my skull.

My wallet was on the floor, its contents spread in a pile. He didn't snatch the two hundred bucks; he didn't leave a cheery good-bye note, either. The encounter was as odd as the first time I'd met him. I never saw Chuck Fairchild again, nor did I care to.

Whether or not he truly believed Sunday was alive, I didn't know. But that wasn't why he came to Vermont. He'd yearned for that visit with me. With someone Sunday had loved. More than wanting it, he needed it. He knew she and I had that bond, he knew he'd lost her long ago. And that he did care for her in his own sick way. In an equally bizarre fashion, he respected me for being the guy with whom she'd found love and some semblance of happiness. In a strange, backhanded way it was a show of respect. That, more than anything, is probably what saved my ass.

News got back to me what became of Chucky. Barely a year later, he was put on trial in Valparaiso County for attempted rape of a girl from the St. Mary's Shelter For Young Women. The young lady he'd messed with was courageous. Not from my spoiled Generation Green, but from the new emboldened generation. The generation that had seen their towers fall and learned early how to fight back. She went right after him with the top criminal lawyer in Tallahassee. She was the aspiring news anchorwoman, the one Sister

Jamison had written me about. Her lawyers had rounded up six other victims to testify. At last, Chucky became an MSNBC All-Star and his depraved deeds were known the world over. Spring Break had not been so good to Chucky in the end.

Before the jury could come down with a verdict, however, Charles Witten Fairchild, who was out on a $500,000 bail bond, was found murdered in his Niceville backwater shack. It was said he'd gotten in too deep with some unsavory business associates who thought the sentence he'd receive wouldn't be nearly painful, much less decisive enough. Daddy-Mister, was finally out of commission for good, eight legs and all.

53

Infinity White

May, 2K10

I picked up the pieces of my life in Vermont. I didn't have a plan or program. I was still taking medication, but hadn't sustained any memory lapses or "attacks" since leaving New York. My local doctor attributed it to the reduction in stress, a function of my new surroundings. The big city and my chosen profession in it had never complimented my neurological condition very well.

Still, I hadn't overcome all the psychological setbacks. The visit to the Creek had been cleansing but I wasn't whole. Maybe I never would be, but it did become my goal to achieve a state of balance and peaceful equilibrium for the very first time.

To this end, my little rural farmhouse was the appropriate panacea. I caught up on reading which the high-octane years in New York had not accommodated. I worked around the house and yard. I also outlined a book, a piece of nonfiction concerning the sensational murder case. I wasn't doing it for the money; I was doing it for myself as therapy, if you will.

Then came that cool early spring day in May, fifteen months after the reunion with Chucky at the house. A DHL overnight envelope arrived in my driveway mailbox, sent to me by Aeromexico, Mexico's national airline. I opened it and found a round-trip ticket to Puerto Vallarta. The note attached to it was handwritten in perfect Spanish by a woman. Translated, it stated,

I must speak to you. It concerns Sunday Fairchild. Please come. A driver, Señor Carlos, will pick you up at the Puerto Vallarta Airport.

Warmest regards,

Señora Fernanda Malía.

I remembered the name; Sunday had mentioned her. She was the nanny Chuck had hired to run the household and watch over the girls. Sunday had been close to her and was deeply saddened when Fernanda returned to Mexico.

The thought of an excursion of the sort was unsettling, even eerie, and emotionally draining, too. The idea of jaunting off somewhere Sunday-related, uncertain as to where I was going and knowing little of my hostess, if indeed she was who she purported to be. I pondered whether I should go. In the end, with a fragile but healing psyche and an innate curiosity dueling exhaustively in mind, I had little choice. I had to see the story, if it indeed was a story, to its conclusion. I, too, was writing a book and the trip could be considered research.

The enclosed itinerary indicated that car transportation had been arranged to pick me up in Puerto Vallarta and travel to the final destination, a place called "Tres Angeles," just below the Costa Careyes. I MapQuested and Googled the location, but found no information. Costa Careyes itself was described as a stretch of breathtaking coastline with spotted expensive homes perched on cliffs overlooking the Mexican Pacific with private rocky coves and bays. The flight was scheduled to leave in two days.

With a duffel bag, a Brazilian spiritual tome, and a healing mind thwarting the usual bombardment and downplaying expectations, I boarded the plane at Boston's Logan and was on my way to Mexico.

At the terminal in Puerto Vallarta, Señor Carlos was waiting for me by the Duty-Free shop near baggage claim. He drove a vintage Volkswagen Beetle and was very polite, his English wasn't half bad. We drove for hours down a ribboning seaside road which boasted the most picturesque coastal views I'd ever seen with cliffs and mountains and little beaches tucked away and enormous rock formations hovering over them.

As the coastline flattened, the beach became less rocky and gave way to sweeping stretches and whiter sands. In a remote area, we turned down a serpentining red earthen dirt drive and a half-mile in pulled up before tall and broad iron gates marked "Tres Angeles" in wonderfully ornate blue and gold-tiled inlays. Carlos punched in a code and the gates motored apart. There were palms lining the sidewinding driveway and we came upon a splendidly quaint villa perched on the dune with a Spanish-tiled roof and the blue Pacific as its expansive backyard. As I got out, the sun was slamming down hard and the front door to the villa was barely though invitingly spread and Carlos offered a final nod of permission before driving off.

I stepped through the doorway into an entrance courtyard. In the center, an elaborate marble fountain surged with crystal waters and the Mexican-tiled inlays matched those of the outer gate. I slipped through the open-aired living room. The decor was minimalist but tasteful and infinity white, as in white *everything*. It made for terrific contrast with the ever-changing azure hues of the Pacific.

There didn't appear to be anyone in the house. I figured I was early or Ms. Malía was late. I called out, and my announcement was met with silence. I wasn't too concerned. After another long winter and stunted spring in Vermont, it was pleasant to take in the warm, tranquil setting. I stepped outside to a tiled patio that overlooked the water. A pool was somewhere back there, also the infinity type, as it went undiscovered, giving the appearance that its waters were connected to and flowed right into the vastness. The villa seemed poised on paradise.

I set my bag down on the terrace and removed my shoes and decided on a stroll out to the endless run of deserted beach. As I gazed upon the horizon, I spotted a disturbance in the water. A whale's swollen head popped high and then spew shot from its blowhole. I'd read up it was mating season for the whales and there were frequent sightings. Yet there were no neighbors along this stretch. The house was the only construction on the entire sweep of pristine beach. For all I knew, it was just me and the whales.

In a short while, the sun faded toward the Pacific to perform one of its idyllic watercolor retreats. A spring wind suddenly gusted, whipping across my face. Though sand granules stung my cheeks, the wide and white sand beach looked damned dazzling. And empty. It reminded me of a certain beach I'd come to know recently. And love.

The figure advanced from the south, appearing as a black fleck and grew in increments, to child and then adult size. I'd never met Fernanda Malía but upon first look, she appeared rather statuesque.

As the gap between us narrowed, I could see the woman had long dark hair and was wearing big oval sunglasses. She was dressed in white linen, drawstring pants with the tie dangling in front cut above her navel, revealing her midriff, the pant legs swaying with the ocean breeze lapping up from behind. A black sweater wrapped her shoulders, and she was holding her sandals in hand. As the woman came closer, I got a decent look at her tanned face and wondered if we'd met before. When she got within fifty yards, I was sure of it.

The expression on her face was decidedly stern and remained so; I was not even granted the emerging smile of a polite greeter. She didn't move in closer to me than the seven feet she settled on. She stayed back, her carriage rigid. It made me do the same. I recognized her, all right, the wind snatching a tear out of my eye to tickle my cheek.

"*Buenos días*, Harry."

The voice was deep with scarcely a trace of southern belle and I'd heard her speak this way a couple times. The tone, presently, was even lower and raspier, unrecognizably so.

Under normal conditions, it was a time for rejoicing, to see in the flesh a loved one thought gone and perished, but these weren't normal conditions as nothing about them ever had been.

When I didn't respond, she did. "How are you?"

It was no piece of cake on my interior; I was held immobile in a cold stone state of shock, my pulse quickening, my hands trembling and awash.

"I've needed to speak to you," she proclaimed.

If ever there'd been an understatement...

Though several years older, the contours of her body and face were the same, the skin folded and clothes creased in all the remembered places. The energy surging forth from her frame was far different, however, like that of another person. It kept me frozen in my tracks.

"You've had me all wrong."

"You don't say..." It was more selling herself short. "And from how far back?"

My question coincided with an unearthing of her cotton tank top to wipe her lenses. Her face didn't change in either direction, whether harder or more at ease; it remained consistent and closed down. She was a beauty, all right, a chilled one, and perhaps even colder than that.

"As far as you can remember," she put it bluntly. "I couldn't have it, Harry."

"What?"

"This."

"You mean us?"

"I mean anyone."

"Love?"

"No." She shook too. "Not configured for it."

"By all means, disappear then."

She acknowledged my way of thinking with a short, charitable nod.

"Maybe I was at one time, but—" Surprisingly, her voice cracked and water suddenly seeped into her eyes. "I was too far gone when we met and there was no turning back for me."

"How do you mean?"

"There was no room left," she said. She wiped her eyes and tried to collect herself. "Sure, it was nice those first perfect lays, the morning excitement, the walking on clouds. But soon, very soon, the killer D's got a hold of me, like usual. And I distance, dislike, then show disdain." Her face crumpled, and she broke down partially.

"And then?"

"And then I totally despise," she gasped in between sobs.

"That's the pattern?"

"Doesn't it sound familiar?"

"I think 'despise' covers it best."

"Don't Harry, make it any more difficult."

She lowered her head, which gave her time to regain herself. It took a while before she straightened up. "You're a wonderful man. Exciting, kind. The only one I could take for more than a little while."

"Lovely—"

"My greatest show of love, or caring, or whatever you want to call it is seeing you now." The eyes were leveled ruthlessly upon me to punctuate. She broke from that regard to confuse the signal further, to behave even more unpredictably.

I was in shock and the strength of that was gaining momentum.

"Harry, Harry, Harry," she breezed. "Sweet Harry. Your mind is something, maybe a work of art. Sexy. And so are you. Underneath the tangled and frayed nerve endings, there is a beautiful soul, but you're without essential knowledge. You didn't pick up on it, not that anyone could have. But if anyone could have it was you—"

It was the delivery, her words flowing in a cadence I'd never heard. She wielded a razor's edge, her points laser-guided. The carefree, warm, and loving Sunday I'd known was buried somewhere, perhaps, but that generosity of spirit lay beneath a force of character I'd never witnessed. Frightening.

"Tell me about yourself. The real you."

"My fangs are sharp and I will bite. Perhaps you already know."

"You're full of it and you know it." I wasn't sure, though; I was only half-believing myself, hoping what I posed had some validity.

Her return glower was transmitted from an even darker place. "With respect to me, it's never going to get any better. For you."

I took a while with a response. I needed time. She believed herself too much and I believed in my dying appraisal of her too little.

"Harry Starslinger: The closest thing to male perfection I could have ever dreamed of."

"What the hell does that mean? What do you have to tell me?"

"All right," she spat and she did it brutally. "For two years, Harry, I worked for Dr. Bowden Knowles in Tallahassee. Knowles was a disciple of Dr. Roger Hoskins, your Dr. Hoskins, remember?"

My pump thundered. "How could I forget?"

"In the late eighties, after leaving his practice in Massachusetts, Dr. Hoskins, inspired by your case and others, got a grant from the National Institutes of Health in Bethesda to study the causes of a recently recognized illness, Attention Deficit Disorder, and other related neurological disorders. You probably know that—"

I did.

"What you don't know is Dr. Knowles was part of Hoskins' team. The two of them became pioneers in the treatment of ADD. Knowles returned to Florida to practice privately. He sought out teens in the local area who might be afflicted. The nuns introduced me to him, actually. They'd described to him my hyperactivity, my inconsistent personality, the mood swings, and bouts of unrelenting sadness. They thought he might be able to help. Yes, Harry, I'm loaded like you. According to Dr. Knowles, as much or more so."

The news was stunning, naturally, but anything from her had to be at this point. As I watched her recount her tale, she became emboldened, her delivery became more deliberate and unwaveringly aggressive. It was a persona and modus operandi that I'd never witnessed.

"Knowles tested me for everything and I had positives across the board. Bipolarity, ADD, hyperactivity, the works. To get away from Niceville and learn more about myself, I took a job in his office. It gave me a routine and structure, structure that I sorely needed. Sound familiar? That structure included sleeping with him. I've slept with a lot of men, Harry, I always have. It's a drug for me. Fucking for me is like uppers for you; it has a calming effect. Or it did until I met you. And I didn't need it from anyone else anymore."

"Sunday—"

"No, Harry, wait! And listen! Knowles had a file cabinet of neurological disorder case studies that fascinated me. When office traffic slowed, I perused them. Then, I found you. 'Harvey Starslinger.'"

She paused to angle up, to see this deliciousness register on me.

"You had a thick folder, Harry. A classic case study, an inspiration to all the doctors. I'd known about you for five years. In some ways, you were my idol, but instead of a baseball card to remember you by, I had a copy of your file. And I had to meet you in person to see my match, my 'male counterpart' as Knowles put it. I was magnetized to you in some inexplicable way. I didn't know exactly why other than we shared similar conditions. When we first met I told you I knew you lived at 473 Broome Street. Remember wondering how I knew? Or how I knew about your penchant for going off on creative rants? Yes, I targeted you. Before I met you, I felt that special bond between us, and as soon as we spoke, I wanted to eat you alive. But that's the easy part for me; that's always been the easy part, Harry."

My legs held me up purely from muscle memory and experience. There was little power left in them. I felt gutted.

"I know what you're wondering, but by tomorrow there will be no more questions, no more secrets. I promise."

"Who are you?"

"It's not in our natures to be patient, but try…"

I could only stand there and take it.

"Greer spoke to me of your attraction to danger in romance. It's why you were instantly attracted to me: you knew something didn't fit. Sure, you found me beautiful, but that didn't separate you from the pack. You knew something wasn't right; that's what hooked you, something deep and dark was lying hidden there and you had to go after it, to see what it was, to see if it would scorch and torture your soul. It's very self-destructive to be attracted to something you know can hurt you, but I know all about it—"

"You proposed something I couldn't have and asked for something I couldn't give. Love passed me by long ago. I was too far gone when you met me; I'm further gone now. Mine is a life sentence and it's not a pretty one. Now I'm going to show you, Harry, the real me."

"Nina Pearson's parents were on that Air Florida plane which crashed into the Everglades. There were no survivors. It left Nina with two hundred million dollars and extensive land holdings. Chucky learned of her story and found she lived with her guardian in nearby Destin. She attended the local junior high and took ballet classes at a dance studio. Chucky decided to enroll me in that ballet class, to get to know her and win her confidence, and then influence her to attend Sunday school at the Shelter. Nina was immediately attracted to me and my charismatic high-energy behavior and we became best friends. When Chucky and Floyd made her guardian disappear—yes, forever—Nina was there for the taking. She moved in to the Shelter and eventually he brought her home and soon after Chucky started up with his underage thing having his way with her against her will, at first. She'd been a virgin. But then she fell in love with him. It wasn't long before she wanted to marry him and Chucky proposed to her, but in a different way. Marrying her was against the law, so he legally adopted her, as he'd done for me. At the same time, a few lawyers, some Florida corrupt beauties, took hold of her paperwork. From then on, her bank was in the hands of Chucky, a job easily done in a state that doesn't care as long as you keep paying…"

"Soon, however, the personal relationships started to crumble. Nina was always jealous of me, of other women Chucky'd bring home. So she started up with Floyd. Chucky didn't like that and they fought. She made threats, threats guys like Chucky don't like to hear. Not love threats or money threats, quality of life threats. As in jail. So he threw her in the bay behind the house, held a foot on her back, and drowned her. I tried to stop him, but I was no match. He threatened to kill me too if I said anything. We all backed his story that she'd run away."

"Chucky then had his crooked legal team invent charities to receive 'donations' from Nina's trust until there was no money left. The charities were run through corporations he'd set up and the lawyers were taken care of handsomely."

I was still shaking, sure. "And the rest of the money?"

"When it came time to take care of the others, Chucky was Chucky. He wouldn't pay off Floyd. Floyd got per diem, handyman wages, basically. Chucky promised to settle, but never delivered. When he was let out of prison, Floyd threatened him to pay or he'd go to the police about the murders of Nina and her guardian."

"So he killed Floyd?"

"Floyd disappeared not long after. He's never been found."

I tried my damnest to process what she was saying, but didn't know where to begin. "What was your relationship with him after Nina's murder?"

"I didn't know what to do. I couldn't make a move without being followed, I was trapped. And terrified. Finally I offered up his name to the federal government for his tax-dodging accounting ways at the club and it got him thrown in jail. He never knew it was me."

Sunday employed the past tense, of course, as Chucky had been found murdered three months before.

"Having him incarcerated gave me my freedom and time, time to figure things out. Of course I could have blown the whistle, I was an accomplice, but a minor at the time. But don't forget: I was loaded, ADHD-loaded. I wanted to get control of the issues that had been plaguing me throughout my childhood and teens, all my life. I'd swept everything under the rug, rationalizing my passive behavior with temporary Band-Aids, but the Band-Aids would lose their stick. That's when I went to Knowles to get help, to get knowledgeable, to take control of my life."

"Then you came along, more forcefully than I'd anticipated. You introduced me to a glamorous world. For the first time in my life, I felt alive and believe it or not, normal. It's what people like us crave, isn't it, Harry? To be and feel normal? I was accomplishing on my own merit without anyone looking over my shoulder at every move and I had a sense of self-worth again, all thanks to you. I even told you in the Hamptons, remember?"

I did; I'd memorized it.

But giving someone their life back and a chance to become the person they always could have been, and can still be? Priceless...

"In New York, I felt my best..."

She stopped suddenly then, water flowing to her eyes again.

"Tell me—"

"But it was much deeper than that. I'd gravitated to you in that inexplicable way and when I got to know you and love you I found out why. Of course, your love made me feel worthy and deserving again. But more than that, I saw what you'd gone through and how you'd survived it and it was a fountain of inspiration for me. I thought if you could do it, well... It gave me the strength to help myself. And that's why I called you my angel."

It was difficult for her, her voice quavering, her chin rolling.

"B-b-but in going through my own healing process, I had my down times like you, Harry. I'm bipolar too, and I was capable of those same outbursts, those unstoppable fits of depression. And I didn't want you to see me that way any more than you wanted me to see that side of you."

"The night of the awards I had that kind of night. I was very depressed, I got very drunk. It's why I couldn't say no to stupid spontaneous acts with guys like Nitr8 and women like Greer. That's how I medicated those lows, that's how it happened in the limousine that night. When I phoned you late that night, it was a cry for help. I wanted you to rescue me, to take me away. And you did."

The corners of her mouth nearly curved as the thin line of water edged over the bottom of her eyes and slid down her face.

"But for all the good that happened to me in New York, and you were the best, it was not enough. Having a career or notoriety didn't make a difference, not with my background. I wanted," and then she broke totally, trying to articulate through a heaving chest, "my *life back!!!* As a little girl, as a lady! A respectable young lady! But I could never get it back! All I could get was better. And maybe, just maybe, I could get *even*."

She twisted off and away and released the tempest of pent-up emotions in a deep, enduring cry. I wanted to go to her, but was still unable to move. After recovering, she stood stiff and straight and let her secret be known.

"So I became Nina."

It wasn't necessary to flash through the history. Sunday had taken herself out of circulation and resurfaced as the girl who'd "run away," Nina Pearson.

"I had her documents, the lawyers didn't know what she looked like, no one had seen her since she was fifteen. I changed my look, hired my own attorney and had him take care of it with them. I signed papers without ever seeing them and paid them off generously enough not to ask any questions or get suspicious. Don't forget; they were at risk themselves for their sordid dealings, dealings I had third parties threaten them with."

"But why me?" I cried out suddenly. "Why disappear from me? You could have just told me this!"

"To protect you, to protect me, to protect everyone I cared about."

"From who?"

"Him. And I didn't want you to talk me out of it."

"To talk you out of what? What did you do?"

She said it evenly and with no less cunning. "I got even, Harry. After I left New York I came here and worked on a plan. I set up a legal fund in Florida and paid for a group of lawyers to represent a young woman Chuck had sexually abused recently. I even paid his bail anonymously and I did it for a reason—"

"So you could kill him—"

"I could have done that before the trial, but I wanted him to be indicted and go through the process so the world would know about him. I wanted him to experience at least some public humiliation for his conduct."

I eyed her neutrally. "And the money?"

"It wasn't about the money; it was never about the money. I've given most of it away. The Shelter received a large sum, so did the National Institutes of Health and the American Cancer Society. There's a charity established in Nina's name, as well."

"What about the land?"

"I hold the title for that entire sweep of beach as far as the eye can see. Title to do what I want. It will stay like it is Harry, with no development. The way I've loved it, the way I've cherished it. And the way I've needed it. At times it was the only thing that kept me going. I want it to be there for the little ones, the girls and boys…"

"Forever…" I said.

"Amen."

I stayed fastened on her as she caught her breath. Surprisingly, her features eased and lost their harshness for the first time in the twenty minutes we'd been talking. As she told me how much she'd wanted to see me again, her voice grew quiet. She began to sound again like the woman I'd once known, looked like her too and I was registering in her eyes a way I also remembered, the identical expression I'd never stopped offering her.

She moved a step closer, then embraced me tightly. I was frozen to her and she kept holding on and the warmth passed through me and thawed me and made my arms come to life. I wrapped her as I felt an energy I also remembered from other days, return. She began sobbing into my chest and I felt it creep in and touch my core. It was her, the one I knew and loved.

We stayed in each others arms a good while.

"It's wonderful being here," she said, "with you. And no more pretenses, no more lies, just us. Finally, Harry."

When we pulled apart, her face was puffy and full of water.

"Any regrets?"

She stuttered through it, her chin trembling again. "Y-y-yes, many. Wishing I could have helped Nina; wishing I could have gotten him sooner. Wishing I could have been more honest. And wishing I could keep you, but I know it would never work out."

I wouldn't challenge her, though I hoped to hear her reasoning.

"I'm going away," she said. "That does not make a good partner."

She hesitated.

"And I have other regrets." She broke slightly again, but maintained ahold of herself. "I did my best with what I had. In my youth, I'd had a lot and lost it and by the time you came around it was almost gone. You were my last gasp—"

"Of?"

"Innocence. I felt it for the first time since I was a little girl with you. Our union was the last soft, sweet, pretty bit of it, and for that I'm grateful to have experienced it again. But what I've given to you is the most I'm capable of, the most I've ever been capable of…"

Silence fell upon us for a moment as the wind kicked up again.

I waited, making sure there wasn't anything else she had to say concerning the biggest mystery of all. There wasn't. So I asked.

"Why did you confess all this? Why didn't you just let me go?"

She stood there, riveted on me, her flooded eyes suddenly dropping. Then she kicked the sand. Her foot flopped to its side.

"I had to," she said sparely, in whisper. "I know I could never have made it or even continued on; I could never have survived without you. Seeing you fight to get better and cope and being loved by you inspired me so and gave me that courage. You rescued me and oh, how I've wanted to return the favor. See Harry, you are my angel."

She wiped her face which had not stopped seeping yet and

gripped me even tighter. "And I've missed you so very, very much."

"The little things," I said. "I've missed the little things."

It made her show one fully, finally, that gleaming smile. "You know when I first fell in love with you? I mean really fell…"

I shook.

Through her upset she burst out in laughter, "When you told me about your plans for the Dodo Bar…"

I remembered, our first meeting in SoHo over 'Bucks bold when I discussed the demise of the Mauritius dodos.

"I thought I'd blown it."

"No Harry, you'd sealed it. Forever."

"How?"

"Because it let me know you felt it."

"What?"

"You know, don't you?"

"Yes, but I'd like to hear it."

"The same pain as me."

I stepped forward and hugged her again and we gripped each other and neither of us let go. Sunday bucked and cried into my chest and I didn't want to let her go, until she cracked out once more, laughing through it.

"Will you tell me another one of your depressing human interest animal stories?" She belched even harder and I thought, this is the girl loved, my girl, at long last.

"The kind that depicts the corrupt nature of mankind, man not-so-kind?"

"Precisely."

"A coyote in Central Park comes to mind. And a baby gorilla…"

"Gorilla," she chose.

"'Kay," I said, still in a state of shock that this was all really happening. "In the jungle of Equatorial Guinea in 1966, a group of naturalists came upon a massacre of a clan of silverback gorillas, all killed by poachers. The bodies were hacked up and strewn all over. Amid the carnage was one baby gorilla left alone and alive with his mouth still attached to its dead mother's nipple. This baby male gorilla was albino; it was totally snow white. So the men rescued him and he was placed in a zoo in Barcelona where they named him 'Snowflake.' For the next thirty-six years, Snowflake lived in the Barcelona Zoo and he became the symbol of the city too, his face featured on all the postcard racks. Snowflake mated each year and he sired twenty-two baby gorillas, but never produced another albino."

"Snowflake's skin was pink and without pigment and thereby very sensitive to the sun's rays. So he eventually contracted skin cancer and in 2003, I flew to Barcelona when I heard his death was imminent. We were all on Snowflake death watch, as it was only a matter of days. I visited the Zoo every day to pay my respects to the ailing boy until one day I wasn't allowed to. Snowflake died the next day. Curiously, in all the time he was in the zoo, Snowflake rarely turned around to greet the public. He kept his back to the tourist flow, always. In total defiance of. Surely as a result of the memories of the horrendous murder of his mother and the rest of his family at the hands of you-know-who. The city of Barcelona was devastated when he died; people mourned for days. They buried him there at the zoo in his enclosure and to this day Snowflake is the only albino gorilla ever recorded in history. My Snowflake pin still rides along on the lapel of my jean jacket."

With tears welling once more in her eyes, Sunday raised her hand and gently caressed my cheek. My lids were flooded, too.

"That's my Harry," she said.

I let go of a smile with a face that tumbled around, for so many reasons, take your pick. Water broke on both eyes and ran down my cheek.

"And I will always be in love with you."

I stepped in to her and she squeezed me so very hard. Our faces touched at the sides and the water from both met on our noses and cheeks and lips. We kissed right on through the saltiness.

After a ten-minute embrace, she took my hand and guided me back to the house. We didn't speak the first hour; we laid on a double lounge chair on the patio gazing at each other, holding each other close, watching the waves break. The silence was the way it had to be and it was right.

Not having spoken of ourselves, we went into the bedroom and made love. I broke hard at the moment of climax, a tremendous release of a lifetime's worth of grief, sadness, longing and shock. She held me tight, maternally, sisterly, and romantically, and didn't let me go from her clutches for hours.

We spoke in short exchanges, *you want to stay in here?*, or, *sit on the couch?*, or, *dip your feet in the water at the shore's edge?*

She offered me food and drink but I couldn't eat; I was too dazed. Euphoric. Delirious.

But it was all too true: Sunday was alive. She'd been living in absolute obscurity and serenity on the Pacific coast of Mexico.

54

Beating The Machine

She said she regretted what I'd had to endure and it had killed her to keep it from me. I believed that. She was convinced I'd be too vulnerable and if I ever did come searching for her, which I would have, the person she truly feared on this earth might follow, putting my life in jeopardy too. As long as Chuck Fairchild was alive, he would hunt her down, traveling to the ends of the earth to find her and kill her for having left him. Though life had not felt precious at times, she never wanted him to have the satisfaction of ending hers.

In addition to her fear of Fairchild, Sunday had become disillusioned with her life in New York, especially after the explosive advertising campaigns. It added to the psychological stress and pressure she was already experiencing.

"As much as I loved you," she explained, "I was frightened by what was happening, the media attention, the personal demons. I was hiding too much, the real truths of my life, from someone I loved, someone I never wanted to hurt. But knowing I was doing that added to my fear and insecurity and it led me to make mistakes."

"No one's innocent here," I confessed, referring to my contributions. I'd guided and advised her in the career, after all.

"You did it to help me."

"Sure. From my little corner of my little scando world—"

"And me from mine."

Sunday apprised someone of her fears, a doctor I'd heard her mention once. Dr. Carson Kilmer, a pathologist. He was the only person who knew the extent of her personal tragedy. Kilmer had been a close friend of Sunday's at Florida State University. They'd worked in the same medical office. After medical school, Dr. Kilmer was offered a staff position at a prestigious hospital, Beth Israel in Manhattan, a great opportunity for him. He accepted the offer and moved to New York, where he found a charming one-bedroom apartment in SoHo. On Thompson Street. An apartment I knew well.

Sunday, meanwhile, had had a lifelong yearning to live in New York. When Fairchild was sent to prison, she had her chance. She'd stayed in close contact with Kilmer. When he took the position in Los Angeles, he offered Sunday his apartment and the gesture gave her the incentive to come to New York at last.

The story behind Sunday's disappearance is simple. She'd done exactly what she said she was going to do. She would get out of the business and the city when she felt it was time.

Dr. Kilmer had risen to chief pathologist at Beth Israel, but before resigning, he devised a plan to help his long-suffering friend. To take her out of circulation, to make her disappear forever. His ruse was to give her an injection to keep her heartbeat undetectably low, undetectable to the nonprofessionals with no heart monitoring equipment, in essence, the first wave of policemen at the crime scene. The cause of death, they would assume was asphyxiation by strangulation with acute heart failure. They'd planned it as a murder, which required an autopsy. An autopsy that Kilmer would perform. It had enabled him to control the body. Enhanced medical records in Florida indicated that Sunday had had a history of heart troubles, corroborated by an insurance policy she'd taken out on herself.

Dr. Kilmer had immediately arrived at the crime scene in the ambulance and wheeled her off. He had taken her to his office at the hospital where he performed his examinations. But no autopsy was ever conducted. Kilmer had taken an unidentified, unclaimed Jane Doe's body out of a refrigerated locker and falsified a name tag. There was no need to identify the body, as there was no family to do it and there was no need for a trip to the city morgue. Dr. Kilmer was a friend of the family with impeccable credentials and his signature would be enough to remove any attention from the plan.

Under this false name tag, the body was sent directly from

Kilmer's office at the hospital to the crematorium early the next morning. No suspicion arose, as Sunday's freshly famous name was never written on the identification tag.

The body was cremated under the assumed name and the ashes were retrieved by Dr. Carson Kilmer, designated "family friend." He completed the necessary paperwork, autopsy report, death certificate, and the order for cremation, to make it legal and legitimate. If any questions surfaced, he would attest he'd performed his duties in secret to ensure the privacy of a celebrity, also a close personal friend. There would be no celebrity morgue photographs and no DeadBeauties.org offerings.

Kilmer then notified his superiors he was taking the position offered in Los Angeles. The Machine took care of the rest. It sent the news to all corners of the world, including the Florida State Penitentiary in Oscaloosa that Sunday Fairchild, the Two Lips Girl and a rising star of film, music, and television, had met a tragic end and was gone forever. Which was the fate she'd hoped for.

Sunday never intended for me to find her body in her apartment, to make me go through that anguish. She knew it only compounded my pain of losing her. Also devastated by the fate of Dr. Greer, she felt partially responsible. I felt responsible too, but who can prevent a serial killer from setting a mark?

What had happened was that the locksmith who was charged with Dr. Greer's murder took the opportunity to falsely lay claim to Sunday's murder, as well. In essence for the string of homicides he'd conducted which had no headlining Face appeal, he took credit for the ultimate high-glam murder.

Not many people get second chances, but Sunday Fairchild had gotten one. More than anything, I was happy for that.

55

Adderall Paul

"Slings?"

"Yeah, Paul?"

"Listen up. Don't tell anyone but... Swear you won't tell anyone?"

"Swear."

"Well, here goes. I got a job."

"Really?"

"It's helping out my brother, but still—"

"But still. Congratulations."

"Thanks. You know I don't have so much time on my hands anymore. It's kinna nice." Then he added, "But just keep it between us."

"Zips." I knew paranoia was a healthy first step for a Militiaman to take on anything new, especially joining the ranks of nine-to-five society. Though his new hours were probably more like ten-to-twelve. Baby steps.

"Just remember—"

"Remember what?"

"What you've learned. And pass it on."

"'Kay. And Slings?"

"Yeah, Paul—"

"Thanks for being there. For me. No one ever has been, really."

"Pass it on, brother."

56

Angels

"She's a blonde all right the kind that can have it long or short up or down wet or dry but that doesn't mean all that much because she's one of the rare ones one that can make you happy you're living in the same era at the same time in the same space because it makes you feel so damned human and alive and you know she's had her share of humility and terror and you have too and you think that it's right between you but you're still not sure because of what you've both been through but that kind of a risk is perhaps worth taking because it's what you're on this planet for in the first place and if you lose it's better having loved strong and hard and lost but if you win it will take all that pain and turn it into a flaming positive and maybe just maybe you can get back to those wonderful things you thought life had to offer way back when you were a little princely towhead blond wonder yourself with the happy face and spirit and you had your first crush on someone and you were going to get married and have kids with her and the thought now of finding this in your adult life is all too unbelievable and exciting and you can't wait to find if there is that destiny awaiting you or if it will pass you by but if the tide of fortune is there that girl that exceptional girl will be waiting there and you love her not for what she was or will be but for what she is and how she has shown the type of courage you saw once before in your life and you're lucky if you see that kind of strength once in a lifetime and now you've seen it twice and it's helped strengthen you and given you more courage in your own life and yet that's not it either because it's about you and her and the unique poetry and music that your souls compose together that you're her angel and she's yours a combination not likely to be found anywhere in such an original and profound way and it's that love that love that you've heard about and read about and your heroes like Hendrix and Lennon sang about and you feel like you've received heaven's choicest

blessings because now you've found it and she's compassionate and she's intense and she's engaging and she's the one for you and the one you want to share genes with to mix your souls in the next generation for without her you just don't have that unity of spirit and completeness but with her you envision a long life together with souls forever connected and when it is finally time for you to go you want it to be her holding your hand before you slip off into that unconscious state and pass into dream sleep and have one last fractured longing before expiration that you will meet up again in the cosmos and all that is more than enough to keep you going and it makes you so deeply grateful you prevailed against all the other microscopic entities fighting for life all those years ago and you made it on to this earth against all probability and odds and this very life often maligned and deemed unfair and unjust has rewarded you for having the faith and hanging in there and made you capable of showing the love that you truly feel its privilege and you have no regrets when its all over just the love the love the love and that is what you will pass on with your last breath."

"And if by some twist of fate that it doesn't work out you have no regrets and are so damned happy and content that you had the privilege to know her and you thank God for that and it is your last and dying unconditional wish that she be happy and content herself and that is a cause you would die for."

My heart triple-jumped and my eyes snapped open as I shot up straight in bed, my thumper slamming hard and fast. I didn't know where I was. I saw the whiteness of the bedroom and the cool, silvery blue sea through the window. It wasn't afternoon or night it was morning and Sunday was not laying beside me.

I put on the robe that had been left on the chair for me and stepped into the living room. I called out, but heard no response. Continuing out to the patio and past the pool, I scanned the sweeping shoreline in both directions, but there was not a soul to be found.

Strangely, I didn't feel panic, nor did I feel dread.

A tiny voice could be heard in the direction of the house. It was a fragile voice, punctuated by thin, sharp giggles, a young girl's voice. I moved back up the beach and returned inside to follow the sounds, advancing down a white corridor off the living room to what seemed to be the door to a guest room. There was another voice too, at least one more than the girl's.

I stepped up to the door and knocked gently. After a short interval, the door was spread open and a woman emerged from the room careful to shut the door behind her. She was in her fifties, petite in stature, and she had black shoulder-length hair. Her face was olive and very tan with refined and raised cheekbones. She seemed a proud and dignified woman, perhaps Central or South American. Or Spanish. Or Mexican.

"*Buenos días, Señor,*" she greeted me.

"*Buenos días.*"

"*Mi nombre es Señora Fernanda Malía,*" she proclaimed.

I knew the name, of course. Fernanda Malía apparently did exist, after all. "Hello, Fernanda... Where's Sunday?"

"She's not here—"

"No?"

"She is not coming."

The woman shook her head as well, with resolute eyes underscoring the assertion. She faded back a step to allow me passage to the room. I spun back to her briefly and she relayed a guarded, but no less excitedly expectant expression. She smiled and nodded.

I approached the closed door tentatively.

When I opened it, I skipped a breath at what I saw and my knees buckled and I spiraled to the floor and my eyes were soon brimmed. I held in my gasp and did my best not to cry openly. I didn't want to scare her. It seemed a dream akin to the one the night before in which I'd ranted of sharing genes and mixing souls in the next generation.

She was sitting there quietly on the bed, her hair blonde and wavy with rolling curls. She had a delicate, pretty face, like a face I'd once known. Yes, it was an angel's face. The girl wore a chiffon Easter dress and the color was lavender, also known as light purple.

I wiped my eyes and collected myself, clearing my throat. I looked upon her adoringly and she gazed at me all the while. Though I was a stranger she didn't get uncomfortable or nervous.

"Hello," I tried gently with my voice fighting off emotion.

She didn't say anything. She had a small envelope clutched in her hand. I rose from my knees and advanced to her kneeling again before her. She couldn't have been more than four years old, three-and-a-half tops, though I wasn't an expert on children's ages.

"I know who you are," she said with a fragile smile, her face glowing with wonder and beautiful innocence. "But are you really-really?"

I recognized the phraseology and so many things cascaded into place then.

"Yes, darling. I am."

She paused a moment, the corners of her mouth curving up slightly to an even shier smile, though sparkling and radiant still. She rushed toward me and wrapped little arms around me; the water on a fragile hold in my eyes, fell from my cheeks. I was about to let go uncontrollably, but suppressed it as best as I could.

As we hugged, the envelope dropped to the carpet and the little one picked it up and handed it to me.

Fernanda came from behind taking the hand of the little one whose tiny eyes never left me. I could feel their curiosity, I could feel their penetrating quality. And in all that I could feel their mother.

I slowly opened the letter, a white card which folded open with a written message, the handwriting also familiar.

You were right, Harry. Angels can say good-bye.

I clutched it several seconds as water streamed down my cheeks. With my free hand I took one of hers, so soft and small.

"I'd like to play on the beach now. Will you come with me?"

"Can't think of anything," I said hoarsely, "I'd rather do… more."

We left that room and I dug into my bag and drew out a polo shirt and put it on. Hand in hand, we stepped out onto the patio and proceeded to make our way to the open sand.

Sunday was right; I didn't have any more questions. I realized fully now what she'd done and why she could have never contacted me before. She said that she'd had to "protect everyone I care about," a mother protecting her child, the fiercest, most visceral, and comprehensible instinct in nature. I also understood why she'd brought me to Mexico and named the villa "Three Angels." And for this reason she had to see me one last time.

She'd planned it right down to a house bought in my name. She'd made it end this way; it was the only way it could end with what she'd been through. And what she'd done. She'd fulfilled as many obligations to her conscience as possible and loved as best she could. Now she needed solitude, peace. To remember, to forget.

To be alone, forever.

Though we'd likely never see her again, Sunday had "returned the favor" she'd spoken of, and in that way, she'd been my angel too. No longer distanced and detached, I was connected and she'd connected me. She'd given me her most precious, the ultimate gift, the supreme expression of love, ours. And in that way, too, she would always be with us. For the first time in my life I felt it: complete. Sunday knew to do that, one angel saying good-bye, the other saying hello, with DNA to match. I was not the rejected Harry after all. And hadn't been for years.

I'd found my Christmastown. Only it wasn't any fantasyland; it was real, filled with caring people and a little one with the angel face. I had Sunday Fairchild to thank for it.

The afternoon winds which had been consistently ripping off the Pacific died, and the sun broke through the hazy blanket and shone brightly on the dunes, the water returning to its terrific steely blue. At the shore's edge, the little one watched tiny whitecaps appear and disappear while I said my good-byes.

"Do you know my name?"

"I think I do."

I picked up our cherished creation, the creation I'd unknowingly longed for all my life. A residual surge of breeze came off the bay and the sun lay on our faces just fancy-fine.

And that big blue beyond was our only witness.

Except for that other angel looking out for us, of course. I was certain she couldn't miss us. Little Caitlin's lavender dress and my Bali purple shirt made sure of it.

I would never forget something Sunday and I had articulated also long ago. Angels can say hello again, too. For that we would remain silently hopeful. I couldn't envision a human being with the will, strength of purpose, and conviction of Sunday, someone who'd been able to endure and survive so much, remaining silent to loved ones forever. And yet, if a reunion never did come to pass, I was still forever changed. At last, after all these years, I was no longer Harry Disconnect.

I was Harry, all right, damnit, Harry with the good face.

Author's Note

The following eulogy I wrote and delivered for an old friend who passed away in the summer of 2008.

My Finest Julys

A Tribute to Robert C. Hattersley

(1936—2008)

by

Coerte V.W. Felske

July 16ᵗʰ, 2008

St. John's of Lattingtown Church
Locust Valley, New York

What about Bob Hattersley?

Brilliant, original, movie star handsome, a towering presence; at the same time, an exposed nerve, irreverent, off-color, so very articulate, an inventor of the most succinct, laser-like, yet sledgehammer witticisms and phraseologies, he could string words together like no other; self-effacing, hysterical, kind, generous with a heart as big as a house; in the end, a very complex man. Henry James with a twist, Henry Miller with a boost, let's add a dash of Jay Gatsby in there, too. Only Gatsby *wished* he was that funny. Bob was indeed a figure right out of a novel, of lost innocence in America perhaps; undoubtedly larger than life, mythic even. (And you all must be thinking now, tell me something I *don't* know.)

Well, I'm going to take this from a different angle, to show a side of Bob of which you may or may not be aware of.

I was a bit younger than most of his contemporaries and had the great fortune to meet him early, and I grew up before his own eyes. In my estimation, Bob Hattersley was a man made for summer and indeed that's when I met him.

In July, 1971, we lived on the country club street in sleepy, conservative Quogue, Long Island. I was ten years old, and my recently divorced mother was disturbed by the seemingly endless commotion coming out of the big gray house on the corner. And so, she rang up the household to complain about the noise. And, eventually, she marched on over there to have a meeting. "Why don't we meet in the road?" she was told. In thinking back it was certainly a riff on Lennon and McCartney's "Why Don't We Do It in the Road?" But my mother was unsuspecting at that point. That was how we met Bob Hattersley and his merry band of co-habitators for the first time.

It was an explosive household, a rare groupie arrangement for the residential district in Quogue. It was a collection of youngish, madcap Wall Streeters who lived for their weekends and excess was never above, or below, them. *Animal House* had nothing on these guys. And what was really weird was that they all talked like him, like a crazy bunch of Hattersley Hobbits, running around the lawn, making blood-red drinks, and somersaulting into the pool. With or without clothes. In fact, no one ever knew really how they made it onto Club Lane. But they did, and by leaps and bounds, we were all the better for it. This is my interpretation of those days. And I would soon come to know that this was the beginning of my finest Julys.

Ironically, my recently single mother went over to the Hattersley house to complain about the ruckus, and, as the story goes, she never left. Romances flourished, there were break-ups, swappings too. If it could be done, it was done. At the same time, many of these people became lifelong friends. In fact, Bob married his next-door neighbor Catherine, and his girlfriend at the time, Diane Smith, now Diane Jennings, is godmother to my daughter.

As a Wall Streeter, Bob was a betting man, and he bet on me early. Bob gave me my first job. That summer. (Which is significant because I'm not sure I've had one since.) My job was to clean the pool. Ten dollars a week, which I eagerly tapped him on the shoulder for, as soon as he arrived each Friday night after commuting out. Make no mistake, looking up at this skyscraper guy and hitting him up for cash was pretty terrifying for a barstool shortie.

"Excuse me, uh, Mr. Hattersley—may I have my ten dollars please?"

"*What?*" He'd snap in that delightfully incredulous tone and contorted Hat-man face.

"*There are pine needles all over the pool and YOU, want ME, to give YOU, ten dollars? Oh. Yeah. Sure.*"

"Yes, well, um, Mr. Hattersley, that was the hurricane—"

Then came the bend over with the stomping feet, his head snaking in at you, eyes widening, brows lifting. "*Hurricane???*"

"And, uh, I had a tennis match—"

"*TENNIS MATCH??… Here! Take my wallet! Take my car! Have my house! And while you're at it, why don't you go make out with my girlfriend too, YOU LITTLE WEASEL!!*"

Then, of course, he'd throw me his million-dollar beamer, followed by the Hattersley burst of baby machine gun snickers "*heh-heh, heh-heh,*" meanwhile, MY heart was leaping out of my chest, and he'd say, "Okay, pal o' mine."

Of course, I later figured out that giving me a job with salary was really a payoff of sorts. With me, he'd get the pool semi-cleaned, but more importantly, he'd get my trap shut on anything I'd heard, seen, or witnessed in that wacky house. All for the price of one Alexander Hamilton. Bob knew a good investment too.

All the zaniness aside, my mother said in those early days about Bob, "He's someone you're going to know the rest of your life."

How prescient her words had been.

Later on, Bob came up from the city to attend my football games at Bronxville High School and he took particular delight when I had a good game and was awarded "Bronxville Bronco of the Week" status in the local paper.

For a long time thereafter, when he'd see me, he'd spout, "Hey, it's Bronco of the Week! *Yes!*" with genuine, almost reflected relish.

Bob also used to go way out of his way to drive up from the City, pick me up in southern Westchester, then bring me all the way back to the Meadowlands to see pro football games, then bring me home again. One game, we saw the Bears square off against the Giants. I was a tailback and Bob wanted me to see the best. That day, in the sleet and snow, we watched Walter Payton surpass Jim Brown's career rushing record.

I remember how thrilled Bob was for me when my professional career took off and I was sent to Los Angeles to write a big-star Hollywood movie. But what was more impressive to Hat was the fact they'd put me up in the infamous and at times, tragic, Chateau Marmont Hotel.

"*Y-y-yes!* The kid's co-writing a movie with Mickey Fucking Rourke! And guess what? *HE'S LIVING IN THE JOHN BELUSHI DEATH SUITE!!! YES!!! Heh-heh, heh-heh…*"

I came to learn in life that there is a lot that goes into fathering, but I also learned, no matter what, sometimes one father isn't enough. There are things you just can't discuss if you have that certain breed of parent. For my brother Derek and me, Bob filled that void as a third parent. You could tell him absolutely anything and not feel as though you were being judged. And he was there for you. Like a best friend. A loving father in his own right to his two exceptional daughters, Grace and Lelia, Bob was a father figure to me and for me, and I like to think he considered me, perhaps, like a son he never had.

Along with this larger-than-life persona, yes, came two glorious and beautiful daughters. Grace was about six, I think, in the summer of '71, Lelia slightly older. Lelia was blonde and gorgeous, made cuter by that steel retainer with its snapping rubber bands. Grace had an absolutely angelic face, with Bob's handsome features smeared in there in a special swirl of DNA alchemy which could only produce such an uncommon beauty, at the same time, a wonderfully feminized version of him. In Grace, you saw Bob, and you still do, thankfully, mercifully.

As I got older, I came to understand and absorbed the other unique qualities Bob had, which were, there's no other way to say it, inspirational. It was his use of language, really, that impressed me so; his word mastery, his special ability to articulate, his diction, and the fabulous vocabulary he possessed. I ate up his phrases like cotton candy. The way he tossed off stories, anecdotes, and humorous tales was unrivaled in my experience. Off the cuff, Bob was at his best. And for him it was like showing a little leg, though he wasn't a show-off. With that unique blend of sardonic, acerbic wit, crocodile snappy dialogue, and the best punch line you ever met, he absolutely commanded your attention, any table's attention. Hat was the straw that stirred the drink. He was Hunter Thompson gonzo meets Raymond Chandler noir, delivered with an ease and fluidity, tempo and cadence, that invited you to step right into what appeared to be a thrilling world, his thrilling world, of "mouthpieces," "little weasels," and "filthy swines." He had an entire Field Club afterhour's establishment so terrifically body-snatched, emulating him. Like the Hobbits, it was mimicry, of course, but more accurately, it was always in homage to. And he knew it. And they knew it. Bob was truly an original. Bob was *The Original*.

(How did he have this gift? I can only venture to say he was so specially configured his brain circuitry must have been surgically fissured, more like hot-wired, in the galaxy's finest Formula One race car chop shop, made with a lot of heaven, and a little dash of hell. The man *was* a race car, and if you were going to take the ride, you better strap yourself in and hold on, or, get out of the way. But in either case, don't forget your helmet. – *OMIT*)

If you were going to throw your chips in and play, you had to be on your game with Hat. But he wasn't mean-spirited or cruel. As imposing a figure as he was, he was an absolute Teddy Bear. Verbally, he wouldn't show you up. Because he could have sliced you into shreds in a heartbeat. He embraced the darker ironies of life and infused them with his own special brand of humor. His neologisms and nicknames were legendary and passed through the societal landscape like wildfire. The one time I did rat out that wacky gray Hobbit house, and my mother, to my father, Bob called me "Scoop" Felske, bringer of the news; there was Bronco of the Week; in reference to my regrettable, personally-sheared hair designs in the eighties, very spiky, punked, and gelled, irregularly-shaped and simply awful, he called me "Hair Wars." There was our fearless foot-long Norwich Terrier with a Napoleon complex named Stuart, to whom Hat referred to as "the Wart Hog," the way he aggressively barked at people to back off. When our dog died, Hat put it on the Wall Street newswire media feed, "The Wart Is Dead." His girlfriend at the time was recovering from a car accident and was on crutches. Diane Smith became "Sticks" Smith. My mother Anneke was renamed, too. To "Attica." Why? Because she was such a riot.

With this power arsenal of language, wit, and hard-boiled humor, Bob had that uncanny ability to bring people together in a hyperkinetic way, uniting them, creating friendships and lasting bonds. If Hat was your friend, there was an entire Roman Legion of support that came with him. I like to think he brought out the good cheer in people, the funny in the unfunny, and the funniest in funny people, and at times, even the best in people.

I must confess that when Bob left Quogue, the town was never really the same for me again. Perhaps cherished brother-in-law Botsford, Beatty, Degener and Degener, Murray and Murray, Greeff and Greeff, Disston and Disston, McClean and Moley, will agree. Felske and Felske certainly felt it. A chip was taken out of the town for some; a gaping hole was left in it for me. A rare and unique soul had moved on and a certain spark was gone. And it never returned.

Bob came and went like magic. For me, Bob *was* magic.

Sadly, I didn't see Bob in these intervening years. My loss. Big loss. I like to think that funny little elitist enclave with the funny Indian name cramped Bob's style. Of course he could ruffle feathers and Old Guard Quogue, at times, cast a jaundiced eye at this big, boisterous, unforgettable, magnetic presence. Because this guy had charisma in spades. As far as I can remember, Quogue never encountered a presence like this. And I don't believe it has experienced one since, or ever will again. Hat inspired jealousy too.

Whenever I hear someone boldly boasting absolute quote-unquote "truths" on some subject or some particular person, I always keep that philosophical tagger in mind, a fave quotation of mine by German philosopher Friedrich Nietzsche:

"There are no truths. Only interpretations."

Many things can be said about Bob, I suppose, "interpretations," but I will forever think of him as one of the most original and unique spirits who ever, ever crossed my path.

(I've known only four and I get around. But I must say it's pretty lofty company. – *OMIT*)

High noon July, the sunburned baby face, scratching off the Sunday Times crossword puzzle in minutes in his beach chair, popping into the ocean for some "hydro-therapy," driving his chocolate-brown Porsche; his childish giggle, the giddy delight and pride he took in his daughters, and the exuberance he generated with that big Hat smile, this was a loving, big-hearted man and dedicated father who, in the days I knew him, just burned, rippled, crackled, snapped, and fired with a rare, exceptional form of sensitized life. Bob was about life. And living it. And letting it all hang out, or, letting your hair down, as it were. I thought to give myself a hair trim this week before the service, but then thought, *nah*, this is the way Hat knew me. And remembered me. And accepted me. And didn't judge me. And always let me be me. There was no way I was going to cut it.

I remember Bob telling me one time he wanted to write a book. Not an autobiography, mind you. Just fiction. No doubt in homage to his gonzo alter ego. I even think he'd outlined a few chapters.

"Wanna know what the title is?" he asked me.

"Sure, give it up, Hat-man."

He broke the big wide one. "*Lost In The Fun House*," he said.

"Great title," I said.

"I'n'it? *Heh-heh, heh-heh.*"

In my view, Hat's proposed book had nothing to do with feeling confused, or lost, or out of it. Cause Hat was on it. Hat got it. Rather, it was more like, we all share the same star stuff, we're all in this together, this magical mess and swirl of total inexplicable chaos, we call life. And so, we might as well embrace it, have fun with it, and be a little extraordinary while doing it. To me, that was what Hat was all about.

Did he burn too brightly? Perhaps. (The great ones often do.) But oh, what a glorious flame.

After all those years of making us laugh, now he's making us cry, but they're tears of joy really, to have been spinning around on the same axis, on the same globe, at the same moment in history. *We* were the lucky ones.

It was some kinna magic, wasn't it?

That is *my* interpretation. And those *were,* my finest Julys.

With his health failings behind him, I believe Hat-man is no longer lost, but found.

A touch of noir, a touch of madcap, a touch of Grace and Lels, a touch of greatness, and never a touch of evil, and more than a touch of genius—you were missed, you are missed, and you will be missed.

Okay, "pal o' mine;" hats off to you, Hat Man.

Heaven just got lucky.

Heaven just became a better place.

Heaven just became the Fun House.

Coerte V.W. Felske was born in New York City and grew up in Manhattan and Quogue, Long Island. He attended Bronxville High School and received his Bachelor of Arts degree from Dartmouth College. He did his graduate work in film directing and screenwriting at Columbia University. *The Shallow Man*, originally published in 1995, was his first novel. His second novel, *Word*, came out in 1998 followed by *The Millennium Girl* in 2000. In 2008, the author established his independent online literary imprint, The Dolce Vita Press, founded in conjunction with Amazon.com, to publish and distribute his books. The imprint's inaugural publication was *The Shallow Man: 15th Anniversary Edition* released in September, 2009, followed by the author's first new novel in eight years, *Scandalocity,* released in May, 2010.

The author launched The Dolce Vita Press in an effort to have significant contact with readership, exercise creative control over his work, and to have the artistic freedom to incorporate the talents of top photographers, graphic artists, and book jacket designers. The Dolce Vita Press label derives from the Italian term "dolce vita," which translates to the "sweet life." Felske was influenced by Federico Fellini's cinematic masterwork, *La Dolce Vita*, which tells the tale of a carefree, decadent group of seemingly glamorous partiers, nightclubbers, and exotic women as they navigate their way through Rome's high society, all pursued by a dashing playboy paparazzo. The author has often referred to his literature as "dolce vita fiction," stories about nightclub impresarios, serial womanizers, fashionistas, fortune-hunting women, entertainment business hopefuls, and scandal sheet writers entrenched in a similar dolce vita circuitry; in essence, characters living modern versions of that illusory sweet life depicted in Fellini's film. Felske has three more new works completed and coming soon from the DVP. His next novel, *The Ivory Stretch,* will be released in November, 2010, followed by *Chemical/Animal*, his second written in first person as a woman, in the summer of 2011.

All Coerte V.W. Felske titles for The Dolce Vita Press are available at the author's Web site, www.coertefelske.com, www.thedolcevitapress.com, as well as Amazon. com.

To contact the DVP, request a review copy, or write to the author, please visit the author's Web site at www.coertefelske.com.